Redeeming Hope

Anna O'Malley

POOLBEG

Published 2005
by Poolbeg Press Ltd
123 Grange Hill, Baldoyle
Dublin 13, Ireland
E-mail: poolbeg@poolbeg.com

© Anna O'Malley 2005

The moral right of the author has been asserted.

Typesetting, layout, design © Poolbeg Press Ltd.

13 5 7 9 10 8 6 4 2

A catalogue record for this book is available from the British Library.

ISBN 1-84223-203-7

Typeset by Type Design in Palatino 10/14.5
Printed by
Litografia Rosés S.A., Spain

www.poolbeg.com

About the Author

Anna O'Malley lives in the west of Ireland with her dog, and now writes full-time. Her first novel, *I'm Sorry*, was published by Poolbeg in 2004.

Acknowledgements

Thanks to Gaye Shortland, Edel Hackett, all at Poolbeg, and all the usual suspects!

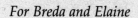

For Breda and Elaine

Chapter 1

The forecast of 'intermittent light showers' was a gross understatement. In Hope Prior's opinion, stair rods would have been a more accurate description. Sitting in the queue of traffic she watched the lashing rain bounce off the bonnet of her car, the wipers at full tilt barely managing to keep the windscreen clear. The road ahead was a blurry mass of red brake lights and indistinct grey shapes scurrying, huddled under umbrellas rendered ineffective by the gale (described equally economically by the previous night's radio forecast as 'light winds').

Dublin in June. Put it down to global warming.

Peering ahead, she tried to get some clue as to what was holding up the traffic. The lights were on green but nothing was moving. The driver in the BMW, so close behind he was almost crawling up her bumper, beeped his horn and others took it as a cue to follow suit.

What was that about? What was it with men beeping their horns when there was obviously nowhere to go? Did Mr Angry in the Fuck-Off Beemer seriously think that she and the rest of the drivers in the unmoving queue were sitting there because they had nothing better to do? Irritated, she glanced in her rear-view mirror, then back at the clock on the dash.

12.45. The meeting with Maurice Redmond at the bank had run over and she was running late. Her stomach muscles contracted. She loathed being late.

The moron was leaning on his horn now. Her eyes returned to the rear view. Late middle-age, overweight, face puce, stressed out close to apoplexy, effing and blinding, free hand flailing the air: a coronary incident waiting to happen. Although she found his overreaction irritating, she could empathise to a degree. The city's traffic management was a joke. Roadworks everywhere. Excavations for the new (and already obsolete) Port Tunnel vying with the still-under-construction LUAS Light Rail system to see which could create the most havoc.

'LUAS' the hoardings brazenly declared. 'First train 2003, then every fifteen minutes.' Already more than a year late and way over budget. The public sector got away with murder.

The cars ahead inched forward but before she had a

2

chance to shift into gear, Mid-Life-Crisis-Neanderthal was at it again. For a split second she was tempted to cut the engine and just sit there, arms folded, but the clock in her peripheral vision, shining luminous green, reminded her that it was not an option – besides, CPR wasn't in her repertoire. Releasing the clutch she rolled forward and joined the moving traffic.

Twenty minutes later her umbrella was disembowelled by a rogue gust of wind as she stepped out of the exit of the Fleet Street multistorey carpark. Fighting with it briefly she managed to pull it back into some semblance of its original shape, then, shielding her upper body as best she could, she battled her way against the storm towards Anglesey Street.

As she turned the corner the gale abruptly ceased, the buildings on either side of the narrow cobbled Templebar thoroughfare acting as a windbreak. She could see Ruby, her PA, up ahead, on the way back from posting a mail shot. She too was carrying the crippled remains of an umbrella, but it was a flimsy affair and the wind and the deluge had been too much for it to cope with so she looked like a drowned rat. As Hope approached, she gave the door a hefty shove open with her shoulder and disappeared inside.

The phone was ringing as Hope entered reception but Ruby was nowhere to be seen. Hope was reluctant to pick up. Recently she had been assiduously screening all her calls. Cash flow was becoming increasingly problematic and her creative bullshitting at the bank would only hold the tide back temporarily.

"Ruby?"

No response. Hope walked over to Ruby's desk and squinted at the caller ID. There were at least five people she didn't want to talk to right now but she didn't recognise the number. After a moment's further hesitation she picked up.

"Prior Engagements."

"Hope? It's Gordo."

Hope cringed. The caterer was on an unfamiliar number. Ruby had been fielding his calls all week.

"Gordo! How nice. Ready for the off?" Hope said, in cheery-voice mode.

There was an uncomfortable pause at the other end of the line. "Um, the thing is, Hope, I ... um, I could do with the rest of the cash up front or I'm afraid I might have to pass."

"*Pass*? Are you out of your *mind*?" Without giving the pocket-sized chef a chance to reply she lashed on. "Still, if you're not up to it I can always call –"

"It's not that," he cut in. "You know I can handle it, it's just ... there's been talk."

"Talk?"

An embarrassed cough. "Word around is that you're going to the wall."

Hope's guts turned over and she was immediately on the offensive. "Gordo, *who* was it gave you your big break in this business? *Who* was it had faith in you when you were an unknown chef starting out?"

4

Ruby walked out of the kitchen at that point, rubbing her wet hair with a towel and, catching the end of the exchange, stopped dead, all ears.

"Gordo, I'm deeply wounded by your lack of faith and the fact that you'd listen to idle gossip. Did I *ever* give you reason to think that I had anything but total confidence in you, Gordo? Did I? *Did I?*"

"Um … no."

"No! And quite rightly. You're top-notch at what you do, and don't let anyone tell you otherwise."

"Well, no, but –"

"Yes, Gordo. Top-notch." A breath. Change of tone. "You managed to get hold of the langoustine all right?"

"Of course – picked it up this morning – but about the up-front money –"

"And the quails' eggs?"

"Yes, yes, I have the quails' eggs too, but –"

"Good man, Gordo. Good man. I knew you wouldn't let me down. If you want something done to perfection and with style, call on Gordo Whyte. I'll see you down there in a while, Gordo. You'll be setting up at around three?"

She heard the outer door opening and glanced over her shoulder in time to see Amy Long struggle inside, loaded down with three hangers of plastic-covered dry cleaning and a small Marks & Spencer carrier bag.

"Uh, yeah. Three o'clock. You'll um … you'll have the cash?"

"If you insist, Gordo. But I hope you realise I

wouldn't do this for anyone else." Positively oozing charm. "See you at three then." Without giving him any chance for a rejoinder she hung up.

"Sorry," Ruby said as she slid behind her desk. "Didn't hear the phone. I was soaked. Had to dry off."

"He was looking for cash up front. Can you believe that? After all the work I've put his way."

Ruby's eyebrows took a hike up her forehead. "Cash? How are you going to manage that?"

"I'll give him a cheque."

"But what if he gets stroppy?"

Hope shrugged. "So what's he going to do with sixty kilos of fresh langoustine?"

"Sorry I was so long," Amy muttered, scurrying past Hope, head down. "There was a queue at the cleaner's and Marks & Sparks food hall was packed." She opened the bag, took out a tuna sandwich, then dumped the bag and a handful of change on Ruby's desk. "No ciabatta, I'm afraid," she said glancing at Hope but avoiding eye contact. "I got you a BLT on wholemeal instead. I hope that's OK."

Hope glanced in her direction. "Whatever. Hang the dry cleaning in my office, would you?"

Amy nodded, then made for the stairs.

"Would you check on Clive at the florist's," Hope said to Ruby as she picked her sandwich out of the bag. "They'll need to be down there no later than half past two if they're to get the table decorations finished in time." Turning the transparent plastic package over in her hand she examined the contents. "How is a BLT a substitute for a cream cheese and roasted ham ciabatta for feck sake?" she murmured.

Ruby grinned. "Oh, shut up! They're both pig, aren't they?"

A thought occurred to Hope so she turned and called up the stairs. "Amy!"

Amy reappeared at the top of the stairs.

"You remembered to confirm the string quartet?"

"Quartet?"

"The Benjaos quartet. For the oyster reception."

The girl nodded. "Oh right. Yes. I did that last week. Don't worry. It's sorted."

Hope watched Amy scurry away and when she was out of earshot turned back to Ruby who was checking her email. "Some gobshite's spreading rumours that we're going out of business," she said in a low voice.

"Who!?"

Hope shook her head. "I've no idea, but I'll make it my business to find out."

Ruby made no further comment but off the top of her head could think of at least four likely candidates, all of whom were owed money by the company.

Hope Prior had set up Prior Engagements six years previously. It was a shrewd move as the company had cashed in on the rich corporate pickings at the height of the Celtic Tiger economic boom. Unfortunately, said Tiger was growing ever more lean and decrepit with each passing month and there were increasing mutterings about tightening belts and cutting costs, so the corporate event business was in the throes of a downturn. In the belief that it was just a temporary glitch, the ever-optimistic Hope discounted the decline and maintained her lifestyle in the certain knowledge that it would all soon revert to normal. Thus did she find herself in the current cash-flow predicament. But lately even she had to admit that contracts were thin on the ground. Apart from tonight's gig, a high-profile event thrown by Icon Software to launch a new accounting package, a small shindig the following week for a fledgling pharmaceutical company courting fresh venture capital, and the unveiling of a new ceramic hair-straightener at the end of the month, her corporate diary was ominously empty of events. The situation had called for drastic action so, persuaded by Ruby, she had been compelled to consider wedding planning. Despite the fact that in event management it was currently one of the only growth sectors, Hope had thus far refused to include it in the company's brief and, on her list of least preferred options, it came ahead of organising children's parties and pushing hot needles into her eyeballs. It had been a case of once bitten twice shy after a brief foray some years previously which had left her of the opinion that all brides were self-obsessed, fatally emotional and totally unpredictable. And as for the Mother of the Bride, well, she didn't even want to go there. So far she had two bookings. One in for a lavish themed bash for three hundred of the bride and groom's closest friends in the Abercorn Castle chapel at the beginning of August, and a smaller affair for a second-time-around fourth-generation Irish-American couple (Mary Kate and Sean) whose dream was to get hitched in 'the old country'. Taking the happy couple's preferences into account, it promised to be Cliché City.

The phone rang again and Ruby picked up. "Prior Engagements. Ruby speaking. How may I – oh hello, Josh." Her eyes swivelled to Hope who made cutting motions across her throat. "Sorry, Josh, she's out of the office right now." A pause. "Yes. She's at a meeting so her phone's probably switched off." A further pause. "OK, I'll get her to call you as soon as she gets in." She frowned as she replaced the receiver. "What did Josh do that you're giving him the cold shoulder?"

Flustered, Hope shook her head insisting, "I don't want to talk about it." So Ruby backed off.

Although avoiding Josh Tierney's calls was a very, very recent development, only since the weekend in fact, avoiding business calls in general was an everyday occurrence of late, but Hope was still for the most part in denial. Tonight she would collect a nice fat cheque from Icon Software which would go a long way towards beating the wolves back from the door. And if tonight was a success, well, every event in itself was a showcase for the company and there was good media interest in this particular launch.

Upstairs in the sanctuary of her office she dropped her lunch on the desk, then peeled off her damp clothes and ripped the dry-cleaner's plastic from an elegantly cut black trouser suit. At thirty-six, barely five feet two inches tall and weighing two pounds in excess of nine stone, Hope Prior could very easily have appeared short and dumpy, but her petite frame, innate sense of style and great posture (the result of three years of Pilates) ensured that she dressed to show off her size-twelve body to its best advantage. She had a more than decent cleavage, good legs, long in proportion to the rest of her, always wore heels and subscribed to the universal truth that a good haircut is an investment and well worth the arm and leg that she routinely shelled out every six weeks.

Slipping on a pair of Patrick Cox mules, then standing in front of the mirror, she ran her fingers through her expensively cropped hair and critically examined her reflection. The waistband of the trousers was sitting a trifle snug. Visits to the gym had been few and far between over the past few weeks and it was beginning to show. A creature of habit – some would say she had become obsessive – the gym had been part of Hope's morning ritual, without fail, three times a week for over eight years. But these days when the alarm went off, truth be told, as a result of a lack of sleep she was too weary, and the thought of a thirty-minute stint on the treadmill out of the question. "Next week," she would mutter to herself as she turned over for another few precious minutes. "Sunday. I'll go on Sunday."

Vowing to join a Pilates class again, go every morning to the gym, give up drink and cut junk out of her diet, Hope sat behind her desk and unwrapped her sandwich, but suddenly the sight of the mayo oozing out between the bacon and crispy lettuce prompted a wave of guilt. Unceremoniously dumping it in the bin she checked her diary and ignored her rumbling stomach. The Icon launch was well in hand. Clive the florist had been a touch problematic, but a postdated cheque and a none too subtle reminder about the weddings on her books had placated him.

Picking up her mail she sorted through it – mostly bills and an official-looking brown envelope with a harp on it, no surprises there. She shuffled them into priority order, pushing them aside for attention later, then checked her email. There was one from Janette Robinson, her Abercorn bride. The tenor of the email suggested unmitigated disaster and as Hope read the text she was reminded why she loathed the wedding sector so much. Janette, in the company of Herbie her fiancé, had spent a weekend at Abercorn Castle, the venue for their reception. Hope had arranged the visit herself, the principal purpose of which was for the happy couple to sample the proposed menu. It was all part of the venue's wedding package. Janette however, according to the email, had discovered to her *"absolute horror"* that Abercorn Castle's white tableware had a thin *silver* border when she had expressly stated that she wanted white tableware with a thin *gold* border.

She was wearing cream shantung silk. *Cream*! And how could anyone possibly consider putting silver with *cream*?

Hope was tempted to email Janette back and tell her to get a life. On average she was receiving at least one email a day from her and there were still six weeks to go. "You're a professional," she said to herself through clenched teeth. "Deal with it." To her knowledge Janette had already changed her mind about the china at least three times. Not surprising therefore that there might have been some confusion.

Picking up the phone she called Lindsey Smith, the functions manager at Abercorn Castle and, after exchanging the usual pleasantries, acquainted her with Jeanette's problem. Lindsey apologised and assured her that if the bride wanted a gold border on her tableware that was not a problem. If however she should change her mind yet *again* that would be no problem either, and perhaps Hope could call her the day before the reception and confirm the bride's *final* preference, just to be on the safe side. Hope replied to Janette's email assuring her that all was in hand and if she had further worries of any nature not to hesitate etc. She doubted that the thoroughly anally retentive Janette would pick up on the irony. Suddenly the undemanding Mary Kate and Sean didn't seem so bad, Irish dancers, traditional pony and trap and fiddle players notwithstanding.

Giving a heavy sigh, she switched on her phone. The

message alarm immediately beeped, as she knew it would. She checked her messages. Four voicemail. One text from her mother. She opened the text. Being one of the last people on the planet to discover mobile telecommunication technology, Maisie Prior had embraced it with enthusiasm. Her texts however were all but unintelligible to Hope, mainly on account of her mother's recent attack of irritable vowel syndrome.

The latest read: *"Dnnr? Nxt sndy? RU cmng? Nd 2 knw? Shll I pt yR nmes in pot?"* In vain she had tried to persuade her to try predictive texting, but she refused to get to grips with it, claiming ironically that predictive text spewed out total rubbish, and how could it possibly know what she wanted to say. Hence the continuing stream of gobbledegook messages, at least four a day.

Lunch, Sunday? Why? Well aware from a lifetime of experience that Maisie always had some other agenda, she couldn't face it. Not with the Josh situation the way it was. Not when her mother made no secret of the fact that she was mad about Josh Tierney. Why couldn't Maisie just mind her own business for a change? Hope gave a sardonic snort.

She quickly checked her voicemail. Two from Gordo. One from Hugh Moore her solicitor, returning her call, to say Martin Beresford had still not replied to his last letter. No change there then. Beresford owed her a lot of money. Money that could ease her cash-flow situation and then some. One from Josh with a brief and to the point: *"Hi, babe. Love you."*

She sighed, thinking, I know, sweetie, but for how long? He'd been away since Monday in Brussels covering some EU crisis and wasn't due home until the end of the week so at least that was a brief reprieve.

As she was writing the cheque for Gordo there was a tap on the door and Amy walked in carrying a mug of coffee which she placed on the edge of Hope's desk.

"Ruby said to tell you Clive might not be able to get down to the venue until three. But he said not to worry, he'll have everything finished in plenty of time."

Hope looked up. She was becoming increasingly irritated by Amy who had been with Prior Engagements for five months. A tall thin girl with lank, mousy, shoulder-length hair, she was around twenty-four or so, and had joined the company on a government employment initiative. Her background was in insurance but she had been a victim of downsizing and had found herself unemployed for over a year which had subsequently qualified her for the scheme. It suited Hope at the time as she had to shell out for only half of her wages and a reduced-rate national insurance contribution. The scheme had only four weeks left to run and Ruby, who got on well with Amy, had lobbied strongly for Hope to give the girl a permanent job on the grounds that she was a good worker, had initiative and the company needed another pair of hands anyway. In a moment of weakness Hope had agreed, but now she was having second thoughts.

In fairness Amy seemed willing to learn, but it was a personality thing. Hope wasn't entirely comfortable with her. She reminded her of a wounded puppy and the chemistry just wasn't quite right. Also, though Hope would never admit it, there was probably some subconscious recognition that Amy's vulnerable victim persona wasn't a million miles away from the kind of individual that Dylan had turned her into, if only briefly, until she had seen sense.

She noticed Amy's brows furrow as her eyes strayed to the waste bin. "You didn't like the BLT! I'm *really* sorry. Can I get you something else?"

The underlying note of panic in Amy's voice raised Hope's hackles but at the same time left her with an irritating twinge of guilt. "No. It's OK. I'll grab something on my way down to the venue."

"Are you sure? It's no trouble."

Hope pushed back her chair, stood up and, unable to keep a note of irritation from her voice, snapped, "No. Really. It's fine. You'd better come with me."

"I'll call a cab."

"A cab? Why? My car's in Fleet Street."

Amy's shook her head. "Er, no. The valet man has it."

Hope stared at her blankly. "The valet man? What valet man?"

"The valet man. He called in this morning. He forgot where you said you'd leave the car so I told him you'd be back around one and you usually park in Fleet Street. He said he'd find it."

Hope frowned. "What are you rabbiting on about, Amy? Why would I hire a car valet? They charge a fortune." Suddenly the penny dropped and she groaned aloud. "Oh shit! You eejit! You fecking eejit!"

Stunned, Amy shrank back a pace. "What?"

Glaring at her, Hope grabbed her coat and briefcase and made for the door. "Quickly," she urged. "*Come on!*"

Chapter 2

Eight minutes later the two women stood at an empty bay on the third floor of the Fleet Street multistorey carpark, breathless after running all the way from the office in Anglesey Street and up four flights of stairs, Hope having refused to wait for the lift. She had no idea of the exact location of her precious red Audi TT but she was certain that its absence from the parking spot had absolutely nothing to do with a car-valeting service.

"Are you sure this is where you left it?" Amy said, though the question bore little conviction.

Hope turned on her heel and marched away towards the lift. After a beat, Amy hurried after her.

The man in the pay booth was smug and unapologetic as he showed Hope the paperwork.

"Repossession, love," he said, tapping the sheaf of A4 printed sheets. "District Court Judgement in favour of the leasing company."

"And you just let him drive out of here?" Hope said astonished. "With *my* car?"

"Strictly speaking it's not your motor, is it?" he said. "Anyway, he had keys, ID, everything. Bradbury & Dunthorp, debt collectors."

Hope blushed to the roots of her hair. The term 'debt collector' had a sickening Dickensian ring to it, and the fact that Amy was hovering two feet behind her caused added embarrassment. "This is outrageous!" she blustered. "It's a clerical cock-up."

Pay-booth man shrugged, a smirk still on his gob. "Take it up with the debt collectors, love. Not my problem."

Back on the pavement Hope strode towards Westmorland Street, livid. Fortunately, the storm and the rain had ceased. When they turned into College Green she spotted taxis waiting at the rank at the top of Dame Street. As they waited at the kerb to cross, Amy opened her mouth to speak but Hope was in no humour for platitudes. "Don't!" she snapped as she set off at a rate of knots, weaving her way between the traffic waiting at the lights. Amy had the sense to shut up and just followed her boss meekly towards the taxi at the head of the queue.

Hope thought she had sorted the problem with the leasing company on foot of her promise of a cheque for the arrears the following week. Obviously not, considering the fact that they had gone ahead with the threatened court action. Then the official brown harp envelope came to mind. She was gutted. She loved her little Audi sports car. She wasn't convinced that the way they had gone about the repossession was entirely legal (as far as she was concerned they were still in discussion). She made a mental note to call her solicitor and check it out. Then a thought occurred.

"Fuck! My iPod was in the glove-box." She cast an accusing glance in Amy's direction. "Shit! And my new Gucci sunglasses."

Amy winced and continued to stare out of the cab window, determinedly avoiding her employer's eye.

The traffic was moderate despite the roadworks, so they made it to the Waterfront Hotel, the dockside venue for the Icon launch, in less than twenty minutes.

As the cab pulled up outside the service entrance, Amy was relieved to see the caterer's truck being unloaded. "Oh look, Gordo Whyte's here," she said, glad to have something positive to say.

The sight of Gordo and his team unloading the food placated Hope to a degree and she cheered up further as she noticed Clive's Hiace parked close by and ahead of schedule. Perhaps the day wouldn't be a complete washout. She hurried inside to check on progress in the function room, Amy two paces behind.

As the lift doors opened near the entrance to the Gandon Rooms her senses were assaulted by the sight of two men and a girl, all sporting dreadlocks, incongruously clad in the striped blazers and white pants of a barber's shop quartet, straw boaters precariously perched on top of the dreads, all manically playing banjos. They were standing just inside the door of the function room in a huddle, close to where the waiters were setting up the table for the champagne and oyster reception. Hope stopped dead causing Amy, whose eyes were on the carpet, to crash into her back.

As Hope stared open-mouthed and lost for words, the banjo players segued seamlessly from 'The Campdown Races' into a frenzied version of 'I'm a Yankee Doodle Dandy'.

"I'm really sorry," Amy said. "I could only get three. I tried for the quartet but they only come in threes."

Still stunned, it took a moment for Amy's words to register. "*You're* responsible for this?"

Amy gulped. "I'm sorry. I did my best. But no one else was available. I just couldn't get a quartet."

"So you got three fucking *banjos* instead?" Hope said. "*Banjos*? What the fuck possessed you?"

"But you said," Amy bleated, "you *said* banjos."

Light dawned. "I *said* a string quartet. *Benjaos*, you moron. Two violins, a viola and a cello playing Mozart. Not the Beverly Hillbillies meet Bob Marley playing fucking banjos!"

Amy, her face a whiter shade of pale, opened her mouth to speak but no sound came out.

Gordo walked into the Gandon Rooms at that point

and made a beeline for Hope. She pasted a smile onto her lips. "Gordo! Everything in hand?"

The chef nodded and before he could say a word, Hope delved into her briefcase, produced the cheque and handed it to the diminutive caterer. "Here you are, Gordo, full payment in advance as promised. Now, what desserts did we finally decide on? I hope you brought your lovely scrummy, sinful chocolate and raspberry roulade."

Gordo was staring at the cheque, seriously contemplating throwing a hissy fit, but, as Hope had predicted, at the same time wondering what he was going to do with sixty kilos of prime fresh langoustine if he decided to get stroppy.

"Come on, Gordo, chop, chop! Time's marching on." Then spotting Clive and one of his young minions across the room, Hope grabbed Amy's arm. "Oh, sorry, Gordo, have to have a word with Clive. See you in a bit."

Halfway across the room Hope hissed, "How hard is it to follow a simple instruction, Amy! *A string quartet!* How fucking hard is that?"

"But I thought you –"

"You're not paid to think. You're paid to carry out basic instructions. If this event is compromised – well, I just hope I can salvage something from this disaster for your sake, or you're history. You hear me? History!"

Amy looked stricken. "Oh please, I need this job. Please let me sort it out. I'll phone that booking agent woman back and sort it out. I promise!"

"You *are* joking?" Hope snarled. "Just get out of my sight."

She left Amy standing impotently in the centre of the room and, a beaming smile once more cemented to her gob, hurried over to Clive.

The florist was his usual camp self, faffing around with the table centrepieces, barking orders at a petulant-looking helper. "No, Rodger. Not there!" Eyes cast to the ceiling, hand laid gently on Rodger's left buttock, he reached over and adjusted the angle of the floral arrangement a nano-smidgeon, then stood back and admired his handiwork. "There. That's better."

Rodger, a slim young man in tight T-shirt and tighter jeans, stood back looking sulky.

"The tables are fabulous as usual, Clive. Well done!" said Hope.

Clive returned her smile. "You can't beat the simple orange gerbera for effect. Understated but at the same time injecting a note of high drama."

"Absolutely. Couldn't have put it better myself," Hope agreed, despite not getting the "high drama" element.

"Masterstroke, the banjos," he added, casting a glance towards the oyster table where the three white hillbilly Rastas had stopped playing and were standing in a loose group talking together.

Hope, on the defensive despite the lack of sarcasm in Clive's tone, frowned. "Just a temporary breakdown in communication."

Clive gave her a puzzled look, then turned to Rodger. "Run along, Rodg, and finish off the tables." Rodg hurried away towards the service exit and Clive's hungry gaze followed his arse, making it clear that his mind at that moment was firmly on rogering Rodger.

Hope gave him a nudge. "Behave yourself, Clive."

She left him drooling and rooted for her mobile in the bottom of her briefcase, then dialled up Ruby. "We have a problem."

"As in?"

"As in Amy fucked up, big-time."

"I know. She was just on to me," Ruby said. "What did you say to her? She was really upset."

"Say to her? What do you think? She booked three fucking demented dreadlocked banjo players instead of the string quartet!"

There was a stifled snigger at the other end of the line. "She didn't mention the dreadlocks."

"It's not funny, Ruby. I'll bet she didn't mention getting my car repossessed either."

"Ah, come on, Hope! The car was hardly her fault. How was she to know?"

"That's beside the point," Hope blustered. "She's got to go. If this launch is ruined, so are we."

"Calm down," Ruby soothed. "It won't be ruined. I'm in a cab on my way over to help you with the goody bags. I'll call Irene Goldstone. Maybe the string quartet's available."

The banjo trio launched into 'Cotton Eye Joe' just as,

in her peripheral vision, she saw the CEO of the Icon board enter the room and stop dead two steps away from the musicians.

"Shit! Too late. Dermot Hudson's just walked in."

"What are you going to do?"

Hope felt faint. "Revert to plan B?"

"Plan B?"

"Persuade Dermot Hudson that white Rasta banjo trios are the new black, I suppose."

"No better woman," Ruby said.

Hope gave a heavy sigh. "Try Irene anyway. If Hudson kicks off I want to have a fall-back position."

Hope felt that her face was going to crack with the effort it was taking to appear calm and relaxed. Hudson, a tall man in his late fifties, impeccably dressed in a bespoke charcoal three-piece suit, was still standing transfixed a couple of feet away from the musicians who, as she approached, drifted into 'It's a Long Way to Tipperary'.

"Terrific, aren't they?" Hope said, inwardly wincing. "We were lucky to get them."

"We were?" Hudson looked a tad bemused, but at least he appeared to be calm.

"I know we discussed getting Benjaos, but then I remembered that Epic Software had used them for a product launch not long ago so I thought it was imperative to have something original and a bit off the wall for yours." This was in fact, a total lie, but Hope was banking on the assumption that Hudson would be none the wiser.

"Epic? Really?" he said, half to himself, then nodded. "Good call, Hope. Good call. Banjos are certainly original, and very . . . eh," he searched for a word.

"Jolly?" Hope offered.

Hudson smiled. "Yes. I was going to say up-beat, but *jolly* seems appropriate." He checked his Rolex. "Minus one hour twenty-six minutes to lift-off. Everything on schedule?"

"Absolutely," Hope assured him.

Looking around the large function room, she felt a surge of relief. Up on the stage Icon's technical bods and the sound-equipment contractors were setting up the audio-visual gear and PA system for the presentation. The tables were looking great. Gordo, placated, was setting up the buffet. Clive was creating his usual floral genius despite the fact that she still couldn't see the drama in orange gerbera. She had personally checked the security arrangements, double-checked the guest list with Icon's marketing manager and confirmed that there would be a good media presence, so she was satisfied that everything was in place. Mentally ticking the elements off her checklist, all that remained to be done was the filling of the goody bags which were currently waiting for her in the hotel's office along with the goodies. Dermot Hudson hadn't known what she was talking about when she brought up the subject until she explained the concept, but then he warmed to the idea, particularly when he discovered that all Icon had to pay for were the bags. A large cosmetic company, clients of Icon, had donated product samples; an executive gym, vouchers for reduced rate membership; a whiskey distillery, miniatures of a new whiskey-based liqueur; and she had persuaded a corporate gifts company to part with small boxes of handmade Belgian chocolates and dinky stainless-steel business-card holders. All that was left to do was stuff the gift-bags which she had carefully chosen: Tiffany blue sporting Icon's corporate logo.

Dermot Hudson's mobile went off at that point and he excused himself. Crisis averted, Hope gave a sigh, this time of relief, and left the Gandon Rooms to set about the goody bags. She looked around for Amy with a view to getting her to help, comforting herself with the thought that surely she couldn't cock up a simple task like stuffing freebies into bags.

The hotel had been very accommodating and had suggested that she fill the bags in a small empty office to the rear of the health spa. When there was no sign of Amy in the vicinity of the Gandon Rooms she headed on to the health spa in the hope that she had used some of the initiative Ruby was always banging on about and had made a start. With no sign of her in the allocated room, she was on her way outside to see if Amy was there when she bumped into Ruby on her way in.

"No chance of getting Benjaos, I'm afraid. Irene said they're doing a recital up in Dundalk tonight."

Hope grinned for the first time that day. "Haven't you heard? Banjos are the new black."

Ruby returned the grin and they slapped a discreet high five.

As they set about stuffing the little blue gift carriers, Ruby said, "Where's Amy by the way?"

Hope felt a stab of guilt. "Um, I think I might have inadvertently fired her."

Ruby stared at her.

"Don't look at me like that. She told the car repo man where the car was and then there was the banjo debacle. I was – well – understandably a bit pissed off."

"So you fired her?"

"Well, not exactly. I said if I couldn't salvage the situation she was history, and after I'd sorted that and went to look for her, I bumped into you, and then I forgot about her."

"She probably went home," Ruby said. "She was very upset. You'll have to phone her and tell her it's OK, that you were angry and that she isn't really fired."

Hope, although she felt a touch guilty, wasn't sure. On the face of it, it seemed like a good opportunity to let Amy go. And strictly speaking, the way things were going, she wasn't altogether sure she could afford to take her on permanently anyway. "I don't know," she said. "You know what cash flow's like at the moment."

Ruby looked horrified. "But you can't sack Amy, Hope! We need her."

Hope gave a snort. "You're kidding. After her banjo

fiasco? If it wasn't for my brilliant quick thinking, Dermot Hudson could well have gone off on one when he walked in to 'It's a Long Way to Fucking Tipperary' instead of some tasteful Mozart."

"I'll grant you have a PhD in bullshit, Hope, but we really do *need* her," Ruby countered. "Just after you left the office I took another wedding booking." Hope groaned and Ruby glared at her. "Stop it! It's a big fuck-off mega-bucks do. Boozaboyz. The skinny darkhaired one with the tattoos. He and his fiancée want to get married in Ballintubber Abbey and have the party in Ashford Castle for four hundred. We'll need an extra pair of hands if we're to pull it off."

"Boozaboyz? The boy band?"

Ruby shrugged. "Well, the sort of punk-revival-meets-Westlife-ish-white-rapper boy band. And she said *OK* magazine have paid, like a gazillion pounds sterling for exclusive photo rights. We couldn't *pay* for that kind of publicity, Hope. Think of the business it'll bring in."

"'She' who?"

"Debbie – some assistant or other, suffice it to say one of their *'people'*." She etched quote marks in the air with the first two fingers of each hand.

"And it's a definite booking, not just an idle enquiry? Or worse, a wind-up?"

Ruby's head nodded vigorously. "Absolutely genuine. Janette and Herbie recommended us. Apparently Herbie's their road manager and Jeanette's a bridesmaid, or the bride's sister or something.

Anyway she was impressed enough with us to sell Prior Engagements big-time." She paused when she wasn't getting whoops of joy from Hope. "This is big, Hope. This could get us out of trouble. Think Posh and Becks. Think purple velvety thrones."

Hope gave an involuntary shudder, but pragmatic by nature she realised that beggars can't be choosers, and if getting into the high-end wedding market would save the business, then she'd have to grin and bear it until the corporate sector picked up again. In that case, Ruby's point about needing additional help was valid. But Amy? Surely she could do better than Amy.

"There has to be someone better qualified than her out there," she said, voicing her thoughts. "Someone a bit less ... I don't know ... a bit less wet."

"I'm sure there is," Ruby agreed, "but not for what you'd be paying. Anyway, despite today's – eh – misunderstanding, she knows the ropes and she's willing to learn." She paused and, appealing to Hope's better nature, added, "She really needs this job, Hope. She was unemployed for over a year before you took her on. And she has Lily to look after."

"Who's Lily?"

Ruby gave her a withering look. "*Lily*. Her four-year-old daughter. She's a single mum. Didn't you know?"

Hope shook her head. "She never said."

More like you never asked, Ruby thought.

"Perhaps I was a bit hard on her," Hope conceded after an awkward guilt-laden silence.

"So you'll keep her on?"

Hope sighed. "For now. But if there's one more cock-up ..."

"There won't be," Ruby promised. "By the way, the bride's calling in with her mum, Friday week at eleven for a preliminary meeting. Apparently the band's away on tour in Australia until the end of the month."

Hope gave a smirk. "Big down under then?"

Ruby nodded. "Looks like it." Then after a beat, "So you'll call Amy?"

Hope sighed. "Oh, all right! I'll call her."

It took a little under forty minutes for the two women to finish stuffing the goody bags after which, with the help of the hotel porter, they carted them into the Gandon Rooms and placed one on every seat. Clive, job complete, had left, and Gordo, who had already put the finishing touches to the amazing-looking cold seafood buffet, had the waiters lined up for a pep talk. Small he might be but he had a fearsome reputation so she was in no doubt that the service would be flawless. The banjo trio who, after checking the acoustics of the room, had settled on a play list and gone off for a coffee before kick-off, had now returned and were tuning up ready to start.

Hope glanced at her watch. "That's us done, and still fifteen minutes to spare."

"Looking good," Ruby commented, glancing around the room

As the first guests started to trickle in, the musicians

launched into 'Zipppity-doo-dah'. Hope couldn't fault their choice as an opener on the grounds that it is virtually impossible to hear that song and not feel positive.

"Can you hang around here for a while?" she asked Ruby. "And I'll see if I can get hold of Amy to tell her she's unfired."

Outside in the service area Hope dialled Amy's mobile. The call connected but after four rings switched to voicemail, suggesting that Amy had rejected the call. She felt a rush of annoyance that here she was, the bearer of good tidings, and the girl couldn't even be bothered to take the call. When the tone sounded she hesitated for a beat, then just said: "Call me, Amy. I need to talk to you."

After she had terminated the call, though, the irritation subsided. The prospect of a big-bucks contract, even if it was a wedding, was a step in the right direction. And as Ruby had pointed out, a splash in *OK* magazine wouldn't do them any harm either. She had learned never to underestimate the power of celebrity. Where Posh and Becks led, or in this case, skinny tattooed Boozaboy and his intended, others would follow. She cheered further remembering Ruby's comment about her car. Maybe she would be able to do a deal with the leasing company to get it back. Resolving to call Hugh Moore to check out the legality of the way in which the debt-collecting company had repossessed it, she headed off in search of Amy.

Pushing open the service entrance, she stepped outside. The wind had picked up again and the area was deserted.

"Fecking global warming," she muttered. "You'd think we'd at least get a couple of decent summers out of it."

Pulling up her coat collar, she walked in the shelter of the wall towards the side of the building leading to the front of the hotel, picking her steps to avoid ruining her new, totally scrumptious designer mules.

As she reached the corner she glanced over towards the quayside and what she saw caused her to stop dead in her tracks. Amy was standing precariously on top of the wall staring down into the water. The wind was ferociously whipping at her hair as she hugged her arms around her lean body. Momentarily stunned, Hope was just getting her head around the scene when a rogue gust buffeted the girl, causing her to wobble and throw out her arms for balance.

Shit, she's going to jump, thought Hope, appalled. *Oh, no! Not again!*

"*Amy! No!*" she yelled, but her voice was lost to the wind. She ran across the grass towards the wall, losing one of her mules in the process, looking around wildly for someone to help. "*Amy! No! Don't be stupid! You're not fired! It can't be that bad!*" But the wind swallowed her words once more.

Within a few yards of the girl, she yelled again. "*Amy!*"

The girl turned her head just as another strong gust hurled Hope forward into the stonework and Amy's legs, toppling her over the wall and into the water.

Hope struggled to her feet. Shaking, hanging onto the wall, she peered into the dock. At first she couldn't see Amy, but then her head bobbed to the surface for a few seconds before disappearing under the water again.

"Shit! Amy! Oh fuck!"

Hope looked around frantically. She had no idea what to do. Then she spotted a red-and-white lifebuoy hanging from a post a couple of yards away. Amy's head bobbed to the surface again a few yards from where she had sunk and Hope saw her gulp in a breath before a wave swamped her and she disappeared from view for a second time.

Only one more time, Hope thought. A drowning man sinks three times.

Peering into the murky water, she searched for any sign of Amy and then a head bobbed up again. Amy was fighting for breath, thrashing her arms.

Hope scrambled up on top of the wall and, clinging onto the wooden post, chucked the lifebuoy into the water. The wind caught it and carried it out too far but then a wave washed it to within six feet of the girl's back. Amy was looking directly at Hope now, still bobbing up and down in the water, waving one arm.

"Grab the ring, Amy! It's behind you! Grab the sodding ring!" Hope yelled.

Amy made a futile attempt to turn in the water but then another wave swamped her and she sank out of sight again. Jumping off the wall, Hope quickly peeled off her coat, jacket, pants, the remaining mule and clambered back up on top of the wall. Then sanity kicked in. I can't do this, she thought. It's madness. I'll fucking drown. At that point Amy broke the surface again, making liars out of the old wives, and the decision was taken out of Hope's hands as a further gust hit her square in the back, hurling her forwards and off the wall.

"Oh! Fuuuuuck!"

Plunging into the freezing cold brackish water knocked the breath out of her. It was deeper than she had anticipated. Kicking her legs she fought her way upwards, breaking the surface and sucking in a desperate breath. Amy was about ten feet away. She was struggling towards the lifebuoy but, as Hope swam towards her, her head disappeared under the water again. Hope waited a couple of seconds for Amy to resurface, but when she failed to appear, panic rising, she filled her lungs and dived under. Opening her eyes, she found visibility was next to zero. She swam in the general direction of where the girl had gone down, stretching out her arms, searching the water. A strong swimmer once upon a time, Hope kicked her legs up behind her and dived down towards the bottom. Her lungs were at bursting point. Suddenly her arm brushed against something. Fabric, a coat. Feeling her way in the muddy water she found an arm. Amy's. Grabbing it, she pulled her upwards towards the surface. Amy, totally panicked and disorientated, was fighting her every inch of the way. Hope thought her lungs would explode. She let a little air trickle from her mouth to ease the pressure. Suddenly Amy was climbing up Hope's body, making for the surface, in the process giving her a hefty kick in the stomach. A cascade of air bubbles escaped from Hope's mouth as Amy's frenzied efforts for survival knocked all the air out of her.

Suddenly she was light-headed and pretty lights danced before her eyes. It was a lovely warm comfortable feeling. Floating. Light as a feather. Stretching out her hand, she gave Amy one final push towards the surface.

Chapter 3

A gentle breeze rustled the leaves in the verdant canopy above her head. The ground was soft beneath her and an aromatic waft of rosemary and wild sage permeated the balmy air. This is *so* comfortable, she thought, feeling more relaxed than she had in months. She could feel the warmth of the sun on her face as dappled shadows danced over her skin. A bird was twittering concealed in the branches above her, a bee buzzed close by and somewhere she could hear cicadas.

Cicadas? In Ireland?

Abruptly she sat up.

In front of her a gentle slope descended towards a high overgrown hedge close to which three nanny goats grazed. She was lying in a field.

A field?

Disorientated, she tried to remember how she had come to be lying in a grove of trees in the middle of a field. And in the sun. It was a warm sunny day. This is mad, she thought. Then, looking down, she realised that all she was wearing was her underwear and a crumpled, slightly damp white shirt.

"Oh. You're awake."

Hope's heart did a somersault and her head shot around to the source of the voice as she simultaneously scuttled on her knees away from the sound.

He was sitting with his back against the trunk of the tree, legs outstretched, ankles crossed. Thin face, long bony nose, shaved head, odd-looking white jerkin and baggy pants, bare arms and feet.

"Shit! Who are you?"

"Reuben," he said. "Did you have a good kip?"

"How long have you been sitting there, you pervy creep," she snapped, self-consciously wrapping her arms around her body. "What have you done with my clothes?" Then a grotesque thought struck her. "This isn't some kinky kind of creepy Rohypnol thing is it?" She shuddered, anxiety rising as the implications dawned. "How did I get here? What did you do to me?"

Reuben stood up in one easy gliding motion, brushing grass off the seat of his pants. Hope shrank further away from him, glancing around in alarm, looking for help.

"Do? Me? Nothing," Reuben replied. "Why would I

do anything to you?" Shoving his hand in his pocket he took out a tin of tobacco and proceeded to deftly roll himself a cigarette. "Sorry about George," he said. "That was uncalled for, and in the strictest sense, cheating. He had no right."

Hope was on her feet now, edging away from the tree, eyes scanning the field for other people, for some means of escape. "Who's George? Did he spike my drink? How did I get here?"

Reuben tapped his pockets looking for matches and, finding them, lit his roll-up, inhaling deeply before throwing his head back and blowing a plume of smoke up into the branches. The way he held the roll-up between his index and middle finger, arm bent and raised close to his shoulder, looked very girly and alien, which was comforting in a weird kind of way. Observing the ritual, she silently weighed him up. He looked harmless enough but that meant nothing. And who the feck was George? She cast a glance over her shoulder expecting so see some threatening feral-looking Ted Bundy type called George creeping up on her, but apart from herself and Reuben the field was completely empty.

"Who's George?" she repeated. "Did he bring me here?"

"No one brought you here," Reuben said before taking another drag of the noxious weed. A bout of coughing ensued as the smoke went against his breath. When he had recovered sufficiently he said in a strangled voice, "You just arrived."

"*Arrived*?"

Reuben stared at her for a few seconds, then turning, reached behind the tree, withdrawing a sack which he threw in her direction. It landed six inches away from her feet. "You might want to put those on," he said.

Hope looked down at the bag, then back at Reuben. "Not until you tell me how I got here," she snapped, her patience wearing thin.

He shrugged. "Please yourself." Then after a pause he cocked his head to one side, staring at her from under sceptical hooded lids. "You really don't remember?"

Anger had displaced the fear now. "If I did I wouldn't be bloody well asking you, smartarse! Now for the last time, how did I get here and, more to the point, where the hell am I?"

"Where the hell? Depends on how you look at it," Reuben said. "Tell you what. Why don't you slip into the duds and I'll show you around."

Nonplussed, Hope just continued to stare at him.

Reuben stepped forward and, leaning down, picked up the sack, emptying the contents onto the ground in front of her. "Skirt, socks, jumper and boots," he said, then after a beat, "unless you want to walk round all day in your knickers."

Feeling suddenly vulnerable, Hope looked down at the proffered clothes and with one eye on Reuben picked up the skirt – long, tie-dyed, maroon and pink crinkly cotton. "I can't wear this. It's horrible. And the boho look is so last year."

"Knickers it is then," Reuben said, taking another hit of nicotine.

Hope raised the skirt to her nose, gingerly sniffing it, and was surprised when it smelt fresh and clean. "Don't you have anything else I could put on? Jeans maybe?"

Reuben shook his head. "Sorry."

"Look, I have to get back," she said, giving in and stepping into the skirt. "Do you have a mobile and a local cab number I can call?"

"No."

"No, you don't have a mobile, or no you don't have a cab number?" He was pissing her off big-time now.

"No to both." He flicked the butt end of his cigarette away into the grass. "Are you ready for the tour now?"

With the skirt fastened around her waist, Hope felt less vulnerable. Bending down, still with one eye on Reuben, she picked up the jumper. It was somewhat thickened as if it had seen the boil-wash more than once, but it too smelt clean and odour-free. This is fecking surreal, she thought. Better humour him though. Dropping the jumper back on the ground, she pulled on the socks and boots. Reuben in the meantime stood by passively, staring down the valley.

Hope picked up the jumper again, wondering whether or not to take it, then, deciding that it would be a good idea just in case it got cold before she made it back to Dublin, she tied it around her waist. "Won't you at least tell me where I am?"

Reuben shrugged. "I told you. It depends on how you look at it." Then without giving her a chance for further comment, he strode past her down the incline towards the hedge.

Hope hurried after him but found it hard to keep up in the oversized boots. "Where are we going?" she asked, struggling to keep in step. "Please tell me where I can get a cab."

"I told you. No cabs," Reuben said before taking an abrupt left through a gap in the hedge.

Hope stepped through the gap and stopped. Ahead of her in a flat field, half a dozen round buildings with felt roofs were grouped around a central area where a fire blazed in a rusty old oil-drum. A couple of beat-up caravans, a rusting VW campervan supported by bricks where the wheels used to be, and three Native American teepees were dotted around the opposite side of the clearing.

"Yurts," she said aloud, recalling a documentary she had seen not a week earlier about the traditional nomadic Mongolian round houses. "Those are yurts."

"Top marks," Reuben said pleasantly.

"Where did you say we were?" she asked again. "Is this some sort of New-Age traveller camp or something?" Then remembering a news report about a protest camp close to a contentious motorway currently under construction, she had it. "We're in the

Carrickmines and this is a crusty protest camp."

Reuben set off across the field towards the yurts, loping over dried mud-ruts. "Wro-oong! There's no crusty camp at Carrickmines."

Hope took off after him. "Look, joke over. I want to go home."

As they neared the largest of the yurts, Hope heard a fiddle playing, then she heard singing – women's voices. A Percy French piece – 'Eileen Oh'.

Hope stepped around Reuben. The singers were not crusties – not a dreadlock, tattoo, body-piercing or Mohawk in sight – but three hippie refugees from the sixties, except two thirds of the group looked too young, early twenties at most. Long hair, long skirts, not unlike the one Reuben had given her to wear, cheesecloth shirts and sandals. The third woman was more mature, fifty odd, with wrinkled weather-beaten skin that had obviously never seen moisturiser, and grey hair hennaed to an uneven orange colour. They were all sitting there on a log, swaying in time to the music. As Reuben approached they stopped singing and one of the younger women, the one playing fiddle, stood up.

"Hi, Reuben! Back again." She smiled at Hope. "Hi! I'm Celia. You're welcome." Then indicating the other two women added. "That's Skye, and this –" indicating the older one, "is Flo."

"So this is our new soul," Flo said, leaping up and darting forward in an attempt to hug Hope who deftly stepped out of range.

Shit, they're a fecking cult, was the first thought that
sprang into her mind. She had heard all about cults,
how they love-bomb pathetic people at airports and
bus stations, then attempt to brainwash them. Not that
she felt in any danger of that. She had no intention of
letting these mad women try it on with her. But not
wanting to create a scene, she decided that discretion
was the better part of valour.

"Look, there's been a bit of a mix-up and I need to
get back to Dublin. I have an important product launch
to manage today. Would you possibly have a phone and
the number of a local taxi firm?"

Flo looked at Reuben. "She doesn't know, does
she?"

Reuben shook his head. "Not yet. I wanted to show
her around first. Sort of break it to her gently. You have
to have a bit of sensitivity about these things, you
know."

"She does have a right to know, Reuben," Skye
piped up.

"Absolutely," Celia agreed.

"Look. This is all very pleasant, and I'm sure you
mean well, but the clock's ticking. I really *do* need to get
out of here," Hope said.

"Would you like something to eat?" Flo asked.
"Some tofu perhaps, or I think we might have some
cold nut roast and brown rice and red lentils left over
from last night."

Frustration setting in, Hope's voice took on an edge.

"No really, thank you. I just want to get home."

"The thing is," Reuben said, apologetically, "you *are* home."

Frustration gave way to anger. "That's what you think, sunshine! Look! For feck sake, will someone tell me what's going on here? Where am I? How did I get here, and how do I get back to Dublin?"

Reuben and the three Woodstock asylum-seekers all just stared at her, their expressions worryingly ranging from uncomfortable to sympathetic to pitying.

Reuben was first to break the silence. "What exactly do you remember about the last couple of hours?" he asked.

"Not a lot," Hope said flippantly. "I woke up under a tree in that field back there."

"No. Before that?" Reuben prompted. "This afternoon, at the Waterfront Hotel."

Hope looked down at her crumpled shirt. The truth was she could remember little of the afternoon. The banjo fiasco, yes. Filling the goody bags with Ruby. Going out to look for Amy. Then it hit her. "Amy. What happened to Amy? Is she OK?"

"Amy's fine. She could have drowned but she's fine. Mind you, it could have been a different story if it wasn't for George sticking his oar in."

George, again. "Who the fuck is George?"

Flo stepped forward and held out her hand. "I think you should sit down, dear."

Hope wasn't listening. It was coming back to her

now in a sort of mental video replay. Amy in the water. The gust of wind knocking her off the quay wall into the dock. Diving under to find Amy.

"That's it," she said. "I nearly drowned and was washed downriver, unconscious, and landed near here."

"Like Robinson Crusoe?" Flo said, then smiled. "In a way, I suppose."

"You must have found me and carried me to that field." Hope felt a flood of relief. "Right, now we've established that, perhaps you could point me in the right direction so I can hitch a lift back to Dublin."

Reuben gave a heavy sigh. "God, I hate this part." Then inhaling a deep breath he looked directly onto Hope's eyes. "The thing is, Hope. Well, the thing is . . . there's no easy way to say this, but actually you drowned. You're . . . well, not to put too fine a point on it . . . you're dead."

Hope stared at him. He was obviously deranged, either that or this was one of those embarrassing unfunny Jeremy Beadlesque TV shows. She glanced around looking for the hidden camera. The three women were all staring at her as was Reuben.

"Dead?" She laughed. "That's a bit weak."

"But true," Flo said. She wasn't laughing. Neither were the others. Not even a twitch.

"You drowned in the dock saving Amy. George pushed you in."

"Oh, shut up! I remember well what happened now.

45

I was on the wall and a strong gust of wind blew me in."

Reuben shook his head. "Sorry, but that was George. He panicked."

"I've had enough of this," Hope said. "You're all mental. Dead?" she snorted. "Give me a break."

Pushing past Flo she purposefully strode past the fire and the yurts towards the field's perimeter about seventy or eighty metres distant where she had spied a gate. "I'm out of here."

The field, although green and lush, was uneven and furrowed with dried mud-ruts, and Hope had to watch her step to avoid stumbling. The boots didn't help, neither did the long skirt which she had hiked up to avoid tripping over the hem. After fifty metres or so she looked up expecting to be close to the gate but in fact it seemed to be further away. She stopped, glancing back over her shoulder, where Reuben and the three women were still standing looking in her direction. Reuben even gave her a wave.

Well, at least they're not coming after me, she thought, relieved. She was further relieved that no one she knew could see her in the awful mismatched boho clothes. "God!" she muttered. "Do they all need the services of a stylist or what!" She set off again towards the gate, carefully watching her step. There had to be a house somewhere, she reasoned. I'll knock on the first door I come to and ask them if I can call a cab.

"There's really no point."

Spinning around, she almost lost her footing as her boot stubbed against a small rock. Reuben was walking beside her at an easy pace, not even out of breath.

Looking past him she saw that the three women were sitting back on the log some fifty metres away, and although they were out of earshot, from the collective swaying it was obvious they had returned to their singing. "How did you do that?"

"There's really no point," Reuben repeated. "And the sooner you come to terms with the fact that you're dead the better. Trust me, denial is futile."

Pursing her lips Hope determinedly quickened her pace, eyes fixed on the gate, teeth gritted. I shan't talk to him, she thought. Talking is only encouraging him. If I ignore him he'll go away.

"Sorry. That's where you're wrong. Ignoring me will do you no good. I'm going nowhere."

It took a half a second for Hope's brain to catch up. She stopped dead, certain that she hadn't voiced her thoughts aloud. Whoever this weirdo was, he appeared to have the ability to read her mind. She turned around. Reuben had stopped a pace behind her. "How did you do that?" she demanded. "How did you know what I was thinking?"

Reuben smiled and gave a little shrug but made no reply.

Hope turned her head and looked towards the gate. It seemed further away than ever now. Weird. Surreal.

Bizarre. She had no idea what to do. It occurred to her that maybe she had ingested some hallucinogenic drug, magic mushrooms or something. Maybe Reuben had found her by the river (though, even more weirdly, there wasn't any sign of a river in the immediate vicinity) – maybe he had found her by the river, wherever it was, and drugged her in order to get her to join the cult.

"This isn't a cult," he said, unnerving her further.

Hope spun back around to face him. She was both angry and disturbed. Angry that he was playing silly games, angry that she now found herself in the middle of nowhere when she should have been in the Waterfront Hotel keeping a weather eye on the Icon product launch. Disturbed that this nutter wouldn't go away.

"Who the fuck *are* you?" she demanded, hands on hips, feet planted.

He sighed. "I told you. I'm Reuben and I'm your Guardian Angel."

Anger boiled up inside Hope. "Oh puh ... leeease!"

Picking up her skirts and turning back towards the gate, she ran at speed towards it, leaping over the rocks and ruts in an adrenaline-fuelled dash. She was sweating, hyper, determined to reach the gate and flag down the first car she came upon. Glancing over her shoulder, Reuben was nowhere in sight which was something of a relief, but when she turned her head back towards the gate there he was, five yards in front of her.

This can't be happening, reason told her. He was behind me. I didn't see him pass. That was the point at which her boot found a large rock and she tumbled over heavily, whacking her head off the ground, then she was tumbling head over heels into darkness, like Alice down the rabbit hole.

Chapter 4

Opening her eyes she found she was lying on her back on a hard narrow bed in a dimly lit space. A coarse wool blanket covered her, and she could hear rain lashing down outside and smell wood-smoke. Pushing herself up she saw that she was in a round room at the centre of which stood an iron pot-bellied stove, embers glowing red through the glass panel of the door. I'm in one of the yurts, she reasoned.

As her eyes became accustomed to the light she made out Reuben sitting on the floor at the end of the bed, quite still, legs crossed, with his back against the wall. Aware that she had stirred, he glanced in her direction.

"How are you feeling?" he asked, standing up,

moving over to the side of the bed.

Hope squinted at her watch but the glass was cracked so she couldn't see the hands. "What time is it?"

"Time means nothing," Reuben said.

"Maybe not to you, but I have things to do. You can't keep me here, you know!" She swung her legs over the side of the bed and stood up to face him, swaying slightly after the sudden activity. "If you let me go now, call me a taxi, that'll be an end to it. No police. It's forgotten. OK?"

Reuben shook his head, sighed, then placed his hand on her shoulder. Later, if asked, she would be unable to explain how it happened, but at that precise moment, as soon as Reuben's hand touched her shoulder, a comforting warmth suffused her entire body – call it peace – and she knew. Knew for certain that what he had told her was the truth.

"Denial is futile, Hope," he said with sincere compassion.

It took her a moment to get her head together. "So I really *am* dead?"

He nodded. "I'm afraid so. Drowned. By the time the emergency services got there and fished you out, it was too late. The paramedics couldn't revive you."

Hope sat down heavily on the bed again, dropping her head into her hands. "But it's too soon. I'm too young." She stifled a sob. "It's all Amy's fault. It's not fair."

"Not Amy's – George's fault."

George, again. She lifted her head and looked up wearily at Reuben.

"George is Amy's Guardian," he explained. "It wasn't her time and George isn't fond of water, so when she fell in, he shoved you in after her so she'd be saved."

"But what about me? It wasn't my time either."

"Sorry about that. But if it's any consolation I'm not over the moon about the situation either. I'm supposed to be your Guardian. I'm supposed to keep you safe until your allotted time, so it doesn't look good for me if you cross the great divide ahead of schedule. Believe me, Management take a very dim view."

"Management?"

Reuben cast his eyes briefly towards the ceiling and she understood.

"So where am I now?" she asked.

"Sorry to be so noncommittal, but it's like I said earlier. It depends on how you look at it."

"I don't understand."

Reuben took her by the hand and led her towards the door, pushing it outwards. Outside it was still daylight, but the day had turned grey and chilly. The rain she had heard on waking had ceased and the field was muddy, the ruts filled with rainwater which had turned to a sticky viscous consistency. As she stepped through the door, raindrops dripped from the felt roofing down the back of her neck causing her to shiver.

Over the clearing in front of the doorway of a teepee near the oil-drum fire, Celia was playing a fiddle whilst a guy with a beard was playing a button accordion. Flo was giving a tin whistle some wellie and Skye, also on fiddle, was beavering away like a dervish on speed, tapping her foot in time to the music, whilst a couple of thin mangy-looking mongrels sniffed around their feet. Hope didn't recognise the tune drifting across the clearing but it sounded like another never-ending Irish traditional diddly-eye air.

"How would you describe this place?" Reuben asked.

"Hell," Hope said flippantly then her hand shot to her mouth. "Shit! I'm in hell! Hell is a hippie commune. A muddy, damp crusty camp. One long interminable traditional music session with tofu, nut roast, brown rice and red lentils!" Across the clearing the musicians, eyes closed in concentration, played manically on. The only thing that could possibly make it worse in her estimation was if someone struck up on the uilleann pipes or started bashing a bodhrán. As the thought entered her head, the flap of the teepee moved aside and a weasily guy with a Mohawk and nose-piercing exited carrying a set of pipes under his arm. He was followed by a crusty woman with dreads, around the same vintage as Flo, carrying a bodhrán which, as Hope watched, she settled on her knee and began rattling away at with a bone. Despite the rain, the damp, the mud and the chill however, the motley group of musicians appeared to be enjoying themselves.

"That's the point," Reuben said gently, creeping her out again with his mind-reading act. "See what I mean?"

Hope looked up at him. "How very Jean-Paul Sartre," she muttered, the concept leaving her decidedly tense. "Hell is other people." She let out a groan. "Do I really have to stay here, Reuben? Isn't there a Prada Heaven or even, at a push, the Stella McCartney version?"

Reuben shrugged. "You each get what you deserve. Those are the rules."

Hope shivered. The damp chill was seeping into her bones. "The only thing worse than this would be the fiery furnace concept," she said. "On second thoughts, forget I said that. It's fifty-fifty, and at least I'd be warm."

The monotonous wail of the pipes and the scrape of the fiddles were depressing. "Please tell me they're going to stop soon," she pleaded. "This isn't fair. What did I do that was so terrible? What did I do to deserve this?"

Reuben averted his eyes and mumbled, "Haven't seen the file."

Frustrated by the sparse information, she persisted. "But surely you'd have noticed if I'd committed some heinous crime against humanity, because God knows if I did. I can't remember."

The angel rubbed his hand over his shaved head, his body language indicating that he was uncomfortable with the topic. "Look, it's not my place to be judgmental. I just do guardian duty."

"Evidently not that well," she snapped.

"Granted," he conceded. "I saved you more than once during my tenure though. Remember the snow drift incident on the mountain road in Wales?"

"That was you?"

"And when you couldn't find your passport at the airport when you were supposed to fly out to New York for that wedding on September 9th. 2001?"

The memory came back to her with a jolt. She and Josh were heading out to his brother's wedding in Boston and had planned to spend a couple of days in New York, the highlight of which was supposed to be breakfast in the restaurant at the very top of the World Trade Centre on the morning of September 11th. At check-in she couldn't find her passport which she'd distinctly recalled putting in her bag along with Josh's and the tickets. They'd been unable to get another flight until three days later by which time all flights had been cancelled.

"I thought that was just luck," she said. "Fate."

He shook his head. "Yours truly," then placed the palm of his hand on his chest. "But for me you'd have either fried or frozen to death. Today was the first time I slipped up."

Gratitude forgotten, she muttered, "Don't I know it! And I'm in fecking trad-music, New-Age, crusty hell as a result."

Reuben sighed. "I'm not too thrilled about it either. For us it's three strikes and you're out."

"What do you mean?"

"You're my third strike. I'd already lost two other souls before their time. When you were born into my charge, I was on a warning."

Intrigued, despite her agitation, she asked, "So who were the other two?"

"Glen Miller, the band leader, was the first one." He frowned. "That wasn't my fault either, but would they listen? There was more to that incident than meets the eye, you know? Some covert stuff going –"

"Yes, yes," Hope cut in. "So who was the other one?"

Disappointment that Hope, like His Omnipotence, wasn't interested in his explanation flashed across his face. "Janice Joplin," he said grudgingly, his thin features taking on a sulky expression.

"You were really Janice Joplin's Guardian Angel?" Hope was impressed.

Cheered by her enthusiasm, he nodded. "She was tricky, that one. I felt it a tad unfair to blame me considering her lifestyle. And choking on her own vomit wasn't something I expected. I thought she was just snoring …" He stared at the floor for a moment, remembering, then gave a sigh of resignation. "Those are the breaks. I suppose Management thought you'd be less challenging."

"So let me get this straight," Hope said. "You were fired. God gave you the boot."

"In a manner of speaking. More like a three-match suspension. It's a 'go sit over there and think about what you've done' situation. Depressing, isn't it?" He kicked at a stone, sending it skidding across the mud into a glutinous puddle. "George's fault, of course. He had two strikes against him too, so I guess that's why he panicked. Can't blame him, I suppose."

"So who were his failures?" she asked.

Reuben waved his hand dismissively. "Oh, no one you'd have heard of."

"I didn't realise it worked like that. I always pictured angels as …" she searched for the words.

"What? Ethereal beings in white robes?" he said a half-smile on his lips.

Hope nodded. "Well, yes. And wings. I thought angels had wings."

"No wings either. Don't need them to get around."

"So I noticed," she concurred. "I didn't imagine for a moment an angel would look like you though."

"Strictly speaking I don't look like this," he said. "I only have this form for my time here, to help me blend in. Actually I'm just pure energy. No substance at all."

"So they dumped you here too."

"Yes." He sighed. "Believe me, I'd far rather be on the earth plane in my capacity of Guardian. Most of the time it's a very satisfying existence. And this place doesn't appeal at all. I suppose at least we have that in common."

Then a thought struck her. "Hang on a minute. I just

saved someone's life. That has to be worth something."

Reuben raised one eyebrow. "Strictly speaking that's debatable."

"Oh, come on! Despite the fact that George pushed me in, I was up on the wall. I'd taken my clothes off. I was going to dive in anyway."

The hippie angel gave her a leery look.

"Oh all right, I was a bit reluctant, but I would have. I wouldn't have just stood there and let her drown. And I did save her. You're not going to tell me it was this George character, considering his aversion to water."

"So what's your point?" he asked.

She shrugged. "I'm not sure. This has to be a mistake. Isn't there any sort of appeals procedure? Surely sacrificing my own life in order to save another has to give me some clout for getting out of here?"

Reuben made no comment, but she could see that he was thinking it over.

"And it wouldn't do you any harm. I mean if I get promoted to Prada Heaven, at least you can sit out your suspension in comfort."

"I'll look into it," he said and promptly disappeared.

Hope wasn't sure which aspect of Reuben disturbed her most, the mind-reading, or his ability to dematerialise and pop back up at will. That's angels for you, she thought, surprised by how quickly she had bought into the whole concept.

The crusty trad band came to the end of the tune, and relief flooded Hope's head as she basked in the ensuing delicious silence, rolling her neck to get rid of the tension. The grim grey clouds parted showing glimpses of clear blue sky, a shaft of sunlight bathed her face with warmth and light, and a soft balmy breeze wafted sandalwood smoke from the fire towards her. Maybe this place isn't so bad after all, she thought, closing her eyes and raising her face, luxuriating in the warmth of the sun. But she held that thought for only a split second before the ensemble ruined it by breaking into some unrecognisable but depressing dirge, the grimness only accentuated by the droning of the uilleann pipes. Clamping her hands over her ears she retreated back through the mud into the yurt, shoving the door closed in an attempt to dampen the noise.

The sight of Reuben sitting on the bed startled her.

"I thought you'd gone off to plead my case," she said, indignant.

Reuben held up a box file. "Done and dusted. I'm back."

"Already?"

"Time means nothing," he repeated, then picking up a briar pipe he proceeded with the lengthy process of getting it to light. He looked oddly incongruous holding the pipe, the way a child does when he mimics a largely adult occupation, and if she were to be picky, a touch effeminate too. Hope watched him sucking away at it and, scowling impatiently, fanned away the sickly sweet cloud of tobacco smoke that enveloped her.

"And?" she repeated.

Reuben took another couple of puffs, then convulsed in a coughing fit. At that point Hope wished that he would give up altogether on tobacco and give a less noxious vice a try. *"And?"*

He smiled, revealing a set of perfect white teeth, his eyes crinkling at the corners. "It looks as if we're in luck."

Chapter 5

"Run that by me again," she said.

Reuben tapped his pipe against the pot-bellied stove, emptying the ash over the stone hearth, wrinkling his nose with distaste. "It took some persuasion, but I pleaded your case and my supervisors were amenable to your request for an appeal."

"I got that part. You said there were certain conditions."

He nodded and tapped the box file with the back of his pipe. "It's all in here," he said.

"What?"

"Your transgressions."

She reached out to snatch it from him, but he pulled it away. "Sorry," he said. "Confidential. More than my job's worth, and I'm skating on thin ice at the moment as you well know."

"You said something about returning to the scene of the crime. What did you mean by that? I'm not a criminal. What am I supposed to have done?"

"Sorry," Reuben said. "Crime was probably the wrong word. The thing is, the powers-that-be total up every transgression, and there's a sliding scale of tariffs depending on the final score."

Hope was incredulous. "What? Like SAT scores? That's ridiculous."

"I don't see why." He opened the box file and flipped through the printed sheets therein. "It's all down here in black and white. Just like the nuns told you in scripture class."

Hope snorted. "So if someone, say, kills someone but for the rest of their life is a paragon of virtue, and someone else, me for instance, commits a whole load of small sins, technically we could both end up here?"

Reuben shook his head. "No, no. It's way more complicated than that in practice, but in theory I suppose you could be right, working on the tally principle."

It seemed a very arbitrary system to her and grossly unfair. "So what about the concept of forgiveness?"

He gave her a wan smile. "Ah, there's the rub. One has to ask for forgiveness in order to be forgiven. Therefore one has to acknowledge one's sins. Take responsibility for one's actions." He paused. "Correct me if I'm wrong, but I can't say I remember you ever beating a path to the confessional box."

"It's a concept I have difficulty with," Hope said, defensively. "I don't suppose there's a chance I could do it retrospectively?"

Reuben smiled. "Funny you should ask that. The thing is, considering the breakdown in communication, it's been agreed that you'll have the opportunity to do just that." He waited for some comment from her but when none was forthcoming he continued. "This is a first, Hope. Never been done before. And I have to say with some modesty, that but for me it would have been a non-runner." He paused expectantly, waiting for her to at least show a modicum of appreciation, but her senses were numbed by the surreal nature of the situation. "It was only when I pointed out their cock-up in the sacrifice-for-the-sake-of-another category, which you hadn't been credited with, that they caved in."

"I should think so," she muttered. "Least they could do considering."

Miffed by her lack of gratitude, he frowned. "A *thank you* would be nice."

Hope snapped. "For what? I shouldn't even be here. I'm not supposed to be dead. You were supposed to be my Guardian for feck sake."

"Well, maybe if you'd acquitted yourself better on the earth plane, you'd be in Prada Heaven," he countered. "Anyway, the point is, what happened, happened. What you did, you did. George did what he did. But at least you have a chance of making amends – a way out of here." He patted the box file again.

Frustrated, Hope pleaded, "But if you don't tell me what I'm supposed to have done, how can I defend myself or make amends? How can I ask for forgiveness?" Reaching out she made another attempt to grab the file. "Give it here."

Reuben deftly snatched it out of range again. "Sorry. No can do. We'll deal with the incidents individually, starting first thing in the morning."

"Deal with in what way?"

"Like I said. We return to the scene of the cr – the incidents," he amended. "You'll discover the consequences of your actions, and in some cases will get the opportunity to take different action."

"I don't understand. If it's already happened, how can I change it? Won't that upset the space-time continuum thingy?" she asked.

Reuben sniggered. "You've been watching too much science fiction. And if you don't mind me saying so, you have a very inflated opinion of your importance in the grand scheme of things." Placing the box file on the end of the bed he turned and stood with his back to the stove, savouring the heat. "We're not talking about the big picture here, which is fortunate. In the global scheme of things your actions only affected a limited number of souls. And as far as I'm aware you didn't start or prevent a world war, or tragically meet your end whilst on the brink of discovering a cure for AIDS."

Ignoring the sarcasm Hope felt a slight tingle of, well, *hope*. "So I could change things? Make different choices?" she said, a number of possibilities springing to mind mainly in the "total-fuck-up-if-I-had-my-time-over" category.

"Not those choices," he said, exercising his mind-reading ability. "The only things you can change are actions that wounded or caused other souls hurt, loss or trouble. But that's not the point of the exercise – the main purpose is for you to acknowledge your transgressions and seek retrospective forgiveness."

Disappointed by his swift put-down, she opened her mouth to protest but Reuben raised his hand to silence her objection.

"No, Hope. Your life will remain the same. You cannot change those choices. And if I may reiterate, the whole point of the exercise is for you to acknowledge your wrongdoing and where applicable and possible, make small changes to lessen the negative effects on others. Only then can you seek forgiveness."

"Bummer," she said. "So I can't change my mind about Dylan?"

"I'm afraid not," he said. "But you could make amends."

Hope scowled. "What for? Are you mad?"

The angel cocked his head to one side and gave her a long steady look. She waited for him to expand on the ridiculous amends-to-Dylan statement but was disappointed when after a few more seconds he gave a sad sigh. "That's what I'm talking about, Hope. You just can't see it."

"Can't see *what*?" she pleaded, frustrated to the point of screaming.

"Hope, face it, you're totally self-centred. It's always *me – me – me*, poor me. Always someone else's fault." He paused, examining his fingernails for a beat, then thrashed on. "You never take responsibility, do you?"

He might just as well have walloped her across the face.

"That's a bit harsh," she said, cut to the quick. "I'd challenge that statement. And you're not one to talk. As I see it you haven't taken responsibility for your cock-ups either."

Ignoring her indictment he said, "So name me one instance. One time where you've thrown up your hands and said 'It was my own stupid fault!'."

She felt colour flooding upwards from her neck to her face. "I thought you weren't allowed to be judgmental."

"I just tell it like it is," he said, picking up the box file again. "Some things would test the patience of an angel." He smiled then to take the harm out of it, his eyes crinkling attractively at the corners, before adding in a more friendly tone, "Are you hungry? I'm starved."

Despite feeling hurt and affronted by what she perceived to be unwarranted criticism, at the mention of food Hope realised that she was very hungry having eaten nothing since breakfast. She was also relieved that he had changed the subject. She wasn't up for a fight, particularly with Reuben, aware that he was her only ticket out. "I am quite peckish," she said.

He smiled at her again. "Come on then. Let's go across for supper. Flo's cooking."

Untying the boil-wash sweater from around her waist, she pulled it on over her head in preparation for going outside. "So what's on the menu? Nothing I'd call edible for sure."

Reuben put an arm around her shoulder. "Close," he grinned, shepherding her towards the door. "Flo's doing her red lentil and nut roast with tofu, and if my memory serves me correctly, soya milk pudding for dessert. How's that?"

Hope groaned and a mental image of her discarded BLT lying in the bin oozing creamy mayo sprang to mind causing her mouth to water. "Couldn't we just head back to the earth plane right now and grab a gourmet pizza in the Temple Bar Milano?"

Whilst Reuben tucked into his plate of nut roast and grey, unappetizing, gelatinous tofu, Hope could only move hers half-heartedly around her plate. It wasn't just the food, and in fairness to the crusty hippies, they had made every attempt to make her feel welcome (and thankfully had stopped playing their instruments, for the duration of supper at any rate) but the ramifications of her situation were only just sinking in. She had never given death, let alone the after-life much, if any, thought, and the fires of hell story that the nuns had drilled into her was certainly way too far-fetched for her to give it any credence. But neither had she expected this. Then there was the whole other matter of eternity. Reuben's repeated phrase, "time means nothing", took on a completely new and thoroughly terrifying resonance. Eternity. What was Estée Lauder thinking when she named her perfume after such an appalling hypothesis?

Reuben leaned towards her and, in a low voice, said, "She didn't mean eternity in the true sense – she was referring to eternal love until death us do part. Of course, it could be argued that love transcends death, but that's a whole other argument."

"Will you stop doing that?" she hissed. "It's rude to listen to other people's thoughts."

"Well, sorry. But I can't just tune out, you know," he said, then raising his palms and theatrically placing them over his ears, he turned away and started talking to Flo who was sitting on his right.

Great, she thought. Of all the angels in the whole of the firmament, I have to get the precious queen.

Skye, who was sitting across from them at the other side of the stove, having finished her supper picked up her fiddle. As she did so, the bearded guy, whom Hope had heard someone call Lucas, retrieved his button accordion from behind the log they were sharing. Hope didn't wait for the crusty to pick up his uilleann pipes, but quietly placed her plate on the floor and slipped outside.

The sky was cloudless and lit by an ethereal light which, had they been on earth, would have been the moon. Behind her the others were all tuning up their instruments and she could hear the murmur of conversation.

I have to get out of here, she thought. I can't stay here for eternity, I'd rather ... Shit! I'm already dead. Then another thought struck her. Unless ... She barely dared think it, in case Reuben was listening in, but she couldn't send the notion away. Unless ...

Trotting across the field, mindful of the muddy ruts, she made her way back to her allotted yurt. In the morning, Reuben was going to take her back to learn some kind of lesson, to give her the opportunity to achieve forgiveness and thus promotion to Prada Heaven. And, he had said, that would involve righting some wrongs – so presumably she'd have to relive parts of her life in order to do that. Well, if so, she thought, I'll go along with it. I'll do every thing he asks, but when it comes to Amy, I'll be devious. I won't let her get to me. I'll be so nice to her she won't want to jump in the first place. And if she doesn't jump, I won't drown ... after all, Reuben had admitted it wasn't my allotted time to cross the great divide ...

She shivered with excitement. It has to work, she thought. I won't be breaking the rules because I won't be changing *my* life as such. I'll be changing Amy's. I'll just make sure that Amy's life is so wonderful, suicide will be the last thing on her mind.

The more she thought about it, the more she felt it was doable. Being nice to Amy, making her life better would be a breeze compared to the alternative.

Pulling her bed closer to the stove, she wrapped herself in the coarse blanket and settled herself down for the night in the hope that if everything went according to plan, this would be her first and last night in hell.

* * *

"OK," Reuben said. "Here's the thing."

They were sitting under the tree in the copse on the hill above the encampment. It was quite early and the mist had not yet burned off in the valley. Earlier, hunger had driven Hope to consume a large bowl of porridge which tasted surprisingly good, despite the drizzle of goat's milk and the lack of sugar. Reuben had offered her a spoon of honey but as she had never been fond of honey she had passed. Wally, the uilleann piper, was just tuning up as she swallowed her last mouthful, and Celia looked set to pick up her fiddle, so she cast a glance at Reuben and they both baled out before fiddler and piper had time to get into their stride.

"If only they'd play something less dreary. And short. Something short would be preferable," she muttered as, noses wrinkled, they picked their steps through the muddy ruts, past the pig pen towards the gap in the hedge.

"I think it's a case of the piper calling the tune," Reuben observed as behind them Wally's pipes wailed the first sorrow-laden notes of a lament.

Even a distance away under the trees, occasionally the wind carried the sound in snatches to her ears. Under normal circumstances she would have been able to tune out, but the incessant nature of it was like an itch, and however she tried to ignore it, it impinged on her consciousness.

"Here's the thing," Reuben repeated, as if trying the phrase out for size. Then satisfied with the sound of it, continued, "We're going back very soon, so it's important that you understand the rules of engagement."

"I know," she said, anxious to get on with it. "I can't change my own life, just minimise the way I caused others hurt or harm. I get it. Now can we go? It seems I've a lot to make up to Amy for."

The angel stood up and offered her his hand. "First things first," he said.

For Hope who was bent on cutting to the chase, this didn't bode well. "But shouldn't Amy be first?" she asked, innocence personified as she struggled to her feet, impeded by the long peasant skirt.

"All in good time," he said.

Hope, swallowing her impatience, smiled at him. "I thought time meant nothing."

"Only in the afterlife," he said and she shuddered at the implications of eternity as she reached out and took his hand.

Chapter 6

The air was stuffy, suffused with cigarette smoke and the smell of stale beer. Coming to her senses she found that she was slumped on the floor in the corner of a bar. She felt fuzzy-headed and disoriented, though not drunk, and had no memory of how she had got there. The bar was crowded. A few feet away a rowdy group in rugby jerseys were singing 'The Fields of Athenry' and she experienced a brief flash of déjà vu.

As the impromptu choir came to the final dubiously executed harmonies of the anthem, she felt suddenly both claustrophobic and nauseous. Struggling to her feet she looked around for Reuben but he was nowhere in sight. Where the feck am I, she thought, panic rising, not sure if she was in some other hell or back in the land of the living. Then the floor moved beneath her feet and she was thrown forward into one of the singers, knocking him off balance, spilling half his pint. There was a good-natured whoop of "Whoa, Neddy!" as he steadied her with his free hand. Embarrassed, she muttered an apology, then the floor shifted again and she lurched back into the wall, whacking her elbow against hard metal. It took a second for her brain to unscramble the information. She was on a boat, or more accurately, a ship, evidently in the teeth of a gale. With this realisation the nausea immediately developed into a full-scale need to hurl, so she pushed her way through the crowd towards an exit sign, flailing her arms to make passage. Her ears were ringing, she felt faint, she was sweating profusely and her mouth was filling with saliva.

The rush of a salty wind hit her full in the face as she staggered outside to the deck, clinging onto the wall to keep her feet. Beyond the deck railing it was pitch black which made the heavy swell all the more alarming. The need to vomit however superseded caution and she made for the side, the pitching of the ship accelerating her passage, smacking her against the rail as she puked up her breakfast, dry-retching violently even after the contents of her stomach had long been evacuated. Groaning, she clung on, wishing for death as a better alternative, alive to the irony that she was already dead – livid that God, or whoever, appeared to be having a laugh at her expense. Suddenly an eternity of uilleann pipers seemed marginally less awful than infinite seasickness, particularly when the release of death was no longer an option. The dizziness subsided after a brief while and she shivered with cold, only her thin cotton shirt and the boil-wash jumper, now peppered with a few rogue splashes of vomit, between her and the elements. The crinkly peasant skirt, damp with spilt beer and sea-spray, clung to her legs and she was hard pressed to think of any one time when she had felt more desolate.

Feeling a hand on her elbow she turned her head expecting to see the elusive Reuben, but instead recognised the singer in the beer-stained rugby shirt.

"Are you all right?" he yelled, his voice half carried off by the wind.

"Do I look all right?" she moaned, irritated, holding on with both hands, laying her forehead against the cold metal.

He leaned in closer. "Sorry? Didn't catch that. The wind …"

Shaking her head she feebly waved him away but he was clearly bent on being a Good Samaritan. She had neither the strength nor the inclination to argue when he took her arm and led her out of the wind into the shelter of a covered walkway.

"Can I get you a port and brandy?" he asked. "It's great for seasickness."

Wishing he would just leave her alone in her misery, she shook her head again, a pathetic moan escaping from her lips.

He wouldn't take no for an answer though. "You look in a bad way. Sit down over there before you fall down, and I'll get you that drink." He guided her over to a bench by the bulkhead. "Terrible thing, seasickness."

Rugby Guy went back inside and Hope slumped down on the bench, bent double, her arms wrapped around her waist to ease the pain developing in her guts, her head in her lap. Although a strong swimmer, the sea and she had never been close friends, and she utterly detested boats, the mere sight of one enough to bring on instant queasiness. What the feck am I doing here, she thought. Despite Reuben's assurance that he was taking her back to her past life, she was afraid that this was some kind of celestial sick joke and, like the Ancient Mariner, she was doomed to sail stormy seas forever, which to her mind was grossly unfair considering that, for the life of her, she couldn't remember shooting an albatross.

"You're on the ferry. Don't you remember?"

Reuben was sitting at the other end of the bench, long legs stretched out, hands dug deep into the pockets of a heavy brown overcoat, back against the wall.

"What ferry?"

"To Wales. January 1989."

She sat up abruptly. "I'm back in 1989? Why, for pity's sake?"

"Think about it."

The door to the bar opened and Rugby Guy walked back out onto the deck, a glass cupped in his fist, and stood in front of her, feet planted apart for balance. "Here," he said, handing it to her. "Take small sips. It'll settle your stomach." Without invitation he sat down next to her, paying Reuben no heed. "My name's Eoin." He offered her his hand. "Are you going to the match?"

Ignoring the proffered hand, she felt too ill to entertain small talk. "*What*?"

If he noticed her ungraciousness he ignored it. "Munster and Cardiff." He was full of enthusiasm.

"Don't be stupid!" she snapped, then put the glass to her lips, taking a tentative sip. She was afraid she wouldn't be able to keep it down, and was relieved when the warmth of the spirit sliding down her gullet instantly calmed the nausea and eased the pain.

"That wasn't very nice," Reuben said. "He's only trying to help. See, that's what I'm talking about. Your historical disregard for the feeling of others."

"Oh, piss off!"

Rugby Guy looked wounded, so she glanced past him towards Reuben. "Not *you* – him," she said to make a lie of Reuben's last remark.

Eoin turned his head to look.

She took another sip from the glass. "This is 1989, right?"

He nodded, a touch bemused.

"You doubted my word?" the angel said.

Hope leaned forward again to address Reuben. "Just

checking. You still haven't said why I have to come back here."

Eoin was lost. "I'm sorry?"

Her eyes shifted back to him. "Not *you*, stupid," she repeated impatiently, her eyes swivelling once more to Reuben. "*Him!*"

"*Who?*"

"*Him. Reuben.*"

"He can't see me," Reuben said. "He thinks you're a nutter."

Confirming Reuben's assumption, Eoin edged a little further away along the bench. "Are you on something?"

Hope gave an impatient sigh. "Forget it." Then knocking back the remainder of the port and brandy, she gave a shudder as the strong spirit took her breath away. To her ongoing annoyance she realised that Eoin wasn't about to give up.

"Um …are you on your own?"

"Afraid I've escaped from the asylum?" she snapped. "You don't know the half of it, sunshine."

She felt helpless. Out of control. She wanted to scream. To open her mouth and shriek with despair.

"I'm dead," she wailed dejectedly. "Fucking dead and I'm only thirty-six. It's not fair."

"Look, is there someone to meet you when we get in to Pembroke?" He sounded concerned.

Despite that, he was getting right up her nose, prattling on at her when all she wanted was for him to leave her alone so she could find out what Reuben expected her to do. "Why don't you just piss off!" she snarled.

Even Good Samaritans have their limits. His face hardened and he stood up. "Please yourself. I was only trying to help."

"Hit on me more like," she countered tersely.

He laughed at that. "Don't flatter yourself. Have you taken a look in the mirror lately?" Turning abruptly, he stomped off back to the bar.

"He was trying to hit on me. Take no notice," Hope said.

Reuben smirked. "I don't think so. You look dog-rough right now."

Self-consciously she ran her hand through her hair. "It's these awful clothes. Anyway, there was no need for him to so pass-remarkable. He's no oil painting. Did you see the belly on him?"

"Speaking of clothes," Reuben leaned down to the side, produced a navy duffle coat from nowhere and offered it to her, "here. You look cold."

She felt like telling him to stuff it, that she wouldn't be seen dead in a duffel coat, (ha ha) but a blast of cold salty wind changed her mind. "Thanks," she muttered grudgingly, struggling into it, digging her hands in the pockets for warmth. "You still haven't told me why I have to come back to 1989 of all years. What did I ever do to Dylan? He had a good shot at ruining my life, for feck sake."

"There you are! Always on the defensive," Reuben said triumphantly. "OK. So tell me your version of events."

"My *version*?" She gave a snort. "Like there's another way to tell it?"

He sighed and cast his eyes skyward. "So humour me."

Hope wrapped the duffel coat tightly around herself, pulling the sleeves down over her hands. She felt like telling him to fuck off, but was smart enough to realise that under the circumstances she wasn't in any position to, that unless she was prepared to spend eternity in a yurt, in hideous hippie clobber, she would just have to comply.

"You're absolutely right," he said, creeping her out again. "The sooner we get this show on the road, the sooner you can move on."

Then a thought struck her. "If I'm back in 1989, and I'm presumably on my way over to Wales to Dylan, how come it's so stormy? It wasn't like this. As I remember it, it was quite calm. I wasn't sick at all."

"It's all a matter of perspective," he said. "Your mind was full of Dylan, you were so desperate to get to him, you didn't notice the storm. You were high on love, on adventure."

She closed her eyes trying to recall the crossing, but she couldn't. He was right. All she had been thinking of at that time was following Dylan back to Wales.

He gave her a nudge. "So go on. Tell me your

version. And, of course, you don't have to tell it aloud –
just run through it in your mind – I'll hear you
anyway."

An ironic chuckle escaped her. "What's to tell?" she
said. "It wasn't one of my better decisions. He was a
pathetic, jealous, philandering control freak."

"Not good enough. Tell it from the beginning – what
happened – how you felt."

Hope felt a flash of irritation. She was loath to talk
about her feelings and didn't relish the prospect of
some half-baked, cringe-inducing, daytime-TV-type,
soul-baring session. "But you know all this. You were
there," she protested.

"You're missing the point again," he said. "You're
supposed to be analysing your actions. Searching for
transgressions with a view to forgiveness. Just tell it
how it happened, Hope. From start to finish, then we
can move on."

The reiterated promise of moving on was an
incentive to comply.

"Oh, all right. He had a cottage on this mountain in
bloody West Wales …"

"No. From the beginning," Reuben insisted. "The
very beginning."

Chapter 7

Hope paused and cast her mind back.

Porter & French, January 1987. New Year. New start. Her first job in PR, assistant to Roddy French. Working for Roddy, bombastic bullshitter extraordinaire, who could put a favourable spin on Hannibal Lecter's motivation for eating human flesh, was a steep learning curve. He had a ferocious temper, didn't suffer fools, and exploded at regular intervals, but she quickly learned not to take it personally. He expected her to be available at the end of the phone at any time of the day or night. The use of personal initiative and creative thinking was both encouraged and expected. The P&F mission statement – *"There is no situation, however serious, humiliating or merely embarrassing, that cannot be spun to the client's advantage and no occasion that cannot be used to exploit a photo opportunity"* – was an oft-repeated mantra.

Thrown in at the deep end she quickly learned the ropes and thoroughly enjoyed the excitement of the cauldron that was the publicity industry. It was a small company: Roddy, Paul Porter, Polly Hughes the office junior, Paul's assistant Lainie McLoughlin and herself. The company specialised in both promotion and damage limitation in the entertainment, publishing and media sectors and had a respectable number of pretty high-profile clients.

At the time she shared a small house in Sandymount with Lainie McLoughlin and had a lively social life. Work was fun. Life was good.

Then Dylan Jones upset the applecart.

Nine months after Hope joined P&F, Paul head-hunted Dylan Jones. They were old friends, having worked together in London before Paul had returned to Dublin to set up P&F with Roddy. There was a buzz around the office about the new whiz-kid PR man for a couple of weeks before Dylan put in his first appearance. Paul repeatedly regaled them with tales about their young free and single days in London, to the point of nausea. At a critical point, the *"we were so drunk"*, and *"Dylan did this or that outrageous thing, it was hilarious"* stories, ceased to be amusing. Hope and Lainie both suspected that Paul, pushing forty, married with two kids and one on the way, was in the throes of a mid-life crisis and hankering after the freedom of youth. Truth be told, he appeared to be a little in awe of Dylan Jones, who, if the stories were to be believed would probably turn up for work in a blue satin cape with his knickers on over his trousers. But bearing in mind Paul's penchant for exaggeration, more probably he was a five-foot overweight dwarf with facial hair, a squint and sticky-out ears.

She was therefore somewhat surprised when she and Lainie walked into the office on the second Monday in September to be greeted by Polly, all of a dither about Dylan Jones. "He's a ride and a half," she said. "Bleedin' gorgeous."

Taking Polly's taste in men into account – anyone with a motorcycle and a pulse – this statement was questionable. Before Hope had a chance to test the validity of Polly's account however, Roddy sent her out to the photographer's to pick up some prints. When she returned it was Lainie's turn.

"He is pretty fit," she confided. "Not really my type. A bit lean and hungry in a sort of Liam Neeson meets Daniel Day Lewis kind of way, but fit nonetheless."

Hope's ears pricked up at this. The Liam Neeson/Daniel Day Lewis hybrid might not have been Lainie's cup of Earl Grey but, if the description was correct, he was definitely hers.

"Married though," Lainie added, bursting her bubble.

When she walked into Roddy's office after lunch she

had a chance to judge for herself as Dylan Jones, all six foot three of him, was sitting on the sofa leafing through a sheaf of papers. Lainie's assessment turned out to be pretty accurate. Mid-thirties, Liam Neeson body with brooding dark Daniel-Day-Lewis-during-his-tortured-longhaired-period looks. Jeans, black T-shirt, loafers. For Hope, despite the fifteen-year age differential, he was, as Polly had so succinctly put it, a ride and a half.

Roddy was sitting behind his desk, a cup of coffee in his hand. "Ah, Hope. Meet Dylan Jones," he said. "Dylan, this is my assistant, Hope Prior."

Dylan Jones looked up from the papers he was reading. "How's it going?" he said, then dropped the papers on the floor beside the sofa. There was a charming hint of Wales in his accent. He made eye contact. His eyes were an intense heart-stopping shade of blue and she felt herself flush.

"Hi," she muttered glancing away to hide her confusion. "Um, Roddy, Gavin O'Mahony said he's not up to the meeting this afternoon. He said he'll call to reschedule."

"Bollox!" Roddy said. "Call him back and tell him to talk to no one until I've briefed him." He glanced at Dylan, who had wandered over to the window and was looking down on Merrion Square. "Stupid bastard shagged the nanny, and his wife's in hospital with breast cancer."

"Who's Gavin O'Mahony?" Dylan asked.

"TV presenter. Does an afternoon magazine programme for old biddies," Roddy said. "Took yer woman to the bloody Shelburne. Someone tipped off a photographer from a red top and he got them with a long lens in the nip. Didn't even have the wit to close the sodding curtains."

Dylan Jones caught Hope's eye. "So what's he like, this O'Mahony guy?"

Surprised that he was asking her, Hope flushed again. "Um, middle-aged, perma-tan, boring old fart, basically."

"So how would you spin it?" Dylan asked.

"*Me?*"

He nodded. "Yeah."

She thought about it for a moment. "OK. I suppose I'd get him to beat his chest in abject regret. Publicly beg his wife for forgiveness. Have mutterings about the stress of the wife's illness. Generally play the sympathy card. Get the public feeling sorry for him, but at the same time raise his profile from boring old fartdom to rural housewives' fantasy shag ... Oh, yes," she added. "Can't have him blaming the nanny either. Wouldn't look good for him to slag off the nanny."

Roddy grinned. "Good girl. Glad to see you've been paying attention. Exactly my plan. Now run along and get me Sinead Hogan on the line."

"So what do you think of Deadly Dylan?" Polly asked later. "Wasn't I right? Is he a ride, or is he a *ride*?"

"He's OK," Hope said casually, her pelvic floor

contracting at the memory of his amazingly sexy blue eyes. Polly sniggered and glanced over at Lainie who, knowing Hope's preference in men, was equally unconvinced by her blasé appraisal.

For the remainder of the week, due to the Gavin O'Mahony incident, Roddy had her run ragged, typing out press release after press release, not to mention having her practically living out at the O'Mahony's Sutton home to baby-sit Gavin in order to prevent any off-the-cuff statements to the ever-present press pack at his gate. So she saw little of Dylan Jones. He was equally busy in meetings with Oran Mulcahy concerning a strategy to promote his latest discovery, Lucy Aragon, a gorgeous and talented eighteen-year-old of Afro/Irish extraction, with a big voice, big boobs and an even bigger attitude.

On the Friday evening, there was a photo call at Gavin O'Mahony's house to record a solicitous and bowed Gavin returning from the hospital with his frail-looking, post-operative wife. Roddy had already issued a statement to the effect that Gillian O'Mahony had decided to stick by her husband and, although she hadn't yet got over the hurt, she had decided to forgive him; that as a cancer sufferer she was all too conscious that life was too short to hold a one-off lapse against her husband of twenty years.

It had been touch and go and had taken a lot of persuasion on Roddy's part to convince Gillian that she had more to gain from putting on a brave united front than by throwing him to the wolves, but Roddy being Silver-Tongued Roddy, had talked her into it. An achievement, particularly in view of the fact that this was far from a one-off lapse, just the first time he had been stupid enough to get caught in *flagrante delicto* by the tabloids.

As they stood at the front door, Gavin with a protective arm wrapped around Gillian's shoulder, a thin smile on his appropriately shameful phizog, whilst the photographers snapped away and the hacks shouted inane and (taking into account Gillian O'Mahony's fragile appearance) insensitive questions, Roddy muttered in Hope's ear, "This'll cost him, big-time. A new convertible Beemer for her if he's lucky. His career, if he fucks up again." He paused then gave a heavy sigh. "Still, I suppose we should be grateful he's just into young crumpet and not bum-boys."

Once the press was satisfied with their pictures, quotes and sound-bites, and Gavin and Gillian were safely inside the house, Roddy gave Hope a lift back to town.

"She took the pay-off. A measly three grand," he confided. "Cheap at ten times the price considering she could have done a Kiss and Tell and fucked up his career."

"She didn't strike me as the gold-digger type," Hope said. "I think she's genuinely in love with him."

Roddy snorted. "Give over. She took the cash, didn't she?"

"Only so she could get away from that circus back there," Hope protested.

She had visited Alice, the nanny, with Roddy the day after the story broke and had felt genuinely sorry for her. As far as Hope was concerned Gavin bloody O'Mahony was a pervy old git, so she couldn't understand what an attractive girl like Alice, blonde, sweet-faced, and sweet-natured if gullible, saw in him. About ten minutes after they arrived, Roddy had left them alone, ostensibly to make a phone call, but in reality so that she and Alice could have a girl-to-girl chat to ascertain the danger factor: if she intended to go to the Sundays or if there was a chance she could be bought off by Gavin. After hearing Alice's side of the story, she was surprised by her naiveté. The girl had really believed that Gavin and she had a future together, that he was going to leave Gillian, that he loved her as much as she loved him, that his marriage was over, that his wife didn't understand him – blah, blah, blah. But as far as Hope was concerned he had exploited his wife's illness and his celebrity to get inside the nanny's knickers, with declarations of undying love and all the other balderdash. What a bastard!

By the time they had negotiated the evening traffic it was well past six, so Roddy drove straight to Baggot Street, parking on Waterloo Road, and they walked across to the Waterloo, the regular Friday-night watering hole for P&F staff. Hope immediately cast her eyes around the pub in search of Dylan, and felt a surprising stab of jealousy when she spied him up at the bar in the company of Paul and a tallish woman, late twenties with mid-length curly red hair, in navy linen trousers and a white shirt. She had her hand laid proprietorially on his shoulder.

"That's the wife," Lainie whispered in her ear. "Monica. Twenty-nine, actress."

"You interrogated her then," Hope muttered, mortified that Lainie had caught her scoping out Dylan.

"Not her. Paul," Lainie said. "And put your tongue back in, you're dribbling. Besides he's taken, and he's way too old for you anyway."

"Piss off," Hope said. "Do you want a drink?"

"Glass of Guinness," Lainie smirked. "I'll be at that table over there."

Hope went up to the bar and ordered two glasses of Guinness, watching Dylan through the mirror while she waited for the Guinness to settle. Monica still had her hand on his shoulder, but he wasn't taking much, if any, notice of her, concentrating instead on Paul who was listening intently to whatever he was saying. Suddenly Paul threw back his head and roared with laughter. Dylan turned his head and caught Hope's eye in the mirror for a split second before she glanced away. Cursing under her breath, she felt the heat rise up her neck again, a marauding flutter of butterflies was making fast and loose in her stomach, and she wanted to throw up. This is stupid, she thought. Fecking stupid. Get a grip. He's married. Unavailable.

It didn't stop her from fancying the boxers off him though. Lainie was right. He was *so* her type, it hurt to look at him. Tall slim frame that would look good in a bin-liner, and those dreamy blue eyes.

"So how did old Gavin fare?" Lainie asked as Hope put the two glasses on the table.

"Stuck to his script," she said. "I think it went OK, though if you ask me, he deserves to be hung out to dry. If I were Gillian O'Mahony I'd castrate the miserable bastard. I'd dump his clothes in a bin-liner on the step and have the locks changed."

"You and me both." Lainie shuddered, wrinkling her nose! "Yuk. Imagine all that orange wrinkly flesh. What did the nanny see in him?"

Hope took a sip of Guinness, one eye straying back to Dylan's reflection. "She's still mad for him, poor cow. She thinks he's being noble, staying with Gillian because of the cancer, when in reality he's just doing what he's told in order to hold onto his job, the house and avoid a mega-bucks divorce settlement."

"I'd never let a man use me like that," Lainie said.

"Me neither," Hope agreed.

The following week, with the Gavin O'Mahony incident successfully put to bed, his career intact, the nanny out of the country and Gillian busily extracting her pound of orange flesh, Hope was back in the office. At around five-thirty on the Wednesday evening, just as she was getting ready to leave, Roddy dumped a couple of tapes on her desk. "I need these letters sent out tonight," he said cheerily. "I'm off. See you tomorrow." And without a *'Do you mind?'* or *'Do you have to be anywhere?'* he was gone.

Hope groaned. She had been sitting idle for most of the afternoon and had planned to catch the six o'clock showing of *The Untouchables* at the Carlton with Lainie and Polly, Kevin Costner being the girls' preferred eye candy of the month.

"I do have a life, Roddy," she shouted at his back as the door swung quietly closed behind him.

"Bugger!" Polly moaned. "We'll miss the start."

Hope sighed. "No. You two go on. I'll catch it some other time."

"Well, if you're sure," Lainie said.

It was pushing 6.45 by the time Hope printed out the last of Roddy's correspondence, though apart from a contract which needed particular care and careful proofreading, considering the content of the rest she couldn't see what was so urgent that the job couldn't have waited until the following morning. Roddy's thoughtlessness left her feeling grumpy. It wasn't the first time he'd dumped on her, ruining her plans, but there was little she could do. She enjoyed the job, it paid well, and on the double-plus side, she'd just been given a rise without having to ask. Also she was learning all about PR which she had never expected to when she had joined the company at the start of the year with just basic computer skills and no reference. Truth be told, she was surprised that Roddy had given her the job as his PA in the first place, her interview had been such a disaster.

She'd arrived late because the bus hadn't shown up, and bad-tempered because she was dripping wet as the result of a truck deliberately swerving in to hit a large puddle, soaking her with a sheet of dirty rainwater. There were two other candidates ahead of her, both immaculately turned out, blonde, and very efficient-looking. The fact that by the time her turn came she was dying to pee and had developed a raging headache didn't improve the situation. He had then kept her standing in front of his desk, damp, crumpled, with head throbbing, while he took a long phone call. When he finally hung up, without any preamble he asked, "In your opinion what qualities are essential in a good PA?"

"The patience of a fecking saint, for a start," she'd snapped. Roddy's jaw had dropped and, because she knew she'd blown it, she added for good measure, "And I'd teach you some basic good manners."

As she stomped towards the door she heard him bellow with laughter, then: "Where are you going?"

"Home," Hope snarled. "If the sodding bus shows up."

By the time she got to the bus stop she had cooled down and the realisation that she had totally fucked up began to sink in. She needed the job. She was broke, and if she couldn't find the rent, imminently homeless in view of the fact that the dole was woefully inadequate to keep body and soul together. Miraculously an almost empty bus glided into the stop and she hopped on. More miraculous perhaps was the fact that by the time she got to her flat in Ranelagh, a shiny new Merc was sitting outside the building, Roddy French leaning against it, chubby arms folded across the front of his camel crombie, a cigar in his gob. It appeared he liked her forthright no-nonsense manner (his words) and offered her the job on the spot.

After sticking down the last of the envelopes and shutting down her computer, Hope heard someone walk into reception. Assuming it was the cleaner she paid no attention until Dylan Jones poked his head around the doorway of her office.

"Don't you have a home to go to?" he asked.

"Roddy wanted some letters sent out tonight," she said. "I was supposed to be going to a movie with the girls."

He stepped inside the office and leaned against the doorframe, his head only centimetres from the top. Faded denims, white T-shirt, trainers. He ran his hand through his hair, pushing it out of his eyes. "That's a bit off," he said, glancing at his watch. "It's going on seven."

Her stomach churned at the way his soft Welsh cadence stressed the first syllable. "*Sev*-en."

"Hmm," was all she could manage. Then a nervous giggle. "Well ... must go home or it'll be nearly time to come back." Cringing at how wet she sounded.

"You've nothing else on then?"

"No. No. Just a night in front of *Corrie*." God, how sad does that make me sound, she thought, wincing.

"What's *Corrie* when it's at home?"

"Um, *Coronation Street*. It's, um …just a soap."

"Oh, right. *Coronation Street*."

Hope gathered her bag, glancing out of the window so as she wouldn't have to meet his stare. Out on Merrion Square the trees swayed in the breeze.

"Fancy coming to The Baggot Inn?"

Stunned, she wasn't sure she had heard right. Was that an invitation? "Sorry?"

"The Baggot Inn. Lucy Aragon, this chick I'm doing publicity for, she's got a gig there later. I've got *Hot Press* lined up so I have to be there to make sure she doesn't mess the interview up." When she didn't reply straight away, mainly because she couldn't get her brain to engage, therefore couldn't guarantee a coherent sentence, he coaxed, "*Come on*. You deserve a couple of pints on expenses to make up for missing the movie."

Walking around the square, he took her arm to guide her across the road, and his touch was electric. Get a grip, she reminded herself. Don't be a complete eejit.

"You're an old friend of Paul's then," she said in an attempt at some semblance of lucid conversation. She had to quicken her pace to keep up with his long loping stride.

"Paul and I go way back," he said, then laughed. "How anyone as straight as Paul did so well in this business is a constant source of amazement to me."

Connn-stant. There it was again. *Amaaaze-ment.*

"Really? The way he tells it the both of you got up to some pretty wild stuff when you were young, free and single in London."

He laughed again and his delicious eyes twinkled. "Well, if you call smoking the odd joint and getting occasionally bladdered *wild.*"

"Occasionally?"

"Oh, all right, every time Birmingham City lost a match which was ..." he timed the pause perfectly before he continued, "well, most weekends and whenever there was a mid-week game really." He laughed and she laughed too at the shared joke.

The Baggot Inn was packed even though it was still quite early. Dylan took her arm and guided her through to the back where a skinny guy in a Deff Leopard T-shirt was belting out a cover version of some U2 song, supported by three grim-looking mates on guitar and drums. They didn't sound bad either despite the fact that they weren't singing original material.

"Who's the band?" she asked.

He leaned down so his ear was close to her mouth.

"I said, who's the band?" she repeated. His scent and his closeness were intoxicating.

Cupping his hand so it was close to her ear he shouted, "They're called Mad Bastards. Oran

Mulcahy's just got them a three-record deal with Sony. Apparently they're the next big thing, apart from our Lucy Aragon of course." Then spotting Mulcahy sitting at a table on the other side of the stage, he took her arm. "Come on. There's Oran. What would you like to drink?"

* * *

Reuben coughed to attract her attention, startling her considerably. Lost in the past, she had forgotten about his presence beside her on the bench.

"Um, can we move along a bit," he said.

"You're the one who said 'from the very beginning'," Hope grumbled.

Reuben sighed. "I *meant* from the beginning of the affair."

Chapter 8

Lucy Aragon came on stage at ten and did a thirty-minute set. She had a gutsy bluesy voice and looked funky in leggings, black high-top Docs, and a white baggy off-one-shoulder top, cinched in tight at the waist by a wide pink patent belt. Her hair was in beaded braids and her coffee-coloured skin shone almost luminously in the stage lighting. She ended the set with 'Mustang Sally', which had the crowd stomping and whistling for more.

Dylan stood up. "Have to go to work, petal. See you in a tick."

Petal. He called me *petal*, she thought, her stomach muscles clenching.

She watched him as he ushered Lucy Aragon to a

table in the corner where Sam Duffin from *Hot Press* was waiting to start the interview, and felt a stab of jealousy as Dylan placed a guiding hand on her back. Sam jumped up as they approached, then they all sat down together.

Oran Mulcahy, who had disappeared just as Lucy had finished her set, returned to the table with a glass of Guinness for her and a gin and tonic for himself. He was a small man, tubby with close-cropped hair, never seen in public with a woman and reputed to be gay, although he was so far back in the closet his home address should have been Narnia.

"Lucy's great, isn't she?" he said.

Hope nodded. "Yes. Terrific."

The interview lasted about fifteen minutes, then Lucy got up, and Hope was disappointed to see Dylan sit down again with Sam Duffin. Lucy made her way over to Oran Mulcahy and sat down next to him. The two of them chatted together, ignoring her, but she was too intent on watching Dylan to care.

* * *

Reuben cut in on her thoughts. "Look, is all this relevant? Can't we just cut to the chase?"

"I thought this was about me?" Hope snapped, irritated. "I'm just trying to find out what I'm supposed to have done that was so awful. I need to get it clear in my mind."

Reuben leaned back, spreading his arms out along the back of the bench, then gave a theatrical sigh. "OK, if you *must*."

* * *

Hope closed her eyes. She could see the scene in The Baggot Inn as clearly as if it were yesterday. Feel the disappointment as she watched Dylan across the room talking to Sam Duffin. He's forgotten about me, she thought desolately. Glancing around she noticed that Mulcahy and Lucy Aragon had gone, leaving her alone at the table, her half-finished glass of Guinness in front of her. She felt uncomfortable. Conspicuous. Hope-no-mates. Then Dylan looked across and beckoned to her and she felt a flood of relief.

By the time she made it through the crowd to his table he was standing, shaking Sam Duffin's hand. She stood awkwardly looking on as they said goodbye, then Sam left.

"Fancy a nightcap. My flat's just up the road," Dylan said. Brooking no argument, he took her arm and led her out into the street. The autumn night had turned chilly as they crossed the street and walked down towards Pembroke Road.

"You live very handy for work," she said, cringing once more at how inane she sounded.

"And where do you live?" he asked.

"Lainie and I share a house in Sandymount. I suppose I really should be looking for a cab."

"Don't be daft," he said laughing. "You'll be queuing at the rank for the best part of an hour at this time. Come in for a coffee and I'll call a hackney from the flat."

The flat was at the top of a tall Georgian terrace halfway down Baggot Street. Hope wondered if Monica would be there, and what she'd think of Dylan bringing her back, then reasoned that she'd probably be fine about it. Why wouldn't she? They worked together.

But of course Monica wasn't there. "Over in London shooting a commercial for yoghurt," he explained.

"Oh," was all she could think of in reply to that, anticipation tingling in the pit of her stomach. She could hear him clattering about in the kitchen as she mooched around the bijou sitting-room looking at photos in frames. Dylan and Monica, he standing behind her, his arms wrapped around her waist, both grinning at the camera. Monica in Victorian costume on stage in some production. A publicity shot. She squinted at the bottom of the picture. *Monica Rhys-Jones. The Importance of Being Earnest.* There was another of Dylan and Monica, this time on a tropical beach holding hands. A helmeted Dylan hanging from a rope, rock-climbing.

Suddenly he was standing behind her. "No milk," he said, then slipped his arms around her waist and the next moment his lips were on hers and she felt faint with pleasure. Suddenly he pulled back from her.

"Sorry. I shouldn't have done that." Struck dumb,

she just stared at him confused. "It's just …" he stammered. "Well, the thing is I'm so attracted to you, I couldn't stop myself, but I shouldn't have taken advantage, I'm sorry."

"Your wife …" she replied, whilst thinking, No, no, it's fine, please don't stop.

"Monica?" he gave an ironic snort. "Monica and I …well, we've drifted in the past few years. This was supposed to be a new start." He wandered over to the window and looked down at the street. "But it's not working out. That's why she's in London."

"I thought she was shooting a commercial?"

He nodded. "Oh, she is. Very ambitious, my Monica."

My Monica.

"We lead largely separate lives these days," he said, turning back from the window. His eyes were sad. "I don't think we'll last that much longer before she decides to up sticks and sod off back to the UK."

"I'm sorry," Hope said. "Must be tough. Do you still love her?"

"I'll always love her," he said wistfully. "But I'm not *in* love with her." He turned his head and caught her eye. "If you understand the subtle difference."

"Oh, I do," she said. "That's so sad. So what are you going to do?"

"Nothing I can do now. We're done. Finished."

He was still standing by the window looking soulful. Hope took a couple of steps towards him. "She must be mad." Her voice was barely audible.

Turning his head he smiled. "More like she was mad to get mixed up with me in the first place."

"Oh, don't say that!"

He stared at her for a long minute then took a step to meet her and wrapped his arms around her, pulling her head into his chest. "Do I sense that you've been hurt too?" he said.

His empathy brought tears to her eyes. Looking up at him she blinked and he wiped a rogue tear away with his thumb and licked it.

"Come on," he said, voice husky, and led her toward the bedroom.

* * *

"Oh, please!" Reuben scoffed. "You sound like Mills & bloody Boon. I can't believe you bought that load of codswallop!"

"I was young and impressionable."

Reuben snorted again. "You saw straight through Gavin O'Mahony," he pointed out. "As I recall you couldn't understand how the nanny could be so gullible."

"That was different. You could hardly compare Deadly Dylan to Gavin the Orange-Faced Geriatric."

"Nevertheless, he was married," Reuben said censoriously. "Don't you think you should have checked out the veracity of his claims of estrangement?"

It was Hope's turn to snort. "Yeah, right. A delectable man I fancy the boxers off comes on to me with a sob story that lets my conscience off the hook and you think it's as easy as that? Great with the benefit of hindsight, Reuben, but I was twenty for feck sake. I can't believe this counts as transgression *numero uno*. It was totally Dylan's fault. He took advantage. He seduced me. I was dazzled."

Reuben clearly wasn't convinced. "So you're seriously trying to tell me you swallowed it."

Hope sniggered. "A girl rarely swallows on purpose."

Reuben frowned. "Don't go there."

She gave a sigh. "Oh, all right then. Yes. I was an eejit. I believed him. He reeled me in hook, line and sinker. Are you happy now?"

He shrugged. "OK, granted he swept you off your feet somewhat, but what about later on? After that."

She shook her head. "No. Really. I believed him. I was besotted. His marriage was kaput. I believed he was in love with me."

Surprisingly, despite the eventual outcome, Hope could clearly recall the sensation of being totally and completely in love with Dylan. The morning after The Baggot Inn, after lazily making love again, he made her coffee then called her a cab. On the drive to Sandymount, she closed her eyes, remembering the small mole just below his shoulder-blade as he sat on the side of the bed, sighing as she relived the night before in her head. The urgent almost rough sex as he took her for the first time, from behind. The gentler more sensuous second time, on the floor in the tangle of the duvet, her on top, looking down into his gorgeous blue eyes.

Lainie wasn't home which was a surprise until she remembered that she had planned to stay at Dave's. She didn't know whether she was relieved or disappointed. She was bursting to tell her. Then, as she was drying herself off after her shower, he phoned.

"Hi."

"Hi, yourself."

"Listen, about the office," he said. "Don't take it the wrong way if I'm a bit, well cool, will you?" then before she had a chance to react he added, "It's Paul, you see. He's very fond of Monica and it could cause friction between us if he knew that we were an item."

An *item*?

She was thrilled senseless. An item. Dylan and her. "Um, an item?" A broad grin spread across her face.

There was a pause before he replied. "Eh … unless you're having second thoughts. I really will understand if you're dubious. I mean it's not an ideal situation."

"Oh no! No!" she blurted out, afraid that he'd misunderstood. Terrified he was going to change his mind. "I understand. We can keep it away from work."

"Thanks, Hope." Another measured pause. "You know I said I'd understand … if you didn't want to get involved, I mean?"

"Yes."

"Well, I was lying. I'd be devastated."

Devvv-ass-tated.

She laughed, thrilled silly. "*Really?* Me too."

"You're amazing," he said.

Amazing. He thinks I'm amazing.

She got into work ten minutes late and bumped into Lainie in the kitchen brewing Paul his morning caffeine fix.

"You've had sex!" was her friend's opening shot.

"I have not!" she protested.

Polly waltzed in on the exchange. "You have so. You've got that 'I got laid' grin right across your gob, for feck sake."

"So who was it?" Lainie demanded. They had her trapped against the fridge and, catching her own reflection in the mirror above the sink she could see what Polly was getting at. She drew an imaginary zip across her mouth. "My lips are sealed."

"Ah, come on," Lainie protested.

Hope wavered. "Can you two keep a secret?"

"Of course not," Lainie scoffed. "Don't be silly."

"Then tough titty," Hope replied, the grin still plastered to her face, and breezed out of the kitchen. Not to be put off by a downright refusal to spill the beans, Lainie followed her at a rate of knots.

"Why won't you tell me?" Then a thought struck her. "Shit! It's not the awful on-again-off-again Derrick again, is it? Please tell me it's not Derrick!"

"It's not Derrick, and even if you reach down my throat and drag out my liver, my lips are sealed." In truth she was dying to tell, but was also enjoying the fact that she knew something that Lainie and Polly were desperate to find out. Through the open door of her office she saw Dylan walk into reception in the company of Lucy Aragon. Lucy had dressed down in jeans and cord jacket, but she still looked sensational. Unconsciously Hope ran her hand through her hair, feeling utterly plain in comparison to the lovely Lucy, but her heart leapt when Dylan winked conspiratorially at her and mouthed 'Hello, gorgeous' as he passed her door.

And that was what it was like. He made her feel special. She lived for any moment alone in his company however brief, inhaling his scent, just being close. They spent illicit time together when Monica was away again on a shoot and Lainie over at Dave's. But true to his warning, he was decidedly cool with her when anyone was around to the extent that Lainie remarked on it eventually.

"What did you do to rattle Deadly Dylan's cage?"

Hope shrugged. "That bollox? No idea." Innocence personified.

She found it increasingly impossible to concentrate, to the point where Roddy blew a gasket. He'd asked her to find a particular file, and when there was no sign of it after twenty minutes, and no reply from her desk, he ventured into the outer office to find her standing by the filing cabinet staring into space.

"What is wrong with you, Hope? I asked for the Harvey Hamilton file half a bloody hour ago!"

Hope snapped back to reality just as, in her daydream, Dylan was licking his way down her body, having just reached her belly-button.

"Oh, sorry. It was misfiled," she mumbled, flipping through the folders until she put her hand on it. "Sorry."

"Shape up, Hope," Roddy warned. "I don't know where your head's been this week but it's certainly not been in the office."

But Lainie wouldn't let it go and, by the end of the third week of guessing, of cajoling, she finally lost it. "What's up with you, Hope? Why won't you tell me? I'm your friend for God's sake. Don't you trust me? Who is it that it has to be such a state secret?"

It was a Saturday and they were in the Alicia Bridal Boutique for the toile fitting of Lainie's wedding gown, and her own bridesmaid's dress. She had been dying to share it with Lainie for days and only Dylan's reminder of the importance of keeping it out of the office had prevented her from blabbing sooner, but the look of hurt on her friend's face was the final nail in the coffin of secrecy.

"You promise not to tell anyone?" she warned.

Lainie frowned. "Why? What's the big deal?" Then it struck her. "Shit! He's married, isn't he?"

Hope shook her head. "No ... well, sort of."

Lainie gave her a leery look. "How can anyone be *sort of* married. He either is or he isn't."

"OK. He's married but it's over."

"So he's separated?"

Hope shifted from foot to foot, uncomfortable. "Well, not exactly, but they lead separate lives. They don't sleep together, at least they don't have sex or anything."

Alicia came in at that point so they shut up as she pinned the side seam on Lainie's dress to fit. "When's the wedding?" she asked.

"The third Saturday in March," Lainie said.

"You're bound to lose a few pounds before then with all the running round despite Christmas, but don't worry, we'll do the final fitting the first week of March, and if you lose more after that it's just a case of a nip and a tuck." She stood back and looked at Lainie's reflection in the mirror. "What do you think?"

Hope stood behind her friend. Even in the calico toile she looked gorgeous, her tall slim figure accentuated by the elegant bias cut.

"You've decided on the ivory satin?" Alicia asked. Lainie nodded. "And dusky rose satin for the bridesmaids?"

"Yes. Yes," Lainie said, anxious for her to leave them alone so she could continue the interrogation. Alicia was oblivious however and wittered on for a further ten minutes about Hope's colouring and what a good choice the dusky rose satin was, and about veils, and headdresses and the cost of photographers. Eventually, after extricating Lainie from the mock-up garment, she left them alone.

"So who is it then? Where did you meet him?" Lainie demanded the moment the door closed behind the designer.

Hope bit her lip. Suddenly she wasn't quite so anxious to share.

Lainie however wasn't going to give up. "Is it anyone I know?"

"Promise you won't tell anyone. The shit would really hit the fan if you tell anyone. Paul would –"

Lainie looked appalled. "*Paul*! You have to be joking!"

"No! Not Paul … Dylan."

Lainie's jaw dropped.

"Paul's really fond of Monica," Hope continued, "and Dylan said it could make things a bit awkward at the office if he found out."

"Awkward isn't the word! Paul's fond of Monica all right. She's only his sodding sister-in-law. I'll bet Mister I'm-Not-Shagging-My-Estranged-Wife Dylan Jones didn't tell you that?"

Instantly on the defensive Hope came back with, "So what? That doesn't alter anything."

Lainie's expression had evolved into one of pure horror. "Only that he isn't being honest with you, you eejit. And how do you know he isn't shagging Monica? How do you know the marriage is over? They looked very together to me in the pub last night."

Hope hadn't made it to the pub the previous evening as she'd had a hair appointment, but Lainie's comment stopped her in her tracks. "How do you mean, very together?" she asked trying to sound unconcerned.

Lainie shrugged. "You know? Together. He had his arm around her. They seemed fine together. He was reminiscing with Paul and …"

"Well, there you are!" Hope cut in, feeling a flood of relief. "He was talking to *Paul*. Don't you get it? Of course he had to put on a show."

Although unconvinced, Lainie relented. "I suppose." Then after a pause, "You're really mad about him, aren't you? It's written all over your face."

Hope smiled dreamily. "He thinks I'm amazing. And he's so talented, Lainie. He really wants to be a writer and he plans to take time out to write an important novel."

Lainie frowned. "Look, Hope, Dylan's well …" she groped for the right words. "The thing is … I mean …"

Hope laughed. "I know there's the age difference, you don't have to tell me. But he loves me, Lainie. He really loves me. We're soul mates."

"Soul mates? Where did that come from?" Lainie scoffed.

Hope found her friend's attitude wounding. "Why can't you just be happy for me?" she said, thoroughly disappointed. "He loves me, Lainie." She sighed.

"We're an item."

"An *item* … so when does he plan on mentioning it to Monica?" Lainie asked, not bothering to disguise the sarcasm.

"Soon," Hope replied. "When the time's right."

Lainie groaned. "Jesus, Hope. Listen to yourself. You sound like that pathetic nanny Orange Gavin was shagging."

Anger rose instantly. Anger and offence. "How dare you compare Dylan to that – that gobshite!" she snarled. "He's nothing like Orange Gavin! He loves me. He thinks I'm amazing. Why do you find that so fecking hard to believe?"

The passion in her voice made Lainie relent once more. "I don't, Hope. Really I don't. You are amazing, I'm just afraid you'll get hurt, that's all."

Hope smiled, the tension dissipated. "He loves me, Lainie. He wouldn't hurt me. I know it. I just know it."

* * *

She heard Reuben chortle beside her on the bench. "Stop being so bloody smug," she snapped. "This is my recollection. I was young."

"Precisely," he replied. "But you're being a touch subjective if I may say so."

"I'm just remembering it as it happened," she countered. "And so far I can't see anything I did that was so wrong. As far as I was concerned his marriage was over. I was in love with him, and to this day I still believe that he loved me in his own selfish way."

"Really?" He sounded surprised by that. "Strange thing love, wouldn't you agree?"

Hope shrugged. "What do you mean?"

"Well, after what happened, how can you possibly believe that he loved you? Love is supposed to be unselfish, love is supposed to be kind, love is … well, the Saint Paul definition." He rubbed his hand over his bristly scalp, frowning as he tried to get a handle on the quandary. "Tell me, is it just an ego thing? Do you need to believe it to placate your conscience? Or, how is it the psychologists put it these days, do you have to believe it in order to boost your self-esteem?"

"Salvage, more like," Hope muttered.

"What?

"Nothing."

They sat in silence for half a minute, then Hope glanced at him. "Why would I need to placate my conscience anyway? I acted in good faith. I was the wounded party."

Reuben shorted. "Is that so? And what about Monica? What about the letter?"

She'd been hoping he wouldn't bring that up.

Chapter 9

Despite Lainie's reservations, Hope was dizzy with love, floating a couple of thousand feet above cloud nine for the remainder of November. Then suddenly, for no apparent reason, Dylan started to blank her. The first couple of times she could excuse it because Paul or Roddy or Polly was around, but by the middle of the second week of December she was becoming alarmed. She hadn't been alone with him or had a conversation of any nature for ages and he appeared to be actively avoiding her. She couldn't think of any reason, anything she had done to cause the sudden coolness, and it was eating her up inside. She was desperate. Knowing he had to work late that evening to finish a proposal, she hung back to be alone with him. She stood watching him for half a minute from the doorway of his office as he sat staring at his computer monitor. Then tired of waiting for him to catch her eye, certain that he was aware of her presence, she walked behind his chair, wrapped her arms around his neck and kissed his ear.

Without taking his eyes off the screen he reached up and brushed her hand away. "Don't, Hope. I'm trying to concentrate. I have to get this finished."

"But I haven't seen you for ages," she said, cajoling, stroking his neck in precisely the spot just below his ear that usually turned him on. "Everyone's gone home. We're all alone."

"Cut it out, Hope!" he barked, roughly dragging her hand away. "Grow up, will you? I have to finish this proposal."

Tears sprang to her eyes. He might as well have slapped her across the face. Pushing past his chair, she blindly ran from the room to her office, tears streaming down her face, confused, hurt. She heard him curse, then call her name, but she didn't answer. Sitting at her desk, she had no idea what to do. Lainie's concerns over her relationship with him came to mind and she felt physically sick.

Then the door opened and he poked his head in. "What's up with you?" he asked with an air of detached casualness.

She was stunned. How could he not know? She just stared at him.

He took a couple of steps towards her. "Look, I'm sorry I snapped at you, but I really have to get that proposal finished. Snaffling Jack Ingram's account from Redmond Heart would be a real coup. You know that, Hope."

He sounded like a stranger. Standing there, preaching to her about presentations and proposals and winning contracts when her heart was about to break.

"And the presentation's –"

"Why are you doing this?" she cut in. Then in case he was in any doubt as to why she was upset, she lashed on. "You've ignored me for nearly three weeks." Saying it aloud brought the tears spilling from her eyes again. "What did I do? What's the matter?" The desperation to know was a like a physical pain in her chest cavity, just below her heart. "Don't you love me any more? Tell me what I did. Please. I need to know." She was aware that she sounded pathetic but she couldn't stop the words from tumbling out. She was aching to run to him. To cling to him, to wrap her arms around his neck, to make him want her again – the only thing stopping her, the need to hold onto the last shred of her dignity.

He stared at her, his face expressionless, then after a long minute he shook his head. "I'm so sorry, Hope. I've been a complete arsehole." He took a couple of steps closer to her desk. "It's not you. It's me."

Here it is, she thought. The 'It's not you it's me' speech, which usually meant exactly the opposite. He sat on the edge of her desk and she unconsciously drew back in her chair away from him, angry, humiliated and hurt.

"I've been a total arsehole," he repeated." I've been under pressure these last few weeks. Things are pretty bad at home and then there's this sodding proposal and stuff, and we haven't had a chance to talk at all."

"I'd sooner you were honest," she said eyes cast down, face burning, feeling totally patronised. "If you've gone off me, the least you could do is to say so."

He groaned. "That's *so* not true, petal. I'm aching for you." He grabbed her hand, but she still refused to look him in the face. "But it's Monica, see," he continued. "She's …" He sighed. "Monica has problems. She suffers from depression, her nerves are bad and she's very insecure."

She waited and when he didn't elaborate she looked up at him. "So?"

"Well, like I said, before we came here we hadn't been getting on for months. I was going to call it a day back then, but she tried to top herself, see. Took the best part of a bottle of bloody Valium. Nearly knackered her liver in the process."

"Jesus!"

"Yeah," he agreed. "I felt so bloody guilty. She could have died. Anyway, I agreed to give it another go. This was our new start, but as soon as we got here she was up to her old tricks again."

"I don't understand. What do you mean?"

116

His eyes were sad. "Don't get me wrong – like I told you, in one way I'll always love Mon, but God, she's not an easy woman. Totally self-centred. Completely driven by her career. She reckons she loves me, but she doesn't, Hope. She's totally self-absorbed. She just can't bear the thought of me being happy with someone else. Anyway, I decided to come clean. Tell her it was finally over, that I was leaving, and I got home to find her in a state. She'd been for an audition for the next Abbey production, some Sheridan play, and she didn't get it. At least that's what I'm guessing caused her to kick off."

"Kick off?"

"Pills. She was like a bloody zombie. Slurred speech, eyes out of focus." He shook his head and closed his eyes. "I don't know what to do, Hope. How can I tell her I don't want to be with her now? What if it caused her to take another overdose? What if she died? I couldn't handle the guilt."

"She needs help," Hope said, stating the obvious. "Shouldn't she see someone? A shrink or something?"

"She is. She's getting better, but I don't think this is the right time to tell her. Not yet, do you?"

"You were really going to tell her?"

He nodded. "I only wish to God I'd said something sooner. I feel like I've missed my window of opportunity, if you know what I mean?"

She shook her head, not willing to agree that it was too late, alarmed that that might be it, that he'd missed his chance and that was that. *Finito.*

"So what about us?" she asked.

He grinned at her. "Can't help myself," he said, sliding his hand into the front of her shirt, cupping her breast. "I've really missed you."

She didn't protest. Neither did she protest when he pulled her up from her chair and took her there and then on the carpet, her ripped tights and knickers around her ankles, she was so overcome with relief.

"You're amazing," he whispered just before he came. "Bloody amazing."

Afterwards, as they were straightening their clothes he said, "In a few more weeks, petal. I'll tell her as soon as she's finished the treatment. I won't miss my chance, again. I promise."

* * *

"The cow!" she said later to Lainie. "The rotten manipulating cow. Fancy doing a thing like that. Taking pills."

"Obviously a cry for help," Lainie commented. "You believe him?"

Hope was taken aback by the question. "Of course. He wouldn't lie about a thing like that. I just can't believe she could be so scheming. I mean what's the point? He's not in love with her any more. End of story. She doesn't love him, just can't bear to think of him happy with someone else. Why doesn't she just get over it? Selfish cow!"

"She knows about you then?"

Hope shook her head. "No, but Dylan was going to tell her the night she threw the wobbly after she failed an Abbey audition. It's just an excuse, of course."

"What, for Dylan?"

"No!" Hope snapped irritated. "Monica. She doesn't want him, but she won't let him go. He's her security blanket."

"I suppose Dylan's a bit anxious too," Lainie commented. "I mean Paul won't be too pleased if Gwen starts giving him grief because Dylan's walked out on her sister. He'd probably get the boot. You, too, come to that."

Lying in bed that night, fantasising about Dylan lying beside her, it came to her. Maybe there was a way she could spare Dylan the guilt of leaving Monica. What if there was a way to make Monica leave Dylan, or better still chuck him out? They could be together. And what if Paul did fire both of them? Dylan was wasted in PR anyway. They could take off. Leave Ireland. He could finally get down to writing his important novel. Monica was just holding him back, clinging to him like a leech, making his life a misery. It wasn't fair.

Slipping out of bed she padded out to the sitting-room and rummaged in the sideboard until she found a notepad. Creeping back to bed, smug with the satisfaction that only a cunning plan can generate, she drafted the letter.

* * *

"You really thought that was an OK thing to do?" Reuben asked.

"Yes," Hope said. "In my opinion I was just hurrying along the inevitable. She was a manipulative bitch."

"So you wrote an anonymous letter telling her that her husband was having an affair. You didn't have the courage to be straight with her, to put your name to this epistle?"

"It wasn't about courage," Hope snapped, defensively. "She was going to find out sooner or later. She was wrecking his life. Holding him back. Anyway, if I'd put my name to it, Dylan might have ..." She stopped abruptly.

"Dylan might have what?"

She felt uncomfortable again and cast her eyes down so she wouldn't have to meet his gaze. "OK. I didn't want him to know it was me in case I pissed him off."

Reuben grinned. "That's more like it." He stood up and held out his hand to her. "Come on," he said.

"Where?"

Taking her hand he pulled her to her feet. "Just come with me."

He led her to the door of the bar and opened it, stepping through it ahead of her.

Chapter 10

To her utter surprise she found herself standing not in the crowded ferry's saloon but in Dylan's sitting-room in the Baggot Street flat. Monica was sitting on the sofa staring into space, her face ashen, her eyes swollen from crying. It took a moment for Hope to gather herself together and realise where she was, and as Monica glanced in her direction, she shrank back.

"She can't see you," Reuben said. "We're back in November 1987."

"December surely," Hope corrected. "He left just before Christmas 87."

"No, this is November," Reuben said. "The time he started to blank you."

Hope nodded. "Ah, the audition. She's upset about

the failed audition."

The door opened and Dylan walked in, a glass of amber spirits in his hand. She was surprised to see him looking so thin. In her recent recollection he'd had more meat on his bones.

He walked over to Monica and held out the glass. "Here, petal. Drink this." His voice was gentle, soft. Even from the distance of almost fifteen years, taking the context into consideration, she felt a flush of annoyance that he had called Monica 'petal'. That was his name for her.

Monica took the glass. Her hands were shaking as she lifted it to her lips and took a sip. Dylan sat down beside her and put his arm around her and as he did, she broke down in tears. "There there, petal," he soothed. "It'll be all right." She buried her head in his shoulder and the sobbing subsided.

"How can it be all right?" she said. "It's over. Finished." Wiping her eyes she gave a shuddering sigh.

Dylan stroked her hair and Hope's hackles rose.

"It wasn't like that," she hissed at Reuben. "She was in zombie mode, he told me. Zonked out on Valium, raving incoherently at him. He told me."

Reuben cocked his head to one side. "Is that so?"

"You never wanted it," Monica said. "I didn't want it to start with. It must have known. It's my fault. All my fault."

"No, it isn't, petal. You can go again in a couple of

months," Dylan said. "I know I wasn't too chuffed when you told me, but I'd got used to the idea."

"Used to what?" Hope asked. "She's been acting for as long as he's known her. It was only a sodding audition. What's he so upset about?" but Reuben raised his hand for her to be silent.

"Just look, listen and learn," he said.

Irritated, Hope opened her mouth to protest, but then Dylan echoed Monica's shuddering sigh. "It was my baby too, love."

"Baby!" Hope couldn't believe her ears.

"Baby," Reuben confirmed. "She had a miscarriage that morning."

"But he never …" She stopped.

"No. He never," Reuben agreed.

"But why is he being so nice? It was over. He didn't love her any more."

"That's not strictly true," Reuben corrected. "'I'll always love Mon, but I'm not *in* love with her.' Remember that old chestnut?"

Hope felt gutted, stupid. Even after everything that had happened during the two years that they were together, she had believed that at the start he had loved her and that he had told her the truth about his relationship with Monica.

"No," she said. "Despite the miscarriage, it was over. Of course he was supportive and kind to her. She'd just lost a baby. That was why he cooled off with me at that point. He was in an impossible situation. She suffered from depression. She'd tried to kill herself before."

"Then why did he lie, and come to that, if they weren't having sex, how did she get pregnant?" Reuben said. "He told you they hadn't had sex for months. She was only six weeks pregnant. If he lied to you about that, how do you know what was true and what was a lie? Was there an audition? Was that another big porky to get him off the hook with you?"

He looked sickeningly smug and Hope wanted to slap the self-satisfied grin off his face. "Well, smart-arse, stop playing mind games and you tell me," she snarled, anger a more comfortable emotion than humiliation. "Was there a sodding audition?"

Reuben nodded. "As a matter of fact there was, but she didn't go."

Hope glanced back into the room. Dylan was still sitting on the sofa next to Monica, his arms wrapped around her. He was stroking her hair and whispering to her, but Hope couldn't make out what he was saying.

"Trust me, you don't want to know," Reuben said, grabbing her hand and hurrying her reluctantly back through the door and onto the ferry deck again. "The point I'm making is, he was lying through his teeth to you. As far as Monica was concerned, her marriage wasn't on the rocks. Dylan had no intention of leaving her, neither was Monica about to sod off back to the UK, as he put it. She had no idea. She thought they'd sorted out their problems."

"But why say it then?" she said.

Reuben gave a humourless snort. "Oh grow up, Hope. He was a serial womaniser. He had no conscience. He'd had one affair after another all the time he was married to Monica. You were just the last in a long line."

"Not the last," Hope said remembering.

"The last during his marriage to Monica," he corrected. "Except for Lucy Aragon, of course, but that wasn't really an affair."

"He was shagging Lucy Aragon?" she was stunned. She'd had no idea, not the slightest inkling.

Reuben sat down on the bench by the bulkhead again. "Well, that's the thing about Dylan Jones," he said. "He has a talent for making every woman he's unfaithful with believe that they're the only one in his life."

"There you are then," Hope said, triumphant. "I told you it wasn't my fault."

Reuben didn't comment on that, just continued with his train of thought. "Lucy dumped him for the drummer of her backing group. It was the first time his ego had been dented like that. Couldn't believe the old charm wasn't working. Told him straight out, she did. 'You're too old for me, Dylan.' He was terribly upset."

She smiled, despite herself. "I'd love to have been a fly on the wall for that."

"Anyway," Reuben continued, "we're straying from the point. Sending an anonymous letter to Monica was not a nice thing to do."

"But effective," Hope said.

* * *

The shit hit the fan three days after she had posted the letter to Monica. She had ripped it up half a dozen times, not because she had any doubts or second thoughts, but because she wanted to get the wording exactly right. She wanted to be certain that the text read as if it had been written by a well-meaning third party. At one point paranoia had led her to cut words out of a magazine with a scissors *á la* ransom demand, but she junked that version feeling it looked too sinister. In the end the simple one-line missive read: *"Your husband is having an affair."* Less is more. She had pondered over the term *"affair"* as opposed to *"in love with"*, finally settling on the former as it sounded more detached. *"Your husband is having an affair."* She had considered being specific and naming herself, but lost courage. The object of the exercise was for Monica to chuck Dylan out. Hating confrontation, she certainly didn't relish any immediate fallout at work, so it was time enough for them to find out after she and Dylan had gone.

She had been on tenterhooks since depositing the envelope in the letterbox, cursing the delays of the Christmas post, so it was something of a relief when on the third morning Lainie dragged her into the kitchen mid-morning, shutting the door and standing with her back against it.

"What's going on?" she hissed. "Did Dylan come clean to Monica?"

Although she had been expecting it, it was still a shock. "Why do you ask?" she said feebly.

Lainie grabbed her shoulders. "Like you don't know? Dylan's done a runner."

She wasn't expecting that. "A runner? What do you mean?"

"He's gone. Upped sticks and moved out. I heard Gail on the phone to Paul. There was this big bust-up with Monica and he's gone."

"She chucked him out?"

Lainie nodded. "Clothes in the proverbial bin-liner on the step."

Strangely, Hope hadn't been expecting that either. She had no idea it would be that easy and she felt a flood of relief. "He must have told her then," she said.

"So where is he?" Lainie asked. "Not at ours, I hope?"

"I don't know," Hope replied truthfully, the first stirrings of alarm churning in her guts. "Why? Have you heard something?"

"Oh, come on," Lainie persisted. "Haven't you spoken to him?"

Hope shook her head just as Polly forced the kitchen door open.

"What's the story with Deadly Dylan?" she demanded. "You can't talk about it without me. Paul's in a huddle with Roddy and they're not takin' any calls."

"Monica chucked him out," Lainie said and Hope was grateful for the economical nature of the statement.

"Why? What for?"

Lainie eyes strayed briefly to Hope, then she shrugged. "No idea."

"Well, Paul wants his guts for garters, so it must be pretty serious. You reckon he's shaggin' that Lucy Aragon?"

"No way," Hope snapped and instantly felt the colour rise up her neck. "I mean, I, um … I doubt it," she added, averting her eyes, guilt written all over her face.

Polly, however, too intent on getting to the bottom of such a juicy piece of gossip, failed to notice. "I'll bet he is," she said.

The fact that Polly didn't know left Hope optimistic that she could avoid unpleasantness in the office. She didn't relish the prospect of a scene and of having to justify herself to Paul. Just because Monica was his sister-in-law, it didn't give him the right to preach to her about her private life.

After Polly had returned to reception to answer the phone, echoing Hope's thoughts, Lainie said, "Hang on a minute. How come Paul's not on your case? If Dylan owned up, surely Monica would have told Gail, who in turn would have told Paul?"

"Maybe he wasn't specific," Hope prevaricated. "He was probably protecting me and just said he was leaving, or it was over, or he was in love with someone else, or something."

"Maybe," Lainie said, but her tone didn't carry much conviction.

When she hadn't heard a peep from Dylan by lunchtime however Hope became increasingly concerned. "He's protecting me," she repeated to Lainie when her friend enquired if she had heard anything. "He won't phone here." She had assumed though that when Monica threw him out, he would go straight to her place. In fact she had fantasised about it. The two of them tucked up in her bed, high on love. Free to be together. Without telling anyone where she was going, she took a cab back to the apartment in the hope of finding him there waiting for her, but of course he wasn't.

"He's not at ours," she confided to Lainie when she returned.

"So where is he then?" Lainie replied, unable to hide the relief that she wouldn't have to explain to her boss why his sister-in-law's errant husband happened to be staying under her roof.

"I don't know," Hope said. "But he's bound to call me soon."

But he didn't.

Christmas came and went, but Hope barely noticed. She skipped the Christmas party, feigned a bad bout of flu to avoid going home for the holiday, afraid to leave the apartment in case he phoned. Unable to explain why he hadn't been in touch, she was beginning to suspect that far from throwing him out on to the street,

Monica and Gail had conspired with Paul to murder him, and all the hoo-hah was just a ruse to cover their tracks.

It was at this point that Lainie totally lost patience with her and told her to get real.

"Face it, Hope, he's just a cowardly bollox and he's run off with his tail between his legs!" she said.

But still she couldn't bring herself to believe that he would just go without a word.

Unless … unless he guessed that the letter was from her. Unable to consider such a disaster, she dismissed that thought from her head, the consequences being too much to deal with.

Then on New Year's Eve, just as she had given up hope and was sinking into a decline, he phoned. Lainie was out at a party, the two of them barely on speaking terms.

"Hi, petal," he said.

That was it. "Hi, petal." No apology. No explanation, just "Hi, petal," as if he'd just popped down to the off-licence for a packet of fags.

Although relieved to finally hear from him, anger bubbled up inside her. "Where the fuck have you been? Why didn't you fucking call me? What's fucking happening?"

"Hey, petal, petal, chill. Chill, will you?" His voice was lazy and laid-back.

"Chill? You bugger off without a word for nearly three weeks and you tell me to chill?"

He laughed. "I'm sorry, petal. But it was all out of the blue. We had this big bust-up over you, and she threw me out. She was like a fucking banshee. I was afraid she'd take my eyes out. I had to get away. I had to give myself time to think."

"Think about what? Why didn't you call me? I was really worried." Then his words registered. "You told her about me?"

"Of course. That's what the bust-up was about."

"But what about –" she was going to say 'the letter' but stopped herself in the nick of time. "So how come Paul isn't on my case?"

"That's why I didn't mention you by name. I just said I was in love with someone else. That it was over. Then, petal, well, I just had to get away. I didn't want to risk Paul taking it out on you in case, well, in case when push came to shove, you had second thoughts about us. It was enough to burn my own bridges without putting a match to yours."

She clearly remembered the flood of relief and gratitude, yes gratitude, that he had been so thoughtful. Worried that she might have changed her mind. So insecure that he didn't want to take anything for granted and make life difficult for her if …

* * *

Reuben guffawed. "I can't believe you really bought that load of old tosh. Wanted to save you from grief?

Was afraid you'd changed your mind? Come on!"

Hope whacked him in the side with her elbow and he flinched. "Easy for you to say with the benefit of hindsight. We've already established that I was a touch gullible," she snapped.

"A touch? Do you want to know what really happened?"

Hope hesitated. Not that she still harboured any illusions about Dylan, but facing the past was proving to be a mortifying experience and she wasn't sure she was up for more humiliation.

She felt Reuben's elbow nudge her gently back. "Come on, you know you want to."

She had no idea of how it happened, of the mechanics, but the next moment, before she had time to say yea or nay, she was standing in an unfamiliar room. It was small and extremely untidy. A bed settee unmade, the bedclothes spilling on the floor, the sheets grubby. Clothes were strewn around and there were unwashed mugs on almost every surface. Dylan walked through the door then, followed by Lucy Aragon.

Conscious of Reuben standing beside her she said, "I thought she dumped him." But he made no comment, just smiled. It was a kind smile though, not smug.

"I told her," Dylan said. "I told Monica about us." He stepped closer and wrapped his arms around her. "I've left her, petal. I've moved out."

Lucy pushed her hands against his chest, disengaging herself and stepping away from him. She looked totally aghast. "What the fuck for?"

He looked surprised for an instant by her reaction, but recovered quickly. Catching her hand, he drew her towards him again and gave her his puppy-dog eyes. "Can't live without you, petal. We can be together now."

"Are you out of your feeble mind?" she said. "*Nothing serious*, you said. *No strings*. Remember?"

He looked less confident and the puppy-dog countenance slipped a fraction. "Petal? I've left Monica for *you*."

Lucy Aragon shook her head and laughed. "You can't be serious!"

"But why not?" He looked totally flummoxed now.

Lucy Aragon's face, on the other hand, was a picture. "For starters, you're too old for me, Dylan …" And she continued at length to tell him exactly 'why not'.

"You expressed a wish to be a fly on the wall," Reuben whispered in her ear, and she found herself smiling.

"I can't believe the lying hound went straight to her," Hope said. Despite the satisfaction of retrospectively witnessing Dylan being unceremoniously dumped by Lucy Aragon, she still felt disappointed and sad at the extent of his duplicity.

"Duplicity? You're hardly one to talk," Reuben said, all sympathy put aside.

"I know, I know. I get the message, but this is all new to me. I'd no idea he was seeing Lucy Aragon."

"Or the chick from Oran Mulcahy's office, the small blonde one with the lisp?"

"Jesus, Reuben, hit me when I'm down, why don't you?" she said, flopping back on to the bench. "Is that it, or do you have a list?"

The angel sat down beside her. "Face it, Hope, he couldn't keep it in his pants." He paused. "Funnily enough it's not so much the sex he's addicted to, more the thrill of the chase, the subterfuge, and the need for adulation."

Hope gave a bitter snort. "He came badly unstuck with Lucy then, didn't he?"

He smiled. "You could say that. Despite what you think of him though, he had quite low self-esteem. Quite common in bullies, I'm told."

"You must be joking. He had an ego the size of the Royal Albert Hall."

"Believe me. Not so." He gave her a gentle nudge. "Feel any better, seeing him dumped."

She smiled. "A bit."

"And how about the letter? You still think that was an acceptable thing to do?"

She thought about it for a moment. "To be honest, given the circumstances, given the fact that I totally believed him, I still don't think I was the villain of the piece. He was way more culpable then I was."

"Thou shalt not commit adultery."

"I didn't. I wasn't married."

"OK," Reuben said, "If you want to nit-pick, how about, *'Thou shalt not covet thy neighbour's wife'* or in this case, *'husband'*."

"Got me there," she conceded. "But I still say, all things considered, he was more to blame than I was."

"But what about Monica?"

"I probably did her a favour."

Leaning back and laying his arms along the back of the bench again, he sighed. "I suppose in one way I can't argue with that. He was, and still is, a very flawed individual, but at the end of the day, that wasn't your decision to make. And the way you went about it caused poor Monica an awful lot of pain."

In light of Reuben's revelation, for the first time she felt a certain empathy with Monica, and experienced a tingle of guilt. "What happened to her?"

"You mean apart from the breakdown?"

Hope cringed. "She had a breakdown?"

Reuben nodded. "In fairness, it was a long time coming, and you were just the last nail in the coffin. Ironically enough she assumed the woman alluded to in your letter was Lucy Aragon."

"Really? That makes me feel a bit less guilty."

"You're actually experiencing guilt?" He sounded surprised. "That's a start, I suppose, but just because she assumed the letter was referring to Lucy, I don't think that lessens your guilt to any great degree. She was still dealing with the miscarriage. Your letter on top of that was too much for her. His womanising was the reason for the new start. She'd found out about one of his women and he'd promised her it would never happen again, so your little bombshell was enough to make her unravel."

She shuddered. "Unravel? You make it sound like she was in a straitjacket. A basket-case."

"Not quite. But close. Grief piled upon grief, and Monica, like many thespians, is a sensitive soul."

"OK, you win. I shouldn't have sent the letter. It was a bad thing to do."

"A very bad thing."

They sat in silence, Hope uncomfortable with thought of sending another woman to the psychiatric ward. There but for grace, she thought.

"Indeed," Reuben concurred. "But you are made of sterner stuff than Monica."

"So what happened to her?" she asked after a pregnant pause.

Reuben was silent for a further half a minute, then he gave her a sly sideways glance. "After she was discharged from the psychiatric clinic, she developed a cocaine dependency. But she was a talented actress. She got regular stage work and a few decent parts in a couple of small independent films, but the cocaine habit coupled with an escalation in her drinking got a hold of her and she had to go into rehab."

Hope groaned. "Now I feel really awful."

"And so you should."

"So is she clean now? Did she get her life back on track?"

He shrugged. "If you could call it that. She met a man in rehab. An American. Another actor. They kept in touch after she completed her course." He trailed off and stared off into space.

"And?"

"He invited her out to LA." He glanced back at her, a sly grin on his chops. "Happily married now with three kids and regular work in a daytime soap."

"Thank God for that!"

The wind had died down, the sea was calmer and she could see the first glow of dawn on the horizon. It seemed somehow appropriate. "What now?" she asked.

"Let me see," Reuben said, closely examining his fingernails. How about: *'Thou shalt not steal'*?"

Chapter 11

He took her back to January 1988. She knew it was January 88 without his having to tell her, because they were in her bedroom at the Sandymount apartment, her case was lying open on the bed, and 'Fairytale of New York' was on the radio.

"'Heaven is a Place on Earth' was Number 1." Utterly disgusted, Reuben curled his lip. "Belinda Carlisle. Can you believe that?"

"Better than Bros, I suppose," she said distractedly, wondering what he was going to throw at her next.

"'When Will I be Famous?'"

"Sorry?"

"Bros. 'When Will I be Famous?'. Down to Number 19 that week. But they were back in the charts by April with 'Drop the Boy'."

"What are you? The fucking Pop Music Police?" she snapped, anxious to get the next sixteen years out of the way, so she could deal with the Amy situation and hopefully get her life back.

Reuben however chose to ignore her ill temper. "Actually, after my involvement with Janis I got to be a bit of an anorak. Always preferred rock to pop, mind you; Bruce Springsteen and U2 to Kylie, until she went indie that is." He frowned. "Although …"

"Although what?" she asked, unable to keep the impatience out of her voice.

"Although, there was a certain catchy boppy thing going on in her Pete Waterman days." Half a tone flat he started to belt out the chorus of 'I Should Be So Lucky'. She gaped at the incongruity of a six foot-three angel clicking his fingers as he popped his head from side to side, approximately in time with his singing. "Number 1 in March 88, if my memory serves me correctly," he added as he tapped out the beats of the instrumental riff.

"Why am I here?" she demanded before he could break into a second round of the chorus.

He stopped singing abruptly. "Clearly not a Kylie fan," he muttered. Sitting down on the end of the bed, he looked her straight in the eye and repeated, "I told you. *'Thou shalt not steal'.*"

A defensive surge of anger rose up inside her and the words *"scumbag"*, *"maggot"*, and *"cheat dirty faggot"* came to mind as Kirsty McColl vocalised her thoughts. "I didn't steal," she protested vehemently. "It was a *loan*. I sent it back ... well, most of it."

*   *   *

He was in Wales. West Wales. Dyfed, the county formerly known as Carmarthen. She had been through there once as a child with her parents and sister Charity on the way to Hereford for the wedding of some relation, and remembered it as a small bustling country town where everybody seemed to be speaking Welsh.

Dylan's brother Owen lived there, but was conveniently heading off to work in Saudi Arabia for a year.

"I'll be looking after his house for him while he's away," Dylan had said once he had calmed her down. "Things couldn't have worked out better, petal. His place is fabulous (*faaab-aless*). And it's the perfect opportunity to make a start on my book."

His enthusiasm was infectious and by the end of the call her spirits had lifted, and she was intoxicated by his voice. It was only after he had hung up she realised that, although he had asked how she was, and if Paul was giving her grief, and had she heard how Monica was dealing with it, there had been no talk of her going over to join him. Plenty about his plans to be disciplined about his writing day. About taking long walks through the Brechfa forest. About the stunning scenery and an encounter he'd had with a fox on the Brecon Beacons, but nothing about her joining him. She didn't even have his address, other then a vague reference to a village called Lanlooney or something like that, and he had called her from a public phone as he claimed his brother didn't have one.

Lainie was scathing. "Of course there was no talk of you going over," she scoffed the following morning. "He's a bollox! He was only using you."

"He loves me," Hope retaliated. "He left Monica for me."

But Lainie was having none of it. "That's a touch revisionist. As I recall, Monica chucked him out."

She had so wanted to believe him, she'd completely expunged the fact from her memory that it was her letter that had prompted the end of his marriage; that he hadn't left voluntarily.

"But he didn't deny it," she countered feebly. "He told her it was over. He told her he was in love with someone else."

"And you know that for sure?" Lainie said.

She didn't, but couldn't afford to let herself doubt it. "He's phoning again tomorrow," she lied. "We'll talk about it then."

But he didn't phone for over a week, by which time she was imagining all sorts of terrible reasons for his silence. Lainie was sympathetic, not because she had any illusions about Dylan, or believed even remotely that he wanted Hope to join him, but because she was a good friend, and because slagging Dylan off had proved to be totally futile. Anyway, she hated to see Hope so miserable. She assumed that as the days went on she would cop onto what a lying bastard he was, finally admit it was over, lick her emotional wounds, and chalk it up to experience.

"But what if he's had an accident?" she'd wailed when Lainie tried to talk sense into her. "He could be lying in hospital right now."

Lainie lost it then and gave her the full rant, throwing diplomacy to the wind. She told her exactly what she thought of Dylan Jones, for the way he had treated his wife, for the way he was treating her, and expressed her amazement at Hope's naiveté. Then, just as she was running out of steam, the phone rang.

Hope froze for an instant then they both made a dive for it, Hope winning by a whisker. It was Dylan, of course. In the nick of time.

"Sorry not to have called before, petal," he said, "but I've been getting myself organised."

With Lainie standing there ear-wigging and mouthing things such as 'Tell him to fuck off,' she found it hard to concentrate. "That's nice," she heard herself say.

"Yes. And I've the use of Owen's Land-Rover. She's a touch ancient but still in good nick."

"That's nice," she repeated as Lainie threw up her hands in frustration and stomped from the room.

"There's this great pub in the village too. All old

beams and real ale. A few amazing old characters in there. Got talking to –"

"I was thinking of coming over," she cut in.

The silence at the other end of the line was deafening.

"Hello!" she said. "Are you still there?"

She heard him cough and clear his throat. "What? For a visit?"

"For good," she said, her heart pounding.

A further silence, followed by a tentative, "OK, petal. When were you thinking of?"

She heaved a mental sigh of relief. "As soon as I can organise it. Is that OK?"

"Um, yeah, of course. But I'd leave it a few weeks, till I get properly settled, if I were you, petal. Weather's shit at the minute. See, I want to get a start on the book and with you there there's no way I'll be able to concentrate." He laughed but she didn't feel like joining in.

"But I wouldn't get in the way," she heard herself saying. "And I could cook for you and look after you so you wouldn't have to bother with day-to-day stuff."

* * *

"Listen to yourself," Reuben said. "Good grief, woman, what were you thinking?"

"Shut up. This is my recollection. Anyway, it did the trick, didn't it? I was over there the next day."

He laughed. "Like he could turn down such an offer. His very own housekeeper/sex slave. The only thing that would have made life better for him was if he was living over the pub. Anyway, he didn't exactly encourage you, despite that."

"Yes, he did. We agreed."

"No. *You* agreed. You said you were coming and chose to ignore the fact that he was less than enthusiastic."

Hope sighed. "Look, Reuben, if you're going to keep interrupting like this ..."

Reuben raised his hands, palms out in capitulation, then drew the imaginary zipper across his lips. But he was right. She knew in her heart and soul that she had closed her ears to Dylan's attempts to put her off. Refused to believe that there was the slightest possibility that he didn't really want her there.

Behind her, the bedroom door suddenly opened, and Lainie poked her head in.

"Listen, the step-class crowd are going to that new club on Harcourt Street tonight. Fancy –" She stopped dead as she caught sight of the half-packed suitcase. "What are you doing?"

Hope was somewhat surprised that Lainie could actually see her.

Reuben gave her a shove in the back. "Well, answer the girl," he said, and it was obvious from her lack of reaction that Lainie couldn't see or hear him.

"Um, packing," Hope muttered.

Lainie pushed the door fully open and stepped inside the room. "Are you sure this is a good idea?" She sat down on the end of the bed close to the spot Reuben had just vacated. He was now standing, leaning against the dressing-table.

Catching sight of her reflection, Hope was stunned to see her twenty-year-old self staring back at her. Scrunched hair, stiff with product. Black 501's and crisp white shirt with shoulder pads. She had no idea how to respond to Lainie, but before she had a chance to marshal her thoughts, she found herself saying, "But he loves me, Lainie. Why do you find that so hard to believe?" It was a thoroughly surreal experience. Her brain wanted to say one thing but her vocal chords were totally out of her control.

Lainie shook her head. "He's a lying bollox, Hope. This is going to end in tears. I know it."

Hope wanted to say, 'I know. You were absolutely right, and I'm so sorry' but the words wouldn't form. "You're *so* wrong," she heard herself say.

She remembered the incident clearly. It was the Saturday morning after Dylan's last call. She was utterly on the defensive and blind to the obvious, and Lainie's pleas for sanity had fallen on deaf ears. It had ended in a bitter row with Lainie stomping out, reiterating her opinion that she was a stupid naive cow and deserved everything she got. In a fit of pique, Hope had finished packing, then, noticing Lainie's PASS card lying on the mantelpiece, and very short of ready cash to fund her journey, on impulse she had picked it up. On the way to the station she had asked the cab driver to stop off at the nearest cash point, where she had withdrawn two hundred pounds from Lainie's account. She felt ashamed at the memory of it, and although she had sent most of it back, the fact that she had done such a thing had put an end to their friendship.

But now, second time round, Lainie was still sitting on the end of the bed.

"I'm sorry but I have to do this, Lainie," Hope was relieved to find herself saying. "However it works out, I know you're only trying to help, and I really appreciate it, but I don't want to fall out with you. I just have to go, and that's it."

Picking up her wash-bag she packed it at the side of her case and shut the lid. She had difficulty with the zip, and Lainie gave her a hand, holding down the side so that the fastener could slide around the corner of the bag.

"He'll break your heart," said Lainie.

"Probably," Hope replied, then smiled. "I don't suppose you could lend me a couple of hundred quid?" It felt good to have power over both her vocal chords and her actions again.

Lainie sighed. "You're really determined, aren't you? Nothing I say's going to make the slightest bit of difference, is it?"

Hope shook her head. She wished that she was in a position to let Lainie talk her out of it, but Reuben had been very specific about not changing her own life, so she shook her head.

"I've no option, Lainie. I *really* have to do this, even if it is against my better judgement."

"When are you heading off?"

"Now. As soon as I've finished packing. There's a ferry tonight from Rosslare."

Lainie nodded resignedly, then stood up and hugged Hope. Hope felt tears in her eyes, as her friend gave her a kiss on the cheek.

"I'll be here to pick up the pieces," Lainie said. "I'll see you off. We can stop at the cash point on the way."

"There, see? There was no need to steal," Reuben said, but Hope just glared at him over Lainie's shoulder.

Inside, however, she felt relieved that she had managed to undo a major regret of her life.

Chapter 12

He wasn't at the ferry terminal in Pembroke to meet her as she had hoped. Fatigued and cold after the rough crossing she had sat around in the waiting-room for two hours, both anxious and angered by his non-appearance. Fears that he might have had an accident surfaced again, and an odd echo of the fear she had felt sitting on the primary school wall waiting for her mother to pick her up, always late. Always the last.

Hunger drove her to the cafeteria after a while where she consumed a greasy fry, which made her feel a little better. "Excuse me," she said to the woman behind the counter, whose name-tag declared her to be Ellen. "Do you know a village near Dyfed called Lanlooney?"

The woman's brow furrowed for a moment, then she shook her head. "Sorry, love." She called over her shoulder, "Hylwyn? Do you know a Llanllwni? Near Dyfed?"

Hylwyn emerged from the kitchen, but she could be of no help either. "Isn't no one meetin' you?" she asked.

Hope shook her head. "He was supposed to be here by now, but he must have been held up."

"Can't you phone 'im?"

"No phone," she said gloomily.

"Best get the bus to Dyfed, then, love. They'll be able to tell you there, I should think."

It took her two hours to reach Dyfed and she had to wait a further four hours for a bus to Llanllwni, so it was going on for 5.30 in the afternoon before she stepped stiffly off the bus in the darkness, in front of a pub, The New Inn. It looked about a million years old. Dylan had been right about the weather: it was bone-numbingly cold and after the oppressive heat of the bus she shivered as she watched the rear-lights recede into the distance. Lugging her case after her, she ventured inside the pub. Two old farmers in wellies were standing up at the bar, half-empty pints in front of them, talking to the barman. The conversation (in Welsh) however ceased as she entered, then the barman looked over at her, his eyebrows questioning. The two old guys turned around for a gawk too.

"I'm looking for Dylan Jones," she said. "His brother Owen has a house somewhere around here." The barman just stared blankly at her, the two farmers likewise. It was all too much. Exhausted by the journey, the cold and anxiety, she slumped down on her case and burst into tears.

Twenty minutes later she was sitting by the fire, a mug of tea warming her hands, a rug thrown around her shoulders. The two farmers, Hugh and Aled, were sitting opposite, discussing which Owen Jones she meant, as if she weren't there. The barman, Wayne, however, was very sympathetic. There were three candidates.

"That'll be Owen Jones over b'there in Salah," Wayne said finally, after she had mentioned that he was off working in Saudi Arabia. "A teacher, he is. Went off just after Christmas. Used to work in the comp in Dyfed, is it?"

"Dylan's his brother. He's staying at the house while Owen's away," she said, grateful to have made some progress.

Hugh and Aled exchanged looks and Aled nodded sagely. "That'll be the writer up the mountain."

Salah was a small-holding on top of high moorland hills. Hugh drove her up there in his ancient Land-Rover and she had to hold on to avoid whiplash as it rattled along the rutted road at surprisingly high speed. They'd been steadily climbing in the fifteen minutes the journey had taken and appeared to be in the middle of nowhere. The wind was whipping the grass on tufty mounds at the side of the road and everywhere was pitch black.

"Have to leave you b'here," he said as he swerved around a speckle-faced sheep grazing at the side of the road, and pulled to a halt. "Swore I'd never set foot in that place."

"Why's that?" she asked.

"Bad blood."

"What? You and Dylan's brother?"

He shook his head gravely. "My great-great-grandfather, Morgan Evans was cheated out of that land by Ira Hopkins."

Hugh looked ancient and raddled, seventy if he was a day. "Your *great-great*-grandfather? But that must have been, what? Over a hundred years ago? Nothing to do with Dylan's brother at all." Then, turning on the helpless charm, added, "Are you sure you couldn't just drop me a little closer? You wouldn't technically be stepping foot, would you? You needn't get out."

But he just continued to stare ahead without comment.

"It's really dark out there," she added after a further few seconds of stubborn silence. "I might get lost."

Gripping the steering wheel, staring determinedly ahead he said, through gritted teeth, "I will never set foot on that land," then clammed up.

Hope peered through the dirty windscreen looking for any sign of a light, anything that would identify her destination. "Where's the house?" she asked, panic rising. "I can't see anything out there. You can't leave me here."

He rummaged under the seat and handed her an old bicycle flashlight, then pointed through the passenger side window. "Down that track b'there. About half a mile."

"Half a mile? You can't be serious!"

"You can leave the lamp at the pub."

He wouldn't be persuaded to take her the rest of the way. "Bad blood," he repeated when she tried to appeal to his better nature. "Wouldn't piss on a Jenkins if he was on fire."

"Who's Jenkins?" she asked confused.

"Thomas Jenkins. Ira Hopkins's great-great-grandson."

She had no idea what he was talking about or how it related to Owen Jones, but he was adamant and unapologetic, so she had no option but to climb down from the Land-Rover and head on foot down a track.

There was no moon, and ahead of her she could see absolutely nothing, the thin beam of the torch of little help. With each step the suitcase got heavier and, because she had to hold the flashlight in one hand and the case in the other, after a hundred yards she had to give up and leave her worldly possessions by the side of the track. To add insult to injury, her coat was in no way equal to the wind-chill factor and she was soon shivering again with the cold, tears streaming down her face as she trudged along the track, not even sure it led anywhere. Then as she reached the top of an incline she spotted a light in the distance. "Thank God!" she cried in relief and quickened her pace, breaking into a run. She tripped and fell a couple of times in her efforts to reach the light, the final tumble just inside the gate, tearing the knees out of her Levi's. Crying uncontrollably she staggered to the door of the stone cottage and banged her frozen fists against it. Footsteps, the door opened and Dylan was standing there, the light behind him. She threw herself into his arms, her face wet with tears and snot.

His first words of greeting were, "What the fuck are you doing here?" A pause. Then, voice softer, "I thought you were coming next month, petal."

"Which part of *tomorrow* didn't he understand?" Reuben enquired.

"I suppose, with hindsight, he was hoping that if he didn't meet me, I wouldn't be able to find him," she said. "But why phone me in the first place if he didn't want me? That's what I'd like to know. If he hadn't phoned, I'd have got over him."

"The man had no backbone. He was lonely. And talking to you was a way of finding out what was happening back at home. At that point he was still hoping Monica would take him back."

"He did ask a lot of questions about what was happening with Paul, and if I'd heard how Monica was dealing with it. I thought he was just being kind. But I suppose I wasn't really listening. I mean I thought he was just trying to find out if they'd sussed I was the other woman." She groaned. "God! How stupid was I?"

Reuben put his arm around her shoulder and gave her a squeeze. "You were in love. You interpreted it the way you wanted to hear it."

"I must have been insane."

He nodded in agreement, disengaging himself. "Romantic love is a form of insanity."

"I can't argue with that, though I suppose good old-fashioned lust came into it too."

Reuben chortled. "It's on the list," he said, eyes twinkling.

"Oh, piss off," she groaned. "I thought we were doing the Ten Sodding Commandments, not the Seven Deadly Sins."

"I can hardly discount the Seven Deadly Sins, can I?" he said. "Particularly as you made a career of chalking them all up."

"I did not!" she protested, vehemently. "I never killed anyone. I didn't worship, what is it, strange gods or anything."

"Granted, with the exception of Mammon, I suppose, but those are commandments not the Seven Deadlies. What about Pride, Envy, Sloth?" He paused. "OK, we can scrub Sloth and I suppose Gluttony in the usual sense, apart from you being a glutton for punishment that is, but that still leaves Anger, and Avarice."

"Jesus! I'd have to be a fecking saint to avoid all that."

"There you go again. *Thou shalt not take the name of*

the Lord thy God in vain'," but he was smiling and there was no harm in the comment. "The powers that be don't expect you to be a saint, Hope. Just to recognise and acknowledge your – shall we say, lapses from the path of righteousness."

She sighed. "OK. I get the message. So what now?"

"You tell me," he said. "This is your journey." Then digging his hands deep into his pockets he casually started to whistle a familiar tune that she couldn't put a name to.

Chapter 13

At the conclusion of his first year-long contract, Owen Jones had signed up again for a further two years, loath to return to teaching a bunch of unwilling kids at the comp for a relative pittance, too well accustomed to his tax-free high earnings, so they were still living in his place in Llanllwni. Eighteen months – two miserable winters – in a stone cottage with neither damp-proofing, central heating or an indoor loo had been a sobering experience. Hope's initial view that her life was a romantic adventure had palled somewhat, especially when she found her clothes going mildewed in the wardrobe. Dylan was plugging away at his Important Novel which, a year and a half on, he was having difficulty finishing. He had secured a literary agent the previous year who had been very excited about the initial chapters Dylan had submitted, but who was getting increasingly agitated that the work didn't appear to be nearing completion. It was becoming something of a runaway train. It was well over one thousand three hundred pages and, due to Dylan's precious nature, his agent's advice about cutting large chunks of it had fallen on stubbornly deaf ears.

Things hadn't been going well on the relationship front for some time either. Dylan's attitude to her was increasingly proprietorial and controlling. The velocity of the downward slide had been in direct relation to the gestation of the Important Novel and he was like a wasp with a toothache most of the time. He had the unerring ability to make her feel inadequate and intellectually inferior and, because of the insidious nature of his criticism, as time progressed this undermined her confidence to a huge degree. Blinded initially by love, she considered him to be thoroughly remarkable, and when he said he was going to write an Important Novel, she had no doubt in her mind that said novel would be a literary triumph. Perish the thought that Dylan Jones would write anything run of the mill. Move over, James Joyce. Make way, Dylan Thomas. She put up with his moods and constant carping criticism because she was in love, was in awe of him, and so made allowances for his creative temperament, placating and humouring him, tip toeing around.

Years later, with the blinding clarity of hindsight, she could see that far from a tortured genius, he was a moody, needy, shallow, selfish old fart, with little talent and an inflated opinion of his own intellectual capabilities.

Initially though, life had been good, and they had fallen into a cosy domestic routine quite quickly. They would rise latish, at around ten, when Hope would cook him a full Irish, after which she would tidy up and sit quietly reading while he got down to work on Owen's computer. At around 1.30, she would wander out to the kitchen and make a light lunch, usually soup and a sandwich, then probably go out for a long walk leaving him to carry on with the Important Novel, popping into the pub for a coffee or a lager before making her way back to the cottage to cook his dinner. Twice a week she drove into Swansea and, while the lady in the laundrette did a service wash, she went to Sainsbury's to stock up. Dylan's taste in food was somewhat conservative so chips, eggs, sausages, burgers and beans figured largely, with the odd tinned steak and kidney pie, which was just as well because she wasn't much of a cook and Owen's Aga range was unreliable to say the least. Occasionally, after a good day, she would sit at his feet in front of the fire with rapt attention and he would read out a few pages of the Important Novel. She was astounded by him. She thought he was a lyrical and poetic writer and she let the words wash over her. She couldn't distinguish any sort of plot line in his stream-of-consciousness style, but didn't dwell on that. It only confirmed in her mind that it must be a really Important Novel, recalling the fact that she hadn't managed to make head or tail of *Ulysses* either, and that was an acknowledged literary masterpiece.

On the bad days she learned to keep a low profile and, as the honeymoon of a damp spring and summer drifted into the first misty days of autumn, the bad days increasingly outnumbered the good. He would slide into a prickly decline, looking for any excuse for confrontation, sighing like a furnace if she made a sound or tuned the radio to any station other than BBC Radio 4. He would whinge about her cooking, complain vociferously about her appearance, about her housekeeping skills, the fact that his savings wouldn't last forever and it was about time she went out, got a job and started pulling her weight. At the time she took all his criticism to heart – the relationship was only nine months old – and she tearfully made promises that she'd try harder, after which he would become remorseful and they would end up in bed where, after some vigorous sex, she would reclaim ownership of their problems.

As time went on she became deft at avoiding confrontation by recognising the warning signals and cheerfully whisking him down to the village pub for the evening, soothing his ire by reinforcing the notion that his work was indeed a work of genius, and what did his agent know anyway? Those who can do. Those who can't become agents.

The pub regulars were a motley crew. Hugh and Aled of course and their respective wives, Maureen and Sadie (but Sadie only on Saturday nights). Maureen was a round happy woman, with pale Weetabix hair, partial to floral polyester, Yardley's Lavender scent, drawn-on eyebrows and red lipstick. Sadie, thin as a rake and very religious, drank sweet sherry, always wore a hat, quoted the scriptures ad nauseam, and her facial expression suggested she sucked sour lemons most of the time. She went to chapel three times on Sundays and rued the day that the status quo had been so cruelly shattered when Dyfed's pubs started opening on the Sabbath. Hope only attempted conversation with her the once, during which Sadie made her disapproval very obvious.

"Doesn't approve yew livin' over the brush," Maureen confided. "Take no notice of her, *cariad*. Yew young ones have the right idea if yew ask me."

Hope immediately took to Maureen after that. She was an avid *Coronation Street* viewer, and as Dylan wouldn't hear of getting a TV, Hope delighted in the opportunity to keep up with her favourite soap, with liberal helpings of *EastEnders* and *Emmerdale* thrown in for good measure. Maureen and Hugh had two children, young Hughie and Laverne, both of whom were at university. They came home her first Christmas in Llanllwni, and Maureen and Hugh's pride in their kids was very evident. Laverne was small like her mother and on the heavy side. Young Hughie, taller and very thin, sported a wispy beard. He was reading Politics and Philosophy at Newcastle and Laverne Spanish and History at York. Dylan wasn't very impressed however and dismissed Hughie as an arrogant gobshite, no doubt because Hughie's offhand manner made it clear that he was equally unimpressed by Dylan. Laverne he just dismissed as "the fat no-brainer".

To Hope however, it was a welcome relief to meet Laverne and Hughie because normally, with the exception of Wayne and his wife Laura, there were few pub patrons under the age of fifty. Hope remarked on this one Saturday evening in January to Maureen. "Nothin' for 'em, here, petal. They all have to go away to study or to get work."

She could empathise with that having decamped to Dublin from Mayo herself as soon as she left school in the pre-Celtic-Tiger days. Wayne was in his early thirties, a nephew of Thomas Jenkins, Hugh's nemesis, though that didn't stop Hugh from holding up the bar every day come rain or shine. Laura was a tall dark-haired attractive woman of twenty-nine. Some might describe her as brittle. Hope often spent the evening talking to her when Maureen wasn't around. She had lived in London most of her life which was where she had met Wayne. She was a nurse and she'd followed him back to Llanllwni when he'd had to return in order to run the pub for his mother, Gwen, after his father died. Gwen occasionally put in an appearance, generally on a Saturday night when she sat with her friend Sadie. They were two of a kind and attended chapel together. Hope got the impression that Laura and Gwen didn't get on too well, and Gwen regularly made reference to the fact that there was no sign of a baby, inferring that the fault lay with Laura. Sadie concurred, quoting yet another convenient tract about painted harlots. Maureen however had different ideas. "Low sperm count," she whispered to Hope one evening, when Gwen was being particularly scathing about her lack of a grandchild, though how Maureen came by this information, Hope didn't like to ask. Although Wayne and Laura appeared to get on pretty well, Laura didn't much like living in rural West Wales. Hope couldn't blame her, considering the fact that she had to reside under the same roof as the Bible-thumping Mother-in-law from Hell.

Hope was happy enough at that time, despite the fact that her social life revolved around a small village pub full of near-geriatrics, and that she was living beyond the back of beyond with a tortured, if libidinous, genius. It was only after a rather nasty incident in the pub in the September of '89, that she began to re-evaluate her life and realise how much it had shrunk.

Dylan, the worse for drink, and in a foul humour anyway on account of a letter from his agent, the contents of which he wouldn't discuss, had made a complete show of her when she had offered an innocent opinion on the Guildford Four appeal due to be heard the following October.

"Bollox!" he'd roared. "All the fucking Irish, never mind just those IRA bastards, should be shot! Fucking shot!"

Stunned by the personal nature and vitriol of the attack, she had been temporarily lost for words.

The whole bar lapsed into an embarrassed silence, then Wayne, darting a glance at Hope, cajoled, "Steady on, mate."

"Well," Dylan countered, "bloody Ireland! They should hand it back and let them fight it out amongst themselves."

"But what's that got to do with the Guildford Four?" Laura asked. "If they're innocent they shouldn't be inside, should they? It means the guilty ones, the ones that planted the bombs, are walking free."

Dylan had just flapped his hands in reply to that. "Whatever," he muttered.

Nobody commented further, Wayne taking the initiative to start talking about football. The atmosphere lifted but Hope felt deeply wounded.

"If you don't mind me sayin' so, *cariad*," Maureen said as the men were exchanging views about Manchester United, "there was no call for that. He doesn't respect yew, yew know? A blind man can see that."

Hope, though still smarting, was taken aback. "What do you mean?" she said.

"Well," Maureen replied, "he never talks to yew, and when he does he's always criticisin'. Dismissin' what yew have to say as if yew were tup stupid."

"No. It's not like that, honestly, Maureen. He loves me. He's just under a lot of strain at the moment," she said.

"That's bollox," Laura had interjected. "Even if he is stressed out, he has no right to take it out on you."

Maureen pursed her lips, darting a toxic glance in Dylan's direction. "Absolutely. I'd tell my Hugh where to get off if he talked to me like that. Using the F word indeed! And in front of everyone."

Hope felt herself blushing. "Really, he didn't mean it. He'll make it up to me when we get home," she'd protested.

But he didn't. The following day he acted as if nothing had happened and there was no reference or apology for the "fucking Irish" remark. After breakfast he got up from the table, rolled a cigarette and sat in front of the computer.

I'm being oversensitive, she thought as she washed up the dishes, trying not to make any noise.

All the way into Swansea though, Maureen's comment kept niggling her. The more she thought about it, the more she realised that Maureen was right. He never spoke to her when they were out, preferring to stand with the men and talk football, or literature with Aled, who was surprisingly well read. He's under a lot of strain, she told herself, recalling her excuse to Maureen. But then again, as Laura had pointed out, that didn't give him licence to take it out on her. True his savings were getting low. The book was taking longer that he had planned. Maybe that was it. You always hurt the one you love. He doesn't mean it.

Suddenly she really missed Lainie. Missed her mother, missed even her scatty sister Charity. She realised that she had no one to talk to except a fifty-year-old woman, and a pub landlord's wife.

Then there was the matter of sex. She found it difficult to feel sexy and desirable when Dylan criticised her all the time, and when not carping about one thing or another he'd go silent for extended periods of time. In fact, far from lusting after Dylan, now sex was prompted principally by the need to dispel an atmosphere, and sometimes simply the need to be held. She felt a sudden surge of panic followed by a terrible sense of loneliness. Dropping the laundry off at the laundrette she plodded despondently towards the supermarket. I want my mum, she thought.

About a week after she'd arrived in Llanllwni, Hope had phoned home to tell her mother where she was. Maisie's negative response had surprised her. She couldn't understand why her mother would have even the slightest reservations about her daughter running off abruptly to another country with a man fifteen years her senior. (She didn't dare mention the fact that he was also married.) The call had developed into an argument with bitter recriminations, resulting in Hope, after defensively attacking her mother about her own boring unfulfilled life, hanging up abruptly.

* * *

"Bit harsh that, don't you think?" Reuben said, dragging her from her reverie.

"In retrospect," Hope agreed. "But we made it up."

"Eventually."

"Better late than never. And Dylan was partly responsible. I can see now he resented me having any contact with my family."

Reuben sighed. "There you go again. Blaming someone else for your own shortcomings."

Hope felt a surge of anger but bit her tongue.

"When your mother needed you and you turned your back," Reuben went on.

The anger was abruptly supplanted by an overwhelming sense of remorse. "I know. I feel really bad about that."

"And so you should."

Hope sighed. "I wish I'd been a bit more assertive. I wish I'd hadn't listened to Dylan and gone anyway. If Mum had only written."

"She did."

Outraged Hope shook her head. "No, she didn't!"

But Reuben just gave a wan smile and nodded his head.

* * *

After the first phone call, Dylan had been very sympathetic and supportive. Those were, after all, the first halcyon days of their relationship (or so she had thought), but much later down the line Hope could see how well the rift with her family had suited him.

About a week before the 'fucking Irish' incident she had bumped into Jenkins the Post who handed her a letter from Charity. The letter was full of reproach, asking why she hadn't written, hadn't answered letters. The epistle prompted a bout of irritation. It was a litany of rebuke for not replying to letters that, if indeed they had been written, she had never received. She couldn't understand why her mother couldn't just be happy for her, couldn't accept her relationship with Dylan. That was Maisie's problem, she decided turning the page – she couldn't let go. It was only as she read on that good old Catholic guilt kicked in, big-time. Charity went on to tell her how Maisie was heartbroken and needed all the support she could get "what with Dad being so ill".

Ill?

Immediately she ran into the house and told Dylan.

"If he's so ill why didn't your mother write and tell you yourself?" he'd said. "She's just trying to manipulate you through Charity. Trust me. My mother's the same."

"But if he's sick …" she said

Dylan had snorted derisively at that. "Oh, come on!

Of course he's not sick. Not seriously. It's just a ruse to get you to back down and come home. She can't face the fact that you're an adult. That you have a life of your own."

"You really think so?" she'd said.

"If he was really sick she'd have been in touch herself."

* * *

"You didn't know he'd burnt the letters," said Reuben softly.

Hope was genuinely shocked by the notion. "No! But did he? Are you sure they weren't just lost in the post?"

Reuben shook his head sympathetically. "Fraid not. He waylaid the postman, then chucked them in the fire while you were out. But in any case, it wouldn't have hurt you to have made the first move and called your mother. I think we can chalk that one down to Pride, with a *soupçon* of not 'Honouring *thy mother and thy father*' thrown in. How's that? A Deadly Sin and a Commandment all in one go." He let a measured pause hang. "Still …it's not too late."

"Too late?" Looking around, she became aware that they were standing in Sainsbury's carpark and she was wheeling a trolley laden with plastic shopping bags back towards Owen's Land-Rover. She was getting used to the concept of time travel now so didn't wonder at it any more. "What are you saying?"

Reuben looked past her to a phone kiosk. "It's not going to change the trajectory of your life substantially."

Hope frowned uncertainly. "Could I?"

"Go on." Reuben took her trolley and gave her a nudge towards the phone. "You know you want to." With that he thrust a handful of change at her.

It was only as she hurried across the carpark that she realised she was humming the same tune that Reuben had been whistling, and she couldn't prevent a sly smile as she realised that it was John Lennon's 'Maisie'.

Conscience salved, Hope walked back across the carpark to rejoin Reuben. Her mother had been thrilled to hear from her. So thrilled there hadn't been any mention of past disagreements. They had talked for ages until the beeps went as the last of her coins had run out. Hope had painted a happy picture of her life with Dylan so that her mother wouldn't worry.

"Your father's going in for tests. They're afraid that he might have testicular cancer," Maisie blurted out after a while. She sounded terrified.

Hope knew the outcome. It was indeed testicular cancer. She could only imagine how shattering the news must have been, even though she hadn't been around to see the anguish and the worry suffered by her whole family. It didn't really help knowing that he would be successfully treated and would finally get the all-clear three years later. She had been encouraging when Maisie had told her, reeling off imaginary people she knew of who had all made full recoveries from testicular cancer. She felt at the end of the call that her mother had been a lot more positive, and Hope promised to call every week from then on.

Reuben had loaded the shopping into the back of the Land-Rover and was sitting in the passenger seat. As she climbed in she realised he was singing again.

"*I'm too sex-y*," he warbled as he bopped his shoulders. "Right Said Fred. Got to Number Two."

"Actually they made Number Twelve with 'Are You Mine?'. Sadly it was their swan song. It all went pear-shaped on them after that. I think one of them is in musicals now. *Joseph and that Dreadfully Garish Coat* thing. All total fiction of course. It didn't happen like that at all."

"Thank you so much for sharing that with me."

"Happy now?" he asked as she settled herself behind the wheel. "Doesn't doing the right thing give you a buzz?"

She smiled as she nodded in agreement. "What now?" she asked.

He cocked his head to one side and reprised the chorus of 'I'm Too Sexy'. Then stared at her, waiting for her to catch on.

Suddenly she knew where this was going. 'I'm Too Sexy.' It had been playing on the radio as she had walked into the basement offices of KidzStuff on a cold wet day in November 1989. It was the day she'd met Josh Tierney for the first time.

Chapter 14

Dylan had been whingeing on about money again and the fact that he was supporting her. How was he supposed to get to grips with the Important Novel if he had to worry about money? She took him at his word and on her next trip into Swansea bought the local paper, sat down in a coffee shop and scanned the Situations Vacant columns. She was disappointed that there didn't seem to be many jobs going for which she was qualified, and she didn't fancy a run-of-the-mill, boring, office job. One advertisement caught her eye however.

"Receptionist/Girl Friday required for busy party-plan company."

She rather fancied the term Girl Friday as it

suggested, if nothing else, variety. Rather than a box number the ad carried a phone number, so she found a pay phone and called straight away. The man to whom she spoke, and whose name she didn't catch, invited her along for interview straight away. He sounded excessively hassled so she didn't get the chance to enquire as to what the company actually did. Was it party plan, as in selling the likes of Tupperware or Ann Summers, or was it actually parties as in birthdays and the like? She hadn't expected an immediate interview and felt self-conscious about turning up in her jeans and heavy sweater rather than a smart business suit (not that she even owned a business suit any more), but went nonetheless, thinking, nothing ventured . . .

The sign above the basement door read *KidzStuff*. It was a colourful sign with balloons and a clown's face at either end of the script. Rechecking the number to confirm that this was indeed the address she was looking for, she was in two minds about going in. It didn't take a Mensa-esque intellect to work out that the parties referred to were very obviously children's parties. The ad called for a receptionist. Looking at the small basement premises it occurred to her that this was hardly a venue, therefore if she had to deal with anyone it would be the parents. Then again, the term Girl Friday sprang to mind and suddenly the prospect of variety was less appealing. She was still pondering this when the door opened and a man poked his head out.

"Are you Hope?" he asked, looking up at her. She

nodded. "Thank God!" he said with feeling. "Come in. Come on in."

He was pushing fifty, slight of frame, but with a noticeable basketball-sized beer belly, arms that appeared to be proportionately too long for his body, and sparse sandy hair at the periphery of a bald freckled pate. Hope trotted down the steps.

The small front office was brightly painted if a touch scuffed, but terminally cluttered. The man held the door for her then grinned. "I'm too sexy."

Startled, Hope stopped dead in her tracks. "What?"

"The song," he said inclining his head towards the radio. "Very catchy, isn't it?" He reached over to the radio, which was sitting precariously on the window ledge, and reduced the volume, then stuck out his hand. "Tudor Evans," he said, "aka Custard."

"Sorry?"

"The clown." He pointed to some framed photos on the wall and she recognised Tudor Evans in a clown's get-up. Blue tufty wig, oversized red satin pants with yellow braces over an emerald green shirt. Clown make-up, red nose and those long joke rubber shoes also favoured by one Ronald MacDonald. As a kid Hope had been terrified of clowns. She took a pace back.

Tudor though was oblivious and indicating another photo – recognisably Tudor in civvies with a tatty, moth-eaten but evil-looking ventriloquist's dummy on his lap – volunteered, "Me and Chalky. Thank God you're here." Stepping over to the desk he picked up a pile of papers which were haphazardly strewn across the surface. "Herminie left this mess behind her and between one thing and another the place has descended into chaos. Utter chaos. When can you start?"

"Um, hang on," Hope said. "Shouldn't we discuss what the job involves, hours, pay, that kind of thing?" Tudor Evans looked nonplussed and as the silence lengthened, Hope added. "I mean, you know nothing about me, either."

"I know you look perfect for the job," he said, "but if you insist." He sat down behind the desk, still holding on to the bunch of assorted papers. "Ten till six. Tuesday to Saturday and the odd Sunday. Answering the phone, bit of this, bit of that, you know. Organisation really. Are you good at organising things? Because God knows this place needs some organisation." Hope was about to reply, but he cut her off, obviously thinking that as this was an interview perhaps he should go through the motions and ask some pertinent questions. "So what is your career experience?"

"I was a PA in PR," she said.

"A PA in PR? Perfect. So you could start ASAP then. Tomorrow OK?"

"Eh, when you say organisation, organisation of what? The parties, the office, paperwork? What?"

Custard the Clown alias Tudor Evans shrugged. "Bit of everything, really. Why?"

The door leading to the rear of the premises opened then and Custard's mate walked through. Taller, sans beer belly, and much younger than Tudor, he had the orange version of Custard's wig, full make-up, and a baggy check jacket over a purple and yellow tartan kilt with a joke sporran resembling a cow's udders, beneath which he wore horizontally striped, colour-coordinated stockings, but no shoes. The oversized shoes he carried in on top of a cardboard carton which he was balancing on his forearms

"Ah, Josh. Meet our new Girl Friday," Tudor said. "Sorry, love. I've forgotten your name."

"Hope. Hope Prior."

"Hope, meet my colleague Josh Tierney, or as he prefers to be known, Ginger McFling."

Ginger McFling put the carton on the cluttered desk, then offered his hand. Hope automatically took it, then, yelping, leapt back as a minor electric shock shot up her arm.

"Feck! Sorry," Mc Fling said.

"You'll have to excuse our friend here. He fancies himself as a bit of an ac-*tor*," Tudor said. "He's inclined to immerse himself once he dons costume, slap, and gets into character."

Mc Fling pulled off his wig, revealing a mop of curly dark hair. "Take no notice of that old bollox," he said, grinning as he opened his palm and removed the electric shock gizmo. "I genuinely forgot. Sorry. Welcome to the madhouse, Hope."

Hope was surprised by the Irish accent. "Where are you from?" she asked automatically. It was a while since she'd heard an Irish accent, and it was good to meet a fellow Irish person, even if he was got up like a scary, colour-blind, Scottish buffoon.

"Galway. What about yourself?"

"Mayo – Westport," she said. It was hard to judge with the make-up, but she guessed that he was around her own age.

"I know it well," he said. "I have cousins who live out near the Reek. The Fortunes. Do you know them?"

Hope nodded. "The vet?"

He nodded.

"Yes. I was in the same class as Maggie."

"Shouldn't you be getting along?" Tudor said pointing at the face of his watch. "Kick off at two in Langland, remember. Can't keep the little darlings waiting, Mr McFling."

"Keep the wig on, Custard," Josh replied, replacing his own and, picking up carton and shoes, headed for the door. "See you again, Hope."

"So how about it?" Tudor asked, looking around the wreckage that was once an office. "Please take the job. If someone doesn't sort out this madness soon we'll vanish under all this bloody paperwork."

The money was only average, but the anarchic nature of KidzStuff was oddly appealing to Hope so she took the job on the spot promising to start the following morning, bounding home like a Labrador puppy full of enthusiasm with the news.

Surprisingly, despite his whingeing about money, Dylan wasn't keen, fearing that his comfort zone might be disrupted if she wasn't around to see to his every need.

"But why do you have to start so soon? Isn't this all a bit sudden?" Then a plaintive, "What about me?"

Hope was disappointed that he wasn't leaping in the air shouting whoop-di-do. "But, Dylan. As you said yourself your savings won't last forever, and you do need a pressure-free environment to finish your Important Novel. At least you won't have to worry about money now."

Put like that he could hardly object further, so he gave in, small-mindedly commenting that perhaps the cash would come in handy and they'd better make the most of it because the job probably wouldn't last that long anyway. The subtext of the throwaway remark stung, but she let it pass, now accustomed to Dylan thinking of her as intellectually inferior.

In truth, it wasn't just the money aspect that appealed to Hope. She was getting bored with the rural idyll. Life held no challenge any more and she was fast losing her confidence, buried in the country with nothing to do but pander to Dylan's creative temperament. Also, although never exactly flush, she'd always been accustomed to having her own cash so she felt guilty asking him for money. He didn't make it easy either. Living with him for the guts of two years, she couldn't fail to notice that where funds were concerned he was on the careful side, doling out what he thought she should need for the housekeeping, with little to spare. She didn't recognise this as good old-fashioned meanness at the time, acknowledging that as they were living on his savings, they had to conform to some kind of budget. As time had gone on, however, she'd noticed that when it came to spending on luxuries, it was OK as long as said luxury was something to contribute to Dylan's comfort. Her one-time necessities, such as a decent haircut to mention but one, were firmly filed in the Totally Unnecessary Extravagance column.

So it was that she found herself creeping downstairs before dawn had cracked the following morning, leaving the Important Novelist snoring his head off. Nodding to convention she had chosen the black trousers and a black polo-necked jumper for work garb. Whatever about the chaotic state of the office, she felt she should at least try and look efficient. She had hung the clothes over the Aga before going to bed but, as if for spite, the range had gone out in the night so the clothes were cold and a touch damp. The cold of the cottage was something she'd never got used to. Even during a hot spell the previous July the heat had failed to penetrate the thick rough stone walls, and the tiny windows kept out even the most determined ray of sunlight. She contemplated relighting the Aga. Dylan was rubbish at it. But she didn't relish emptying the ashes and spending possibly half an hour coaxing the ornery contraption to cooperate. She decide to feign ignorance on her return from work.

She overestimated the morning traffic, arriving in Swansea by 9.15, so took the opportunity to grab a cup of tea and a bacon roll in a café a few doors down from KidzStuff. Then, set up for the morning, she headed along the street at five to ten. The office was locked up and in darkness, so she sat on the steps and waited.

Tudor hurried along breathless half an hour later.

"Sorry, sorry," he flapped. "Had to get a key cut for you, you see. Took longer than I thought it would."

She followed him down the steps and they went inside. The phone was ringing but stopped before he could reach it.

"Damn! That's what I mean, see. That's why we need you. Can't afford to miss out on business."

Hope picked up the phone and dialled 1471 and used the call-back facility. Tudor was watching her, puzzled. The call connected and when it was picked up she said, "Tudor Evans from KidzStuff for you. Please hold the line," then handed the receiver to Tudor.

The call was indeed an enquiry. Tudor dealt with it, then hung up. "How did you *do* that?" he asked, as if she possessed supernatural powers.

Hope explained the 1471 service.

"That's amazing," he said.

"But don't you have an answering machine?" she asked, glancing round the office. "Or a computer?"

He shook his head. "I'm a bit of a Luddite, I'm afraid

– a technophobe, but if you think it would be a good idea, perhaps we could think about it."

After a brief tour of the offices which took all of three minutes (the back room, piled high with cartons and boxes with party stuff spilling out of them, a bathroom and a small kitchen leading out to a tiny yard), he showed her the diary.

"I have to go out now," he said. "See if you can sort this lot out, would you. There's a treasure." And he was gone.

Hope hung up her jacket and sat down behind the desk. Amongst the dross littering the desktop she found a dog-eared KidzStuff brochure listing the services and pricing structure. She studied the listings. The entertainers on offer were Custard the Clown, Ginger McFling, Tudor Evans and Chalky, and Marvo the Magician. It appeared that clients could hire solely the entertainers, or if they were of a mind, there was the superior package where KidzStuff contracted to organise the whole shindig: food, birthday cake, two entertainers and marquee if required, priced per head, according to the type of menu and service required. Sticking the price list where she could easily find it, she sat behind the desk and wondered where to start. Then, after a moment's reflection, sighed and set to.

Initially she couldn't understand how the place could have got into such a mess in so short a time, Tudor's comment implying that they had been without a receptionist for only a short period. But as she waded through enough paper to have caused the felling of a small forest, she found invoices and bills and receipts from months back. Either said Herminie was totally crap at basic organisation or she'd been gone far longer than a couple of weeks. Once she had sorted the paperwork into piles, filing the stuff that was redundant, placing bills that needed immediate payment and invoices to send out in the In tray, she gave the desk and floor a good clean. Suddenly she could see the wood for the trees. Although she felt grubby and her hair and clothes were dusty, she derived a certain sense of satisfaction from a job well done.

Late morning, there was one phone enquiry. Initially the caller, Alyson Worthington, had been looking only for a children's entertainer, so Hope had acquainted her with the options, whereby Alyson chose Marvo the Magician, after first establishing that no livestock was involved in the act on account of little Jeremy's allergies. Hope had no idea but assured her that she would personally acquaint Marvo with her son's delicate constitution. She then asked little Jeremy's mother if she was having the party catered. When the response was negative, she thrashed on, selling the advantages of the comprehensive KidzStuff package. Far less bother, no mess in the house if she went for the marquee option, and cheaper in the long run etc etc. She was surprised and delighted when, by the end of the call she had sold Mrs Worthington (who had been totally ignorant that such a service was available) the Superior Package for twenty-five six-year-olds, sweet and savoury buffet, Marvo the Magician and Ginger McFling, Ninja Turtles birthday cake (after that preference had been requested), balloons, party poppers and favour bags. Due to the unpredictable nature of the November weather however, Alyson Worthington decided against the marquee, sticking with her original option, a local church hall. The booking was for the following Sunday.

Tudor breezed in at ten past one and stopped dead in the doorway.

"Well, I must say …" He seemed stuck for words. "There, you see. I said you were perfect for the job. Now how about a bite of lunch?"

"I got a booking," Hope said proudly, unable to keep the grin off her face. "Superior Package for twenty-five. Next Sunday."

Instead of jumping for joy, Tudor looked worried. "The superior package?"

"Eh, yes. Is that a problem?"

Tudor rubbed his pate, then gave a shrug. "Can't be done."

Hope picked up the brochure and pointed at the copy. "But it's on the list. I took the booking."

Tudor shook his head. "Sorry. Can't be done."

"But why not?"

"Wouldn't know where to start. My lady wife, Herminie, used to deal with all that."

"Herminie's your wife?"

Tudor nodded. "Yes. My lady wife."

Annoyed that her effort and initiative were in danger of being wasted, Hope protested, "So what's the problem? Why can't she do this one?"

Tudor sat on the edge of the desk. "I dare say she could, but you see she left me four months ago. No warning. Just upped and left with the car, the furniture and Sparky."

"Sparky?"

"The dog."

"Oh."

"Smartest dog ever. Part of my Chalky act." He looked dejected, sitting there on the edge of the desk, staring at the floor.

Hope felt distinctly awkward. There wasn't really any protocol for this sort of situation. If Herminie had died tragically, an "I'm sorry for your loss" would have been in order, but what to say to a man when his wife has just buggered off? She settled on, "I'm sorry. You must miss her?"

Tudor nodded forlornly. "It was the betrayal, you see. I expected her to be faithful."

Uncomfortable, Hope shifted from one foot to the other. "That's not unreasonable, I suppose."

Tudor nodded again, then looked up. "Yes. I really miss that dog."

She studied his face for a hint of a snigger, any suggestion of irony, but realised that he was totally serious. This man is bonkers, she thought. She smiled sympathetically though. "I'm sure you do. But it seems a shame to turn business away. Couldn't we do it? How hard can it be to organise a few sandwiches and buns? The back room's full of balloons, paper hats and party poppers."

"Oh, there's more to it than that," he declared.

Hope wasn't buying it. "Such as?"

Tudor shrugged. "I have no idea."

"But surely you must have had some input? You must know how Herminie did it."

He shook his head. "I'm the artiste. As you've probably gathered by the state of the office, organisation is not really my strong suit."

"Maybe not, but all I'm saying is it's a shame to turn business away without even giving it your best shot. Tell me. Did Herminie do the all catering herself?"

Tudor snorted. "Herminie? No. Couldn't cook to save her life. She bought the food in, already prepared from somewhere."

"Somewhere?" Hope shook her head in frustration. "Didn't you take any active role, even a minor one, in that part of the business. *Any* part at all?"

"I told you. I'm the artiste," he said defensively. "When Herminie ran off with Marvo, I let that end of the business slide."

"She ran off with Marvo? *Marvo* as in Marvo the Magician?"

Tudor gave another heavy sigh. "Yep. One and the

same. The bastard."

Hope winced. "So, tell me," she asked. "How are you at magic?"

Chapter 15

She got home at seven to find the cottage empty and a curt note on the kitchen table. *'Gone to the pub'* it read.

The Aga was cold to the touch and there were dishes in the sink. She was disappointed. She had hoped that he'd be there, happy to listen to her account of the day. And as days went, she'd enjoyed it immensely. She had talked Tudor Evans into giving the Superior Package a go, though it took some persuasion on her part which surprised her, and he only agreed when she promised to root through the files to find Herminie's suppliers. She couldn't fathom why he should be so reluctant. After almost two years of mooching around the house she was anxious for a bit of mental stimulation and was looking forward to a new challenge, so wasn't about to let the opportunity slip through her fingers. Truth be told, she wanted to prove to Dylan that she wasn't useless. She wanted him to be proud of her, and felt that if she was actively contributing to the household expenses rather than being a drain on his savings, his attitude towards her would improve and she would regain his respect.

Granted it wasn't that big a challenge, but beggars can't be choosers, and organising a children's party – no, an *event* – was better than tiptoeing around, humouring a creative genius. There were times when she felt a certain empathy with Mrs Ibsen, Mrs Joyce and Mrs Beckett.

Aled and Hugh were propping up the bar as usual when she walked in, Wayne was leaning on the bar reading the *Western Mail* and Dylan was sitting in a quiet corner alone, an empty pint glass in front of him.

She got a sulky reception, being greeted with: "The bloody Aga's gone out."

"Did you eat?" she asked.

He nodded at an empty plate with the remains of a few cold chips, then stood up. "Come on. Let's go."

"I've had a lovely day," she said trying to thaw the frosty atmosphere in the Land-Rover as they headed up the mountain. "You wouldn't believe how disorganised the place was, but I made a start at kicking it into shape. Honestly, I thought Roddy French was untidy, but you wouldn't believe –"

"I had to have instant packet soup for lunch!" he cut

in like a petulant child. "Bloody packet soup!"

"So why didn't you light the Aga and cook yourself something?" she asked in a reasonable tone.

"I didn't have time," he bleated. "I had a major edit to do, but I was so fucking cold I had to abandon it and cycle down to the pub."

Under normal circumstances she would have been riddled with guilt at the thought of him sitting at the computer shivering because she had been careless enough to let the range go out, but his huffy tone of voice annoyed her.

"Wouldn't it have made more sense to light the sodding Aga?" she snapped back.

It was probably the fact that he was so accustomed to her humouring him that caused her short-tempered response to take him by surprise.

"Possibly," he replied curtly.

They drove on in silence. She had been looking forward to telling him about her day, but he didn't appear to be in the least bit interested. She'd been hoping that he'd make some gesture of support like perhaps cooking dinner but, by the evidence, that was obviously too much to ask. Just as she was building up a head of steam to say something, for the first time in ages, he apologised, totally taking the wind out of her sails. Reaching over, he placed his hand on her thigh.

"I'm sorry, petal. I'm being selfish, but the work isn't going too well. Tell me all about your day."

The anger immediately dispelled and she reverted

to her usual role. "Oh, no, Dylan. *I'm* sorry. I should have lit the Aga before I went out this morning."

"Well, never mind. We'll just have to make sure it's well banked up every night. The bloody thing hates me. You know you're the only one who can handle it. I don't know what I'd do without you."

His puppy-dog eyes and lopsided grin tugged at her heart-strings. *He needs me,* she thought. *He really needs me.*

When they reached the cottage, she immediately set about lighting the Aga and all talk of her day was forgotten.

The following morning, with only three days to go before the Superior Package party, Hope sprang into action. That morning, still troubled by a hint of guilt, she had left the cottage cosy and warm, the Aga banked up. Dylan's lunch of ham sandwiches was wrapped in tinfoil, and a tin of Heinz Cream of Tomato soup left out with the tin opener within easy reach. (Perish the thought that he'd have to make do with instant packet soup two days in succession.) The components of his breakfast fry she assembled on the draining board, and even set a place at the table.

Arriving at the office at 10.15, she opened up, then sat at the desk and wrote a to-do list. By the time Tudor put in an appearance at ten fifteen with two steaming takeaway coffees, she had searched through the filing cabinet and found the name of the caterer that Herminie usually used, and made a note of the marquee supplier for future reference.

"Everything's under control," she said. "I just have to call the caterer, organise the party favours – by the way what's the budget on that?"

"Budget?" Tudor asked, blinking like a myopic mole.

"For the party favours," Hope repeated. "How much can I spend on party favours?"

Tudor shrugged. "I don't know. Not my –"

Hope sighed and cut him off. "I know, not your department. Don't worry. I'll work it out. By the way, how can I get hold of McFling? I need to tell him about Sunday's booking."

"Josh? Oh, he'll be at college. He's only part-time here, but I dare say he'll call in this afternoon."

After they had drunk their coffee, realising that Tudor Evans desperately needed to be managed, she gave him a list and sent him into the back room to sort out balloons, party hats, party poppers, and to see if there was anything resembling party favours in amongst the general tat overflowing from the numerous haphazardly stacked boxes. Then she called the caterer. By lunchtime she had the food sorted. Bronwyn Ironside, the caterer, after ascertaining the age group of the guests, suggested sausages, mini-pizzas and chips, with orange squash and Coke, and marshmallow tea cakes, chocolate fingers and jelly and ice cream for dessert. Getting a touch carried away and announcing herself as the new Operations Manager, she'd even negotiated a discount on the basis that she was a new broom and was searching for the *best* food and most *attractive* deal. It surprised her how easy it was, proving the universal truth that those who ask get, those who don't pay through the nose.

Tudor emerged dusty but triumphant with a big box of balloons, half a box of party poppers, paper hats, and a carton of assorted lucky bags and yellow sherbet dips for going-home favours.

"That just leaves the cake," she said, ticking the accomplished tasks off her list. She had seen a Ninja Turtle cake in the window of a confectionary at the top of Saint Helen's Road, and Ninja Turtle paper plates and cups in WH Smith's in the shopping precinct.

"There you are then," Tudor said a wide smile on his face, piggy eyes twinkling. "I don't know what Herminie thought was so complex about all this. Always led me to believe it was really difficult." He smiled at her. "Now that's all sorted, why don't you go and get some lunch. I can cover the phone till you get back."

Suddenly hungry, Hope agreed. "OK. Would you like me to bring you a sandwich or anything back?"

Tudor seemed genuinely touched. "That's remarkable thoughtful of you, my dear. Egg and cress will do nicely, if it's not too much trouble." Rummaging in his pocket he produced a crumpled fiver. "The Dairy Maid's your best bet. They do a cracking egg and cress."

Hope took the proffered bank note and, shrugging on her jacket, headed off to lunch.

Sitting up at the counter of the Dairy Maid with a bowl of steaming soup in front of her, she felt a tap on her shoulder. She turned her head and had it not been for the voice she wouldn't have recognised Josh Tierney minus the scary clown make-up and dodgy get-up.

"How are you getting on with Custard?" he asked sliding onto the stool next to her.

"Grand," she said grinning. "He's a bit disorganised though."

He grinned back. "You reckon?"

"Oh, speaking of Custard, you've a booking for Sunday. Superior Package. Twenty-five six-year-olds. Unfortunately I also booked Marvo the Magician."

Josh winced. "Oops!"

Hope sighed. "Yes. But how was I supposed to know? I'll have to call your woman and make some excuse. Hopefully she'll be happy with Tudor and Chalky as substitute."Then as an afterthought, "Always assuming the loss of Sparky doesn't put the kybosh on that too."

The waitress took Josh's order for a toasted BLT, then he glanced at Hope and his brow furrowed. "How come Tudor's taking Superior Packages again?"

"He didn't. I did," Hope replied. "It's on the brochure after all. But apparently his *Lady Wife* led him to believe it was beyond his capabilities, but we muddled through. I think he was surprised that it only took half a morning in all to get it sorted."

"So what are you doing about the games?" he asked. "Tudor doesn't do games."

"Games?"

"Party games. The little blighters expect to be entertained."

It was news to Hope, but then she had never been to a Superior Birthday Party. Her most lavish experience as a child was when Breda Ronayne's uncle tried to do some inept conjuring tricks and almost severed a finger, which as an eight-year-old she had admittedly found very exciting.

"But isn't that what the entertainers are for?" she said.

"Not entirely. You have to organise party games with prizes before the food. Then it's the entertainers, then the disco."

Hope felt the first stirrings of panic. "The brochure didn't say anything about a disco."

He grinned at her again. "OK, so I was winding you up about the disco, but I'm deadly serious about the games. You know – Musical Chairs, Pin the Tail on the Donkey, Pass the Parcel, that kind of thing."

Hope shrugged. "Oh, well. I'm sure Tudor can manage that much."

"Don't you believe it. Like I said, he doesn't do games. When he's not Custard the Clown or Chalky's alter ego, he's terrified of kids. Absolutely scared shitless."

She gave a sly grin. "You're winding me up again."

He shook his head. "Fraid not. Herminie always did that bit. A regular Brown Owl she was. The kids had a healthy respect for her which, believe me, is no harm. So I'd say it's a racing certainty that the party games are down to you."

Hope exhaled then bit her lip, half regretting that she'd talked Tudor into it. Party games meant she'd have to organise prizes ... *be* there, for God's sake! She hadn't expected that to be part of the deal. And what would Dylan's reaction be to the news that she'd be working Sunday?

"Look. I'll give you a hand before I terrorise the little bastards with my Ginger McFling, if you like," Josh volunteered. "How many kids did you say?"

"Twenty-five."

"OK. So you can string out Pass the Parcel for a good fifteen minutes with twenty-five layers of wrapping. They'll all want to have a turn at ripping a sheet of paper off. Have to fix it though so the kid whose party it is, wins. Then say another fifteen minutes for Pin the Tail on the Donkey and, if none of them end up impaled on the door, you can finish up with a speedy session of Musical Chairs. It only needs to go on for an hour."

Put like that it didn't seem so bad, but as she'd never had that much contact with small children en masse she did find the prospect more than a touch daunting.

After they had finished their lunch and she had

collected Tudor's egg and cress, Josh walked her back to the office.

"So what brought you to the wilds of South Wales?" he asked they crossed at the lights at the end of the Kingsway.

"My boyfriend," she said. "He's a writer."

"Really? What's his name? Have I heard of him?"

"Dylan Jones, but you wouldn't have heard of him yet. He's in the middle of an Im – of a novel at the moment." She felt a flush of embarrassment that she'd almost referred to Dylan's book as an Important Novel. And although she always thought of it in those terms, somehow to a relative stranger the words didn't sit comfortably. In fact when she thought about it, the term Important Novel seemed a bit premature.

"So where do you live?"

"Oh, miles away. The other side of Dyfed, a village called Llanllwni. What about yourself? What brought you here. Tudor said something about you being an actor."

He laughed. "Me? No way! Ginger McFling is as far as my acting abilities go, and that's just to earn a crust while I finish my degree. Mind you, I'm not sure I'll stick it out to the end."

"Seems a shame," she commented. "What degree are you doing?"

"Journalism and Communications," he said.

"So how did you get involved in kids' entertaining?"

He shrugged. "By accident really. When I was a kid my Uncle Bertie was a part-time kids' entertainer and I used to help him out to earn a few bob. The Ginger McFling clobber's his. He passed it on to me when he retired."

"So you've no ambition to run off with the circus then?" she said, cracking a smile.

He laughed. "No. But McFling's keeping the wolf from the door right now, though I dare say he'll go into retirement as soon as I get a proper job."

Tudor was full of enthusiasm about the Superior Package when they returned to the office, singing Hope's praises which she found quite sweet, but also gratifying. It was a long time since she had felt truly appreciated. Dylan needed her, she knew that, but despite what he had said the previous night, she doubted that he really appreciated how much effort it took to keep him happy and looked after.

She was surprised later that night when, after carefully picking her moment, she mentioned to Dylan that she would have to go to work the following Sunday, and he didn't fly into a strop.

"OK, petal. Don't you worry about me." The 'don't worry about me' bit was said with genuine sincerity, in perfect good humour and devoid of any trace of the usual sarcasm as in 'Don't worry about me – I'll just sit here in the dark'.

*   *   *

Reuben guffawed beside her in the driver's seat of the Land-Rover. "I suppose you thought he was being supportive."

"Yes, actually."

Ahead, through the windscreen she recognised the road leading to Caswell, a village on the Gower peninsula.

"What are we doing here?" she asked.

"Little Jeremy's party," he said as they swung in through the gate of the church hall. Tudor's ancient Morris Minor Traveller was parked close to the door and the rain was coming down in sheets just the way she remembered it.

She glanced back in Reuben's direction to ask why they were there, but he had vanished.

Chapter 16

Tudor and Josh were already in the hall blowing up balloons with the aid of hand-pumps when she ran in out of the deluge, lugging a box containing the birthday cake which had been in the back of the Land-Rover all night. There was a sizeable number of inflated balloons wafting about the hall in the draught, and they had already hung up a *Happy Birthday* banner over the small stage upon which stacks of chairs were stored. Long trestle tables lined the walls. A ghetto-blaster was playing a Kylie Minogue tape, which made Hope think of Reuben and wonder where he was and, come to that, why he had brought her back here. What did he expect of her? For the life of her she couldn't recall anything she had done here that could be even remotely construed as bad.

Despite the appalling weather outside, the hall was warm and glaringly bright due to strip lighting. Hope groaned inwardly and prayed a silent 'Do I really have to go through this again?'. But Reuben was conspicuous by his absence so she knew it was a given. Resigned, she took out her list and prepared to go stoically through the motions, despite knowing the horrors that lay ahead.

Twenty minutes later the tables were set up at the end of the hall nearest the kitchen, where Bronwyn Ironside, the caterer, a large well-upholstered jolly woman, was unpacking the party food in readiness to be reheated. The hall was festooned with balloons and the tables were set, in every place a party hat, Ninja Turtle cup and plate, a party popper, a paper napkin, a plastic fork and spoon. As an afterthought, aware of a six-year-old's fondness for what her father had always referred to as 'muck sweets', she had bought large economy-sized bags of jelly beans, jelly babies and dolly mixtures and emptied them into Ninja Turtle paper dishes which she spaced strategically along the table. The birthday cake took pride of place in front of Little Jeremy's setting, so all in all, the hall looked appropriately festive. At least it had back then. Now, as Hope scanned the room, she realised that actually it all looked rather tatty, sad and amateurish. It made her realise how far she had travelled. From a tatty party in a church hall for twenty-four kids and the six-year-old Antichrist, to big-budget software product launches and celebrity weddings.

But no time for regrets. Time was marching on and the sooner the games were over and done with, the more rapidly this day from hell would pass. And the sooner the better as far as she was concerned.

Time to set up musical chairs in readiness for the two o'clock kick-off.

"I'll give you a hand," Josh offered, leaving Tudor to finish the tying of the last balloon. As he was passing the chairs down from the stage to her, Hope shot a sneaky glance in his direction. He hadn't donned the McFling clobber as yet and it occurred to her that she had never really looked at him properly back then. She'd thought she was still in love with Dylan so he was just Ginger Mc Fling, a nice Irish guy with a natural easy but uncheesy charm, and a weird sense of humour. A good friend in the making. She felt a sudden stab of regret, but pushed it aside. No use crying over spilt Guinness.

Alyson Worthington and Little Jeremy turned up then. Alyson was younger than she sounded on the phone. Late twenties, attractive and dark, dressed in expensive-looking casual clothes that were too old for her – the kind that always sport a gold-embroidered nautical detail somewhere, and appear to come only in white, navy or red, or a combination of all three. Her bobbed hair was held back by a velvet hair-band and she wore a thin string of pearls at her throat. Little Jeremy was the spitting image of her, but totally hyper, and by the way his mother reacted, Hope got the impression that this was quite usual. As she stood talking to Alyson he dashed around the hall bursting all the balloons within his limited reach, screaming at the top of his lungs.

"Nuts," was the first word out of Alyson's mouth.

Hope nodded. "Yes. He is a bit."

"No! I mean I hope you made sure that none of the food contains nuts," she said, a frown creasing her porcelain brow. "Little Jeremy's very nut-sensitive."

She could have told Alyson that no, the food didn't contain any nuts. She could also have pointed out that perhaps if she checked up on the amount of artificial food additives, sugar and Coca-cola that Little Jeremy was consuming, he might be more manageable, and had she ever heard of ADHD?

At the time though, Hope had felt a stab of panic. As far as she could recall Alyson Worthington had only mentioned livestock in the context of allergies. "Um, actually, you didn't say anything about nuts."

Alyson raised her perfectly tweezered eyebrows. "Oh, I'm sure I did."

Hope was just as sure that she hadn't, but knew that there was no point in arguing the toss. "OK. No problem. If you'll just hold on, I can check to make sure," she replied, scurrying off to the kitchen to ask Bronwyn Ironside if Little Jeremy would be able to get through the party tea without an attack of anaphylactic shock. Bronwyn assured her that neither the sausages or mini-pizzas contained nuts and, as she stood waiting, Bronwyn checked the bag that the oven chips had come in and, after a tense thirty seconds, declared all the food was Little-Jeremy tolerant which, the way things were shaping up, was more than could be said for Hope.

The guests started to arrive then along with a straggle of mothers who all bore a rather alarming Stepfordesque resemblance to Alyson Worthington. Little Jeremy was getting increasingly excited, which was in itself an achievement, ripping the wrapping paper off each gift as it was handed over, immediately losing interest in the contents as soon as the next one was proffered.

Josh had disappeared off to a back room to get changed and Tudor was lying low, presumably with Chalky, determined to avoid contact with the kids for as long as possible. Hope suffered through interminable rounds of Musical Chairs, a jolly smile plastered to her face, past experience making her determined to change history and make sure that Little Jeremy won. The winning wasn't the point. With the clarity of the twenty/twenty vision that is hindsight, she was set on avoiding the fall-out caused by his accidental elimination in the second round: he had spent the duration of the game shoving and tripping up any kid that came into range, intermittently emitting a high-pitched scream. He had also clipped her ankles quite painfully a couple of times in the course of the game, during which the mothers present, who numbered eight in all, had sat in a circle at the far end of the hall drinking coffee, apparently immune to the noise, and taking no interest whatsoever in the proceedings.

By the time the last two kids (three counting Little Jeremy) scuffled for the final chair, Hope had a splitting headache and a strong urge to throttle the Birthday Boy. For peace's sake she had declared the result a three-way tie and handed out three prizes.

For safety's sake, second time around, she abandoned Pin the Tail on the Donkey. Little Jeremy and sharp pointed objects were not a good combination. She shuddered at the instant recall of the hoo-ha when one of the guests had been left permanently scarred as a result of LJ trying to determinedly pin the tail to his coccyx. That only left Pass the Parcel.

It took some time to get the kids organised in a circle on the floor. In fact she'd had no idea that the attention span of small kids was so limited. It took Josh in his McFling persona to grab their attention. Exhausted and much wiser, Hope once more customised history by playing an accelerated version of the game at warp speed. She succeeded in getting through all twenty-five layers of wrapping in a swift nine point five minutes, with Little Jeremy shredding the last layer to expose a packet of crayons which, from his reaction, left him singularly unimpressed. She thanked providence that cynicism was evidently an unknown concept to this crowd of six-year-olds, as there were no cries of "Fix! Fix!".

The next trial was to get them settled at the tables for tea. The Stepford Mothers lent a hand with this, assisting also in the serving of the food. Little Jeremy was, by this time, high as a kite on sugar and chemical-additive overload and was still stuffing his face with jelly beans. Hope had got the brunt of it when she found herself in the flight path of his dish of jelly and ice cream which he had launched at the kid sitting across the table. She got it full in the face which caused much hilarity. This time round however she kept well out of his line of fire and felt quite smug when tea was drawing to a close and it was almost time for Tudor and Chalky. Lulled into a false sense of security now that the moment had passed, she ventured over to the vicinity of Little Jeremy to light the candles on the birthday cake, exhorting the kids to sing along. *"Happy Birthday to you! Happy Birthday to you!"* Halfway through the third *"Happy Birthday"*, Little Jeremy, now sugared up close to spontaneous-combustion level, let fly with the jelly and ice cream, scoring a direct hit. It was only then, as she stood there, melted ice cream running down her face and dripping onto her shoulders, that she understood; only then, when she caught sight of Reuben doubled up with mirth, did she realise.

Later, Ginger McFling acting as MC got the kids

sitting quietly in a circle (even Little Jeremy) and they were all awestruck by the Tudor and Chalky act, which, despite the moth-eaten appearance of the dummy, was very funny, even from an adult perspective. After that, McFling had led them in a singsong. It was at this point that she was overcome with admiration at the way the kids related to and cooperated with the scary-looking Hibernian clown. He had them eating out of the palm of his hand, doing all the actions as requested, making them laugh in between ditties by producing feather dusters and silk hankies from up his sleeves, and generally holding their rapt attention. Hope quietly wondered, despite Josh's insistence that the tedious games be included, why they hadn't just cut to the chase.

After the Stepford Mothers finally led their offspring home, worn out but happy, each clutching a lucky bag and a sherbet dip, and Tudor and Josh were getting changed

* * *

Hope found Reuben sitting up on the counter in the kitchen eating a piece of cold pizza.

"I didn't do anything wrong, did I?" she said.

Reuben leaned over and flicked a stray lump of jelly off her shoulder. He was expressionless, then his shoulders started to shake, his mouth twitched and he was laughing again, to the point where he had to wipe away a tear.

"No," he said when the laughter subsided briefly, "but you have to admit it was very entertaining. And I *so* wanted to see it again. *Wallop! Splat!* It was hilarious."

"You know, Reuben," Hope said as he was once more overtaken by a fit of mirth, "for an angel you have one very evil streak."

"OK, so I owe you one," he said, finally pulling himself together.

Her irritation soon evaporated as his happy humour was infectious and she found herself grinning back at him. "I *will* hold you to that," she promised. "But tell me again. Why did I talk Tudor into doing the Superior bloody Package?"

The guardian angel sighed. "Because, as I found out to my cost, you're a sucker for a challenge."

Little Jeremy's party had been a steep learning curve. Or more accurately, a hard lesson learned. Hope considered the event to be something of a disaster, despite Tudor and Josh's attempts to persuade her otherwise when they went for a post-event drink at a local hostelry.

"You have a definite talent for organisation, my dear. And you're way better than Herminie," Tudor insisted. "The kids were terrified of her. They had a far better time with you at the helm."

"He's right," Josh agreed, cracking a grin. "*I* was afraid of Herminie. And they really enjoyed the jelly and ice cream slapstick. In fact, I think you should make it part of the package, Tudor."

"Over my dead body," Hope cautioned, still not convinced. "Anyway, I doubt Alyson Worthington and the rest of the Stepford Mothers were that impressed. You were right first time, Tudor. KidzStuff should just stick to supplying entertainers. You were both really good by the way."

Josh laughed. "Don't sound so surprised!"

"Well, I am. To be honest, I don't know what I was expecting. I was kind of afraid of clowns as a kid, and I've always thought ventriloquists' dummies a bit creepy, but you and Chalky were really good, Tudor. I didn't see your lips move once."

Tudor blushed. "That's most civil of you to say so, my dear. Chalky and I go back a long way."

"Have you ever thought of expanding? You'd go down really well with adults, you know."

"Oh no, my dear. I'm afraid for an adult audience I'd have to … how can I put this delicately?" He frowned. "I'd have to change my material, you see. Make it smutty, and Chalky wouldn't like that."

"But how do you know?" Hope protested. "I'm an adult and I really enjoyed your act."

Tudor was adamant. "Sadly you are in the minority, my dear. I did try to play an adult audience some years back when I did a season at Butlin's – in fact that's where I met my Herminie – she was teaching ballroom dancing – but, not to put too fine a point on it, I went down like a lead balloon."

That was a disappointment. Though Hope's opinion

was entirely sincere, she did have another agenda in trying to persuade Tudor to up the age level of his audience, namely her wish never to organise kids' party games again.

Conscious that Dylan had been on his own all day, Hope only stayed for the one then, gratified that Tudor seemed so happy with her efforts, drove home. Despite his lack of objections to her working on Sunday, she was nonetheless a touch anxious that the Important Novelist might throw a moody when she got home. She was pleasantly surprised however to find that he had a shepherd's pie in the Aga and had the table set for dinner. After they had eaten, when Hope gently blew in his ear and suggested an "early night", he said he'd rather a trip to the pub on the grounds that he was too tired or, as he put it, "totally shagged out", subsequent events proving his choice of words to be very much to the point.

Tudor and Josh's assessment of how Little Jeremy's party had gone was justified the following Wednesday when, just before lunch, she took a call from a Rosemary Williams who announced herself as Little Rhodri's mother, as if it should mean something to Hope. All became clear however when Rosemary mentioned Alyson, and the fact that Little Rhodri had such a good time at Little Jeremy's party last Sunday. Mrs Williams, it turned out, wanted KidzStuff to organise a Christmas bash for Little Rhodri and thirty of his friends on the first Saturday in December.

"Entertainers, you mean?" Hope said, fingers crossed.

"No, no. I want, what's it called? The Superior Package. The whole thing."

Hope's guts churned, then Rosemary continued, "Oh, and a marquee. I'd want a marquee. Tell me, how much would all that cost?"

Hope, who had been rearranging the filing system at the time of Rosemary Williams' call, just happened to have the brochures handy. She scanned the charges and reeled off the various elements, adding roughly fifty per cent across the board with the expectation that this would put her off.

But no such luck. Rosemary wasn't fazed in the slightest. "That sounds very reasonable," she said, surprising Hope, and making her wish she'd just doubled the price and been done with it.

"The weather's very cold though," Hope cautioned. "You'll need heating. That could be very costly."

"Look, just organise it and put it on my bill," Rosemary said, adding in a patronising tone, "We have a very extensive garden, you know, so we could have quite a *large* marquee opening off the dining-room French windows."

Realising that far from putting Rosemary off she was only encouraging her, Hope gave in and accepted the booking, which included the top-of-the-range children's menu and *large* heated marquee. Then Rosemary enquired if, in addition, KidzStuff could supply a finger-food buffet for the adults who would number approximately twenty. Never one to shirk a challenge, and with Bronwyn Ironside's price list in front of her, Hope gave it one last shot, assuring Mrs Williams that the *Platinum* Package included a finger-food buffet for the adults and one hot dish such as buffalo wings or lamb kebabs. With no guide as to what price to charge, she just doubled the cost of the Superior kids' menu and added a further ten per cent for luck.

"So let me see," Rosemary said. "What are we up to now?"

Hope punched the numbers into the desk calculator and read off the growing total to Rosemary who seemed delighted, particularly with the concept of a *Platinum* Package, despite the exorbitant cost. She did however let the cat out of the bag big-time when she made a disparaging comment about draughty church halls, leaving Hope in no doubt that her largesse had much to do with outdoing Alyson Worthington.

"And chairs," Rosemary said with a note of triumph, as if she just discovered the theory of relativity. "I want those little gold chairs. The type they have at fashion shows. I assume one can hire that kind of thing?"

Hope hadn't a clue where she'd be able to hire little gold chairs, but kept her mouth shut, making a mental note to check with the marquee company to see if they had a contact, or better still, hired out said chairs themselves.

"And the ventriloquist and the clown," Rosemary continued, now well in her stride. "Do you have a conjurer by any chance? Alyson said something about a conjuror and I'd really like *three* entertainers."

Oh course, you would, Hope thought. "Um, I'm afraid Marvo is no longer on our books, but leave it with me and I'll see what I can do. There would be an extra cost for a third entertainer, of course."

Josh walked in at that point in time to overhear the end of the conversation. After Rosemary agreed to the extra cost of a third entertainer, she then asked if the marquee would be decorated, preferably with a Christmas theme. With absolutely no idea how much that would cost Hope said it could be done but that she would have to get back to her with a price.

Business satisfactorily concluded, at least as far as a smug Rosemary was concerned, Hope ended the call, put down the phone and shook her head. "Bloody hell. You'll never guess what I just did," she said, then filled him in on Rosemary's call.

"And she didn't argue about the price?" Josh remarked.

Hope shook her head "No. Not a murmur. Not a quibble. The more it cost the happier she got. I think it was the *Platinum* Package thing that really swung it, she's so determined to outdo Alyson Worthington. To be honest I was just trying to put her off with the price hike."

Josh grinned. "No kidding. But you know what this means?"

"Means?"

Josh nodded.

Hope shrugged, not sure what he was getting at. "KidzStuff makes twice the profit for half the effort?"

"Hardly half the effort."

"I'm not with you."

Josh parked his bum on the edge of the desk and folded his arms across his chest.

"Well, for the cost of the *Platinum* Package I expect Rosemary and her Little Rhodri are sure to want party games. Lots and lots of party games."

Chapter 17

Tudor was very impressed by Hope's skills not only as an organiser, but also as a saleswoman. Doubly so when, by the following day, she had worked out the grossly inflated profit margin on the booking.

"Good grief! That's outrageous," he said. "Are you sure this woman's aware of the expense she's incurring?"

"Absolutely," Hope confirmed, waving Rosemary Williams' deposit cheque, which had arrived in the post first thing that morning. "Evidently the more we charge, the more credibility we have."

Tudor shook his head in wonder. "I can see that I'll have to put you on commission, my dear. You certainly deserve it."

"The thing is, she wants a third entertainer. A

conjurer preferably. Do you know anyone who would fit the bill?"

Tudor scratched his head. "Apart from Marvo, I'm afraid not."

Hope had a thought. "But surely there are agencies. Didn't you ever have an agent?"

"I never needed one. I did the holiday camps, you see, and the cruise ships before that. Then I met my Herminie and we started this place. But I think you're on the right track. I'm sure there's one in Cardiff if my memory serves me correctly."

A call to Directory Enquiries gave her the number of a theatrical agent in Cardiff. The agent, Terry, sounded hassled, and hummed and hahed for a while, muttering about the busy season. But after Hope switched on the charm he relented and promised that although he couldn't promise any specific magician, he would definitely make sure to send her someone for the date specified.

After she had paid a visit to Rosemary Williams' Mumbles home to measure the space available for the marquee, she called the marquee rental company and put in an order, specifying that she needed the space to be heated and lit. The chair problem was also sorted. The company supplied both chairs and tables, and could certainly supply the gold numbers that Rosemary had set her heart on. They didn't do decorations, but Byron, the salesperson she spoke to, gave her the name and contact number of a freelance display-design service. Assuming that such a service would charge through the nose, that was a non-runner, so she declined. Then he helpfully suggested a wholesale display-goods outlet where all the requisite stuff could be purchased, and even gave her a ballpark estimate of the cost, taking the size of the marquee into account.

The following day she headed off with Tudor and his cheque book.

"You know, although Rosemary's paying for the stuff, she won't want it afterwards so we can recycle it," Hope commented. "Next time you get a marquee booking we can make even more profit."

"Is that entirely honest?" Tudor asked. He was sitting in the passenger seat of the Land-Rover, looking apprehensive.

"Of course it is," Hope assured him, stunned by the question.

"But if Rosemary Williams is paying for the decorations, doesn't that mean they belong to her?"

Hope was flabbergasted. "Don't be silly. She's paying for a *service*. Do you really think she has the time or inclination to schlep off to the wholesaler's to choose a load of fake holly, tinsel and sparkly stuff, not to mention the imagination to decorate a marquee? Anyway, it's a waste to just chuck it away, not to mention a crime against the environment."

"Well, when you put it like that," Tudor said, relaxing a little.

"Exactly."

Hope signalled right and turned into the wholesaler's carpark.

"You know, my dear," Tudor said as they were loading the boxes of decorations into the back of the Land Rover, "you can be quite bossy if you don't mind me saying so, but I think you came along not a moment too soon. Without Herminie to keep an eye on things, KidzStuff was becoming something of a sinking ship."

Hope had never thought of herself as bossy, but considering her subordinate domestic situation she wondered what a psychologist would make of her newfound professional assertiveness.

On the drive home that night her head was full of plans for KidzStuff. A new brochure, different packages and obviously a new price structure. That afternoon, after she had organised the food with Bronwyn Ironside, and with the summer in mind, she'd scoured the Yellow Pages looking for suppliers of balloons and general party stuff, bouncy castles and such. In doing so she came across a company that hired out tableware, glassware, linen and cutlery, large indoor plants even, in fact anything to do with events. She was really surprised, having had no idea that such services were available. It got her thinking. She was excited. Although Tudor's offer of commission was some incentive, two years of aimless domesticity had hardly been taxing and it was a long time since she had felt challenged. Her job at Porter & French had been, for the most part, stimulating, and Roddy had brought out the best in her, allowing her to use her initiative, which was a good thing. Truth be told, even though looking after Dylan had been the deal, she missed the satisfying feeling of a demanding job well done. Now, the way things were shaping up at KidzStuff, it looked as if Tudor was going to be an equally good boss, if for different reasons, namely the fact that he couldn't organise a riot at an England away game. There was also the added bonus that she would have her own money again, earned on merit.

She was bursting to tell Dylan about her day. She had been so taken up with organising Rosemary Williams' party, she'd only had a sandwich at her desk at lunchtime so was ravenous by the time she got home. Dylan was sitting at the computer but there was no sign of any food on the go.

"What's for dinner?" he snapped as soon as she walked through the door. He didn't even look round.

She felt suddenly deflated. "And how was your day, dear?" she asked slumping down on the sofa.

If he noticed the sarcasm in her tone, he ignored it. "As you ask, it was shit," he said. "Geoffrey's still insisting on cuts. Can you believe that? The man's a fool." His eyes still hadn't left the computer screen. "A bloody cretin."

This was an oft-repeated conversation. Dylan would hear from his agent, Geoffrey Mandelson. Geoffrey would (quite reasonably in Hope's opinion) suggest cuts from the manuscript which was growing like a virus in a shanty town, and Dylan would go into a precious strop. Generally the protocol was for Hope to commiserate. To say, what did Geoffrey know about literature, and cite the difficulties that HG Wells and George Orwell had experienced before being recognised as literary geniuses. This time however something snapped.

"Do you not think he might have a point?" she said, more sharply than she intended. "I mean, it is his job, after all. And you have to admit, it is a bit, well … long."

There was an audible intake of breath from the other side of the room. "Long! What has *long* got to do with it? Was Vikram Seth asked to make cuts!"

Hope really had no idea. "Yes," she said. "I heard him interviewed once and he said *A Suitable Boy* started out at two and a half thousand pages before his agent and his editor slashed huge portions of it." This was a total fabrication but she couldn't back-pedal now.

"Two and a half thousand pages? How many words is that?" Dylan asked, sidetracked.

Hope shrugged. "No idea."

Dylan frowned as he made a mental calculation, then remembered that he was supposed to be irate. "And your point is?" he barked, flustering her; making her forget that it was he who had asked the question in the first place.

"Um … well, I'm not sure … maybe you should listen to Geoffrey."

He thrust back his chair in a fit of temper and stood up. "That cretin?" Dramatically throwing his hands in the air in frustration, he roared, *"Fucking hell! Why am I surrounded by bloody illiterate idiots?!"* He was red in the face. Fuming.

"Look, it was only a suggestion," she said in an effort of calm him down. "What do I know?"

"Exactly! So don't offer an opinion when you don't know what you're fucking talking about!"

Simmering with rage he stomped towards the door, grabbing the keys to the Land-Rover which Hope had dropped on the dresser. "I'm going out. Don't wait up."

The door slammed after him and a few moments later she heard the engine rev as he sped away down the track towards the road.

Hope sat in the silence, wondering what she'd said that was so terrible. So the manuscript needed cuts. So what? It was hardly a reflection on his writing. In fact, surely it was a case of an embarrassment of riches. Now why hadn't she thought of that? *An embarrassment of riches*. She filed it away for future use.

She was awake when he came in at around midnight, but feigned sleep, aware that if he'd had drink on top of a bad mood he would be up for an argument.

Creeping out to work before he woke, she left his lunch ready, a large glass of water and Solpadeine by the bed, and stoked up the Aga in the hope that his mood would have blown over by the time she got home.

The atmosphere remained distinctly frosty for some days, however.

The following week as Hope was sorting through the dusty chaos that was the KidzStuff back room, Josh dropped in to see if there was any work for him in the diary. Hope roped him in to help her shift boxes into some semblance of order.

"Balloons over there," she instructed. "And if you come across a box of party poppers, let me know."

Josh stood to attention and saluted. *"Ja, mein Führer!"*

Hope gave him a good-natured shove and they got on with it.

"So how's your boyfriend's book coming on?" he asked a while later.

Normally Hope would have given her stock answer of "Great," but a week of tiptoeing around Dylan had worn her tolerance levels thin. "Don't ask," she said.

Josh looked surprised. "Like that, is it?"

Hope sat down on a carton of party hats. "Dylan's acting the tortured genius lately, and to tell you the truth it's a bit wearing."

"And is he?" Josh asked, sitting down beside her.

"Is he what?"

"A tortured genius?"

Hope laughed. "Well, he's certainly tortured, and he always refers to his book as the *Important Novel*, so *he* thinks he's a genius at any rate."

"Then it must be true." He smiled. "And what's it

about, this Important Novel?"

"Actually I don't know. It's a sort of stream-of-consciousness thing. He used to read out passages to me but he doesn't any more."

Josh nodded. "Oh. I see."

"Actually, if I'm honest, Dylan doesn't think I'm smart enough to understand it."

Josh guffawed. "A legend in his own lunch-time then."

Suddenly Hope felt guilty that she'd been so disloyal. "Oh no! He is a good writer. That's his problem. He's just a perfectionist," she protested.

"But he thinks you're an eejit?"

On the defensive, she was about to object, to make excuses, but the fact that there was more than a kernel of truth in what he had said made her stop to think. She had always considered Dylan to be her intellectual superior, but in reality she had no evidence of that other than his own assertion. That, and his often patronising attitude toward her. At the start she'd been so in awe of him – she couldn't believe her luck that he wanted her. She had viewed him through rosy contacts. "Well, maybe not an eejit, but ..."

Josh guffawed. "But not smart enough to understand his great literary masterpiece? Come on! If you don't mind me saying so, Hope, your boyfriend sounds like a bit of a wanker to me. You're one of the smartest people I know."

It was Hope's turn to guffaw. "Then you need to get

out more," she said, anxious to change the subject which was so uncomfortably close to the truth.

The day before Rosemary Williams' party dawned wet and very cold. Hope arrived at the office before eight. She'd had no time to leave Dylan's lunch ready or to bank up the Aga before she left as she'd slept through the alarm, so she'd been late waking. This was largely due to the fact that she'd spent a sleepless night worrying about everything. Dylan hadn't been encouraging either, sulking like a child because she had something other than his day, how cretinous the literary establishment was, or the progress of his Important Novel to worry about.

Tudor was at the office when she arrived and the boxes containing the marquee decorations were stacked by the door. After loading them into the Land-Rover they headed off to Mumbles together. Things started well when the marquee arrived on time. Rosemary was all of a dither, not a bit happy with the weather forecast as if that was down to Hope and Tudor, but she cheered up by lunchtime when the sun broke through the clouds, the marquee was up and the floor was in the process of being laid. She did have a small bleat about damage to the lawn, but Hope deflected her attention by commenting on how efficient the gas heaters were. Rosemary didn't even offer them so much as a cup of tea, so by lunch-time, after hanging round watching the progress of the marquee people, Hope and Tudor headed off for a bite of lunch. The afternoon was taken up decorating the party space. Josh turned up to lend his support, but despite the purchase of three large boxes of Christmas glitz it all looked rather sparse and meagre when they had hung up the last bit of tinsel. Hope improvised though. She and Josh lugged in some large plants, namely two six-foot palms from the conservatory, and an equally large yucca plant from the hall, then she dispatched Josh off on his bike to B&Q to get several sets of fairy lights. The lights and the plants were a definite improvement, but disappointing as far as she was concerned. She had visualised something far more sumptuous. Josh commented that sumptuous would cost a lot more, and anyway it was a kids' party and, the last he'd heard, kids weren't that pushed about sumptuous. Tudor was equally encouraging, delighted with everything. Thankfully his enthusiasm was infectious and Rosemary Williams didn't seem in the least disappointed, her criteria for the day being evidently anything as long as it was better and more expensive than Alyson Worthington's do. By four o'clock, everything on the list had been achieved, with the exception of wrapping the prize for Pass the Parcel. Due to Rosemary's insistence on three entertainers, Hope felt somewhat off the hook as far as party games were concerned and planned to string out one game of Pass the Parcel.

Tudor tapped her on the shoulder. "Let's call it a day," he said. He looked whacked and Hope suspected that he too had experienced an anxious sleepless night.

Josh tore off on his bike and she dropped Tudor back at the office where he'd parked the Traveller, then she headed home herself.

Arriving home an hour and a half early at five, she parked the Land-Rover beside Wayne's van. She was surprised to see it as Dylan wasn't that friendly with Wayne and he never called out to the cottage. She was further surprised when there was no sign of either Dylan or Wayne when she walked into the living-room. The Aga was lit however which she thought a good sign.

Kicking off her shoes she padded upstairs to get changed. Halfway up she heard a groaning, panting sound. The bedroom door was open and from the tiny landing she could see a trail of clothes discarded between the door and the bed. She could also see that Dylan was in the bed, and that he was clearly not alone. At first the thought that he was in bed with Wayne stopped her dead in her tracks, until she realised that the feet resting on his shoulders couldn't possibly belong to Wayne. Not unless he had taken to wearing patent stiletto-heeled ankle-boots and fishnet stockings. By speedy process of elimination that left Laura, also in the noisy throes of passion. Hope's motor ability deserted her and she was rooted to the spot. She caught sight of her reflection in the wardrobe mirror, but didn't recognise herself, her mouth agape, her skin the colour of putty. She could hear her heart thumping in her ears and felt nauseous.

Whether he heard something, or merely sensed her

presence, Dylan suddenly paused and glanced over his shoulder towards the open bedroom door. Then, a look of horror on his face, he leapt from the bed muttering, "Oh fuck! Fuck! Fuck! Fuck!" leaving Laura, who still hadn't copped on to what was happening, protesting loudly,

"Hey, you selfish bastard! What are you doing?" Then she too caught her first glimpse of Hope. Her jaw dropped and she echoed Dylan's expletive, drawing her knees up to her chest defensively, pulling up the sheet to cover herself.

"This isn't what it looks like, petal," Dylan said. He had the quilt in his hand and he too was trying to cover himself in an inexplicable show of modesty, which was in itself a bizarre touch.

The ridiculousness of the statement was enough to bring Hope to her senses. *"You bastard!"* she screamed at him, frustrated that she couldn't think of anything more original. But then again, as explanations went, *'This isn't what it looks like, petal'* was hardly a winner in the Nobel prize for the *'clever things to say in a shit situation'* category.

Laura had slithered out of bed and was pulling on her clothes. Dylan took a step towards Hope. He was sweaty and red-faced, his hair on end, which was more than could be said for his erection which had died a death. Standing there naked but for his socks, he looked pitiful.

"Please, petal, let me …" he inclined his head in

Laura's direction. "This is nothing ... nothing . . ."

"Nothing? You bastard!" she heard Laura echo as pillow hit him squarely on the back of the head, bursting from the force of the blow, causing an explosion of feathers. Humiliated and still in a state of shock, Hope fled downstairs. Struggling into her shoes, she had to fight the urge to vomit, but the flight response was stronger. Dylan thundered down the stairs after her, feathers stuck to his sweaty torso and head which, in a surreal moment, brought Big Bird to mind.

"Hope, petal, please listen to me!"

But she didn't hang around. Grabbing the keys off the dresser she stumbled out of the door and jumped into the Land-Rover. Gunning the engine she sideswiped Wayne's van as she swerved towards the gate and hurtled down the track. Fifty yards down the road, she pulled in to the side, opened the driver's side door and barfed noisily onto the grass verge, narrowly missing an irate ewe who was innocently grabbing an evening snack.

She had no idea where she was going, no idea what to do next, so she just drove. Forty minutes later she found herself outside the office. She felt calmer, but no less humiliated and betrayed.

I don't know why you're surprised, a small voice in her head said. *This isn't the first time Dylan's played away*. Too true, but at the time she had been the other woman, and had been convinced that he loved her, that his marriage was dead and buried, and that this was for keeps. Recalling Josh's comment that Dylan considered her an eejit, she felt just that. A thorough eejit. Then questions flooded her head. How long has it been going on? Did he give Laura the same guff about his relationship being over? Instant recall and she heard the words, "We haven't slept together for months, petal. It's all over bar the shouting."

Cold seeped into the cab, so she started the engine and let it idle, switching the heater on to full. The temperature had dropped and the windscreen had iced up in the short time that she had been parked. It had crossed her mind to spend the night in the Land-Rover, but now she realised that it wasn't an option. On top of everything else she didn't want to die of hypothermia. She had no money with her bar a couple of quid so a hotel, even a B&B, was out of the question. The cold shouldn't be a problem, she thought bitterly, not with the residual heat from all those burnt bridges.

There was still a fair amount of traffic around, early Christmas shoppers ahead of the posse, the last of the rush-hour traffic making its way out of the city. I need a drink, she thought but, on reflection, finding a pub and drinking herself senseless wasn't an option on two quid. But what to do? Where to stay? The thought of going back to Llanllwni, facing Dylan and of actually sleeping in the same bed, still damp with sweat, in which she'd just witnessed him humping Laura, was unthinkable. She didn't know where Josh lived, and anyway she felt too embarrassed to just show up on his doorstep. That only left Tudor, kindred spirit, fellow dumpee. Slipping the Land-Rover into gear, she signalled and joined the line of traffic heading out of town.

Tudor answered the door of his neat semi-detached in the Uplands, in his woolly dressing-gown and slippers. Nineteen fifties man. Seeing no point in prevarication, she just blurted out what had happened, then, to her mortification, burst into tears. He was kindness itself though and invited her in, insisting that she join him for a bite to eat. "Only beans on toast, you understand. Never been much good in the kitchen, but I've always found baked beans to be good in a crisis."

Once she had calmed down and had reprised the story, this time in a more lucid fashion, Tudor pursed his lips and tut-tutted. "What a terrible state of affairs! But what's to be done, my dear?"

Hope shrugged. "I don't know."

"Well, do you think it just an aberration, a temporary lapse, or are you of the opinion that it might be more serious?"

Hope sighed. "I don't know. I had no idea he was bonking Laura behind my back if that's what you mean. I feel such a fool."

Tudor nodded sagely. "I know. I had no idea that Herminie and Rodger, that's Marvo to you, my dear, were … you know …"

"Rogering?" Hope offered without even a hint of humour.

Tudor nodded, equally solemn. "Quite so." He picked at a loose thread on the cuff of his dressing-gown, then, after a short silence, he looked up and met her eyes. "So is that it?" he asked. "Or are you going to forgive him?"

"I gave up everything for him, job, friends, family. I followed him over here. I feel so stupid."

"But can you forgive him? Do you want to forgive him?" Tudor persisted. "I'd have Herminie back at the drop of a hat." He paused again, then frowned. "At least I would have. But perhaps not now."

"You didn't catch them in the act though, did you?"

He shook his head. "No. And I was blind to all the tell-tale signs."

"How do you mean?"

"Oh, you know. The way they were together. They were so cold to one another when I was around, it should have been obvious really. Hardly gave each other the time of day, yet whenever I came home unexpectedly he'd be there, allegedly to see me, but for no good reason. I wonder I didn't ...what's that expression you use?" He scratched his head and frowned. "*Cop on*, that's it. It's a wonder I didn't *cop on* sooner. It was all rather ambiguous though. No obvious signs."

Hope gave a humourless cackle. "The one time I came home unexpectedly I found them at it. No ambiguity there." A mental image of Dylan and Laura flashed unbidden into her head. "In our bed," she muttered. "In our bed, can you believe that? God! How could he do that to me?"

"You still haven't answered my question," Tudor said. "Are you going to forgive him?"

The vision of Dylan, standing naked but for his socks, by the bed, spewing out futile wimpish denials, caused her to see him in a new light. He was no longer a heroic figure, and suddenly he wasn't the least bit attractive either (the Big Bird moment compounding it). With the blinding clarity that only betrayal can induce, she realised that not only did she no longer respect him, no longer love him, but she didn't even like him that much. On reflection it had been a long time coming, his lack of respect for her a major part of it. She felt angry with herself for being so emotionally needy and dependent on him, mentally kicked herself for the compromises she had made to accommodate him. Then her grandmother came to mind. A strong lady who had been the backbone of the family business, saving it from the bailiffs when her alcoholic husband nearly drank it into the ground. "If you accept the unacceptable," she said once when Hope had marvelled at how strong she'd been to stand up to her truculent and unbiddable husband, "if you accept the unacceptable, you make it acceptable, therefore you only have yourself to blame." And Hope realised that she had done just that. Accepted his moods, his mostly unwarranted criticism, his pompousness. But enough.

"No," she said. "No. That's it. It's unacceptable. I can't forgive him. Not for this."

Tudor didn't comment. He was sitting motionless staring at the flames of the gas fire.

"Can I stay here tonight?" she asked. "There's no need to go to any trouble. I can sleep on the sofa."

Tudor blinked then looked up. "By all means, my dear. But I have a perfectly comfortable spare bedroom. And you must stay as long as you like. In fact, I'd be glad of the company. I remember what it was like when my Herminie ..." he stopped, suddenly conscious that she might get the wrong idea. "No strings, of course. All above board. No hanky-panky, I can guarantee."

The thought that Tudor might assume that she'd see him as some sort of seducer, of something other than a perfect gentleman, made her smile. "Thanks, Tudor. That's really kind of you."

He stood up abruptly. "Now. Perhaps you would be so good as to make the toast. I'm afraid I have a terrible habit of burning toast, but you can trust me implicitly with the beans."

After tea, they sat together in the front room, like an old married couple, one each side of the fire, drinking their cocoa. It was years since Hope had drunk real cocoa. In fact she wasn't sure if she ever had, or whether she just thought she had. The same way she had never tasted ginger beer, but felt sure she knew what it must taste like having grown up on the Famous

Five, and *Swallows and Amazons*.

"About tomorrow," he said, putting his cocoa mug down on the hearth, "if you're not feeling up to it . . . that is to say, after this business with ..." he paused, not sure what to call Dylan. "Well, I know how distressing it is. I was beside myself with grief and I ..."

Hope put him out of his misery. "I'm fine, Tudor, honestly, and I'd rather just get on with things. To tell you the truth, I want to make sure everything goes smoothly tomorrow. Besides, I want to give the dust the chance to settle before I go back to collect my things."

"Well, if you're sure," he said with a note of relief.

Rightly assuming that Tudor would probably have another sleepless night, if for different reasons, Hope insisted on making them mega-strength hot whiskeys before they turned in for the night, and by the sound of the snoring emanating from his bedroom it was a good call. She passed into an uneasy sleep herself a short time later but dreamt troubled dreams.

Chapter 18

Hope awoke before dawn and it took a moment for her to get her bearings. Dylan had invaded her dreams and her restless night had left her tired and stiff. Strangely though, she didn't feel sad, but angry. This surprised her considering how much Dylan had meant to her. She had thought that they'd grow old together. He the successful novelist, she the irreplaceable and supportive partner, basking in his reflected glory. How pitiful did that sound? Her mouth was dry after the hot whiskey so she slipped out of bed, pulled on her jeans and sweater, and crept down to the kitchen. After she had made a pot of tea she sneaked out to the Land-Rover and brought in the Pass the Parcel stuff, then sat down at the table to wrap it up. Despite her efforts to leave

Tudor sleeping, he put in an appearance in his dressing-gown before the tea had had a chance to go cold. He took out a cup and saucer and joined her at the table.

"So how do you feel this morning?" he asked. "As far as um … as the *Dylan* situation is concerned?"

"Angry. And the more I think abut it, the more livid I get," she said, as she slashed at a piece of wrapping paper with a scissors that she'd found in the cutlery drawer. "The rotten lying bastard!"

With one eye on the flailing scissors, Tudor pulled out a chair and sat out of reach. "So what action do you propose to take?"

Hope hadn't give action much thought, too taken up with fanning the flames of her rage, with mentally running over the last few months for the telltale signs Tudor had referred to. It was totally unproductive because she had never actually seen Dylan and Laura exchange more than a couple of words, but maybe that was the point. "Well," she said after a while, "I suppose after today's gig, I'll head home, disembowel Dylan, and pick up my things. Is it still OK to stay here until I can find somewhere else, by the way?"

Tudor still had a weather eye on the scissors. "Oh, absolutely, my dear. For as long as you want."

Despite her brave talk about disembowelment, she felt apprehensive about going back to Llanllwni and facing Dylan. Although she was determined that it was over, she didn't have a lot of faith in her resolve if he turned on the famous Dylan Jones charm. And conversely, what if there was a scene? She hated confrontation and, although Dylan had never raised his hand to her, she was well acquainted with his temper, having spent close on two years placating it, soothing his ego, calming him down. She glanced over at Tudor. Sitting there nibbling at a slice of toast, he had the look of a helpless, follicly challenged hamster, so it didn't seem fair to involve him.

As if he had the ability to read her thoughts he looked up and caught her eye. "You know, if you're nervous, that is to say, if you'd rather not go to collect your belongings on your own, I'm sure Josh would be only too happy to accompany you."

"You think so?" she asked, relieved, but at the same time embarrassed that she'd have to explain the situation to McFling after all the talk of her *amazing* boyfriend.

"Would you like me to have a word on your behalf?" he asked.

After a moment's thought she shook her head. "Um … no, thanks all the same. I'd better ask him myself." It occurred to her that if Tudor asked, it would be easier for Josh to refuse, and she really needed some support. Also, it was unlikely that Dylan would make a tit of himself in front of company. "But, Tudor, there's another problem. You see, much as I'd like to hang on to the Land-Rover and let the bloody bastard cycle, it's not actually his – it belongs to his brother Owen – so I'll have to leave it at the house –"

"Josh can take the Morris Minor," Tudor cut in.

That settled, she felt more relaxed. The plan was sorted. Move out of Llanllwni, move in with Tudor until she could find a place of her own.

How a day, no, less than a day, could turn a person's world upside down . . .

After she had finished wrapping her multi-layered parcel, Tudor insisted that she run herself a bath and have a wallow, as he put it. Apparently there was nothing like a good wallow in a hot bath in a crisis, apart from baked beans on toast that is. Tudor proved to be correct in his assessment, as she felt revived and refreshed after soaking until the water had gone tepid and the skin of her fingertips grew white and wrinkly.

They met Josh in the Dairy Maid at twelve and had lunch together.

After several meaningful looks and a couple of nudges of encouragement from Tudor, Hope bit the bullet and filled Josh in on her revised domestic situation.

"The rotten whooer," was his first reaction, then after a pause. "I know someone who could give him a good kicking if you want."

Hope was horrified, but when the corners of his mouth twitched into a smile she realised he was joking.

"The thing is," she said awkwardly, "I was wondering –"

"We thought it might be a good idea if you were to accompany Hope back to –wherever it is, to collect her belongings," Tudor cut in.

"If you've nothing better to do," Hope added. "I'd appreciate the support and, besides, I'll have to leave the Land-Rover at the house – it belongs to his brother and I'm sure it would give Dylan the greatest of pleasure to accuse me of theft and set the police on me – so I'll need a lift back. Tudor says he'll lend us the Morris Minor.

"*No problemo*," Josh said and Hope relaxed. "Just give me the nod when you want to do it."

Tudor diplomatically changed the subject to Rosemary Williams' party then, and after they had all finished lunch, they headed off to Mumbles.

The marquee looked very festive with the fairy lights switched on. Bronwyn Ironside had arrived ahead of them and was laying out the buffet. She had brought along linen tablecloths for the adult's buffet, but had judiciously laid the kiddies' food on a separate table covered by a paper cloth with a Christmas theme. A small birdlike Asian woman in a starched white overall was polishing glasses as she took them from a crate, and there were a dozen bottles of white wine cooling in a wooden tub of ice. A case of red sat on the floor waiting to be unpacked. Tudor couldn't find a spare plug for the ghetto-blaster so Josh went off to find a three-way adaptor. Rosemary put in an appearance then, a glass of red wine in her perfectly manicured hand. She was wearing navy trousers, a navy and red sweater with the inevitable gold nautical logo, and flat gold leather shoes. She was wound up tight as a spring which didn't bode well, the pressure of outdoing Alyson Worthington obviously getting to her big-time. Little Rhodri, a chubby unfortunate-looking child with hair so blond he appeared bald, and protruding teeth that promised to go a long way towards some orthodontist's holiday home in Marbella, followed his mother into the marquee from the conservatory. He was wearing a stripy T-shirt and looked very Larsonesque. Hope recognised him from Little Jeremy's do and recalled that the pintsized Antichrist appeared to have some vendetta against him as the poor kid had been on the receiving end of many a dig. She made a mental note to keep an eye on Little Jeremy and ensure he didn't spoil Rhodri's day.

"Is everything ready?" Rosemary asked anxiously, her voice so stressed it was three octaves higher than normal.

"Everything's under control," Hope assured her. "Bronwyn's finished setting up the buffet, and the hot dishes are in your oven keeping warm."

"Good, good," Rosemary said, eyes darting round the marquee.

Tudor was off in the downstairs cloakroom getting changed, Josh had returned with the adaptor and, after plugging in the ghetto-blaster, had put on a Christmas tape. Rosemary relaxed a little as Bing Crosby warbled the first soothing strains of 'White Christmas'. She drained her glass and immediately refilled it with chilled Chardonnay from the ice tub. Despite the fact that

Rosemary looked liable to be rat-arsed before the hour was out, Hope breathed a sigh of relief that everything, other than the hostess, appeared to be in order.

What could possibly go wrong?

No sooner had the thought formed in her brain, than she spotted Little Rhodri crouched by the large yucca tugging the electric plug in and out of the adaptor, causing the fairy lights to flash on and off. She hurried over.

"Oops, don't do that, Rhodri," she said, forcibly dragging his reluctant hand away from the socket. "You might electrocute yourself." He gave her a vicious kick in the shin for her trouble. She yelped and jumped back, still with a good grip on his arm, but he was determined, and made a lunge for the plug again. Hope stuck out her foot and he tripped over it, but made a soft landing on a bean bag. Nonetheless he set about wailing unintelligibly as if she had just amputated his arm without an anaesthetic, along the lines of *"Muuummmyyy-she-kicked-myleg-waaaahhh!"*

This caught his mother's attention but she didn't appear overly concerned other than to snap, "Oh, do stop blubbing, Rhodri!" and the waterworks instantly ceased, but Rhodri shot Hope a glance of pure unadulterated hatred.

"The magician!" Rosemary suddenly screeched, oblivious to the fact that Hope had just prevented her son from frying, or at least had stopped him from fusing the entire neighbourhood.

Hope looked around expecting to see a magician on fire or something, but all became clear when Rosemary demanded, "You did *book* the magician?"

"Don't worry. He'll be here in plenty of time," Hope assured her, praying that Terry, the theatrical agent, wouldn't let her down.

The guests started to arrive so Rosemary hurried off, glass in hand, to let them in. Hope took a last glance around the marquee in time to see Little Rhodri back at the socket flashing the lights again. With his mother out of the way she was a tad less diplomatic. Grabbing him by the collar she yanked him away. "Look, kid! That's dangerous. Stop it or I'll set Little Jeremy on you."

Rhodri, furious that she'd spoiled his game again, attempted another robust kick, but she neatly sidestepped him, whipping his legs out from under him again, just as Alyson Worthington, Little Jeremy, and a tall ruddy-complexioned man in Pringle golf sweater and brown stay-pressed slacks walked in. Thankfully two small boys hurtled through the entrance at the same time, pushing past Alyson, Mr Alyson and Little Jeremy, which distracted Rhodri.

Soon the marquee was filling up with both adults and kids, and Josh had disappeared to get changed into his McFling outfit. Hope found Rosemary and suggested that they start a game of Musical Chairs before tea, so she enlisted the aid of a couple of mothers and they helped to organise the kids.

With the experience she had gained from LJ's

shindig, she was careful that neither he nor Rhodri were eliminated in the early rounds. The parents looked on all smiles at first, watching their little darlings, but then their collective competitive spirit surfaced and shouts of encouragement could be heard as they got down to the last six chairs. There was a pile-up at one point when Mr Alyson tripped up the kid behind LJ, leaving the way clear for his son and heir to safely grab a chair when the music stopped. She should have let Little Rhodri win, but with her shin still stinging from his assault, she made sure he got his comeuppance and he was beaten to the last chair by a lanky boy with glasses and a pudding-bowl haircut.

Time for tea.

The kids tucked into the food and the adults looked on, drinking, chatting and picking food from the buffet. There was laughter and the general hum of conversation over the sound of the Christmas music. Pleased that it was going well, she found Tudor and Josh in the kitchen drinking coffee, with Chalky propped up on the counter.

"Would tomorrow suit you to get your things?" Josh asked, as he handed her a restorative mug of coffee. "It's just I'm heading home on Monday night."

Hope's guts turned over, but she agreed nonetheless, with the thought that it was best to get it over with. Then she heard the doorbell, so went out to the hall to answer it.

A moustachioed man with something resembling a

small beige furry mammal on his head, stood on the step, suitcase in hand.

"You must be the magician," she said, relieved, addressing the remark to his toupee, unable to drag her eyes away from it.

"Terry sent me," he said. "Am I late?"

"Not at all. They're just sitting down to tea, but Mrs Williams wants you on first, if that's OK?"

"Good," he said. "I've another gig at five in Llanelli. Where can I get changed?"

Giving the toupee directions to the downstairs loo, she returned to the marquee. The adults had made inroads into the buffet and the wine, and seemed to be having a good time. Hope's eyes drifted in the direction of Rosemary's high-pitched brittle laugh. The hostess looked fairly well oiled as did Mr Alyson, who had his hand planted on her navy nautical bum. Hope approached her.

"The magician's arrived, Rosemary. He'll do his act as soon as the kids have finished tea. OK?"

"Oh, how tremendous!" Rosemary squealed. "I so love magicians!" Tottering slightly, she disengaged herself from the group and clapped her hands for attention. "Children! Children! The magician's here."

Ginger McFling made his entrance on cue and organised the kids in his usual efficient way. With the help of a couple of sets of still sober parents he lined the chairs up in four rows facing in the direction of the marquee's entrance.

"Did the magician get here yet?" he asked under his breath as they ushered the last child into his place.

"Yes. That was him at the door. He's getting ready in the downstairs loo."

As the last kid was seated, two others were up and, being boys, were tussling with each other. It had only taken the one previous experience for Hope to learn that attempting to get twenty-odd six-year-old boys to sit down quietly was like trying to contain spilled mercury. "The natives are getting restless – maybe you should warm them up at bit," she suggested.

McFling caught the kids' attention and started to whip up some enthusiasm by producing a coin from behind Rhodri's ear and telling silly fart jokes and doing a couple of pratfalls. He had the kids in stitches. Hope was looking anxiously towards the marquee entrance, wondering what was taking the magician so long when suddenly, in an explosion of movement, Tudor erupted through the entrance grappling with the moustachioed one, the tufty hairpiece in one hand and Chalky enveloping his other arm. Ping-ponging off the startled adults they ended up in a heap on the floor, Tudor and Chalky on top. The magician, who was trying his best to protect his face from the onslaught, managed to roll over, then it was Tudor who was on the receiving end. It was a surreal sight. Tudor and the magician struggling, with a scarily animated Chalky head butting the magician at every opportunity. The words "Bastard!", "Cuckold!", "Despicable!",

"Betrayal!" were being bandied about at lot.

The crowd that had gathered around the mêlée were all open-mouthed and unresponsive due either to alcoholic stupor or the abrupt and unexpected nature of the spectacle. With the exception of Rosemary who was screaming. At least Hope assumed she was screaming because her mouth was open and her eyes wide, but above the shrieks and clapping and laughter of the kids she couldn't be heard. They thought it was great *craic* and all part of the entertainment, a bonus on top of Ginger McFling's pratfalls, particularly in view of the fact that most of them recognised Tudor and his pal Chalky from Little Jeremy's do.

Josh was the first to come to his senses. "Is this some kind of sick joke?" he hissed.

Hope frowned a 'What are you talking about?' kind of frown.

"Getting fecking Marvo?" he said. "What the hell were you thinking of?"

"*Marvo?*"

It took a second for the name to register, then she groaned aloud. Of all the magicians in all the world, Terry had to send bloody Marvo. *Marvo!* Tudor's nemesis.

Josh dived in and yanked Marvo off Tudor, catching a couple of blows from his elbows and ripping off Chalky's arm in the process, which prompted a collective gasp from the kids. But Marvo shook himself free and grabbed Tudor around the waist, inadvertently whacking him with Chalky's remaining flailing limb. To add to the confusion, a dove, newly liberated from somewhere about the magician's person, after flapping about in panic, had landed on Alyson Worthington's head, wings still aflutter. Alyson tried to beat it off, screeching close to hysteria. An unidentified hand slapped it away and, terrified, it flew off into the house dropping liberal dollops of white guano on anyone in its flight path. Two stay-pressed fathers took the hint and lent a hand then, aiding Josh in separating the two men, then physically restraining them. Tudor was still wild-eyed and livid, and still throwing punches in Marvo's direction with the partially mutilated dummy. Marvo on the other hand, his right eye already showing signs of swelling, was trying to regain some dignity by replacing his toupee. It sat at a cockeyed angle over his left eye.

Needless to say, Marvo didn't perform at the party. Grabbing his suitcase from the hall and legging it, he muttered something abut the police and grievous bodily harm. While Josh calmed things down in the marquee, placating Rosemary as best he could, Hope hurried Tudor to the downstairs cloakroom where she cleaned up his bloody nose, the ventriloquist still clinging to Chalky and his dismembered arm.

"I'm *so* sorry," she said. "I had no idea Terry would send Marvo. *Honestly.*"

Tudor winced as she put a touch too much pressure on his rapidly swelling schnozzle. "I don't imagine for a moment that you did," he said. "But it was the shock, you see. I don't know what got into us. There he was standing in the hall and we just snapped. Completely lost it."

"Understandable under the circumstances," Hope assured him.

The party broke up after the excitement finished. The kids still appeared to be under the impression that it was all part of the fun and were not the least bit pleased when their traumatised parents dragged them swiftly home. Rosemary Williams was not a happy bunny either. When Hope had sought her out to apologise she'd been scathing, threatening all sorts of legal action (Mr Williams, it transpired, was a solicitor). She also stated that she had no intention of paying the balance on her account, and there was a veiled inference that she might even demand her deposit back.

Hope felt dreadful. She felt responsible too, even though it was due to a horrible coincidence, and she fervently hoped that Rosemary's sundry threats would come to nothing. Apart from the prospect of legal action, the twenty per cent deposit, if they managed to hang on to it, would barely pay for the marquee, so that meant that Tudor would be out of pocket for the catering, the Christmas decorations and all the other bits and bobs.

"I'm so sorry, Tudor," Hope repeated for the umpteenth time as she parked the Land-Rover in the driveway of his house.

"Please stop apologising, my dear," he said, though it came out as *"Pleede top apododisig, by dear"* on account of his mangled nose. His eyes, though not swollen, were discoloured with angry purple bruising and his left cheek grazed from contact with Chalky's floundering hand.

Josh arrived just after them and tapped on the driver's side window, so they all went inside.

She waited until they were all seated at the table with restorative mugs of tea in front of them before she mentioned Rosemary. This wasn't difficult as Tudor spent the time it took to get the tea ready in boasting about how he had *"whacked"* Marvo.

He seemed quite gleeful and a touch smug which surprised Hope as she had assumed he would be a *'discretion is the better part of valour'* type of man if it came to violence. And she expected he would at least be a bit shamefaced about it. Not a bit of it though. Although he admitted to having lost it, his face was shining with excitement and he was more animated that she had ever seen him.

"I must say, I feel marvellous!" he declared. "Up to now he was, what's the expression? Unfinished business, that's it. It was unfinished business."

Josh, who was also showing signs of bruising around the temple area, due to Marvo's thrashing elbows, smiled. "Well, you and Chalky gave as good as you got, Tudor. I'll say that for you. And good on you!"

Tudor, still full of it, grinned, then patted Chalky on

the head. "Yes, we did acquit ourselves rather well, didn't we, despite a few injuries?"

"Nothing that can't be fixed," Josh said, picking up Chalky's arm, attempting to reattach it, then giving up.

"I hate to burst your bubble," Hope said, pouring herself a hot drop, "but as a result of your little rumble, Marvo could well make a complaint to the cops, Rosemary's threatening to sue, and she made it clear that she has no intention of paying the balance of her account. She might even demand her deposit back."

"A small price to pay," Tudor commented, wincing as his cut lip came into contact with the hot mug of tea.

"But what if you end up in court for GBH?" She was a millimetre away from including Chalky in her question but stopped herself in time.

Tudor snorted. *"Pwah!* Then I'll make a counter-charge. He hit me first, you know? And look what he did to Chalky!"

"Um ... that was me, I'm afraid," Josh admitted.

"Oh ... well, anyway, even if he does, at the risk of repeating myself, it will have been a small price to pay."

"Not so small," she pointed out. "It's hardly likely any of her friends will book KidzStuff now. Not after that."

"Oh, I don't know," Josh said grinning. "The kiddies seemed to enjoy it."

Hope glared at him. "I'm being serious here, Josh."

Tudor threw up his hands in a dismissive gesture. "Allow me my moment of glory, my dear, before I have to face reality. It's not often one gets the chance to settle an old score, you know."

Hope shot a glance at Josh, but he was obviously of the same mind as Tudor because he was nodding in agreement. "Too true, Tudor. Too true."

"But what if Rosemary sues you?" she protested.

"Then she sues me," Tudor said philosophically. "What's done is done." He paused, then his battered rodent face lit up again like a Christmas tree. "And getting even with that weasel will have been worth every last brass penny!"

Chapter 19

Not too bright and early the following morning Josh turned up at Tudor's. He joined Hope at the breakfast table – Tudor was still in bed – and after the initial refusal followed by the usual "you will, you will, you will," took the proffered bacon sandwich.

"So what's the story?" he said after he had polished off a further two despite his preliminary reluctance.

Hope shrugged. "Show up. Grab my stuff. Leave," she said, adding, "I don't think there's any danger of Dylan doing a Tudor and Chalky. I mean I'm the wronged party after all. Anyway, beneath that bluster, my guess is he's a coward at heart."

Josh grinned. "Maybe I should bring Chalky for back-up just in case."

As it turned out, there was no need for back-up, Chalky or otherwise, as Dylan was conspicuous by his absence when they reached the cottage, Hope driving the Land-Rover, Josh, Tudor's trusty Morris Minor Traveller. She was relieved, but also surprised. It wasn't like Dylan to be up and about on a Sunday before midday.

The place was a mess, with dirty dishes in the sink, an overflowing ashtray on the table and the Aga cold to the touch.

"Maybe he's just gone out for the Sunday papers," Josh offered. "You said he's got a bike."

It was a possibility.

"Then I think I'll just grab my things and get out of here as soon as possible," she said, handing him one of the bin-liners off the roll. "Those paperbacks and CDs on the desk are mine."

She headed upstairs. The bed was in the same state as it had been in when she had last seen it. She wondered it he'd slept there since, or whether the general disarray of mangled sheets and duvet were a result of his getting straight back in again and continuing where he and Laura had left off. Walking over to the window she flung it open to relieve the musty musky smell of stale sex and man sweat. The thought of him humping Laura in their bed prompted a flood of jealousy. Then the breeze from the window wafted feathers from the burst pillow, still lying on the floor where Laura had dropped it. She gave a wry smile. Little hope of him getting into her knickers again after his 'this means nothing' crack, particularly taking her reaction into account. It was a small consolation.

Packing her clothes didn't take long – only one bin-liner – her suitcase and most of the clothes she had brought with her having succumbed to mildew the previous autumn. Taking a last look around the room she was about to close the window, then changed her mind. Let him freeze his bollocks off, she thought malevolently, then hurried downstairs.

"Is that it?" Josh asked, obviously surprised by the one bin-liner she was carrying and his own only half filled.

She nodded. "That's it. Travel light. That's me."

She left the keys to the Land-Rover on the table and walked outside. It was a pleasant day, sunny and dry if cold, which was a change. Usually in November the Llanllwni mountain was covered in an ever-pervading damp mist that seeped up through the stone floors, through the walls, into the bones and through every tiny crack and crevice in the aged warped window frames.

"I'm not sorry to be leaving this place," she said, unaware that she had spoken her thoughts aloud.

Josh opened the back of the Traveller and stowed the black plastic bags. "Really? I thought you liked the country life. Back to nature and all that."

She shook her head. "No. Not really. I'm a city girl at heart. I only came here because of Dylan, and look what a mistake that was."

253

"All part of life's rich tapestry," Josh commented. "Shall we go then?"

Hope nodded and got into the passenger seat. "I never thought for a minute it would finish like this," she said sadly, then sighed. "I mean, am I a total eejit or what?"

"Only as far as yer man's concerned," Josh said starting the engine and driving off down the track towards the road. "And, safe to say, you won't make that mistake again in a hurry."

"You better believe it."

As they turned out onto the road, about fifty yards distant, Hope spied a lonely figure on a bicycle labouring up the hill.

"Shit! There he is. Step on it, Josh! Let's get out of here."

Josh gunned the elderly engine and roared off in the opposite direction at a stately thirty-five miles an hour. Hope leaned over the back of the seat and peered through the rear window. Dylan had stopped and was standing in the middle of the road watching them drive away.

Josh didn't stay long after they returned to Tudor's. He had something on that night and had to pack for his trip home, so after a quick coffee he left. She was disappointed as she could have done with the company, needed a sympathetic ear to have a good bitch about Dylan to, and Tudor was out, she had no idea where. The possibility that he'd been arrested briefly crossed her mind, but the fact that there was no note made it unlikely. Chalky however was very much in evidence, his arm reattached, slumped on the countertop in the kitchen, the scuffs on his face newly touched up with enamel paint.

"Fat lot of good you were," she said to the puppet. "Why didn't you stop him?"

Upstairs in the spare room, Hope unpacked her clothes, then the bag of stuff that Josh had filled. Amongst the books and half dozen CDs she found a box of computer disks, and on reading the label of the topmost one realised that Josh had taken Dylan's backup disks of the Important Novel by mistake. Groaning inwardly she sat on the bed, the box in her hand. Dylan's bloody Important Novel. The result of two years' work, still nowhere near completion. She recalled her reply to Josh's question, "What's it about, this important novel?" – "A sort of stream of consciousness thing." Recalled also, in the days Dylan had condescended to read passages to her, his scathing remark when she had asked him to explain a particularly obtuse paragraph, how he'd thrown up his hands in despair and said that there was no point explaining as she wouldn't understand it anyway. Arrogant bastard! Then she had an evil thought. Grabbing her coat, the disks and Tudor's car keys, she ran downstairs and slammed the front door after her.

At one a.m. the following morning, she pushed back her chair and stretched her aching back. Ten hours earlier she had fed the first disk into the newly leased KidzStuff computer and started reading the text. Some of it was familiar and she recognised the names of his central characters, Gandalph (in homage to Tolkein, though she knew he had never actually read *Lord of the Rings*) and Rosenkrantz. In a moment of evilness, she did a global change. Gandalph to Graham, and Rosenkrantz to Roger. Graham and Roger. Then she randomly shaded large chunks of text and hit the delete button. Warming to the game, she then globally changed the locations from the islands of Gozo and Malta to The Little Known Isles of Stockport and Rotherham, and the time from the present day to a century into the future. Scanning through the text she came across other characters and changed their names too, this time settling on a floral theme. Sylvia to Pansy, Angelique to Our Violet, Marisa to Daisy, Roderick to That Bastard Dylan. That done, she did a global change on random words. Love to potato, death to mango, hate to artichoke, fuck to doodle, penis to winkle and destiny to apothecary. By the time she had finished playing with the text of the first disk she realised that it now numbered only fifty pages instead of two hundred and fifty. Before continuing she slipped out to the off-licence and bought herself a bottle of wine. Warming to the task, she fed the remaining disks into the drive and continued her edit. By the time she had finished the bottle of Barolo, Dylan's Important Novel was a more manageable four hundred pages. The content read like total crap, but then, she thought, laughing out loud, "What would an eejit like me know, eh, Dylan?"

On finishing the task however she realised that in the grand scheme of things, it made no difference. This was only a copy. Dylan still had the original, and all he had to do when he realised that his precious disks were missing was to make another copy. A troublesome detail, but nonetheless doable. She felt suddenly deflated. Dylan would never know, for what was the point of returning the corrupted disks. He would only chuck them in the Aga, if he ever got the damn thing to light again.

Having eaten nothing since breakfast, the bottle of wine had gone straight to her head. At least that was the excuse she gave herself, for who but a drunk person would think of printing out the newly edited version of the Important Novel, stuffing it in an envelope with a covering letter, and posting it off to Dylan's agent Geoffrey Mandelson?

The moment the post office clerk took the padded envelope out of her hand and franked the postage stamps, she had second thoughts, but it was too late. She didn't tell Josh or Tudor what she had done and tried to put it from her mind, but jumped every time the office door opened or the phone rang in case it was Dylan. But he didn't call, didn't come looking for her, didn't make any attempt at an apology. It left her feeling hollow. Had she meant so little to him? Evidently, was the conclusion she came to when, heading towards Christmas, there was still no contact. She wondered how long it would take Geoffrey Mandelson to get back to him, and her stomach turned over in fear of what his reaction would be when he found out what she had done, in the same way it had over the anonymous letter she had sent to Monica.

Tudor was spending Christmas with his widowed mother in Chepstow so, rather than spend Christmas alone, and with some encouragement from Maisie, Hope decided to go home. She was excited by the prospect of a family Christmas after the three she'd spent away. Josh too was heading home to Galway so they took the train together to Liverpool and caught the ferry for Dublin. It was a nightmare crossing with high winds and a very angry Irish sea. Most of the passengers were seasick but, recalling the medicinal brandy and port of two years previously, they kept sea sickness at bay by imbibing a fair amount of the concoction, huddled together in the corner of the bar, where they had spread out their rucksacks and set up camp for the overnight crossing. It was at that point, after three hefty measures, that she confided in Josh. He laughed like a drain. He thought it was hilarious and when the hysteria had died down said, "So what? He still has his fucking Important Novel complete and uncorrupted on his computer, hasn't he?"

It made perfect sense so she put it from her mind.

"What do you reckon he's doing now?" Josh said after a while. "You reckon he's still living on that mountain?"

Hope had no idea. In fact it occurred to her at that moment that far from wondering what Dylan was doing, the only time he crossed her mind was in the context of the Important Novel and her fear that, in light of her creative editing, he might be a bit pissed off, and thus she might suffer some fall-out. She certainly wasn't pining for him which surprised her, though the mental image of him naked but for his socks, hair on end and covered with feathers from the burst pillow was something of a turn-off.

"Do you know," she said to Josh, "I don't really care one way or the other."

"Good for you," he said. "He didn't deserve you."

It was one of those moments. He was looking deep into her eyes and she could feel his breath on her cheek. For a moment she thought, hoped, that he was going to kiss her, but the moment passed and he glanced away.

"Anyway," he said, "bollox to him, I say."

She laughed to hide her disappointment. "Bollox to him!" she repeated lifting her almost empty glass.

"One for the road?" he asked, pushing himself to his feet.

When the bar closed for the night they settled down. Josh opened out his sleeping bag and covered them with it as they laid their heads on their rucksacks. Lulled and relaxed by the amber spirits she soon fell asleep.

When she opened her eyes again she was lying cosy and snug in the crook of his arm and he was snoring gently, out for the count. She lay still enjoying the closeness for a while then dropped off again. When she woke again, for a moment she was disorientated. She was still lying under the sleeping bag but she was alone. The sea was noticeably calmer though. Sitting up she rubbed her eyes. There was a dull brandy ache at the back of her skull and her teeth felt as if there was grass growing on them. The rest of the bar was gradually coming to life too, and as she scanned the room she saw Josh picking his way through the supine bodies, two mugs of coffee in his hands.

"Here," he said, handing one to her. "How's the head?" He sat down beside her again and pulled the sleeping bag over his knees.

"Bit fragile."

Digging into his pocket he pulled out a packet of Nurofen. "Here. Wash a couple of these down with the coffee."

She gratefully took the tablets and swallowed them with a slug of fairly putrid beverage, but it made a pleasant change to be the mindee as opposed to the minder. Dylan was such a hypochondriac. A slight sniffle and he'd be in bed for three days with the 'flu'. Any minor ache or pain was magnified out of all proportion. On one occasion he had insisted that she drive him into Swansea to the A&E because he was convinced that a small spot on his scalp was a melanoma. "It's just a pimple," she assured him, it being three in the morning. But he wouldn't be persuaded and became quite upset so she'd given in for peace's sake. After a four-hour wait his melanoma had indeed turned out to be a common or garden pimple, but he was unapologetic.

When the ferry finally docked they caught the bus to Heuston Station. The Galway train was about to leave so there was only time for a swift goodbye before he did a bomby legger to catch it before the barrier closed.

She had to hang around for an hour before the Westport train left. Feeling tired, grubby and sweaty, she fell asleep as soon as the train pulled out of the station, despite the fact that the rest of her fellow passengers were full of Christmas cheer. She dreamt about Josh, a disjointed but unashamedly erotic dream, and only surfaced again as the train pulled into Westport station three and three-quarter hours later.

* * *

After three days however she wondered what had possessed her to go home for Christmas. It got her to wondering if the phenomenon of Christmas was like childbirth, in as much as apparently one suffers total memory loss about the horrors as soon as it has passed.

The main problem centred around her mother and her sister Charity who had a difficult relationship at the best of times. Added to their constant squabbling was the ordeal of the relations, amongst their number the normally mild-mannered Uncle Jack who, given but a whiff of whiskey, turned into a creepy seven-handed letch, and Auntie Nora, she of the Snide Aside. She got through it however without alienating anyone, and as soon as her train pulled out of the station bound for Dublin again she felt a pang of loneliness watching her father waving from the platform as the veil of amnesia settled.

* * *

Marvo's threat to go to the cops didn't materialise but, as she had feared in the wake of the party fiasco, business for KidzStuff was non-existent. Bad news travels fast. Rosemary didn't demand her deposit back, and in the end she didn't sue Tudor, but her threat of 'you'll never work in this town again,' clichéd though it was, proved chillingly accurate. Four months later after a dismal Christmas season, and with only a few bookings for Mr Custard and Tudor and Chalky in the diary, Tudor admitted defeat. Hope, although she couldn't be held responsible for Tudor's reaction, still felt guilty about the whole debacle. Then he announced that he was winding up KidzStuff because Terry, the theatrical agent, had found him a gig on a cruise liner. He was apologetic in giving her two weeks' notice, but under the circumstances she could hardly blame him. They weren't making enough to pay the office rent, let alone her wages.

"Well, make sure Marvo's not on the bill," she said.

"Any fisticuffs and you could be clapped in irons and confined to the brig – whatever that might be."

Tudor packed his bag, packed Chalky in his case, and went off to sea. He let the house to her at a nominal rent and she signed on with a temp agency, mainly because she had no plan 'B' so hadn't come up with a better strategy.

Because he was studying for his finals she saw little of Josh in the months after Christmas. At least that's what she put it down to, but at the end of May on a sunny Friday evening, he turned up unexpectedly. She had been sitting out on the back step enjoying the last of the evening sunshine after being cooped up all day in the windowless insurance company's dungeon of an office. She hadn't seen him at all in a couple of weeks and, although resigned to the fact that he didn't fancy her in the slightest, she was genuinely glad he'd called.

"So how did it go?" she asked as she opened the bottle of wine he'd brought along.

Josh rummaged in Tudor's kitchen cupboard and extracted two tall tumblers. "OK, I suppose. If I'm lucky I'll get a two-two. So how about yourself? How's the temping going?"

Hope filled the two tumblers with wine then sat down on the back step, leaving room for him. "Grim," she said. "I'm bored out of my brain and I feel like a fecking pit pony. The office has no bloody windows."

He sat down beside her and stretched his legs out into the yard. "So what are you doing there?"

Hope shrugged. "Boring stuff. Typing, photocopying, making tea."

"No. I mean what are you *doing* there? Chuck it. Come to the States with me for the summer."

"The States. With you?"

Josh nodded. "Yeah. Why not? I'm heading to Boston for a week to see my brother, then on to Martha's Vineyard until September. He reckons he can get me seasonal work on one of the ferries."

"But I'm broke."

"And bored out of your tree. Come on. It'll be fun," he coaxed.

"But I've nowhere to stay, no job, no visa, nothing," she protested.

"So what? Cian won't mind. He can put us both up for the first week, and we can play it by ear after that. I'm sure he can find you a job too, or at least point you in the right direction." When she didn't reply he nudged her in the ribs. "Come on! Give it a lash! Live dangerously! Take a chance!"

"Done there, been that," she said, "and look where it got me."

He gave her a wry look. "And temping in the black hole of Calcutta's better because …?"

His attitude annoyed and flustered her. Granted he had a point, but at the end of the day it was way simpler for him than it was for her. He had a student visa, a job and presumably a plane ticket. "Don't be such a smartarse," she snapped, but he wasn't easily put off.

"OK. Give me one good reason why you'd rather stay here than go on another adventure," he said and anticipating her reply, added, "and yer man, Bollox-Head, doesn't count."

Despite herself, she cracked a smile. "*Bollox-Head*?"

He grinned back at her. "It works for me. Or 'Wanker' if you'd prefer."

"No, no. Bollox-Head works ... better than Important Fecking Novelist, anyway."

He topped up their tumblers. "So how about it? Throw caution to the wind, or go back down t'pit?"

It was a tempting offer but, truth be told, it wasn't just about being too broke to afford the air fare – it had just as much to do with the fact that in the two weeks Josh had been off the scene, she'd really missed him. The realisation left her feeling suddenly uncomfortable and a touch awkward now he was sitting close beside her on Tudor's back step. Since running after Dylan and landing beyond the back of beyond she'd had no social life outside the village pub, and Josh and Tudor were the only real friends she'd made of her own accord. In the five weeks that she'd been temping she hadn't stayed anywhere more than a few days which hadn't given her the opportunity to make new friends through work either.

That made her officially Hope No-Mates.

Then there was his almost offhand suggestion: 'Come to the States with me.' Did that mean *with* me, or with *me*? Was it just a throwaway remark or had he given it serious thought? Still wounded and a touch vulnerable after her experience with Dylan despite her denials, she was afraid to make assumptions. All she managed was, "Um …".

"Tick-tock-tick-tock," he said grinning and rocking his head from side to side. "I'm off on Sunday."

"Sunday!"

He nodded. "Yep."

Hope gulped back her wine to hide her confusion. He was staring at her, waiting for an answer, but she still had no clue if he had another agenda, or indeed if he was that bothered one way or another whether she went with him or not. The words frying-pan and fire flashed across her mind.

"Um … sorry, can't," she said, looking away. "No chance I'd be able to organise money and stuff by Sunday."

She heard him sigh beside her, then push himself up.

"Pity," he said.

They said their goodbyes at the door, both over-animated and jolly. There was a clash of noses as they exchanged an awkward kiss on the cheek, then he was gone.

As she watched him walk away down the road she was overcome by a sense of regret, but didn't have the courage to run after him.

* * *

One lunch-time towards the end of the summer, while strolling through the shopping precinct, she suddenly came face to face with a huge poster of Dylan Jones in the window of WH Smith. It was a suitably arty poster, black and white with him looking broody and very Daniel Day Lewis. Confused, she just stared at it open-mouthed. *Stockport Pier: International Number One Bestseller*, the legend at the bottom of the poster read.

Stockport Pier?

Inside the store there was a huge pile of hardbacks on a table close to the door with a smaller version of the window poster hanging overhead. Hope picked up a copy and opened the fly leaf.

"Dylan Jones, 37, lives with his partner, Laura, in rural West Wales. This is his first novel" it read. His *partner* Laura? She felt a flood of resentment that the copy didn't read his partner *Hope*, but then mentally slapped herself for being pathetic. Curiosity got the better of her and she idly flicked through the pages. The names, Graham, Roger, Our Violet, That Bastard Dylan and The Little Known Isle of Stockport leapt out at her. Her stomach turned over. The Important Novel, or more accurately her cocked-up version of the Important Novel, a Number 1 bestseller? How come? It was total crap. This is crazy, she thought. Absurd. It doesn't make sense.

In a state of disbelief she went back to work but couldn't concentrate, so she left early feigning sickness.

Still unable to grasp the fact that Dylan's Important Novel, the novel that she had spent a drunken ten hours totally adulterating, was now at the top of the bestseller list, she found herself back at WH Smith. The pile had reduced considerably since lunch-time. Dithering for a moment she picked up a copy and took it to the pay point. When she got home she attempted to read it but gave up after two chapters, which admittedly was a chapter further than she had managed with *Ulysses*, but did that mean it was a great novel? Hardly. Am I missing something here, she thought and ploughed on for a further chapter but was once more defeated. It did made more sense now that it sported commas, full stops and the odd semicolon, and there was less stream-of-consciousness crap, but she was still stumped as to how it was at the top of the bestseller list, and the *international* bestseller list to boot.

By accident she caught an arts programme on BBC2 later that night and *Stockport Pier* was given a glowing review by all the panel. "Satire at its most brilliant," was one quote. "Side-splitting funny, but a shrewd tongue-in-cheek analogy of the consumer society" another, and Dylan was quite favourably compared to both Samuel Beckett and George Orwell, but she suspected that was solely down to the satirical title. Tolkien was named as a major influence (more crap – to her knowledge Dylan had never read *Lord of the Rings*) and there was reference to the two-book, seven-figure deal the author had signed across the pond. Talk also of the film rights allegedly bought for another frightening figure, and conjecture amongst the panel as to which actor would be most suitable to play Roger. Richard E Grant topped the poll with Kenneth Branagh as Graham, and Angelica Houston to play Our Violet. Ironically the general consensus for the part of That Bastard Dylan was evenly split between Daniel Day Lewis and Liam Neeson. There was even talk of a Booker nomination.

Enough!

She switched off the TV. But there it was. The bitter realisation came to her that if she didn't wake up within the next five seconds, Dylan's Important Novel actually was *important*, at least as far as the literary establishment was concerned, and this caused her to finally agree with his often-aired opinion they must all be cretins.

* * *

"Funny thing, fate," Reuben said. They were in Tudor's Morris Minor Traveller driving along the Mumbles Road, around the elegant curve of Swansea Bay.

"Fate? If I hadn't been drunk I'd never have done it," Hope said.

He grinned. "My point exactly."

"So you're telling me it was fate that all that happened? Destiny? Because if that's the case then it means I had no control over my actions, so how can I be held accountable? Bit like poor old Judas."

"Ah, Judas. Poor fellow. The victim of propaganda in my opinion, but all the same, sadly, we are all still accountable."

Hope sighed. "He made a bloody fortune, you know."

"Judas? I don't think so."

"No! Dylan. Made a few million anyway." She'd seen a piece in one of the Sunday supplements the previous year showing his 'Tuscan hideaway' with a smiling Dylan, his arm around Laura, sitting at the edge of the infinity pool. "The next book didn't do so well, but you can't switch on the telly these days without he's up there spouting off, the resident intellectual, pretending to be some kind of sodding Welsh Salman Rushdie."

"Hmmm. Still bitter, I see," Reuben commented as they drew to a halt at a set of traffic lights.

"So why am I here?" she asked after a brief silence. "Obviously my actions, though admittedly not well intentioned at the time, didn't do Dylan any harm. In fact, but for me he'd probably be back on the PR treadmill."

Reuben turned his head and looked over his shoulder to the back seat. Hope followed his gaze and her eyes fell on a large padded envelope addressed to Geoffrey Mandelson.

"Is that it?" she asked.

He nodded. "That's it. *Stockport Pier*. Waiting to be posted."

"So we're back before I sent it?"

He nodded again. "That's right. November 1990. Kylie Minogue released 'Step Back in Time'. Appropriate, wouldn't you say? Got to Number 4. A particular favourite of mine."

Hope stared at the envelope. Although she was long over Dylan, had long since let go of the baggage that rejection and betrayal had laid upon her, she still harboured a niggling feeling that it wasn't fair. How come he got to be so bloody successful when, had it been left to him, he'd probably never have finished the fecking thing? He must have been aware that it was she who had made the changes, she who had posted it off to Geoffrey Mandelson, but had he sought her out to say thanks? Had he ever acknowledged her part in it? Of course not. Why would he?

"It's your choice," Reuben said. "To post or not to post? That is the question."

"You mean I have a choice?"

"Of course."

Leaning over the seat, she picked up the weighty envelope. It would be so easy to chuck it in the nearest bin. Dylan would be none the wiser. She wondered in passing if Laura would have stuck it out had he not made it big. Would she have put up with his tortured genius persona? Hardly. It's amazing what some women will put up with to sustain a lifestyle.

"So what's it to be?" The lights changed. Reuben slipped the Traveller into gear and drove on. "Post office or bin? Bear in mind that if you were to drop it in the nearest bin, *technically* you'd be righting a wrong."

He had a point. She gave a wicked smile. "I would, wouldn't I?"

Reuben signalled and pulled in to the kerb outside the General Post Office. "I think it's make-your-mind-up time."

The fickle finger of fate. There lying in her lap was the instrument of Dylan's success ... or if she chose to dump it, his continued failure. She felt suddenly powerful. But what was the point in being petty? Dylan was history.

Opening the car door she held out her hand. "You'd better give me a fiver," she said. "For the postage."

Chapter 20

It was her mother's accident that brought Hope home to Ireland in the September of '92. Maisie Prior had driven smack into a tractor which was on the wrong side of the road on a sharp bend on a narrow country lane. When Hope dashed into Galway University Hospital after grabbing the first available flight from Cardiff airport, then the Galway train which she'd made by the skin of her teeth, sick with worry, she'd found her father pacing the corridor outside the operating theatre. She ran down the corridor and hugged him. He looked thinner, older and was grey in the face from the shock and the fear. Charity appeared then with two cups of tea from the vending machine and there was more hugging and the two girls cried a lot until the surgeon came out of theatre to tell them that Maisie Prior was a very lucky woman. But for the air bag she wouldn't have stood a chance, and had got away lightly with a badly broken arm and collar bone, a broken jaw and a lacerated right leg. He told them that in time she should make a full recovery. It was sighs of relief all round and more tears, this time of joy. Although the nurse suggested they go home to get some sleep, they refused and hung around, still running on adrenaline, until Maisie regained consciousness and was well enough for a brief visit. Later that day, light-headed from lack of sleep and buzzing from an excess of caffeine, Hope and Charity sat together in the kitchen of their childhood home. Their father, exhausted, was asleep.

Hope commented on how thin he looked, whereupon Charity commented, "Why wouldn't he be? He's been through hell and back what with the cancer and now this."

Hope felt a huge pang of guilt that she hadn't been there, and straight away rashly resolved to stick around to nurse her mother back to health. .

"But what about your job?" Charity said, surprised by Hope's untypical altruism.

Hope shrugged, a touch embarrassed. As far as her family was concerned she had a fabulous job in PR, was doing great, and couldn't possibly consider coming home, when in reality she was just about keeping body and soul together on a boring treadmill of a job. She had told them about her break-up with Dylan when it had happened, but although she'd related to her mother chapter and verse how she'd caught him in bed with Laura, she couldn't bring herself to admit what she'd done to his manuscript. Later that year in a phone call, Maisie had wistfully commented in passing how she'd seen Dylan interviewed by Melvin Bragg on *The South Bank Show,* and how she'd had no idea he was such a talented writer, the subtext being 'what a pity you didn't stick it out a bit longer now he's so successful'.

Three days before Maisie was due out of hospital, Hope returned to Swansea to collect her stuff. She'd been sharing a house with two other girls since moving out of Tudor's two months previously. Not that Tudor had wanted her to move out, but since returning from his last cruise with a nineteen-year-old Filipina bride in tow she had felt, naturally enough, somewhat uncomfortable invading their space, so despite the happy couple's protests, she had replied to an ad she'd seen in the local newsagent's window and moved on.

Maisie was so touched that she'd give up her amazing job and her fabulous life in Wales in order to care for her, was so moved and thrilled skinny, that Hope hadn't the heart to tell the truth that she didn't give a toss for her current job as office dogsbody at a small PR firm. When she had applied for the post of PA to the Managing Director, she'd had hopes that the job would pan out like Porter & French and that she would be given the same level of responsibility, but her new boss was a whole other kettle of fish. An anal-retentive control freak, he had no understanding of the concept of delegation, and initiative was a dirty word. Her expectations certainly weren't realised when she found herself filing, answering the phone and running errands. In reality, when push came to shove, she was pleased to have an excuse to start over.

Maisie took six months to get back on her feet during which time Hope fell into a comfortable routine of housekeeping and cooking the family meals. Her father, a civil servant, had never been particularly house-trained as Maisie spoilt him rotten. Also Hope suspected early on he had resorted to the male gender's cunning plan whereby any household chore that they are nagged into doing is subtly sabotaged, as in sticking a red sock in with the white wash, so there is no fear of a repeat request. It was a lot easier than housekeeping for Dylan, though she found it hard sometimes living back at home and being accountable for her movements. To get out of the house and also to earn some cash she worked four nights a week in a pub. Most of her friends had moved away and the weekend scrum in the disco didn't appeal, so working in the pub, chatting to and sometimes flirting with the punters, was a social life of sorts.

Shortly before Christmas she caught a repeat of *The South Bank Show*, the one with Dylan's interview. Melvin seemed to take quite a shine to him, but then Dylan had adopted his most charming self-deprecating persona. Even after the guts of two years it still rankled when he alluded to the support he had received from his partner Laura who, incidentally, sat beside him, simpering in Donna Karan. Hope wondered fleetingly how long it would be before she caught him shagging some young one.

At Easter, Charity, who never stuck at a job or a relationship for more than six months and was currently a nail technician, arrived home from Dublin to announce that she was engaged. There was a stunned silence.

"You're not up the d … um … well … you know?" her father said, blustering until Maisie gave him a hefty nudge.

"Congratulations, pet," she said, hugging her daughter, whilst making faces at her husband over her shoulder. "Who's the lucky fella? Is it Martin?"

"God, no! I finished with him ages ago. It's Goran," Charity said. "He's an Australian and I met him in Templebar. He's a juggler."

"A juggler? That's eh – nice," Maisie said. "Isn't it, Tom? A juggler."

"A juggler? What class of a job's that?" Tom said, impervious to Maisie's attempt to prevent the rain falling on Charity's parade.

"I worked for a ventriloquist once," Hope butted in, "and he made quite a good living, Dad, honestly."

"He juggles chainsaws," Charity added. "He's very good at it."

"He'd fecking want to be," Tom said. "Jesus! What class of a job is that at all?"

Charity burst out laughing. "Only kidding. He's a journalist really and he doesn't really juggle chainsaws. He's only doing the juggling to earn a few extra bob while he's interning at the *Irish Press*. He's on some kind of exchange programme. But you should have seen your faces. Anyway, we're planning an August wedding because Goran's visa runs out in September."

"August! But that's way too soon!" Maisie wailed. "A wedding takes planning. There's not enough time."

"Sorry, it has to be August," Charity said, "or the groom won't be around." Then, sensing that Maisie wasn't keen on giving ground, added, "Of course I could always go back with him and we could have one of those quickie beach ceremonies in Bali on the way."

Falling for it hook, line and sinker, Maisie folded. "You'll do no such thing! You'll get married here in the church. Do you want your grandparents to be spinning in the grave, God rest them?" She blessed herself. "You might not get a Saturday, mind you. Not now. People usually book two years ahead for these things, you know."

Charity gave Hope a surreptitious wink. "That doesn't matter. Any day suits."

Although she was under the impression that she'd got what she wanted, Maisie suddenly frowned. "It's only four months! How will I arrange a wedding in four months? There's the cake, the invitations, the –"

"Chill, Mum," Charity said. "Hope was in party organising, remember? It'll be no bother to her. Will it, Hope?"

"No bother at all," Hope replied, her stomach churning at the memory of her last debacle.

Maisie was all agog about the guest list. This was, after all, the first family wedding. She had listed some one hundred and fifty uncles, aunts, friends and neighbours before Charity called a halt.

"Mum! Please. I don't want that big of a do. I don't know half of those people, and there's still Goran's list."

Maisie looked disappointed. "Oh. Right." Then, after a brief pause, "So are his people coming over from Australia?"

Charity shrugged. "Don't know, but he's got lots of mates in London."

"*Mates*? But what about family?" Maisie said. "Surely family members should get preference."

"There you go!" Charity snapped. "Taking over again. Look, Mum, this is *my* wedding and I don't want a load of wrinklies I haven't seen for years clogging up the fecking dance floor!"

"Don't you take that tone with me!" Maisie warned, squaring up to her daughter, but Charity was up for a fight.

"Well, if that's how you feel about it, I'll just sod off to fecking Australia!"

"You'll do no such thing, my girl!"

Tom had melted away at the first talk of weddings in

case he was called upon for an opinion. Charity and Maisie had an uneasy relationship at the best of times so he knew the warning signs and was smart enough to know when to run for cover.

Hope stepped between them and yelled, "Hey! Stop, you two! Time out!"

"But it's *my* wedding," Charity whinged. "She's spoiling it, like she always does."

Maisie settled into martyr mode. "Well, I'm only your mother. I only ever want what's best for you. And if you're determined to alienate half the family…"

"Stop it!" Hope repeated. "This is a wedding. It's supposed to be fun, but if you two are going to be at each other's throats at this stage, maybe Charity would be better off in Bali."

Charity never had any intention of buggering off to Bali to get hitched so she quickly backed down. "I never said I didn't want *any* relations. Just not the ones we haven't seen for years, that's all."

"And I never said I wanted *all* the relations – you just jumped down my throat before I had a chance to finish what I was saying," Maisie said. "And I'm sorry if I spoil things for you. That's never my intention." She was in full martyr mode now, even managing to squeeze a tear out of the corner of her eye.

"Charity didn't mean that. Did you?" Hope said, glaring at her sister, and when Charity said nothing, repeated more insistently, "*Did you?*"

"No," Charity mumbled. "I suppose not."

"Well, I have to see to the potatoes," Maisie said stiffly as she made a tactical retreat. "They'll be boiled to a mush."

"God! She's going to drive me nuts!" Charity said when Maisie was out of earshot, then slumped theatrically down on the sofa. "I can't deal with this. You'll have to organise it or I'll be a fecking half-orphan before the Big Day."

Hope shook her head. No change there then, she thought, well aware that it wasn't from the wind that Charity had got her tendency towards histrionics.

After a tense lunch, Hope bit the bullet. "Now, about this wedding," she said with forced enthusiasm. "What's the budget?"

Although Hope enjoyed the prospect of organising the wedding, looking forward to having something to get her teeth into again, the reality was rather different. On almost every occasion that her sister was home before the Big Day, she spent most of the time refereeing and keeping mother and daughter apart, with the exception of the weekend the groom made a visit to meet the folks. Despite Charity's attempts to wind her up, Maisie kept her cool. Hope didn't really take to Goran. Her father was polite, but it was obvious that he was a little intimidated by the tall talkative Aussie. And he was very tall, over six foot six, a slim but muscular surfer-dude type. Longish sun-bleached hair, thin Eastern-European, looking features, his father being from the former Yugoslavia. He was quite charming though and after the event Hope put her lack of enthusiasm for her brother-in-law-to-be down to fact that he reminded her so strongly of Dylan.

On the other occasions when Charity was home without her intended, Tom kept a very low profile. Early on he had decided to make the wine for the reception. A keen winemaker, he made that his excuse to disappear into the garage at the first sign of trouble.

At the beginning of July, Hope travelled up to Dublin and she, Charity and Sandy, Charity's flatmate, best friend and chief bridesmaid, went shopping for the frocks. The whole experience was an eye-opener for Hope. Adidas didn't do wedding clobber to her knowledge, but in the event Charity, whom Hope had rarely seen in a dress after her First Holy Communion (and she remembered that as being a battle of wills between mother and daughter) and who favoured urban sports gear or Levi's, was unaccountably drawn like a moth to the flame to big extravagant meringue dresses. She finally settled on a white silk number with a tight bodice, low back, big skirt and detachable train. Finding nothing in the bridal shop that she and Sandy could agree on, Hope suggested a trip down Grafton Street to Monsoon, where they picked up two identical strappy bias-cut dresses in claret moiré for under a hundred quid each.

At 1.30 they adjourned to the Bad Ass Café where Charity had arranged to hook up with Goran for lunch.

The café was crowded but as they looked around for a table Charity said, "There he is," and they followed her to a corner table.

Goran was on his feet.

"Hi, petal," he said, planting a kiss on Charity's chops, which caused a wave of *déjà vu* to overtake Hope.

It was the way he said it. He could have been Dylan. So momentarily disconcerted was she that she didn't notice the other occupant of the table until a familiar voice said, "Good Grief! Hope! How are you?"

It was Josh Tierney.

Hope felt a flood of happiness. "McFling!"

Josh leapt up and they hugged like the long-lost buddies that they were.

"How do you two know each other?" Goran asked. "And what's with the McFling?"

Hope and Josh both laughed, then Josh said, "Oh, didn't you know, Ginger McFling's my evil twin."

They sat down to lunch. Josh, it turned out, also worked at the *Irish Press* and over lunch Hope and he regaled the others with stories about Ginger McFling, Mr Custard and Tudor and Chalky, finishing off with an account of the Marvo incident, much embroidered for effect, though characteristically Charity was more concerned for the puppet than she was for Tudor.

"Poor Chalky," she said. "Was he hurt?"

"Only a minor temporary limb loss and a few abrasions," Josh said. "Nothing a dab of paint and a couple of screws couldn't fix."

"You should do your Ginger McFling thing with me in Templebar," Goran suggested after their laughter had died down. "Might encourage the punters to McFling a bit more cash into the hat."

"Thanks all the same, but my pratfall days are over," Josh declined.

And Hope was sorry. She'd have quite liked to see McFling in action again.

"So what's Tudor doing these days?" he asked while the others were chatting amongst themselves.

"Oh, didn't you know? He got married again. "

Josh's eyebrows took a hike up his forehead. "Are you serious?"

Hope nodded. "Yeah. A gorgeous Asian girl half his age who he met on a cruise. She's a masseuse."

Josh laughed. "Well, good for him! I hope it works out this time."

"Me too," she agreed.

"And what about the Important Novelist?" he said after a pause. "Did he ever get in touch?"

Hope gave a derisive snort. "Don't be silly!"

"Well, he owes you one."

"A legend in his own lunch-time." She sighed. "I'm afraid it's a case of selective amnesia."

"I couldn't believe it when I saw his ugly mug all over the papers. He did a signing in Boston, you know? I was there. I'd stopped off to see Cian again on my way home from Martha's Vineyard."

"You saw him?"

He shook his head. "No. I was tempted to go into the bookstore and make a show of him, but Cian and I got bladdered instead."

"Pity," she said. "But you'd probably only have been arrested or something."

"So what brought you home?" he asked.

Hope told him about her mother's accident and was about to go into her usual story about giving up the big PR job when she remembered who she was talking to. Lowering her voice, conscious that Charity might overhear, she said, "Actually, it was a good excuse to start over. I was going mental working for this control freak. My folks think I had a big job in PR – but it was hardly a big job. A chimp could have managed it. Anyway, I got major Brownie points for dropping everything and coming home, so don't say anything to Charity."

"Why would I?" he said.

She felt silly about the lie and felt she should explain. "I suppose I was embarrassed because I made such a mistake running away with Dylan. And I wanted them to be proud of me. And technically it wasn't a lie. I *was* the Managing Director's PA. He just wouldn't let me do anything that required an intellect. I just let my mum jump to her own conclusions."

"So how's your mum now?" he asked.

"Oh she's great, thank God. Though I'm beginning to get a bit stir crazy living back at home."

He nodded. "I can imagine. So what are your plans?"

"Plans?" Hope didn't have any. She shrugged. "Well, there's the wedding to get out of the way, but after that, I haven't a clue."

"You're not going back to Wales then?"

Hope shook her head and laughed. "No. No reason to really. No one was tripping over themselves to throw amazing employment opportunities at me, and I'd say as soon as I told my boss I wasn't coming back he called the chimp-keeper for my replacement."

"It's just I have a cousin who has a PR firm. Hackett & McAllister. Have you heard of them?"

Hope shook her head.

"They only started up about six months ago, but they're doing OK. They might be looking for someone, and your CV looks pretty good. I mean you worked in PR in Dublin too, didn't you? Then there was the event management."

Hope laughed. "A couple of kids' parties? Hardly event management."

Josh grinned back at her. "Hey, don't knock it. If it wasn't for Marvo, that party would have been a triumph. Anyway, you could be economical with the details about that and your last job. I mean I wouldn't mention the chimp."

Hope laughed.

"I'll give James a call if you like," he offered.

"That would be great," she said, excited by the prospect.

There was an explosion of laughter from the other end of the table at that point and Goran said, "Hey, Josh, the girls here don't believe I was a drag queen once. Tell them the story."

Josh related an incident the previous January when, for a bet, Goran had dressed up in full drag and had mimed to Diana Ross at an open mike night at the George.

Hope didn't get the chance to ask Josh about himself as, very soon after, he and Goran had to go back to work. Outside the café Josh asked her for a contact number in case he got any joy from his cousin, James Hackett. Hope was a touch disappointed that he felt he had to qualify the request like that, more so that there was no mention of meeting up again.

"Josh is cute," Charity said as they were walking down Crown Alley towards the Quays. "So what's the story there?"

"No story," Hope said. "We're just mates."

Sandy make a *pwah* sound. "Well, I wouldn't chuck him out of bed for eating crisps. Is he coming to the wedding?"

Charity shrugged. "I don't know. I've never met him before, but I can get Goran to invite him if you're interested."

"You bet," Sandy said, and Hope felt a sharp stab of jealousy.

"He's gay," she blurted out before she could stop herself and the other two groaned.

"Wouldn't you bloody know it? "Sandy moaned. "All the fittest men are either married or bloody well gay!"

Chapter 21

As the wedding drew closer, Hope's time was taken up with the final details, such as booking accommodation for the American relations, sorting out the flowers for the bride and bridesmaids, floral decorations for the church, the wedding car etc. Charity had set her heart on a cream vintage Bentley and Hope was smugly pleased with herself when she managed to track one down in Longford which was available on the given day, though the fact that the nuptials were to take place on a Thursday possibly had something to do with it. Maisie was making the cake, and Agnes Walsh, Tom's eldest sister, was decorating it. As there was no love lost between the two sisters-in-law, Hope braced herself for fireworks. Much to her surprise however, both women were models of reserve and self-control and the icing interval passed without a harsh word or any bodily injury to either woman.

Two weeks before the big day, she got a call from Josh.

"I talked to James and he *is* looking for someone," he said. "He wants you to give him a call."

Hope was delighted and took down the number. "Thanks a million, Josh. You're a star," she said, excited at the prospect of a new job and of basically getting her life back.

"Not a bother," he said, then her heart lifted even further when appended to his goodbye was the promise, "See you at the wedding."

It took two days for her to pluck up the courage to call James Hackett and she had the sense to do some serious rehearsal first in front of the bedroom mirror. She disliked interviews at the best of times, aware that when she was nervous she was inclined to come over sarcastic and occasionally aggressive. It did briefly occur to her that in the case of her interview with Roddy French this had proved to be a plus, but then Roddy was a special case and she couldn't count on Josh's cousin being of the same mind. There was also the matter of her CV. If James Hackett asked why she had left Porter & French, which he inevitably would, she could hardly reply, "Well, actually, I was shagging the managing director's brother-in-law, and buggered off to Wales with him."

She mulled over the usual clichés – 'I was looking for a new challenge' – 'I wanted to expand my people skills in another area' – but the time-lapse between leaving Dublin and starting work with KidzStuff looked a tad fishy if she went for that approach. The word 'sabbatical' came to mind, but she felt that could imply she lacked commitment. Priests took sabbaticals after years in Africa. Academics took sabbaticals and wrote theses. Teachers took sabbaticals to keep the psychiatric ward at bay. But taking into account her undistinguished employment record, the term sabbatical sounded like an excuse for unemployment, like a *resting* actor.

On the off-chance that Tudor was between cruises, she picked up the phone and dialled his number and after only a couple of rings, Suki, the new Mrs Evans, answered. Hope identified herself, enquired after her health and asked for Tudor.

After the usual greetings, Hope got straight to the point and asked him for a reference, and if he could possibly bend the truth a little as in back-dating her period of employment, explaining her predicament.

"Absolutely, my dear. No problem at all," he assured her. "I'll get to it straight away and post the reference on to you. I believe there's still KidzStuff stationery in the attic."

"So are you and Suki still on the cruise liners?" she asked, once business had been taken care of.

"My good lady has retired, so to speak, but Chalky

and I intend to return to it," he said. "Though we shan't be doing the autumn Caribbean gig on account of the baby."

"The baby! That's amazing, Tudor. When's it due?"

She could almost hear the broad proud grin spreading across his face. "September," he said. "September the fifteenth. I can hardly believe it myself."

She had an instant mental image of Tudor with the baby on one knee and Chalky on the other and gave an involuntary shudder, as in her mind's eye Chalky's face wore a scary and malevolent expression.

"Let me know if it's a boy or a girl," she said, and Tudor assured her that he would. She worried about how Chalky would react to the baby for a few moments after she replaced the receiver until common sense kicked in.

"He's only a puppet. A bloody puppet. Get a grip!" she said aloud and Maisie, who was passing through the hall at the time, gave her a very weird look.

True to his word, Tudor's glowing reference arrived three days later. On a second reading it sounded a bit over the top, but there was no time to get it amended as her interview was scheduled for the following day. In any case, she was more relaxed about the meeting, having spoken to James Hackett who sounded friendly and enthusiastic. He told her he was impressed by her experience and was looking forward to meeting her.

Taking the Monday evening train up from Westport

to Dublin she stayed overnight with Charity and Sandy. Charity was high as a kite with pre-wedding jitters and had lost at least half a stone. She was worried that the dress wouldn't fit despite the fact that it had been taken in after her final fitting the previous Wednesday. It hung under its plastic cowl on the back of her bedroom door and she obsessively kept taking it down and trying it on for size. She also had a heroic, positively volcanic zit threatening to erupt on her chin. Hope calmed her down and dabbed the offending blemish with Tiger Balm, assuring her that it would be gone by the morning.

After an uneasy night Hope fell into a deep sleep as the first watery rays of the sun poked above the horizon, and didn't wake again until after nine. A touch panicky although there was still a good two hours before her interview, she leapt out of bed and made for the shower. Charity was sitting at the kitchen table, an uneaten slice of toast in her hand, when she hurried into the kitchen, a towel wrapped turban-style around her wet hair. Her sister's chin was still a little red, the threatened spot having all but disappeared, but that fact didn't appear to have calmed her down any.

"Goran's folks flew in last night," she said as Hope helped herself to a bowl of cornflakes. "We're meeting up for lunch. I don't suppose you'd come along for moral support?"

"I'll do my best," Hope promised, "but my interview's at eleven and I don't know how long it will take."

"Hardly two fecking hours," Charity snapped. "Lunch isn't till one."

Hope sighed. "OK. Fine. Where?"

Charity looked at the piece of toast in her hand, then dropped it back onto the plate. "One o'clock. The Elephant & Castle."

Hope wanted to encourage her to eat something, but bit her tongue remembering the hissy fit her sister had thrown the last time she'd been home when Maisie, never one to beat about the bush and noticing the weight she'd lost, had asked Charity if she was developing an eating disorder.

"The sooner this bloody wedding's over the better," Maisie had hissed to Hope after Charity flounced out of the kitchen in tears. "I'll swing for that girl. I swear I will!"

At ten to eleven Hope walked into the offices of Hackett & McAllister on Crowe Street, an apprehensive knot in the pit of her stomach. A girl around her own age was behind the reception desk talking on the phone. Hope stood and waited.

"Gavin O'Mahony on line two for you, James," she said, then hung up.

"The TV presenter?" Hope said to the girl before she could stop herself.

The girl gave her a puzzled look. "Yeah?"

Hope blushed. "Sorry. I'm Hope Prior. I'm here for an interview … nerves."

"Oh, right," the girl said, checking the diary and ticking off Hope's name.

"It's just I handled Orange – I mean Gavin when I worked for Porter & French a couple of years ago – I'm babbling, aren't I?"

The girl cracked a smile, possibly on account of Hope's slip of the tongue rather than the babbling. "Just a bit," she said, then stood up. "Listen, you're early and James is running a bit late. Would you like a coffee, or on second thoughts a gallon of Rescue Remedy to calm you down?"

Hope laughed which relaxed her a little. "I think more caffeine would probably send me into orbit. I hate interviews, but I'd kill for the Rescue Remedy if you've got any."

The receptionist's name was Sonya Gallagher and Hope took a liking to her immediately.

"James is a pussycat," she said as she handed Hope the small bottle of herbal tincture to administer to herself. She squeezed a few drops onto her tongue and felt instantly calmer. Then the phone in reception rang. "Sit down there for a minute and get your breath," Sonya said heading back to her desk. "I'll give you a call when he's free."

Hope sat down and watched the minutes tick by all the way around to eleven fifteen when Sonya caught her eye and gave a nod.

"Last door at the end of the hall," she said. "Good luck."

In reality James was totally different from the mental image she had built up in her mind after speaking to him on the phone. Late thirties, slight, mousy, pale lashes. She'd expected him to be younger. He bounded round the desk as she entered, offering his hand and giving her a firm handshake.

"Glad you could make it," he said. "Sorry I kept you waiting."

"It's fine," Hope assured him. "Sonya said you were running late."

Leading her over to a sofa, he invited her to sit and took the armchair opposite. She could see her CV lying on the low glass-topped table between sofa and chair.

"Coffee?"

She shook her head. "No, thanks. I'm fine."

"I was talking to Roddy French," he said for openers and her heart sank. "He had good things to say about you."

"Really?" she replied, genuinely surprised.

He smiled. "I believe his exact words were, 'She's a great worker, has bags of initiative, but she left in a bit of a hurry'."

Hope winced. "I suppose he gave you the gory details."

"Edited highlights, but your private life's not relevant. And he said he was very sorry when you left. Apparently it was only after you moved on he realised how much you contributed to the smooth running of his life."

"He said that?"

James nodded. "And the way Josh was singing your

praises I thought I'd better see you before someone else snaps you up."

Unaccustomed to being bombed with positive affirmation, Hope just gave a weak stunned smile.

"So you left your last job because of a family crisis, I understand."

Hope nodded. "My mother had a car accident so I came home to mind her."

"And you don't want to return to your previous job?"

"I doubt it's still available. It's been over six months. But in any case I wanted to come home, and to tell you the truth, the job wasn't panning out as I'd hoped. The most challenging thing I got to do was collecting the Managing Director's dry cleaning."

"So tell me about the event organising."

Hope delved into her bag, drew out Tudor's reference and slid it across the table towards him. Picking it up, he perused it.

"Um … well, it … um …the company specialised in children's entertaining and … um … well, it sort of evolved really," she said nervously, anxious to give a good account of herself. "When I joined the company, Tudor, that's Tudor Evans the proprietor, a children's entertainer, mainly did, well – children's entertaining, but I persuaded him to go the whole nine yards, and we started to cater the total package. Marquees, entertainers, catering, decorations, party games, that kind of thing. We were planning to include adult events

– I mean – oh dear, that sounds a bit sleazy but you know what I mean. And I'm in the process of planning my sister's wedding right now, but I'd like to get back into PR. I really enjoyed working for Roddy and …" she paused.

James was sitting back, a bemused look on his face.

Her heart sank. "I'm running off at the mouth, aren't I? I've blown it."

"Not at all," he assured her. "It's refreshing to see someone with a bit of enthusiasm for the job. So … have *you* any questions?"

She frowned, caught on the hop. "Well … um … what exactly does the job entail?"

"Much the same stuff as you did for Roddy." He smiled. "And probably some dry-cleaning-collection duties. Though by the nature of our client list we also organise events such as book launches, charity events, the odd product launch, that kind of thing – so your experience on that front could be useful. The business is growing quite rapidly so I really need a good PA and according to Roddy you could well be it."

She wondered if he was actually offering her the job.

Then he continued, "Of course, you'd be doing work for my partner as well as me."

Ah, she thought, McAllister. I wonder what he's like?

He looked at his watch, a gold Rolex. "In fact, why don't we trot along to her office now and you can meet her."

Her? She had assumed the McAllister of Hackett & McAllister would be a he.

Diana McAllister was around thirty-five, plumpish and quite hard-looking with dark hair cut in a short asymmetric bob, and olive skin. Very well-groomed, very businesslike, she lacked James's warmth.

After James had introduced them she said, "I used to work with Paul Porter when he was with AF&D," without revealing how she felt about him, either professionally or on a personal level.

Appleby Formby & Drew was the London PR company where Paul had met Dylan Jones. She wondered if Diana McAllister also knew Dylan Jones but didn't ask. It got her thinking how small the world of PR was. Undoubtedly they'd discussed her CV and James had called Roddy to check up on her so it was certainly possible that Diana McAllister would be aware that she had run off with her ex-colleague's brother-in-law. If she did though, she showed no sign of it.

"We're a small ship and everyone here pulls together," she said. "So you might find yourself working late from time to time, and I'm inclined to shout a lot when I'm under pressure, but it's nothing personal, unless of course you cock something up. Do you think you could handle that?"

Hope nodded. "I worked for Roddy French, didn't I?"

James's mouth twitched into a smile, then he glanced at Diana who gave a curt nod. "Great," he said rubbing his hands together. "When can you start? How about Monday on a month's trial?"

She almost danced along Crowe Street. After offering her the job, James had filled her in on the type of accounts the company handled. Diana specialised in publishing, as in promoting writers and books, and a number of clients had followed her when she and James had set up the company, notably four of the larger UK publishing houses. James's remit was similar to Roddy's except in the sports sector, but they had recently diversified into the charities area. She was pleasantly surprised too when he mentioned her salary and the fact that she'd be entitled to four weeks' holiday per year. She'd almost forgotten what it was like to earn decent money and the prospect of leaving penury behind was extremely appealing.

As she'd an hour to spare before she had to meet Charity and the Aussie in-laws, she found a phone box and called Josh at work but was disappointed when he was out.

She'd rashly agreed to starting the following Monday which left her only six and a half days to get her act together as well as chasing up the final details of Charity's wedding. She wondered how Maisie would react when she gave her the news that she'd got a new job and was moving to Dublin. Although she had made a full recovery, Hope was aware that her mother had got used to having her around. Then there was the question of accommodation. Charity had suggested (assuming she'd get the job) that she should take over her room and share with Sandy which was an option, but she wasn't sure they'd get on that well. Sandy was very like Charity, OK in small doses, and the apartment was terminally untidy – Hope, although not over-fussy, was used to some semblance of order. Still, she thought, it'll do for now. If it doesn't work out I can always look for somewhere else.

Aware that she was going to get nowhere if she didn't look the part and with the prospect of a respectable pay cheque, she stopped off at Marks & Spencer's and maxed out her credit card, purchasing a smart, well-cut black trouser suit, two crisp white blouses, a pair of black ankle boots, a black polo neck and a three plain white T-shirts – her new Power PA uniform. Standing in front of the mirror in the changing room, she examined her reflection. Since leaving Dublin and living with Dylan beyond the back of beyond for two years, then temping, she'd forgotten what it was like to look this smart. And smart was how she felt, what with her hair freshly cut and coloured by Maggie @ No Problem, her local Westport salon, and the new smart power-suit rig-out.

Carried away by the quest to reinvent herself, at least visually, she was fifteen minutes late arriving at Elephant & Castle. Goran, his folks and Charity were already seated and had ordered. Charity looked relieved when she caught sight of Hope walking down the restaurant towards the table, but she was still visibly tense and a touch manic.

Hope knew that her sister was nowhere near as confident as she generally appeared and that meeting Goran's parents would be an ordeal for her.

"Sorry I'm late," she said. "I had a job interview and it went on a bit."

"How did you get on?" Charity asked, eyeing up her shopping bags.

"I start next Monday on a month's trial." She was unable to suppress the wide grin spreading across her face. There were congratulatory murmurs from around the table then Goran introduced her to his folks. His father, also Goran, was a template for how his son would look thirty years hence. His mother, Mona, a well-upholstered fifty-something, fifth-generation Aussie who boasted how her forefathers were all sheep-stealers transported from Cornwall. Goran Jovanovic Senior was a plumber and Mona a teacher. They seemed like nice people. Hope didn't have to contribute much to the lunch-time conversation which was just as well because her mind was elsewhere, but Mona kept the conversation going, regaling Charity with cringe-worthy but nonetheless funny anecdotes about Goran Junior when he was a kid. She seemed to be conscious that her daughter-in-law-to-be was nervous and was trying to put her at her ease, but for some reason Charity seemed to get more and more tense as the meal progressed. Hope recognised the danger signals as her sister laughed too loud and too long at every opportunity, finally bursting into tears for apparently no reason and rushing off to the loo. Goran looked helpless so Hope hurried after her with a hasty, "I'll just ... um," to the embarrassed Antipodeans.

Charity had locked herself in the loo and refused to come out. Hope could hear her sobbing behind the door. Eventually after some coaxing the door opened and Charity slunk out.

"What's up?" Hope asked.

Charity's eyes remained steadfastly on the floor tiles. "I don't think I can go through with it," she snuffled, then dissolved into tears again, wrapping her arms around her body and rocking back and forth, tears positively spurting.

Hope was at a loss. She stood there watching her sister impotently for a few seconds, then put an arm around her shoulders. "But why not, sweetie?"

Charity just shook her head and sobbed some more, so Hope gave her a squeeze. "Look, is this just the pre-wedding jitters? What's the matter, really? Have you two had a row or something?"

"No."

"Then why the change of heart?"

Charity shrugged.

"Is it the whole rigmarole of the wedding stuff? Is it Mum?" Hope asked, frustration mounting.

Charity shrugged again. "Sort of," she said, and Hope waited for more explanation, but that appeared to be it.

"Sort of Mum, or sort of the wedding stuff?" she

asked, all too aware that there'd been more tension than usual between mother and daughter.

"Both," Charity mumbled. "I just wish we'd buggered off to Bali and had done with it."

"Bit late for that now, sunshine," Hope muttered back. "They've already printed the tea towels."

"What?"

"Nothing," Hope sighed. Charity had calmed down somewhat – at least, she wasn't actually crying, she was staring at the floor looking forlorn. She did a good forlorn. Hope had always envied her ability to look pathetic when the need arose. "Look. You still want to marry Goran, am I right?"

Charity nodded.

"So why not just bite the bullet. It's only one day. And who knows, you might even enjoy it. Anyway," she added after a pause, "cancel now and you'll have to send all the pressies back."

Charity's head shot up. "Even the deep-fat fryer?"

"Particularly the deep-fat fryer," Hope assured her. "You know what Auntie Agnes is like. Anyway, you wouldn't want to waste all those dancing lessons, would you?" Hope had suggested that for the opening dance, rather than the usual inept shuffle around the dance floor, they should wow the watching guests with a dramatic tango. "And then there's the Bentley," she added. "When else will you have the opportunity to swan around Westport in a cream vintage Bentley?"

Appealing to Charity's hidden shallows was an

underhanded strategy, but it did the trick. The two sisters rejoined Goran and his folks at the table. As they approached conversation ceased abruptly, but Charity put on a happy face.

"Sorry about that," she said. "Bit wound up," and that was the extent of her explanation.

Goran pulled out her chair for her and gave her a kiss on the back of the neck as she sat down. His parents, fair play to them, acted as if nothing had happened and Goran Senior diplomatically changed the subject by asking Hope about Westport.

Hope caught the evening train back home. Charity and Goran were driving down the following day with Goran's parents in a rental car, but Hope didn't want to wait over as she was anxious to get down to packing, and to tell her parents face to face that she was leaving. Sandy was taking the train the following morning with some other friends.

As Maisie was equally adept as her younger daughter at making a drama out of almost anything, Hope was trepidacious about breaking the news to her, but with the wedding on her mind and the American relations arriving, Maisie seemed to take it in her stride which was a relief.

Flopping down on her bed just after midnight, Hope breathed a sigh of relief. She was happy and felt optimistic for the first time in ages. New job. New start. Charity's wedding plans running like clockwork. And then there was Josh. What could possibly go wrong?

Chapter 22

Charity, Goran, and the Jovanovics arrived in Westport at lunch-time the next day. Maisie made them all tea after the introductions were made, then the bride and groom headed into town to meet up with some of Goran's mates lately arrived from London. The two sets of parents sat awkwardly around the kitchen table. Hope knew that Maisie was anxious about meeting Goran's parents, and for the first five minutes it was a touch tense, but then Mona broke the ice by complimenting Maisie on her garden, and soon the two women were exchanging notes, wandering around the garden arm-in-arm looking at the shrubs. Tom and Goran Senior talked in monosyllables until the subject of rugby came up. The Aussie also was an *aficionado*, so soon they too were shooting the breeze as if they were long-lost buddies. After a while it was time for Goran's parents to check into the hotel and freshen up for the wedding rehearsal, so they headed off at the same time that Hope had to leave for Knock Airport to collect Auntie Maureen and Uncle Ben who were flying in from Birmingham. She had hoped that Charity would oblige and leave her free to check on the final details, but she'd had an attack of Guinness amnesia and hadn't returned from Mat Molloy's pub. The flight was an hour late and it was well past six before she finally dropped them off at their hotel and returned to the ranch.

As soon as she stepped through the back door, Maisie grabbed her by the arm and dragged her outside again, dramatically putting a finger to her lips to hush her protests.

"While you were out the car man called," she whispered. "The Bentley's broken."

"Broken?"

Maisie nodded, her eyebrows knitted together with apprehension. "Broken. It won't go."

Hope shot a glance over her shoulder at the house. "Does Charity know?"

Maisie shook her head. "God no! She's bad enough as it is without giving her something else to whinge about."

"But surely they have a substitute," Hope said. "A vintage Rolls maybe?" She gave a nervous giggle.

"Surely they love us enough to give us their last Roller."

Maisie frowned. "This isn't funny, Hope. But it's a good job your mother was able to fix it."

"What?"

Maisie had a habit of using the third person occasionally for no apparent reason which could be confusing. "*I* organised a substitute," she said with an air of triumph.

Hope heaved a sigh of relief. "But that's amazing, Mum. How did you manage that?"

Maisie pursed her lips. "That's the trouble with you young ones. You don't give your elders and betters credit. As it happens I have a contact in the motor trade. Paudie Halpin. You know Paudie?"

Hope shook her head.

"Of course, you do. Paudie from Ballinafad. He has the garage. His sister's married to that fella in the planning department who was caught taking bribes." And when Hope continued to stare at her blankly, added with an air of frustration, "You do! He's bald, and he's in the drama group."

Hope still had no idea who she was talking about but for peace's sake feigned recognition, "Oh, *that* Paudie Halpin!" Then a thought struck her. "It is a *proper* wedding car?" She was well aware that Charity was liable to throw a wobbly if Paudie Halpin turned up in a beat-up taxi to take her to the church.

"Of course, it is!" Maisie snapped, annoyed that her daughter would even question it. Hope relaxed, relieved that a car crisis appeared to have been averted.

"And I've another little surprise up my sleeve for tomorrow," Maisie said smugly.

Hope waited for her to elaborate, but Maisie just tapped the side of her nose and, hearing the phone, hurried out to answer it.

The rehearsal went amazingly smoothly and afterwards the two families moved on to the hotel where Hope had booked the post-rehearsal dinner. It had started out as an intimate affair, just the immediate families, the bridesmaids and groomsmen, about twenty in all, but as many of the more distant relations and other guests were staying at the hotel the number had swelled to over forty. After dinner they drifted into the bar to be joined by some late arrivals and the evening developed into quite a party. Around midnight Hope sequestered a reluctant Charity and they got a taxi home. She was in high spirits, all anxiety having disappeared, and after a mug of Ovaltine they both went off to bed. .

The following morning was a different story though and the bride was once again like a bag of cats. But worse than that, a bag of cats with monumental hangovers. It got Hope to wondering if it was obligatory for brides to come close to cracking up before the Big Day, and, if so, was all the fuss really worth it? Maybe buggering off to Bali hadn't been such a bad idea after all. Maisie wasn't much better, stressing about the flowers and reminding Hope every couple of minutes to be sure to collect them from the florist's and to deliver Mona's corsage and the men's buttonholes to the hotel, and were they sure her hat was OK? Not too over the top? And not to forget to bring her corsage and her father's buttonhole back to the house.

"The florist's on my list, Mum. Don't worry. And the hat is gorgeous," she kept assuring Maisie, admittedly through gritted teeth after the tenth time, but to little avail. She did manage however to get both Charity and Maisie to the hairdresser's approximately on time. Sandy was already there her head in the backwash and Sharon was shampooing her hair. Maggie had laid on a jug of Buck's Fizz for them. Hope gratefully took the proffered alcohol, slugged it down and watched as the proverbial hair of the dog had immediate effect on Charity and her prickly humour instantly improved. She mouthed a silent 'thank you' to Maggie who had confided in her on a previous occasion that in her experience brides were a pain in the arse and the only way to manage them on the wedding morning was to ply them with either drink or drugs, and in extreme cases, both.

As her own short hair didn't need attention from a hairdresser between cuts, Hope hurried off to the florist to pick up the flowers while the others were getting their hair done. It was a bright sunny morning and the town was crowded with tourists, it being the height of the season, so she had difficulty parking. In desperation she had to abandon the car on a double yellow and run into the shop. She got away with it though and after delivering the corsage and buttonholes to the hotel, stopped off for a quiet ten minutes and a coffee at McCormack's.

Auntie Agnes was sitting at a table in the corner, her hair freshly crimped, munching on a bacon roll, but before Hope had a chance to effect a tactical retreat, her aunt caught sight of her and beckoned her over.

"Isn't it only wonderful about the weather, thank God?" she said, blessing herself. Hope sat down. True enough it was a lovely day, the forecast of intermittent blustery showers having proved to be inaccurate. But then that was no real surprise as the Met Office seemed to assume that the weather reached no farther west than the River Shannon. Hope often wondered why they didn't just ring up Castlebar or Sligo and ask "What's the weather doing over there, lads?" Their accuracy rating would probably shoot up as a result.

"Yes," Hope said. "It is a lovely day."

Agnes nodded in agreement. "You tell that to your father. If it was left up to him it'd be pouring from the heavens."

Hope was at a loss. "I know Dad's a civil servant, but I wasn't aware he had control of the weather."

Agnes frowned. "Don't be smart. You know perfectly well what I'm talking about." Delving into her handbag she produced a small statue of the Infant of Prague. It was obvious that the head had at one time been broken off as it was glued back on at a jaunty

311

angle. "If I hadn't ignored him and put out the wee statue, it'd be a different state of affairs, so it would."

Hope was about to laugh, assuming that Agnes, possibly for the first time in living memory, was taking the piss, but then she realised that her aunt was perfectly serious and was referring to the old wives' tale that leaving the statue of the Infant of Prague outside for three days before any given date was guaranteed to produce good weather. She wasn't sure but she thought she remembered some old biddy stipulating that the statue's head had to have been knocked off and glued on again for the ritual to be effective, but Hope discounted that as to her knowledge she'd never seen a religious statue that didn't have a badly glued-on head. It appeared to be a basic design fault.

"Well, yes," she said. "Good job you did."

She ordered a coffee and drank it more hurriedly that she'd planned, searing her gullet in the process. Agnes was hard going at the best of times and she didn't need the grief, her patience quotient teetering dangerously close to the red. "Good heavens! Is that the time," she said, pointedly looking at her watch. "Must be off. Have to pick up Mum, Charity and Sandy from the hairdresser's."

Back home it was all systems go. Her father was just back from the hotel having delivered the wine and, deciding that he was peckish, was making toast – much to Maisie's consternation.

"There's no time for that. Will you go and get dressed!" she screeched.

"But I'm hungry," he moaned. "We won't be sitting down to the meal till after five. I'll pass out with the feckin' hunger for God's sake!"

Maisie rooted in the cupboard and grabbed a packet of Digestives. "Well, have a bloody biscuit then!"

Tom gave Hope a hangdog look and sloped down the hall to the bedroom, followed by Maisie. "Did you shave?" Hope heard her say, but didn't catch her father's response.

Hope poured herself a glass of juice and laced it with a hefty measure of vodka, then hurried down to her own room with the expectation of a quiet ten minutes in which to unwind and get ready herself, though she had barely time to slip into the dress and put on her make-up before Sandy pushed the door open.

"Charity's nearly ready and she wants you to help her with the veil."

Irritated, Hope groaned, then followed Sandy next door to Charity's room. Her sister was standing in front of the wardrobe mirror staring at her reflection. When Hope saw her she caught her breath. She looked stunning, her skin as pale as porcelain, her auburn hair shining in the simple 'up' do.

"Wow!" Hope said. "You look gorgeous!"

Charity caught her eye through the mirror and smiled. "Thanks." She appeared lost for words herself, overcome by the vision staring back at her. The door opened and Maisie bustled in, stopping dead at the sight of her younger daughter.

"Oh, my God, you look beautiful!" she said and burst into tears.

If Hope had been Charity she wouldn't have been sure how to take it, but thankfully Charity just smiled and handed her mother a tissue.

"Don't you dare cry," she said. "You'll start me off and I'll wreck my make-up."

Maisie was going to the church with Ben and Maureen, and as Hope was pinning the corsage onto her lapel she whispered. "Wait till you see my surprise!" but again didn't explain.

The house was suddenly quiet after Maisie, Ben and Maureen had gone so there was a hiatus as they waited for the wedding cars to arrive.

As Hope, assisted by Sandy, attached Charity's veil and tiara, Tom beamed at her with pride. "You look lovely, pet," he said.

Hope heard the crunch of tyres on gravel as she was heading into the kitchen to get the bridal bouquet and the bridesmaid's posies. Charity had chosen arum lilies and the florist had done them proud. But as she picked up the bridal bouquet she heard a scream from the hall and hurried out to investigate. Charity was standing at the front door, her mouth agape. Sandy was doubled up in stitches and Tom, well, Tom just looked confused.

"What's up? What's happened?"

Giggling, Sandy just pointed out the front door, then Charity snarled, "Is this your idea of a joke? Where's my sodding Bentley?"

Hope looked past her out of the front door and it soon became apparent what was up. Parked outside was a white stretch limo about twenty feet long, complete with white ribbons and artificial flowers adorning the oversized chrome radiator.

"Er ...the Bentley's broken," she said sheepishly, and swiftly shifting the blame added, "Mum said she'd fixed it."

Charity's face was thunderous. "What does she know about bloody cars?"

"No. I mean, she said she'd arranged the substitute," Hope said.

Paudie Halpin, who had been standing by the gate having a smoke, on seeing the front door open and the bride waiting, topped his fag and hurried down the path. "Are you ready then?"

Charity found her voice again. "Are you seriously expecting me to get into that – that fecking *pimpmobile*?"

"Ah, come on, love," Tom said, embarrassed with Paudie standing there, trying to placate her. "It's not bad. It's a limo. Don't the film stars all ride in limos?"

Sandy piped up, "Hey, Char? You have to admit it does have a certain ironic quality to it. Come on! It'll be a hoot if you turn up in that."

Hope and Tom both held their breath, then, after an anxious five seconds, Charity giggled. "Now you come to mention it, I suppose it is a bit of a hoot."

Paudie Halpin didn't look too chuffed that the bride had called his limo, his pride and joy, a 'pimpmobile', and was even less impressed when she cracked up again on seeing the interior decorated for the occasion with more artificial flowers and white, lace-trimmed, heart-shaped satin cushions. He got into the driver's seat muttering something about lack of taste. Then to add insult to injury, a moment later there was a loud rumbling sound as Mickey Halpin, Paudie's son, pulled up outside the gate in a beat-up Toyota to take the bridesmaids to the church.

This set Charity off again and Hope suspected she was but a nanosecond away from total hysteria, so grabbing Sandy by the wrist she hurried to the Toyota. She didn't want to be around if Charity lost it and felt the best tactic was to get her to the church and be done with it. So this was Maisie's little surprise. What was she thinking, Hope wondered as, in a noisy cloud of exhaust fumes, they pulled up outside the church. Still, she thought, it could have been worse. She could have arranged for PJ Flynn's pony and trap.

The two hundred guests were seated up at the front of the church and the usual onlookers inhabited the benches further back. The aisle was long but the bridal party progressed at a sedate pace in time to Handel's 'Arrival of the Queen of Sheba', one of Maisie's favourites. Tom looked proud as punch and Charity was beaming at all her friends as she passed. Josh was standing at the end of a pew and he winked at Hope as she passed. She'd never seen him suited and booted and he looked great. She smiled back at him and continued on. Sandy gave her a nudge then and whispered, "Are you sure he's gay?" but Hope shushed her.

Goran was standing with Dave, the best man, watching Charity make her way up to him, a soppy but touchingly sweet expression on his face.

As the Jovanovics weren't Catholics, Charity and Goran had decided against the full wedding Mass, opting for a shorter service. It was an ecumenical affair with a cousin of Mona's, Leonard Archbold, an Anglican bishop from Wigan, presiding alongside the priest, Father Donnie, a second cousin of Maisie's. Hope smiled inwardly when, as the ceremony progressed, it became obvious that the celebrants were trying to outdo each other. Father Donnie won by a short head when, towards the end of the service, he presented the newly spliced couple with a Papal Blessing scroll and a candlestick carved out of bog-oak. Just as the bishop was giving his final blessing, in her peripheral vision, Hope noticed Brigie Conway, Maisie's best friend, struggling with a small hamper to one side of the altar. Placing it on the step she loosened the lid, then suddenly there was a flurry of movement and two doves fluttered into the air and flew out over the congregation, to perch, one on the public-address speaker, the other on the crown of Mona's hat. In theory it would have been a nice if somewhat cheesy touch, if wasn't for the fact that Mona was phobic about birds. It was Alyson Worthington all over again as she struggled shrieking from the front pew, beating at the hapless bird, whose claws were embedded in the straw of her hat and who was as anxious to get away from her as she was to get away from it.

Maisie's little surprise had gone somewhat pear-shaped and the look on her face mirrored the fact.

Tom leapt across the aisle and he and Goran Senior managed to disengage the bird, then Tom scuttled to the side of the altar and stuffed it back into the hamper. Meanwhile the organist, Mossie Moran, totally oblivious, was belting out the recessional piece, 'The Grand March' from *Aida.* Both bride and groom rushed over to Mona and attempted to calm her down and after another half minute the music died, Mossie eventually realising that something was amiss. There was stunned silence, until Malachy, Tom's elder brother who was a Garda Sergeant in Athlone, took matters into his own hands and announced to the congregation that there was nothing to see, nothing to worry about, that the incident had been dealt with. He signalled up to Mossie in the organ loft who, somewhat falteringly, resumed 'The Grand March'. Bride and groom, satisfied that Mona was OK, glanced at each other uncertainly, then arm in arm made their way down the aisle at a speedy lick. Mona, a touch dishevelled, took Tom's arm, and Maisie took Goran Senior's and they all followed the bridal party towards the exit.

After the usual ten minutes outside the church when all the smokers lit up and guests took rolls of bad photos, the bridal party set off for the reception. The pimpmobile made a circuit of the town beeping the horn as was customary, the Toyota in its wake, still belching out exhaust fumes.

"Well, that was hilarious," Sandy commented as the taxi embarked on a second lap by mistake. "I thought yer woman was going to lay a feckin' egg. Nice touch though."

"Don't look at me," Hope chided. "I think that was probably my mother's 'little surprise'." Then to Mickey, "Enough with the horn. Just go to the hotel, will you! You're making a show of us."

Sandy sniggered. "Like your family needs any help!"

When they arrived at the hotel there was no sign of Mona, and Maisie explained that she'd gone up to her room for a lie-down. "Did you ever see anyone making such a fuss over a little harmless bird, for God's sake?" she hissed at Hope, obviously disgusted by Mona's performance, and utterly disowning any culpability for her hysterical reaction.

Hope made no comment other than to ask, "You haven't any other little surprises lined up, have you?"

The irony was lost on Maisie however. "No, I haven't," she said, a sour look on her face. "I just hope Mona didn't completely spoil it for Charity. You know how she likes dolphins."

"What have dolphins to do with anything?" Hope asked, mystified.

"Dolphins. Doves. Isn't it all the one?" she replied, leaving Hope none the wiser. "And you've no idea how hard it was to find even the doves." Then she spotted her friend Brigie, the dove wrangler, so she waved and hurried over to her.

"Well, that was interesting," Josh said.

Hope looked round. He was standing behind her, two glasses in his hand, a mischievous smirk on his gob. "Birds are obviously your signature thing,"

Hope took one of the proffered glasses. "Hey, just be thankful she couldn't get the dolphins."

"Dolphins?"

"Don't ask."

He laughed. "You look great, by the way."

She smiled at him. "Thanks. You scrub up pretty good yourself."

"So, how did you get on with James?"

"Brilliant," she said. "I start on Monday."

He raised his glass in salute. "Excellent! Though I knew you'd get it. So where are you going to stay?"

"In Leeson Park with Sandy for starters. It's not ideal. I have a suspicion she'll drive me nuts, but it'll do for now."

She glanced over towards the bar where Sandy was flirting unashamedly with Dave, the best man. He was putty in her hands and hanging on her every word, his eyes drawn to her rampant cleavage like iron filings to a magnet.

"James is sound. I think you'll get on well," Josh said.

"I hope so. Anyway, enough about me. You never told me about your trip to the States."

"You'd have loved it, Hope. Gorgeous weather, great *craic*. I even came back with money."

"I wish I'd gone with you." Then before she could shut herself up, voiced her thoughts. "I really missed you."

His eyebrows took a hike up his forehead and his mouth went into a lopsided grin. "Missed me?"

She felt heat rising up her neck. "Um … yeah. I … um … well, you know, good mates are hard to come by."

He nodded. "Yeah," then after a beat his eyes dropped to his glass. "I fancied you like mad, you know."

Hope's eyebrows went vertical at that. "Really?"

He nodded. "I was gutted when you wouldn't come with me."

"Shit! Why didn't you say something?"

Shrugging, he smiled at her. "Oh, I dunno. You were vulnerable, I suppose. I wasn't sure how you'd react." Then placing his hand over his heart added, "I suppose I was afraid you'd burst out laughing, tell me to fuck off and break my heart."

Hope was almost lost for words and the best she

could come up with was, "Why on earth would I do that? You knew I was over Bollox-Head."

"You *said* you were over Bollox-Head," he corrected. "To be honest, when you blew me out like that, I knew you weren't."

"Oh yes I was, and for your information, if I'd had the slightest inkling that you fancied me I'd have gone with you like a shot."

"Bugger!" There was an awkward silence, then he frowned. "I just didn't get any vibe that you were interested."

She laughed and wagged her head from side to side. "Pot. Kettle. Neither did I. What were we like!"

Before he could reply, Maisie bustled over, red in the face and flustered. "Hope! Disaster! Your Aunt Megan just told me that young Chloe's gone vegetarian."

Hope waited for the punch line, but then gave up. "And …?"

"So what's the girl going to eat? She can't have the beef *or* the salmon! What are you going to do about it?"

"Me?"

Maisie's face was a study in astonishment. "Oh course you! Who else? It's your responsibility. We can't have your cousin eating just spuds and veg."

"But I thought she was a vegetarian," Hope said, quite reasonably in her opinion.

Maisie flapped her hands in frustration. "Oh, you know what I mean. Can't the chef make her something special with rice or lentils or that soya stuff? You know how picky Megan is. She's only looking for something to sneer about."

True enough, Maisie and her youngest sister Megan were extremely competitive and Hope was aware that Megan would dearly love to have something to criticise her mother for.

She sighed. "OK, Mum. Leave it with me. I'll see what I can do."

"Good girl," Maisie said, then her eyes swivelled to Josh. "And who's this?"

"Josh Tierney, Mrs Prior. I'm a friend of Hope's. Nice to meet you."

Maisie went all girly and coy. "And lovely to meet you too, Josh." Then she remembered the threat of imminent disaster and became flustered again. "Oh, do go and sort it out, Hope, or we'll never hear the end of it. Oh, there's Ken." And without another word she hurried off.

"Sorry," Hope said, handing Josh her glass. "I'd better sort this out or Mum's life will be *ruined*."

He laughed. "Can't have Auntie Megan getting the upper hand."

"See you in a bit," she said and went to look for Rhona Fitzgibbon, the banqueting manager.

She had a spring in her step, the tingle of anticipation in her stomach and couldn't stop the smug smile spreading across her face as she thought about Josh.

He fancies me, she thought. He wants me.

She found Rhona in the Cara Suite, checking out the table decorations, and apologetically acquainted her with the snag of the rogue veggie guest. Rhona however didn't seem at all fazed and assured her that the hotel regularly catered for vegetarians and would organise an aubergine bake and veggie stir-fry for Chloe's main course. Once they had ascertained where she was sitting on the seating plan, Hope breathed a sigh of relief and went to look for Maisie to let her know that the catastrophe had been averted.

She found her in the bar talking to Mona and Goran Senior. Mona had evidently recovered from her bird trauma and looked normal again if a touch puzzled. Hope noticed a downy white feather still clinging onto the back of her hair, but chose not to mention it.

"Hi," she said brightly as she joined them, then to Maisie, "Relax, that's all taken care of, Mum."

"Oh good girl," Maisie said obviously relieved. "I was just explaining to Mona about the dolphins."

Hope continued on through the bar to rejoin Josh and, spying him in the corner talking to Goran's brother Ivan, headed over. Just as she was about ten feet away, a tall slim blonde vision in a lilac silk suit hurried past her to join the group.

Josh's face lit up on seeing her. "Casey!"

"Sweetie!" she squealed. "So sorry I'm late, the damn train took forever." She threw her arms around Josh's neck and he kissed her. She had a body and legs to die for and a distinctly American accent.

Hope stopped dead in her tracks just as Josh saw her in his peripheral vision.

"Hope, I'd like you to meet Casey." Casey disentangled herself. "Casey, this is Hope, the bride's sister."

The bride's sister?

"Hi, Hope," Casey said. "Great to meet you." She grasped Hope's hand and gave it a firm shake. Josh still had his arm around her waist. "Your dress is so pretty," she cooed.

"Did you manage to avert disaster?" Josh asked, totally oblivious to her confusion.

"Um ... oh, yeah. No sweat." She felt sick to her stomach and a complete eejit, grateful only that she hadn't thrown herself at him. God, how awful would that have been! Gathering herself together, she attempted a smile. "I'll catch up with you guys later. Have to sort something ... um."

Turning abruptly she fled to the ladies'.

* * *

Reuben was sitting up on the vanity unit humming a tune.

"'What Kind of Fool'. Kylie Minogue. 1992," he said. "No releases in 93, but I think it's pertinent."

"Oh shut up! Why am I here?" she demanded. "Why did you make me go through that again?"

The angel just raised his hands, palms out. "Hey,

nothing to do with me. This is your recollection."

"Then get me out of here," she said, feeling the knife twisting in her back and was surprised at how much it still stung.

"Feels bad, huh?"

"Yeah. He met her in Martha's Vineyard, which made it worse. If I'd gone with him ..."

"But you didn't."

She sighed then a thought came into her head. "I don't suppose ..."

"Not a hope," he cut in before she could finish.

Hope turned on the cold tap and held her wrists under the soothing stream of water. "She followed him back to Ireland, you know. Her old man's loaded so she transferred to Trinity to finish off her degree in economics, which made her a smart blonde to boot."

"I know," he said. "I was there."

"Just get me out of here," she repeated plaintively. "Please."

Chapter 23

Her first week at Hackett & McAllister flew and by the weekend she was exhausted. It was a busy office and as she was PA to both James and Diana she was thrown in at the deep end so didn't have a minute to adjust. The upside was that it took her mind off Josh but also it made her realise that she really loved the job despite the fact that she didn't leave the office any night that week before seven. This was largely her own doing as she was desperate to create a good impression so hung on to finish off all tasks for that day. She was however left with a deep sense of satisfaction at a job well done.

Described as a 'garden flat', Sandy's Leeson Park apartment was at basement level to the front, opening out onto a rear garden, though they didn't actually have access. The fact that the back rooms were at ground level made the flat less gloomy. It was inclined to be a bit damp and as Sandy had moved into Charity's old bedroom, the larger of the two, that left Hope with the narrow rather dingy second bedroom. In fairness, Sandy had given it a good clean before she arrived, so it smelt strongly of bleach and sundry other carcinogenic cleaning materials. It was Saturday before she got a proper chance to unpack her things, but she didn't bother to put her mark on the room as she intended her stay to be a temporary arrangement until she could find something nicer.

James was, as Josh had described him, dead on, and she found him easy to work for. Diana though was a different kettle of fish and lived up to her promise that she was inclined to shout when she was stressed, which appeared to be most of the time.

Sonya told Hope to take no notice, that it was nothing personal. But at the end of the second week when Hope had messed up the wine order for a book launch (by mistake she'd ordered twenty-four cases instead of twenty-four bottles) the wrath of Diana came down on her in spades. She had misheard Diana due to the fact that she was reeling off instructions as she hurried through reception on her way out to a meeting, so she quickly learned to double-check everything Diana asked her to do and to write it down.

Apart from the wine incident however, she didn't make any other major blunders in the first month at the end of which James told her that he and Diana had discussed it and, as her trial period was up, if she wanted the job it was hers.

There was no general Friday night get-together at Hackett & McAllister as there had been at Porter & French, but Hope and Sonya began to stop off at The Palace on Friday nights after the first couple of weeks and she gradually got to meet new people. Sonya like herself was single, but she was reluctant to get involved again after escaping a dysfunctional relationship. She said little about her ex, and when she did she made jokes about him, but Hope sensed that she'd been badly damaged by the experience.

Hope was having no luck in finding somewhere decent to live. She answered a few ads for house shares but they were either too far out of the city, in dodgy areas or she didn't fancy the other tenants. She was slightly miffed when the only promising share in a newly built apartment in Haddington Road fell through because the two girls who interviewed her felt they wouldn't get on. Sonya proved to be her saviour however when one morning she mentioned that her sister Georgina had decided to go travelling and, if she was interested, her room was going spare. Hope was chuffed. Sonya shared a small terraced house with her sister in Drumcondra, in the shadow of Croke Park Stadium. It was warm and dry and her room was light and airy. She moved in as soon as Georgina moved out. It was a huge relief as, apart from the creeping damp in

Leeson Park, Sandy had moved in her new boyfriend and really the place was too small for three people, particularly when two thirds of them were terminally untidy and in Freddy's case appeared to have an aversion to flushing the toilet.

One cold Saturday at the beginning of December when Hope and Sonya had spent the afternoon around the shops they repaired, chilled, to Café en Seine for hot ports. Hope told Sonya about the Dylan interlude, hamming it up as usual for the entertainment value. The subject had come up because his second novel was the full of Waterstone's and Hughes & Hughes, windows on Dawson Street, along with the usual broody blown-up photo. This one was called *Godot Shows Up* (A Satire on the Human Condition). Hope acquainted her friend with her part in Dylan Jones's success. At first Sonya was sceptical until Hope assured her, hand on heart, that it was true.

"And he just took the credit?" she said, appalled.

Hope shrugged. "In fairness, what else could he do? The publishers were chucking huge wads of cash at him. He was hardly going to say 'Sorry guys, you can't publish it'. He might have an inflated opinion of his literary talent but he's not stupid."

"Still," Sonya said, "he could have sent you a few bob for the editing if nothing else."

After two hot ports and much giddiness, Sonya spilled the beans about Gerard. Compared to the Dylan story it was a sobering tale. She'd met him in a club, they'd started dating and moved in together after six weeks.

"I wouldn't mind," she said, "but he wasn't the type I usually go for. He was a gym fanatic and was all muscles and tatts which I've never found a turn on, but ... I don't know, we sort of clicked. It was very romantic."

"So what went wrong?" Hope asked. "Was he playing away?"

"No, nothing like that. As soon as we moved in together he got really possessive. He'd kick off if I so much as looked at another man. Once he decked some poor sod who'd only asked me for a light."

"That must have been grim," Hope agreed. "But you don't strike me as the type to take shit like that." The words pot and kettle came to mind again as Dylan nudged fleetingly into her consciousness, but she pushed him aside.

"I didn't think I was either, but I suppose I was in love with him, at least I thought I was so I didn't want to upset him." She picked up her hot port and took a sip. "Anyway, then he started hitting me."

Genuinely shocked, Hope gasped.

"Oh, he was very sorry and all that, but it gradually got worse until one night he put me in hospital."

"Jesus!"

"Yeah," Sonya agreed. "But a really nice woman cop talked me into pressing charges."

"Talked you into?"

Sonya nodded. "Believe it or not, at first I wasn't going to. I was afraid, you see, but she gently reminded me how the violence had got progressively worse and asked if I really believed it would stop." She paused, remembering, then gave an ironic laugh. "I was bleating on about how he loved me really and garbage like that. But then she said: 'Well, he has a funny way of showing it and odds on he'll kill you next time.' That was a wake-up call I can tell you, so I pressed charges and he was arrested."

"What did he do to you?"

Sonya exhaled. "Oh, broken collar bone, two black eyes, broken nose and ribs. He went berserk, all because I said that I thought Johnny Depp was fit."

Hope was horrified. She'd never been that close to domestic violence before. "So where is he now?"

"Don't know. He skipped the country as soon as he got bail. Last I heard he was in England."

"Well good riddance," Hope said, thankful that as bad as Dylan had been he'd never raised a hand to her. "I don't know about you, but I need a drink after that."

Sonya handed her the empty glass. "Me too." Then, after half a beat, added. "I'm grand now though."

Oh no, you're not, Hope thought as she made her way to the bar, conscious that in the telling of her story, confident out-there Sonya had morphed into a bunny caught in a torch beam. Everything about her was small. Even her voice. It was as if she just wanted to disappear.

It was coming on for 5.30 so the place was filling up and she had to nudge her way through the crush to get service. As she stood at the bar trying to catch the barman's eye the guy next to her tapped her on the arm and said "Hi".

Hope looked around and recognised a friend of Sonya's she'd met in The Palace the previous week but for the life of her she couldn't remember his name. She groped in her memory but without success.

"Luke," he said. "And you're Hope, right?"

"Oh Luke, yes. Sorry. I'm awful with names."

"Pit stop, or are you here for the night?" he asked, catching the barman's eye.

"Pit stop. We were shopping."

"We?"

"Me and Sonya."

The barman came over.

"Pint of Murphy's and ..." Luke looked at her enquiringly.

"Oh, two hot ports please," she said.

"So how are you settling in at Sonya's?" Luke asked as they waited for the order.

"Great."

"And the job?"

"Ah grand." She vaguely remembered Sonya saying something about Luke being in advertising. "You're in advertising, aren't you?"

He grinned. "Well remembered!"

They both laughed. He had a nice laugh.

"I'm a copywriter for my sins."

She nodded and looked interested but she hadn't a clue what a copywriter did. He was obviously used to this reaction because he added, "I write the words and the art director does the pictures."

"Oh, right."

The barman slid the drinks across the bar and Luke proffered a twenty-pound note.

"Oh, you don't have to do that," she protested, but he waved it away.

"Hey, I'm Johnny No-Mates tonight. Mind if I join you?"

The three of them sat in Café en Seine until after seven, then Sonya had to leave as she was going to a family birthday party, so then they were left on their own. Hope found herself really comfortable in his company. He was funny and relaxed and, although he probably was, didn't appear to be obviously coming on to her. It did her ego good after the battering it had suffered. When he went up to the bar to get them one for the road she studied him. Five ten, lean body, shoulders not quite of Liam Neeson-Daniel-Day-Lewis quality, but he looked good in the Levi's and crew-necked sweater. Nice bum. Not exactly good-looking, but no dog either. Floppy brown Hugh Grant hair. Probably around her own age or at most a couple of years older, it was hard to tell. Hmmm, she thought. Nice.

He lived in Ranelagh but he walked her to her bus

stop and waited with her until a bus came along. She got on the bus smiling.

*   *   *

Monday was all go. Diana had a book launch and James, in the middle of organising a promotional shindig for a sportswear company, found he had a crisis on his hands. Winston Murtagh, a middle-weight boxer and Olympic bronze medallist now turned pro, had been caught on CCTV cameras crashing a red light and knocking a cyclist off his bike. He hadn't stopped. The cops, after viewing the footage and identifying his car, had arrested him and he'd been charged with leaving the scene of an accident and dangerous driving. Winston's story was that he hadn't seen the cyclist, so wasn't aware that there had been an accident. As the incident had occurred at four in the morning and the cyclist sustained two broken legs and lay in the road for at least twenty minutes before another motorist stopped to help him, public sympathy was with the victim. Admittedly Winston was an obnoxious, aggressive loudmouth with a taste for glamour models, which had never endeared him to Joe Public, and as one of the top tabloids had printed the attributed quote *"What was the wanker doing out on an effing bike at four in the effing morning anyway?"* James had his work cut out in order to save the boxer's reputation and thus his valuable endorsements. Boxing may be a violent sport but the sponsors prefer all their endorsees to be of the gentle-giant, gentleman-pugilist variety and Winston was more Mike Tyson than he was cuddly Frank Bruno.

When the boxer had turned up at the office for a meeting with James and Isaac Goldfarb his manager, he was all swagger and chunky gold jewellery. When Hope brought in the coffee however it was a different story. Winston was sitting cowed on the sofa looking anywhere but at James as he spelled out how much the boxer stood to lose financially if the sponsors pulled out. Thankfully Winston had once run a ten-K road race in aid of Temple Street Children's hospital, so the strategy was to play up the charity work, visit the injured cyclist in hospital bearing gifts and a large portion of humble pie (photo opportunity), get out his running shoes again and attend every possible charity function going.

Hope was in the middle of typing up a list of events for the boxer when Diana called her in. A man was standing behind her desk looking out of the window.

"Hope, this is my brother Charles. It's his book we're launching tomorrow tonight."

Charles McAllister turned around. Physically he was the spitting image of his sister, same dark hair, olive skin and heavy build, but whereas Diana could carry the weight and was always impeccably groomed, styled and businesslike, Charles was the cartoon version of a flabby absent-minded professor type in old tweed jacket, faded baggy cords, mad hair, thick rimless glasses and beat-up Hush Puppies.

"Hello," she said.

"Nice to meet you," he replied, looking at a point over her left shoulder.

"I need you to baby-sit my brother tomorrow night as I can't make it. I want you to make sure everything goes smoothly."

"OK," Hope said.

"I've got Michael D. Higgins to say a few words before Charles does his reading, but you'll have to introduce Michael D. OK? Think you can do that?"

"Sure. No problem," Hope said, chuffed to have been given the responsibility.

"You know kick-off's at eight?"

"Yes," Hope assured her. "I'll be there by seven to set out the chairs and open the wine and stuff."

"Good. Waterstone's have given us the small room upstairs. I'm expecting about thirty people, and press, of course. The press packs have gone out but bring along some more just in case."

"What's the book about?" Hope asked, directing the question at Charles.

Diana handed her a thick paperback. "Science fiction," she said with undisguised disdain.

"Well, more fantasy really," Charles corrected her. "Time travelling. That kind of thing."

Diana stood up. "You'd better go now, Charles. I have a meeting. But be back here at six sharp tomorrow night. I've pulled out all the stops for you, so don't let me down." Diana at her officious best.

Charles nodded and mumbled "OK, OK", then blinked a couple of times and shambled towards the door.

"See you tomorrow at six," Hope said.

He stopped dead and looked at her briefly before averting his eyes, then nodded, muttering "Yes, yes", and shuffled out of the office.

Diana closed the door behind him. "Families! Who needs them?"

Hope wasn't sure what to say to that, though on a number of levels she had sympathy with the sentiment. "This is his first book, you know? Took five bloody years to write it." Diana was gathering some papers together for her meeting. "He's so bloody useless. Can hardly tie his own fecking shoelaces. An IQ of 145, but what does he do with it? He becomes a librarian. A bloody librarian!" She paused in her rant and looked straight at Hope. "Do you have any brothers?"

Hope shook her head. "No, it's just me and my sister."

"Well, be thankful. The Irish mother has a lot to answer for when it come to raising sons, believe me. Bred to be helpless. Bloody helpless." Snapping the locks of her briefcase shut, she gathered her coat and walked around the desk. "Just make sure he gets there, will you? I've called in a lot of favours for mummy's little darling."

"Can I have a contact number for your brother? Just in case I need to – well, contact him."

"Good idea. Charles isn't the most reliable." Diana scribbled a number and Charles's address on a Post-it and handed it to Hope. "Just make sure he gets there, and keep him away from the wine."

Hope thought she was being facetious, thought it was a throwaway remark, but she realised the following evening that Diana was perfectly serious.

Chapter 24

She spent the greater part of Tuesday running errands for James and confirming that various clients were on the invitation list of a high-profile charity fashion-show fundraiser for a new children's hospice, scheduled for the week before Christmas. Naomi Campbell, Jodie Kidd and Kate Moss were amongst the models. It was when she was covering reception while Sonya was at lunch that she got a call from Luke.

He recognised her voice. "Hope. It's Luke Brannagh," he said. "How are things?"

She was chuffed he'd called. "Great. How's yourself?"

"Ah, you know." He paused. "Listen, do you have any plans for tonight?"

"Oh, well, actually I have to work. There's this book launch I have to take care of."

"Oh." He sounded disappointed.

"But it should be over by nine, if you fancy coming along. It's at Waterstone's on Dawson Street," she said quickly in case he thought it was a brush-off.

"Oh." A more upbeat 'oh'. "OK. What's the book?"

"A fantasy time-travel thing. *The Arctic Troubadour*. The writer's my boss's brother."

"Should be interesting," he said. "What time does it start?"

*   *   *

Just as she was expecting him to walk through the door at six o'clock, she got a phone call from Charles McAllister. "Would that be Diana's assistant?" he asked and when she confirmed that it was, he said, "I'm sorry. I can't do it."

"Do what?" Hope asked.

"This thing at Waterstone's."

Diana's comment about him being unreliable flashed to mind and her heart sank. "But why not? It's all organised."

"I know, but I just can't do it."

"But why, Charles? What's the problem?" She was trying to nudge the panic out of her tone and sound reasonable without much success. Her guts were turning over and the sentence came out in a sort of screech. She knew that Diana was depending on her and would scarify her if she messed up. Whatever she thought of her brother, the event had Diana's name on it and she would be livid if it was less than perfect.

"It's all those people," he bleated. "I just can't stand up in front of all those people and read aloud."

"OK," she said, reaching for a stray straw, any straw. "What if you didn't have to read. What if someone else read for you?"

"Well …" he wavered.

"It seems a shame to miss this opportunity. Michael D. Higgins is going to introduce you and Diana's invited the press, and loads of guests will be there."

"Press?" He sounded horrified, as if this was the first he'd heard about the press. "No. No, I definitely can't do it then. I'm sorry."

"Where are you, Charles?" she asked, panic setting in.

"At home," he said, then went silent, but she could hear his breathing coming in short stressed pants at the other end of the line.

Shit, he's bloody hyperventilating, she thought. "Charles, are you OK?"

"I'm sorry," he said, breathless, then hung up abruptly.

"Hello? Charles?" A pause as realisation set in. "Shit!"

Sonya, who was packing up for the day, glanced over. "What's the matter?"

"Diana's brother. He said he's not coming to the launch."

"Why not?"

Hope wanted to throw up. Her first opportunity to show Diana that she could handle responsibility had gone seriously pear-shaped. "I don't know. I thought it was just nerves and I think I'd almost made him think again but then I mentioned the press and he freaked. What the feck did he think went on at a book launch?"

"Beats me," Sonya said. "So what are you going to do? Diana'll go ape-shit."

Like she needed reminding. Hope thought for a moment, weighing up her options. "I suppose the only thing I can do is to go over to his house and try and reason with him."

Sonya frowned. "But what if you can't?"

"Then I'm stuffed." Shrugging into her coat she checked the address Diana had given her. "He lives in Raglan Road."

She glanced at her watch. It was 6.10. Allowing a minimum of half an hour to forty minutes to get through the rush-hour traffic to the Ballsbridge address brought her up to seven o'clock, then she had to talk Charles into going back to Waterstone's which could take some time if she managed it at all. Sonya was evidently doing the same calculation.

"Listen, would you like me to go over to Waterstone's and set out the chairs and the wine and stuff?" she offered. "It'll give you more time."

Hope was relieved. "Oh, thanks, Sonya. Would you?"

"No problem."

In fact by the time she'd found a taxi, it took nearer to forty-five minutes to get there but she was quietly confident by the time the cab pulled up outside the large Edwardian house on Raglan Road, a quiet leafy street in Dublin 4. It was five past seven.

All the way over she'd been rehearsing what she'd say to him: no need to read at all – she'd read for him if he picked out the passage – they could plead laryngitis so he wouldn't have to say a word to anyone – no more than an hour at most – put in an appearance then he could go home.

How could he possibly refuse? All he had to do was *be* there.

No lights showed in any of the windows which was a touch worrying but the cab driver agreed to hang on to make sure that someone was in before he drove off.

Crunching up the gravel path she felt suddenly nervous. Charles McAllister seemed like a very odd bod and Diana's attitude didn't fill her with confidence. Obviously a black sheep. She climbed the steps, rang the bell and listened at the door for any sound inside. After five long seconds she rang the bell again and knocked the brass knocker a couple of times. Glancing over her shoulder at the cab driver, she was about to give up, then she heard footsteps in the hall. A moment later the door opened a crack and Charles peered out at her.

Not wanting to give him the opportunity to slam the door in her face, she stepped forward, pushing the door wider, and put her foot inside the hall. "Charles ... um ... could we talk?"

The cab driver hooted the horn and after she had waved that it was OK, he drove off.

"I shan't do it. There's no point trying to talk me into it." He sounded like a petulant child.

"Can I come in?" she said, not waiting for his agreement, pushing the door wider and stepping right inside the hall.

He took a step back. "I'm not doing it," he repeated. "Can't." Then he turned and shambled back down the hall towards a door to the right of the staircase. A naked forty-watt bulb was fighting a losing battle, but even in the dimness the cavernous hall looked shabby and neglected.

"Couldn't we at least talk about it?" she said catching up with him. "If you don't want to read aloud, that's no problem. I'll read for you." Reciting her prepared spiel, she followed him through the door, down three steps, along a short dark corridor and found herself in the kitchen. By contrast the fluorescent strip-light in the kitchen was blinding but the room was tidy, warm and cosy, and the armchair, the typewriter on the table and the TV in the corner suggested that Charles spent the greater part of his time there. "We could say you had a throat infection, that you couldn't do any interviews – we –"

"No," he said. "It's no use." He sat down heavily at the kitchen table, a long scrubbed pine affair. In front of him was a full bottle of Scotch and an empty tumbler. Hands flat on the table top, he stared at the bottle longingly.

"What's the problem, Charles?" she said kindly. "What's the real reason you don't want to do it?"

"I just can't face it," he said. "I loathe being the centre of attention. I hate crowds. This was Diana's idea. I didn't ask her."

Reaching out he picked up the bottle, unscrewed the cap and poured a large measure into the glass. Something about his expression rooted out a childhood memory and she recalled Diana's warning to keep him away from the wine.

"How long are you off the drink?"

He looked up at her. His eyes magnified through the thick lenses reminded her of Mole from *The Wind in the Willows*. "Two years three months and four days," he said. "How did you know?"

"My granddad was an alcoholic."

"*Was*? He'll always be an alcoholic," Charles muttered, staring down at the glass.

"Well, no. He's dead actually. The drink banjaxed his liver and killed him in the end."

He didn't react at all to that. The hands of the kitchen clock were edging round to 7.15.

Hope stood up. "Mind if I have a coffee?

He shrugged. "Suit yourself." He indicated a big

346

steel kettle hissing away on the Aga. A jumble of ill-assorted crockery sat on the shelves of a large wood dresser, the sharpness of the carved decoration dulled by layers of gloss paint. Picking up two mugs and a jar of Nescafé she carried them over to the Aga. "Diana went to a huge amount of trouble for you, you know? Called in favours."

"I didn't ask her to."

"All the same. It's not easy to get publicity for books." She set about making two mugs of coffee. "Don't you want your book to sell?"

"If it's good enough, people will buy it," he said.

Stopping in mid-stir she turned round to face him. "Oh, don't be so naïve! Anyway, how are they going to know about it in the first place without publicity?"

He didn't have an answer for that, instead he picked up the glass and held it under his nose, closing his eyes and inhaling deeply. "She thinks I'm a fool. A buffoon," he said.

"No, she doesn't." She paused, conscious that, in fact, he was absolutely right. "Anyway, even if she does, what of it? You wrote a book, didn't you? Diana hasn't written a book as far as I know?"

He put down the glass. "Did you hear the way she described it?"

Hope slid the mug of coffee in front of him and moved the glass out of reach. "Maybe she's just jealous."

"You got that right."

"But why is her approval so important anyway? Your publisher obviously rates it and, odds on, Diana hasn't even read it."

"It's not my fault I was Mother's favourite," he said forlornly as if he hadn't heard her. "She left me this house, you know. Diana's never forgiven me."

Hope groaned inwardly. Family dynamics were a minefield and she realised that if she couldn't pull something out of the bag to get him to Waterstone's sober and willing, she would certainly suffer serious fall-out.

With every second that ticked away, Charles was getting more and more morose and the likelihood of getting him to the launch was diminishing in direct relation to the downward arc of his misery and wallowing self-pity.

She was suddenly irritated by his self-indulgence.

"Is that what this is all about? Getting back at your sister because she's resentful towards you?"

No reply.

"Blood's thicker than water, Charles. Jealous or not she's still trying to help you."

He made a humphing sound and picked up the coffee mug. "Trying to make me look a fool, more like."

"Oh, get over yourself!" she snapped. Then realising that perhaps this wasn't the best tactic in order to get him to cooperate, she consciously softened her tone and tried a different tack. "Look, Charles. You took years to write this book. Why bother at all if no one gets to read it?"

"Don't patronise me, and please, just go away and leave me alone. I'm not going and that's it."

There was finality in his voice and she feared there was no way she was going to be able to persuade him. Time to play the guilt card. Pushing back her chair as if admitting defeat, she stood up. "Well, that's me stuffed then."

He looked up, blinking behind the milk-bottle glasses. "Stuffed?"

She nodded. "Diana'll have my guts for garters tomorrow. This was my big chance to prove myself. If you don't show up Diana will make my life a misery. She might even fire me. No, I'm well and truly stuffed."

"Oh dear," he said. "I'm sorry."

Hope gave an ironic chortle. "No, you're not. You're just thinking about yourself. Just because it doesn't suit you to put yourself out and spend one teeny-weenie hour meeting a bunch of people who might even help your book to sell, you don't give a toss if I get the push."

He frowned and looked distinctly guilty. "I'm sorry. It's the stress, you see. I can't handle stress. Never could."

"Stress? You don't know the meaning of the word, sunshine. When did you ever have to worry about paying bills? You got this fuck-off house handed to you on a plate and your nice cosy public service job in a library. Don't tell *me* about stress!" She was working up quite a head of steam. "No, it's a P45 for me. You can bet on it. A P45 and benefit. I'll be lucky if I'm not homeless by this time next month."

"Homeless!"

Half an hour later Hope hurried up the stairs in Waterstone's accompanied by a reluctant Charles McAllister. Her rant had hit his guilt response a bang-on bull's-eye. They were ten minutes late and the natives were getting restless, but Michael D. Higgins was there, talking to Sonya, who looked distinctly relieved to see them walk through the door. Excusing herself, she hurried over to Hope.

"Bloody hell, you cut it fine. I was running out of excuses."

"You have no idea," Hope said, touching her arm in silent thanks. "Don't let Charles out of your sight until Michael D. introduces him." Heading over to the small table where Charles' book was laid out ready for signing, she grabbed a copy.

"Thank you for coming, Mr Higgins," she said to the politician. "Sorry we're a bit late."

"Not at all. Not at all. My pleasure," he said, his distinctive voice high-pitched and reedy.

"In a moment I'll introduce you, if that's OK, then after you say a few words we'll get on to the reading."

"Wonderful," he said, "wonderful," rubbing his hands together.

Hope hurried back to Charles. "OK. Michael D.'s going to say a few words about the book and about you, then I'll read for you. Have you chosen a passage?"

He nodded, took the book and flipped the pages until he came to Chapter Seven, then handed it back to her. "This bit," he said.

She had to admit he looked truly terrified as he scanned the room. There was a good turnout, and Hope recognised a journalist from the *Irish Times* with a photographer, also one from the *Tribune*. Nell McCafferty and Maeve Binchy, Chris DeBurgh, Twink and Radio DJ Ian Dempsey. Diana had certainly called in favours. Taking Charles by the arm, she guided him reluctantly towards the table. "Come on, Charles. Show time."

She was relieved that she'd got him this far, but was also anxious, afraid that she'd spoil everything and screw up. She cleared her throat, then introduced him to Michael D., and Charles managed a stiff-armed handshake while mumbling something, though didn't manage actual eye contact. He looked utterly terrified by this time.

Hope moved over to the table. "Ladies and gentlemen," she started, then spotted Luke standing by the entrance with Sonya, "Diana asked me to thank you all for coming along tonight to help launch Charles' first novel, *The Arctic Troubadour*, and she sends her apologies that she couldn't be here, but Mr Michael D. Higgins has graciously agreed to say a few words about Charles and the book." She looked over at the elderly white-haired man. "Former Minister for the Arts, Mr Michael D. Higgins."

There was a smattering of polite applause. She stepped back from the table.

The politician, who had obviously read, and attested to having thoroughly enjoyed the book, gave a charming witty speech, praising Charles as a new and exciting talent, with a 'vibrant voice' and described *The Arctic Troubadour* in glowing terms.

She glanced over towards Luke. He caught her eye and gave her a subtle thumbs-up so she smiled at him, proud that she'd carried it off. In letting her attention wander however, she missed Michael D. announcing: "Now Charles will read a short passage from *The Arctic Troubadour*. The author, Charles McAllister, ladies and gentlemen."

More polite applause followed by a deafening silence. Hope snapped back to reality.

"Um … I'm afraid Charles has been cruelly struck down with laryngitis tonight, so he asked me to read a passage for him," she said, grabbing the book from Michael D.'s hands. Charles was white as a sheet and looked ready to throw up. She flipped the book open and started to read. Halfway through the first passage, through the corner of her eye, she was aware of him legging it out the door.

* * *

"And you never thought to go and look for him?" Reuben said. He was sitting on the table swinging his long legs. They were still in Waterstone's but all the guests had left. She'd apologised for Charles, said that he'd got up from a sickbed to be there, but had felt queasy and had to leave.

"No. I was just so relieved that it was all over. I was meeting Luke, and anyway it was hardly my fault he fell off the wagon," she protested.

He gave her a leery look. "You can't be serious."

"You're the one who keeps banging on about taking responsibility for our own actions," she said. "It was his choice."

"And you frogmarching him down to Waterstone's despite his state of mind had nothing to do with it?"

She couldn't meet his eyes.

"He had a full bottle of Scotch for heaven's sake. He was almost dipping his nose in it." Reuben wasn't about to let up.

"But the book did really well," she muttered defensively. "If it wasn't for the publicity it could well have disappeared without trace."

"True enough, the book did well," the angel conceded. "But Diana generated a lot of publicity. It wasn't just down to the launch. The book got great reviews on its own account." He paused. "Pity Charles didn't get to enjoy his success, mind you."

"Oh stop it!" she hissed. "I didn't push him under the bloody train. It was an accident."

"He was drunk."

Both angry and seething with guilt, Hope snapped

back, "He could have fallen off the wagon for any number of reasons."

"And the platform evidently, but how do you know it was an accident?" Reuben persisted. "How do you know he didn't jump?"

Hope's heart started to pound. The news article had stated that one witness was of the opinion that the writer had purposely thrown himself in front of the train as it sped through Kildare station, but the coroner had found that there wasn't enough evidence to support a suicide verdict.

"I thought he'd be OK," she said lamely.

Reuben slid off the table and wandered over to a display of atlases. "That's just the problem. You didn't think at all," he said, lifting the cover of a sturdy glossy-jacketed tome. "The launch went ahead. You'd got what you wanted. Hurrah! Brownie points for Hope. You knew very well that Diana wouldn't fire you if he wasn't there. You might have got a bit of a bollocking, but so what?"

Hope felt awful. "OK. OK. You're right. I didn't think, at least I didn't think past getting Charles to the launch. I wanted to make a good impression on Diana. I wanted to just get it done. Anyway, it's obvious he was really screwed up. It wasn't just the launch."

Reuben was flipping though the pages of the atlas, his disapproval apparent. "All the more reason for you to look out for him."

Hope bit her lip. "Did he?" she asked after a silent hiatus.

"Did he what?"

"Jump."

He flipped a few more pages then closed the book and turned around. "No," he said. "It was an accident. He was drunk and lost his balance."

Hope exhaled. "Oh, thank God!"

"That doesn't negate your part in it," the angel chided. "If you'd looked after him, minded him, which I might add was the least you could have done, considering what he did for you, he might not have gone straight home after the launch and chugged the whole bottle of Scotch. He might not have picked up that first drink.

Hope felt terrible. She had thought of going after Charles, but then got talking to Luke and after everyone had left she, Sonya and Luke had gone on to Nico's for dinner and Charles went clean out of her mind.

"So why are we here?" she asked. "Why aren't we at Charles's right now? I could change things I could save him."

"Could you?" he asked.

Surprised by his reply she frowned. "Isn't that the whole point?".

The angel placed the book back on the table, then picked up a globe from the atlas display. "I don't know," he said, tracing the outline of Africa with his index finger.

"What do you mean, you don't know? Shouldn't I be there now, letting him off the hook. Pouring the booze down the sink so he can't fall off the bloody wagon?"

He glanced over at her. "You tell me," he said.

Frustrated and angry, she wanted to hit him. "For God's sake, help me here, Reuben! You're not giving me any options. I don't know what to do!"

Flicking the globe, he sent it spinning and watched as the continents whizzed by in a blur of colour. "OK. What do you want to do?" he asked after a pause.

"The right thing," she replied without hesitation.

"What? And risk the wrath of Diana. Risk getting fired?"

"Absolutely."

"As if!" he scoffed. A knee-jerk rebuttal caught in her throat as he looked her straight in the eye and added, "That was the start of it, you know."

"The start of what?"

"Your single-minded ambition. You were bitten by the bug. You wanted to be Diana."

Hope guffawed. "Oh please!"

"Don't deny it," he said. "On the surface you might have made little of Diana, criticised her people skills when it came to her staff, but you wanted to be her. Admit it. She was your role model."

He'd hit a nerve. It was true. Diana had been her role model in the early days. "I'm not like her though," she said, then paused. "Well, maybe apart from with Amy, but that wasn't my ..." He gave her a questioning look and she thought again. "OK ... well, maybe it was. Maybe you're right. And if I had my time over I would have minded Charles. It's just I was so relieved that the launch had gone well . . . and then there was Luke ..." She sighed. "I've always felt bad about it – his death, I mean."

"Well, that's a start," the angel said, "You did think he'd killed himself, though, didn't you?"

She nodded, her eyes on the carpet. "That's why I freaked when I saw Amy on the wall." She looked up and caught him staring at her again. "I saved her though, didn't I? I dived in and saved her."

He nodded. "Yes. Yes, you did,"

"So I could save Charles too," she said, desperate to make amends.

"No point," Reuben said.

"No point? I don't understand."

He put the globe down and smiled kindly at her. "Poor Charles. He was a lost cause. The book launch was just an excuse. One way or another the drink would have killed him. Either his liver would have packed up, or he'd have fallen under a bus. He was his own worst enemy."

She felt a palpable sense of relief flood through her. "So it wasn't my fault."

"No, not really," he said, then turned and strolled towards the exit.

Hope didn't move. She just stood there, stunned by

what he'd just said. Relieved. It wasn't my fault, she thought. It wasn't my fault. A broad smile spread across her face. "But you still acted abominably," he said as he stopped by the door.

Quitting while she was ahead, Hope didn't bother to quibble.

"Come on then," he urged impatiently. "We're finished here."

They were walking along Dame Street. It was obviously very late because there weren't many people around, just the last straggle of a queue at the taxi rank, which was a surprise because Hope assumed that it must be only after ten at most. She shivered. There was an autumnal chill in the air and the cobbles by the Bank of Ireland were thickly covered in fallen leaves.

Reuben was humming again and it took her a moment to recognise the tune – then she realised that they had moved on a few years.

"One or two?" she asked.

He glanced round at her. "Two, though when Elton asked Bernie Taupin to write something like 'Candle in the Wind' for the funeral, he misheard so just adapted the same lyrics."

Hope knew that, but didn't comment.

"Found it a bit naff myself," the angel added after a moment's reflection. "Though Elton did play a blinder on the day. Not a dry eye in the house."

Hope remembered it well. She too had been glued to the TV and had blubbed unashamedly. "Why are we back in 97?" she asked. She was anxious to cut to the chase and get to the Amy part. As things were panning out, it looked like her grand plan might just work.

They had reached the Central Bank Plaza.

"Don't you know?" the angel asked.

Exasperated, she shook her head. "If I did I wouldn't be asking." Sitting down on the steps, she sighed. "I can't think of anything I did that year that would merit fecking Crusty Heaven."

He looked down at her. "Really?"

"Really."

"So what about – the end of the endgame?"

Hope groaned. "Oh … that."

"Yes, that," he repeated.

Chapter 25

By the autumn of 1997 Hope had taken over all responsibility for events at Hackett & McAllister. Over the previous four years Diana and James had delegated more and more responsibility for that end of things, and though Diana, unlike James, had never uttered a word of praise, the mere fact that the thoroughly anally retentive woman would trust her was endorsement enough. Anyway, she enjoyed the work enormously, felt she had found her niche, and her added responsibilities were reflected in her salary. She'd suggested to Diana that they expand the events side of the business, but neither Diana nor James was keen. They looked upon the events as a necessary component of promoting their clients' PR interests, rather than an end in itself. So, disappointed, she let it go.

The hours were long but in truth she didn't find that a problem either in light of the fact that the gloss had pretty much gone off her relationship with Luke, and she was glad of an excuse to avoid going home. Had the circumstances been less complicated she would probably just have moved out, but it wasn't that easy as they had bought an apartment together two years previously. It had been the sensible option at the time. Rents were escalating as were property prices, in tandem with the rise of the Celtic Tiger, so it made sense to get on the property ladder before the bottom rung levitated entirely out of reach. Besides, the mortgage came to around the same as they were each shelling out in rent. Perhaps not the most romantic reason for moving in together. What made it more difficult was the fact that they weren't actually fighting. Their relationship had morphed into one of unconditional indifference with occasional, very occasional, sex thrown in. To all intents and purposes they were living separate lives – it was just that neither had acknowledged the fact. Mulling it over with Sonya one quiet afternoon made her realise how little she and Luke had in common. They had totally opposing tastes in music, books, films, even food, and it was only some months after they'd moved in together she realised that his cool laid-back exterior was the cunning disguise of a procrastinator and dedicated couch potato, whose mission statement appeared to be: "*Never put off till*

tomorrow what you can put off till some indeterminate time
in the distant future, except in the case of a Man United
match on the TV."

The only really compatible area of their relationship
had been the sex until even that had gone off the boil.
The problem was she just didn't find him attractive any
more, didn't fancy him.

"And what about him? Does he still have the hots
for you?" Sonya had asked.

"More like the lukewarms, if you'll pardon the
pun," had been her throwaway reply, but in saying it
she realised that it was the truth. They just didn't fancy
one another any more.

Sonya, ever the pragmatist, said, "So what are you
going to do about it?"

It was a case of déjà vu and Tudor Evans came to
mind. He had asked the very same question the day
she'd walked in on Dylan humping Laura.

Hope groaned. "But how do you tell someone you
don't fancy them any more?"

"I suppose you just sit them down and come straight
out with it … or alternatively you could always give
him the it's-not-you-it's-me spiel."

It was a seriously tempting option. "What is it with
me?" she whined to Sonya. "Why does it always go so
wrong?"

"Because you've shit taste in men?" her friend had
helpfully offered.

This came as a surprise as she'd always thought that

Sonya liked Luke well enough. When she questioned this, Sonya stated that she thought Luke was a selfish, lazy bollox, all talk and no substance, whom she'd never really liked.

"Don't beat about the bush," Hope replied, surprised by her vitriol. "*You* brought us together."

"I only introduced you. I didn't think you'd fecking *fancy* him." She said it with her upper lip curled in distaste.

Hope didn't get the chance to ask her why she hadn't said something at the time because the phone rang and she had to take a call for James who was out at a meeting.

The call was from Amber Banner. Amber was the only daughter of Morgan Banner, millionaire entrepreneur, racehorse owner, and former client of James's. Hope had met her once at a reception she'd organised at the Shelburne after one of his horses, Windypharter, had won the Irish St Leger, and remembered her as blonde, on the chubby side with a beaky nose – a sweet but ditzy girl.

"I'm afraid James is at a meeting. Could I help you at all?" she asked.

Amber hummed and hahed for a few seconds, then got to the point. "It's my fiancé's birthday, you see, and I want to throw a party for him."

Hope was about to cut in and tell her that actually Hackett & McAllister didn't do private functions, until Amber brought up the St Leger do at the Shelburne.

"I thought it was amazing, and I want Eric's party to be really special so I immediately thought of James."

"Well, actually, I'm the event coordinator ..." Sonya gave her a weird look but Hope, ignoring her, turned her back. "I organise all the events." She paused for a beat then enquired, "So you really enjoyed the St Leger party?"

"Oh, absolutely!" Amber enthused. "Though I want something different for Eric. Something themed."

"OK. Um ... what sort of numbers are you talking about?" Hope tentatively asked.

"Oh," Amber said, "only our closest friends ... I suppose about ... oooh ... thirty or so."

Hope's heart started to race. "And what kind of budget?"

"Budget?" It came off Amber's tongue as an alien concept.

"Budget. Like, how much do you want to spend?" Hope asked.

Amber laughed. "Oh. I don't know. Lots! You tell me."

Hope felt a drip of perspiration roll down her spine and her heart was still thumping. "The thing is, Amber, the company doesn't actually do private parties, but eh ... well, I could organise it for you myself if you like. I mean, that is my job, so I could stretch a point."

"Oh, would you?" Amber said, gratitude oozing from every syllable, and they set up a meeting at Amber's apartment for that evening.

"*Event coordinator? Could stretch a point?*" Sonya said, a sly grin on her chops. "What if Diana finds out?"

"What of it? I'll be doing it in my own time," Hope said defensively, adding, "and anyway I organise all the events, so I'd say that makes me an Event Coordinator."

Sonya gave her leery look. "If you say so."

Amber lived on Eustace Street not far from the office, where Daddy had bought her a loft apartment for her twenty-first (lucky Amber).

As she had some time to kill before her seven p.m. meeting and it wasn't worth going home, Hope went for a drink at The Palace with Sonya after work. It was then that her friend brought up the Luke problem again. "You have to talk to him about it," she insisted. "Otherwise, knowing the lazy bollox, he'll just go on in his own little comfort zone as if nothing's up."

Hope acknowledged that she had a point, but didn't fancy a row. "What if it gets ugly?"

But Sonya wouldn't let her off the hook. "So what's your alternative? Anyway, what's the worst that can happen? You tell him it's over. That he can either buy out your share of the apartment, or put it up for sale. You pack your stuff and you come over to mine for a while. How hard it that?"

"But what then? I can't afford rent as well as the mortgage."

"Then you'll just have to get a share until the apartment's sold," Sonya said. "My cousin Ruby's looking for someone. Her housemate's getting married at Christmas."

Cash flow aside, given the option, Hope's preference would have been to creep home when Luke was out, pack her stuff and leave a note, and if it wasn't for the fact that they needed to discuss the apartment, she probably would have exercised that alternative. Verbally beaten into submission, she sighed. "I suppose you're right. I'll talk to him tonight, then move some of my stuff out to yours tomorrow, if that's OK? And could you have a word with your cousin?"

Sonya drained her glass and stood up to leave. "Fine with me. I'll give her a call. Let me know how you get on."

At five to seven Hope rang Amber Banner's doorbell and a few moments later the girl's disembodied baby voice said "Hello?" through the intercom.

"It's Hope Prior, from Hackett & McAllister, Amber."

"Oh, super," and she buzzed Hope in.

Hope was surprised when she saw Amber. In the year since they had last met she'd shed at least a quarter of her body weight, her nose looked a lot smaller and had an upturned tip, and her chin – well – now she had one. She was wearing a short leather miniskirt, a black lace top and biker books, her ice-blonde hair carelessly tied up in a scrunchy. She looked very designer rock chick, but carried it off well. Hope wondered what diet she was on, and bearing in mind the nose and chin jobs, speculated as to whether liposuction had played a part in the transformation. Whatever she'd done (or had done) though, she looked great.

Her living space was huge. One complete, mainly open-plan floor incorporating a kitchen and living area, with a mezzanine bedroom and bathroom easily accommodated by the high ceiling, and there were three tall arched windows which overlooked the narrow street.

Hope surveyed the vast room. "Gorgeous apartment."

"Thanks," Amber replied. "I only moved in a month ago. I decorated it myself."

"Really!"

Amber led her over to the kitchen area. "Well, I didn't actually wield the paint brush, but I designed it … at least I chose the interior designer … Coffee?"

Hope sat up on one of the ergonomically designed chrome and leather stools at the broad granite counter. "Please."

"Espresso OK?"

Hope nodded and as Amber set about the espresso machine, Hope's gaze strayed to the furnishings. Two long truffle-coloured suede sofas at right angles to a focal-point raised fireplace where gas flames licked over smooth stones. Pale cream walls with bold artwork. A low chunky dark wood table, a pair of large rosewood oriental cabinets, and a few rugs on the varnished floorboards (which looked original), clever lighting, mostly ambient, a huge ten-foot ficus in a blue glazed pot. All very minimalist, but very chic. Usual hi-fi, video, widescreen TV etc. Stacks of CD's but no books.

"Daniel Morgan Llewellyn," Amber said.

Hope snapped her attention back to Amber. "Sorry?"

"Daniel Morgan Llewellyn, the interior designer." She slid a tiny espresso cup across the counter top. "He's horrendously expensive and a bit of a prima donna about his work."

Hope had often seen him on *Changing Rooms*, the TV makeover show, and the cool elegant interior wasn't what she would have expected taking into account his penchant for turning the bedrooms of suburban semis into scarlet MDF whorehouse boudoirs.

"Would you believe he absolutely forbade me to hang those canvasses?"

Hope glanced at the colourful abstract paintings adorning two of the four walls.

"But well, they're Eric's, so I could hardly not hang them, could I? So I waited until *Irish Interiors* had done the photo shoot." She giggled. "So he'll never know."

"Good move," Hope said. "Is Eric the artist?"

Amber nodded. "Yes, though he's working for Daddy at the moment. Hates it, mind you, but it's just for now."

"So tell me what you have in mind for Eric's party," Hope said. "By the way, when is it?"

"First Saturday in December," she said as she hiked herself up onto the counter top. "And, I'd like something different. I was thinking like a themed do, but I'm not sure what."

Hope, in the absence of James and Diana, had been tossing ideas around in her head all afternoon. "Have you thought of a country house weekend?"

Amber didn't look impressed so Hope elaborated. "I'm thinking an Edwardian house party. Nineteen twenties. Beaded dresses, the men in winged collars, dressing for dinner kind of thing."

Amber gave a cool, "Hmmm."

"A Murder Mystery Weekend. Think *Murder on the Orient Express*. Agatha Christie."

Amber's eyes lit up at that, and she clapped her hands together. "Oh, that sounds like fun!"

"Oh, it is," Hope said, though in truth joining-in events weren't really her cup of tea. "And you could have a traditional jazz band too maybe."

She left an excited Amber an hour later with a promise to get back to her in a couple of days with a detailed plan and the estimated cost, as Daddy was footing the bill. Amber was very enthusiastic about the murder-mystery weekend idea which was a relief to Hope as it was by far the best plan she had come up with. Also she was pretty confident she could pull it off and had a small country house hotel near Greystones in mind as the venue.

She was mulling things over in her mind as she

walked along Westmorland Street towards the bus stop, head down against the cold late October night, and failed to notice that the pedestrian in front had stopped abruptly, so she crashed into his back, dropping her bag and the file she was carrying in her arms. Startled, she gabbled an embarrassed "Sorry, sorry," as they both bent down to retrieve the scattered papers, then she looked up straight into the surprised face of Josh Tierney.

"Fancy bumping into you," he said, grinning.

Ten minutes later, back in The Palace, Josh brought their drinks over to the table.

"So when did you get home?" she asked as he sat down. He looked well, fitter, and he'd put on a few pounds but it suited him.

"About half an hour ago," he said, then took a long swallow of Guinness and sighed with contentment. "Ah, that's good! Can't get a decent pint in Atlanta. So what about yourself? Still working for James?"

Hope took a sip of her drink and nodded. "Yes. I coordinate all the events now."

He smiled. "Good for you. I'm not surprised. Though I thought you'd be running the whole shooting match by now, you're so feckin' bossy!"

They laughed.

"So what brought you home, Mc Fling?" she asked, itching to know how long he was going to be around.

"A funeral, I'm afraid. My best mate's dad died."

"Oh, I'm sorry." They were silent for a moment. "So did Casey come back with you?" She was trying to sound nonchalant but her vocal chords felt vaguely paralysed and it came out as a sort of hoarse shriek.

He didn't seem to notice though. "No. We're not together any more. We sort of drifted. She's engaged to her old college boyfriend now, Hamilton Roebuck the third or fourth or something. Big bugger, size of a small barn. He's a professional footballer, if you can call that stupid American game *football*."

She wasn't sure what to say to that, but he didn't seem too put out. She couldn't stop a big grin spreading across her face. "Sorry to hear that. How long are you home for?"

"Just a couple of days. I have to be back in Atlanta by Monday, so I'm heading down to Galway to see the folks straight after the funeral tomorrow."

A disappointed "Oh."

"And how about you? Are you still with what's his name?"

"Luke? No ... I mean sort of."

He gave her a quizzical look. "Why is nothing ever straightforward with you?"

"Well, we're splitting up and I'm moving in with Sonya for the moment. We bought this apartment together, Luke and I that is, so it's a bit complicated, but Sonya's cousin Ruby has a room going spare after Christmas so I can move in there until the apartment's sold –" She stopped abruptly, realising she was rattling on.

"Yes, you're babbling," he said, amused. "But what else is new?"

She felt herself blush a little.

"This Luke," he went on. "Another bollox-head?"

"Not exactly," she said, grinning at the reference to Dylan. "He's actually very sweet in his own way, but I suppose we sort of drifted too. Nothing in common, no rows or unpleasantness or anything, but no spark either. We could be flatmates for all the interaction we have these days."

"Best to knock it on the head so, if it's going nowhere," he said philosophically.

"Yes," she agreed. "So do you reckon you'll stay in the States?"

He shook his head. "Oh, no. That was never the plan. I'm coming home when my contract's up."

Hopes face lit up. "Really? And when's that?"

"Easter," he said.

She grinned broadly. "Cool."

And he grinned back. Two people just sitting looking at each other, grinning like eejits.

He had to leave after the one pint to go to his friend's house in Glasnevin to sympathise, but before they parted they exchanged mobile numbers and promised to keep in touch. Then just as she was about to walk away he slipped his arms around her and kissed her. A warm affectionate kiss, but then held on to her tighter and for a few seconds longer than a friend would.

She hurried home with a smile on her face.

Chapter 26

"It's just not working out so I think we should call it a day."

"I've been thinking it over and it's just not working."

"I just don't fancy you any more."

"Can't say that. It's too mean." She stared at her reflection in the bathroom mirror, worrying. What if he gets upset? What if he starts a row? She scrubbed that thought. Luke never rowed. He hated confrontation as much as she did. Perhaps that was part of the problem? They never discussed stuff.

"It's not you. It's me." God! How lame did that sound?

She heard the rattle of his key in the front door. Taking a deep breath, she held it for a moment than exhaled. "OK. It's not you it's me ... it's not you it's me." A small voice in her head mocked 'Wimp!'.

He was in the kitchen unpacking a takeaway. Enough for both of them, which left her at a disadvantage. How do you dump someone who's just bought you a Chinese? He turned his head when he heard her walk into the kitchen. "Got you sweet and sour chicken and the fried rice," he said. Then before she had a chance to say thanks, he stopped unpacking and muttered, "Oh sod it!" then turned around to face her. "The thing is, Hope, I've been thinking, and well, this isn't really working." He couldn't look her in the eye and sort of slumped back against the counter top, arms folded, staring at the floor.

The breath was knocked right out of her. "You're dumping me?" she gasped, amazed. "*You're* dumping *me*?" Then she burst out laughing in a fit of hysterical relief, but buried her face in her hands so Luke could be forgiven for assuming that she'd just burst into tears of shock and hurt.

He looked up startled, stammering, "No! Not dumping exactly … at least … I know, this is … look, I'm sorry," he reached out to touch her arm, "but … well, what's the point in going on as we are?" An awkward charged pause. "It's not you. It's me."

Just as she had herself under control the '*It's not you; it's me*' line started her off again. She heard him mutter "Oh shit!" and a moment later felt his arms around her. "I'm really sorry, Hope. I never wanted to hurt you … but … shit!"

Pulling herself together again she wiped away the tears of hysterical mirth and looked up at him.

"I know, Luke, and you're right. And I know you don't want to hurt me. You're too sweet for that, but I suppose if you've made up your mind there's no point trying to fight it."

She felt him relax and exude a sigh of pure relief. "Thanks for being so cool about it," he said. "I've been trying to think of the way to say it for weeks, you know? And it's not as if you've done anything wrong. Not as if I don't *care* about you or anything, but well …"

"I know," she said helping him. "The spark's just gone out, hasn't it?" She felt the hysteria welling up again but managed to keep it together. "So what are we going to do? About the apartment, I mean?"

* * *

"You jammy cow!" Sonya said the following morning after Hope had filled her in on the night before. "So he moves out and you get to stay in the apartment until it's sold?"

Hope nodded. "He's moving in with his brother, so it's not as if it's going to cost him rent, so really it's the fairest option."

"And you didn't say anything about the fact that *you* were going to dump *him*?"

"I didn't see the point." She smiled. "Anyway, this way Luke's the one on the guilt trip."

"So as break-ups go, it was pretty painless."

"Totally pain-free for me," Hope said. "And anyway, at least he has the satisfaction of being the dumper rather than the dumpee. I'd say staying in the apartment is a pretty fair swap for the preservation of his delicate male ego."

"I guess so," Sonya agreed.

Diana buzzed her then so she went upstairs.

"Two things," Diana said without looking away from her computer screen. "I need you to book Eason's for a signing on December sixth, early to mid-afternoon, and then get on to the Morrison and book dinner for a party of ten at 9 o'clock the same night."

Hope made a note on her pad. "OK."

"We've got him on the *Kenny Byrne* radio show on the morning of the fifth so you'll have to meet his flight at eight-o-five and baby-sit him to make sure he gets out to RTE by ten. Oh, and book the Berkley Court for the fifth and sixth. Double room."

"OK. What name?"

"Jones," Diana said. "Dylan Jones."

"Dylan *Bollox-Head* Jones?" she blurted before she could stop herself.

Diana's eyes left the VDU and landed on her. "Excuse me?"

Flustered, Hope backtracked. "Sorry. It's um … just, well, I know … used to know … that is to say … um, I used to live with Bol … with Dylan."

Diana cracked a smile. "Oh, I'd forgotten the

connection. Oh dear, will that be a problem?"

Hope thought about it. "Eh, no, actually. No problem at all."

Diana's eyes narrowed. "Dylan Jones, or more to the point, Icon Publishing, is our client, Hope," she warned, "and I expect you to behave with the utmost professionalism. Do I make myself clear?"

"Crystal," Hope replied, just the merest touch disappointed.

"Oh, and copy this press release, will you, and send it out to the usual suspects."

Hope picked up the A4 sheet. "Anything else?"

Diana's eyes were back on her VDU. "No." Then as Hope reached the door she added, "Sorry about the early start."

"No problem."

Diana smiled. "Good. If it's any consolation, he's requested a limo for his stay so book one and get the driver to pick you up from home."

Hope grinned. "Pimpmobile or something classy?"

Diana laughed. "Oh, I think we'd better go with classy."

"You'll never guess whose book-signing I have to organise," she said to Sonya when she got back to her desk.

"Surprise me," Sonya said, not much interested.

"Dylan Bollox-Head Jones."

That caught her friend's attention. "*Your* Dylan Bollox-Head Jones?"

"The Artist *Formerly* Known as *My* Dillon Bollox-Head Jones," she corrected. "And I'll have to baby-sit him out to RTE for the *Kenny Byrne Show*."

"I'd love to see his face when he clocks you," Sonya said. "Can I come?"

"Sadly I let my connection slip to Diana, and she warned me in no uncertain terms to be professional, so I suppose I'll have to be a good girl."

"Bummer," was Sonya's considered reply.

Hope flipped the pages of her diary to enter the signing before making a to-do list and Sonya returned to typing a letter. "December fifth and sixth." A nano-pause then, "Fuck! Fuck, fuck, fuck!"

Sonya spun her chair around. "What's up?"

"The fifth and sixth. The sixth is the first Saturday in December!"

"And your point is?"

Hope groaned. "Wouldn't you know that fecking gobshite would screw it up for me! Bastard!"

"What?" Sonya said, still at a loss.

"That's the day of ..." she lowered her voice, "of Amber Banner's party."

"So?" Sonya said.

"So how can I be in two sodding places at once?"

Sonya gave her a leery look. "Knowing you, you'll figure something out."

It was almost lunch-time by the time Hope had completed her list for Dylan's stay in Dublin. She'd been tempted, recalling Charity's wedding, to book an all-singing, all-dancing, lights-flashing, pink pimpmobile, but fear of the wrath of Diana got the better of her and she settled for a boring black Merc instead. Reading the press release she discovered that he was still with Laura and they divided their time between their Tuscany hideaway and their home in Wandsworth Common, South London, where they kept their two springer spaniels called respectively Estragon and Vladimir (pretentious git). He was a regular panellist on a BBC Radio 4 arts programme, an occasional contributor to the *Newsnight* review segment, and his 'long awaited' third novel was entitled *The End of the Endgame*. Does that pompous gobshite ever have an original idea, she thought, doubtful that he'd even read the Beckett work from which he'd hamfistedly plagiarised yet another title. The press release went on to list the other two titles. There was some bumph about those, snippets of reviews and quotes from the author, blah, blah, blah, and at the bottom of the page, contact numbers for his agent, Geoffrey Mandelson, Icon Publishing and, of course, Hackett & McAllister, for further information.

Having done all she needed to do for *The End of the Endgame* signing for the moment, and waiting until Diana had gone out for lunch, she settled herself at her desk and set about organising Amber's party. Her first preference of venue was Fitzgerald House, a beautifully restored but modest Georgian mansion set in ten acres close to Greystones. The house accommodated only ten bedrooms, but the coach-house annexe and farmyard buildings had been sympathetically converted to create an additional fifteen rooms and a health spa, so it was eminently suitable. She and Luke had attended a wedding there the previous year and found the service to be superb, though it ranked as a Personal Best in spending for one weekend away. Nonetheless it had been well worth it and she felt sure Amber would approve. The flaw in the plan proved to be the fact that there were only six rooms available in the main house and eight in the annexe. When she explained that she would possibly need at least three to four more rooms, the accommodation manager said there was a strong possibility that they would have some cancellations in the meantime, as two bookings for that date had still to be confirmed, and if not, the remainder of the guests could be accommodated at a nearby up-market B&B. As to the theme of the weekend, she was pleasantly surprised to hear that Fitzgerald House regularly ran Murder Mystery Weekends which was a plus as she'd expected that she would have to contract out that element of the party, so it was one less thing for her to worry about. The Functions Manager promised to email the 'attractive function rates' and menus for Amber's approval. Hope provisionally booked the fourteen rooms in case she lost them, hoping that the majority of Amber's guests would be couples, but confident that even if that were not the case everyone would be accommodated, one way or the other. Easy peasy, she thought as she put the phone down. Next she called her second choice, Albion Place, a country house hotel situated near Avoca. Availability wasn't a problem there, but as they didn't do their own Murder Mystery Weekends she would have to book a group to do it. They didn't do special rates either which made it considerably more expensive, though the restaurant had a brilliant reputation, superb reviews and one Michelin Star. They too promised to post out the rates to her, though she got the impression that the manager was a bit stuffy about the Murder Mystery aspect from the disapproving tone of his voice. Her call to Harvey Holster in order to book the Dixieland Pioneers, a great trad jazz band James had used once before for a charity promotion was equally disappointing. Apparently there was a jazz festival on in Carlow on the weekend of the sixth of December and The Dixies weren't available. Harvey however promised to get back to her with a suitable substitute.

Diana returned from lunch in the middle of this phone call causing Hope a moment of anxiety until it occurred to her that she would probably assume she was making the call for James. Then just as she was dialling Rhona Bucket, a theatrical agent she knew, to enquire about the Murder Mystery players in case Amber chose Albion Place, James walked in. Jumpy on guilt overload and looking distinctly shifty she abruptly hung up before the call connected.

The following lunch-time she called in to see a friend of Luke's who ran an outlet for printed invitations and general party goods. Knowing he was aware that she worked for a PR company she didn't say anything to change his obvious assumption that she was on company business, and he bent over backwards to help her, grateful for the opportunity to get a corporate account. Leafing through his catalogue she selected around a dozen party invitation examples for Amber, along with some cute little art deco style gift boxes for party favours, and he let her take samples of gifts, including handmade chocolates, silver trinket boxes, tie-pins, cufflinks etc. She also priced disposable cameras for the tables, printed table napkins and place cards. Later that afternoon, on the pretext of going out to the post office, she checked out a couple of florists for the table decorations, and quite by chance passed a new confectionary called Over The Top in Crown Alley. The window was full of totally fantastic confections with the ability to send the consumer on big-time sugar and cholesterol overload by the consumption of one tiny delicious morsel. She wandered in, still wearing her corporate cap, inhaling the aromatically luscious aroma of chocolate ganache as she stepped over the threshold, and experienced an instant seratonin fix on the fumes alone. After a bit of chat she secured the corporate price list.

When she got back to the office an hour and a half after slipping away, she met James on his way out. "Where were you?" he asked.

"Post Office," she said, averting her eyes. "Oh, and

um … I had a bit of personal business to attend to. Sorry."

"Personal business? Oh! Right!" He looked embarrassed. "Sorry to hear about you and Luke."

Surprised that he knew, she said, "Thanks. What did you want me for?"

James shook his head. "Oh, nothing. Nothing important anyway." He gave her arm a sympathetic pat and, after an awkward pause, muttered, "Oh well. It'll all work out. You'll see," and hurried off.

Sonya looked relieved to see her when she walked, a tad bemused, into reception. "Jesus! Where were you?"

"Why did you tell James about me and Luke?" she asked.

"Had to say something. He's been buzzing you for the past hour. Where were you by the way?"

Hope sat down at her desk. "Sorting stuff out for the party," she said. "Where do you think?"

"Well, be careful. If Diana thinks you're doing stuff in company time she'll go spare."

"Chill, will you? She won't find out," Hope assured her.

That night, after finally managing to get in the call to Rhona Bucket, she had all the information she needed in order to prepare a quotation. She also had the address of a theatrical costumier, admittedly in London, but from what she'd heard, Amber was a frequent social commuter anyway, and if *VIP* and *Social and Personal* were anything to go by, it was unlikely that any of her chums would balk at the cost. Totting up all the figures and calculating her fee (a percentage of the overall budget) she estimated that she should make close on two and a half thousand pounds. Not bad for a couple of days' work, she thought.

Amber was all excitement about the party when she called to see her with the estimates. When she showed her the brochures for the two hotels though, she frowned, which caused Hope a moment's anxiety, until she went on to say, "I can't stay at Albion Place. I stayed there with my ex, you see, and I don't think Eric would be comfortable with that."

Hope exhaled. "That's fair enough. My first choice would be Fitzgerald House anyway. Much better rates, and they have the health spa too. I stayed there myself last year – a wedding – so I can personally recommend it. The food and the service were superb."

"Terrific!" Amber enthused. "I've heard if it, but never stayed there, but I think Mummy and Daddy have."

"Fitzgerald House it is then," Hope said relieved. Despite thoroughly doing her homework, she was still nervous considering this was the first time she'd had to actually sell a proper grown-up party package, and fervently hoped that she hadn't forgotten anything. It was a long way from jelly, ice cream and Mister Custard.

She went through all the items on her list and Amber chose the invitation cards, on Hope's suggestion sticking to an art deco theme, and decided on the silver trinket boxes and chocolates for the girls and cufflinks and chocies for the boys. In discussing the wording of the invitations, Amber really got into the swing of things and after inviting her guests to a nineteen twenties Murder Mystery Weekend in honour of Eric Dunbar's birthday, she specified that dress for dinner was formal, and period costume preferred.

"This is going to be such fun!" she said, eyes alight, and Hope found her enthusiasm endearing. They discussed the flowers, the menus and the itinerary. Arriving in time for dinner on Friday night. Saturday morning free to enjoy the grounds, the spa, horse riding (optional) and even clay-pigeon shooting and archery, with the murder mystery element commencing after lunch, culminating at midnight, the weekend wrapping up after a late brunch on the Sunday afternoon. Hope then asked if she'd thought of a birthday cake for Eric. Amber had forgotten about the cake and was relieved that she'd mentioned it.

"Well, it's my job to think of details like that," Hope assured her. "There's a new confectionary outlet in Crown Alley, Over The Top, and they do amazing stuff. Would you like to go there with me on Saturday afternoon sometime, and you can choose the cake yourself?"

"Oooh, chocolate! It has to be chocolate. Eric *loooves* chocolate," she said.

"I was hoping to get you a traditional jazz band for atmosphere, but unfortunately there's a jazz festival on that weekend in Carlow so the one I had in mind is booked, but then it occurred to me, what about an old-fashioned orchestra? Think Palm Court. *The Great*

Gatsby. The kind of orchestra that used to play at tea dances? You must have seen them in old black and white movies, and to tell you the truth it might be more authentic. What do you think?"

This was in fact Harvey Holster's idea as he had a suitable seven-piece orchestra on his books who were available on the given dates, so Hope was confident in making the suggestion. Amber was equally keen about that proposal too which Hope found encouraging and she realised that she was actually beginning to enjoy herself. Amber promised to get back to her in a couple of days to confirm everything. Hope had a stab of apprehension realising that Amber had yet to get her father's approval, but relaxed again when she added, "I'm sure Daddy will be fine about it, but I have to run it by him anyway, considering he's paying and all that."

As Amber had promised, Morgan Banner had no problems with the estimate and as soon as she confirmed and paid the hefty deposit, Hope set about booking everything. It was tough going keeping all the balls in the air at once as it was a particularly busy time for Hackett & McAllister and the day job kept encroaching on her efforts, but nonetheless, she managed to get it all booked and confirmed which left her with a huge degree of satisfaction.

It got her to thinking, I can *do* this. I *should* do this.

Chapter 27

The day before Dylan Jones was due to fly in, Luke got back to her with the estate agent's valuation of the apartment, and Hope was staggered. She knew property prices were going through the roof, but she'd had no idea that the value of their snug two-bedroomed Smithfield pad had increased by such an obscene amount. "Are you sure this isn't a typo? Surely there's one too many noughts on that figure," she said, disbelieving her eyes, recounting the zeros.

Luke grinned and shook his head. "Nope. No mistake. See – I told you buying was a good idea. And it looks as if we bought at just the right time."

She couldn't argue with that, and the windfall suddenly turned a mere pipedream into a more substantial concrete concept, as she confided in Sonya.

"*A bird in the hand doesn't make a summer in the bush,*" her friend warned, "or something ..."

But Hope got her mangled proverb and reined in her ambition just a bit. "I'm not stupid," she said defensively. "I'm not just going to pack the job in. But I'll wait and see what comes of this. And who knows? If it goes well, her friends might book me. Anyway," she added, "I'll have to wait until the apartment's sold before I can even think about it."

The following morning, before dawn even had a thought of cracking, Jim, the limo driver, rang her doorbell. Hope had been up and about for two hours, edgy and unable to sleep. She had planned the day like a military operation. Pick up Bollox-Head and Laura, drive across the city to the RTE studios for ten. She'd phoned the producer to find out the approximate time of Dylan's interview, and he'd told her 11.30 to 11.45. No need for Dylan to know that though. That gave her more than an hour and a half to drive on to Fitzgerald House, which was about twenty minutes away from the Donnybrook studios, check that everything was in place and be back in time to pick them up. Then they'd head back to town to the Berkley Court, get checked in, remind Dylan about the press interviews then head back to the office – Diana would be none the wiser – then pick him up again in time for the *Rattlebag* recording back out at RTÉ.

As she sat in the front passenger seat on the way to

the airport it suddenly hit her that she was about to meet Dylan again. In all the excitement of organising Amber's party, the break-up with Luke and just the everyday bustle of a very busy office, the implications hadn't dawned on her. The last time she'd laid eyes on him, in the flesh so to speak, had been through the back window of Tudor's Morris Minor Traveller. But how would he react? How would Laura react? She was pretty confident that she could handle it – after all, he was ancient history and she had moved on, and he had no idea that he was going to come face to face with her. She wasn't sure if she felt smug or anxious.

Checking the arrivals screen she noted that his flight had landed at 8.07, so she headed to the arrivals area and twenty minutes later she saw him walk out of Customs in the company of a young fresh-faced girl of around twenty. Though he'd changed a lot she would have known him anywhere. He was looking around, presumably for a driver with a placard reading *Important Novelist* (or if Hope had had any say, *Arsehole*). He looked older, no surprise there. His head was shaved to a number two which was a surprise, and he'd put up at least three stone. His skin looked dangerously ruddy – more a red-faced John Goodman than Daniel Day Lewis now, the broody good looks having succumbed to the good life. Too much rich food, booze and drugs probably. She smiled to herself, realising that the photo on the flyleaf of his book covers still showed him lean, broody and nine years younger.

She searched the other travellers for any sign of Laura, but she was conspicuous by her absence. Then the words "double room" came to mind when she realised that he and the young girl were together. She wondered why she was surprised. Leopards and their spots.

He was standing, a look of mild irritation on his face. His companion was standing beside him. Petite, dark, pretty, dressed in jeans and parka, a small rucksack slung over one shoulder. Hope approached from his blind side.

"Hello, Dylan – welcome to Dublin."

His head shot round and their eyes met. He was speechless, and his eyes left hers and darted around the area, perhaps looking for help, his brain trying to process the information, perhaps afraid that she was going to stab him, make some kind of scene, or something of that nature.

"Relax, Dylan. I'm Diana McAllister's PA. I'm here to meet you." Her eyes shifted to the girl. "Aren't you going to introduce me to your friend?"

Dylan's vocal chords still appeared to be in a state of stasis so the girl shot out her hand. "Saffron Walters," she said. "I'm Dylan's assistant." She had a crisp English accent with a touch of Sloane.

"Oh course, you are," Hope replied smiling at her. "Shall we go? Your car's outside."

Hope was extremely businesslike on the drive in from the airport, acquainting the Important Novelist with his itinerary. The *Kenny Byrne Radio Show* at ten. The *Sunday Tribune* at 1.30 with photo shoot. Two radio interviews down the line for independent regional radio stations after that, then out to RTE again for *Rattlebag,* the Radio One afternoon arts programme, to record a brief interview with Myles Dungan, and do a short reading.

"Then you're free until ten tomorrow morning when the *Irish Times* want an interview. They're doing a piece for next week's *Saturday Magazine*, so I guess there'll be a photographer too."

"And where's that interview?" Saffron asked.

"At your hotel," Hope said, handing her a copy of the itinerary. "All the interviews, obviously apart from the ones out at RTE, are arranged for your hotel."

Hope was sitting opposite Dylan and Saffron, with her back to Jim, the driver. As Saffron read the printed sheet of appointments, Hope felt Dylan's eyes on her and she glanced over at him. He didn't look away so neither did she and she held his stare until he blinked first and turned his head to look out of the window.

"The signing's scheduled for tomorrow. One o'clock until four at Eason's on O'Connell Street," Hope said, but didn't get any reaction from him as he just continued to stare out of the window. "Then you're done until dinner-time."

He gave a curt nod to that piece of info, possibly inviting her to shut up.

I wonder what's going through his mind, she

wondered, though she was none the wiser by the time they hit the Stillorgan dual carriageway in sight of the RTE studios, as he didn't say another word.

To break the silence on the way, Hope had chatted to Saffron. "Have you been Dylan's assistant long?" she asked, flashing a brief glance in his direction.

"Six months," the girl said smiling. "I've always been in publishing though. I was with Icon until I joined Dylan."

Hope got the picture. Young impressionable girl. How long had she withstood the self-deprecating charm offensive? Had she fallen for the 'my wife and I lead separate lives' old guff? For sure he was screwing her, evidenced by the one double-room booking. Evidenced also by the covert but adoring glances she was giving her hero, coupled with the fact that he was studiously avoiding any reciprocation. *Have to keep it professional at work, petal.* Poor cow, Hope thought. She's got it bad.

"Your table's booked for tomorrow night," she said, addressing him, forcing him to look at her again. "The Morrison, nine o'clock. Diana asked me to book for ten people. Is that right?"

He counted on his fingers, then nodded. "Yeah. Ten people. That's right."

She smiled innocently at him. "Excellent. And there's nothing else you'd like me to help you with?"

He frowned, puzzled. "Such as?"

Hope shrugged. "Oh, I don't know. Book you a

restaurant for tonight, or maybe you'd just prefer *room service?*"

He didn't react, just continued to stare at her,

"No? How about a bit of judicious editing then?" she offered.

She knew she'd scored a direct hit then because she could see the vein in his temple start to throb and the colour was rising up his neck. Saffron looked bemused, a half smile on her lips, obviously thinking this was some kind of joke, and waiting for the punch line.

"Dylan and I are old friends," she explained to the girl. "Years ago, before he was famous."

"Really?" Saffron said. "Wow! What a coincidence!"

"Yes. Isn't it?" she agreed. "What is it they say about chickens coming home to roost, Dylan?"

He was glaring at her now but he managed to keep his tone neutral. "I don't know, Hope." He paused for a beat. "Tell me – do you like your job?"

She had no intention of letting him get the better of her, but equally was alive to the unspoken threat. "Yes, thanks. Very much."

"Then I'd stick to being Diana's PA. Forget about publishing. Editing's not really your thing."

"You think not?"

He nodded emphatically. "I think not. And good PA jobs are hard to come by, so I'd take care, if I were you." He forced a smile. "Thin ice, if you get my drift."

She hadn't expected an actual thank you, but she thought he might at least have had the good grace to acknowledge her contribution to his success in some small way. Perhaps when she'd mentioned that they were old friends. An obvious opportunity to stick in a 'Yes, Hope was a great help to me in those early days', even. Mindful of Diana's warning she hadn't intended to make any reference to the past but witnessing Saffron's obvious adoration had first irritated, then annoyed her so much, she'd found herself unable to resist the temptation to score a few digs at him.

Saffron, detecting the now sub-zero atmosphere brightly piped up, "Oh look! I think we're here."

As the car pulled up at the Radio Centre, Hope said to Saffron. "Just check in at reception and they'll take care of you. I'll wait out here in the car."

Dylan was already out of the car by this time, so Saffron slithered along the seat towards the door.

"OK. *The Kenny Byrne Show*?"

Hope nodded. "Just check in at reception."

Hopping over to the seat just vacated by Dylan she watched as he and his assistant disappeared inside the Radio Centre. "OK, Jim. Can you take me to Greystones now, please?"

On the drive out to Fitzgerald House, instead of calming down she got more and more annoyed. What a bollox! Arrogant wanker! Chill, her alter ego advised. Don't let the bastard get to you. You've moved on, and he'll always be a gobshite.

Morris Boyle, the functions manager, was there to meet her and showed her the Lord Edward suite, a beautiful round room at the rear of the house overlooking the gardens where Amber's party was to be held over the two nights. The tables were all set up for dinner, though the floral decorations hadn't been delivered yet. Hope made a mental note to chase up the florist. The cake however had been, and it was a triumph. A tall cone of chocolate about eighteen inches in diameter at the base, covered in chocolate fudge frosting with white chocolate flowers spiralling from the bottom to the top. She'd confirmed the final numbers with Amber the previous night and rechecked with the accommodation manager that sufficient rooms had been reserved, specifying named guests for the rooms in the main house. While she was waiting for the accommodation manager, she had called Harvey to check up on the orchestra, anxious in case for some reason they wouldn't show up. He calmed her fears, promising that they would be out at Fitzgerald House by six to set up. All this took time however, and it was only when she saw Jim standing in reception trying to catch her eye that she glanced at her watch and saw that it was eleven thirty.

"I had the radio on," he said, "and I heard yer man."

"I know," she said, casting her eyes to the ceiling. "What a wanker!"

"Well, yeah, but the thing is, he's well finished. Aren't we supposed to be there to pick him up?"

"He's finished?! Feck off!"

Jim nodded and took her arm, encouraging her

towards the door. "I'm not kiddin'. He was on just after the eleven o'clock news."

Hope groaned. "Oh shit! Come on then."

They raced to the car and all credit to Jim, he screeched off, displacing showers of gravel as he sped down the drive. Then her mobile went off, Diana's name appearing on the screen.

"Where the fuck are you?" she demanded, without preamble.

"On my way back to pick Dylan up," Hope said. "He wasn't supposed to be ready till eleven forty-five. Kenny Byrne had him on early."

"On your way back from where?" Diana demanded. "You were supposed to sodding wait for him! He's just thrown a hissy fit down the phone to me."

Defence being the best form of attack, Hope said, "Who the hell does he think he is, talking to you like that? Fecking legend in his own lunch-time?"

Probably because she'd come to exactly the same conclusion, thrown off track, Diana agreed, "And then some. Talk about high maintenance. Where are you?"

"Close to the Stillorgan dual carriageway," Hope lied. "Should be there in five. Don't worry, I'm on it."

"Well, get a move on. Anyway, you still haven't told me where ..." Diana said, just as Hope heard her mobile ringing in the background. "Oh, it's Benny Harris. I have to take this, we'll talk later," and she hung up.

Hope's heart was pounding, but at last Benny

Harris's call had given her a temporary reprieve and a chance to think up some story for Diana.

Twenty minutes later, when neither the Important Novelist nor his assistant were in the proximity of the Radio Centre, at the receptionist's suggestion Hope made her way to the canteen, where she found both Dylan and Saffron sitting at a table, two half empty cups of coffee in front of them and the remains of breakfast fries. Anxious to avoid further trouble, and in light of the fact that Dylan's face was like thunder, Hope was all sweetness, light and apology.

"Sorry," she oozed, pulling out a chair and flopping down. "Bit of a hitch on the Press front, but I sorted it out. Heard you on *Kenny Byrne* by the way. You were very good."

Dylan, thoroughly wrong-footed, automatically switched to charming self-deprecation mode. "Oh, I don't know about that."

"Oh you were," Hope repeated, then casting an eye at the empty plates added, "Oh, great! Glad to see I didn't keep you waiting anyway. Sensible move to eat a good breakfast. Might not be time for more than a sandwich for lunch."

To avoid the heavy traffic, Jim drove to the Berkley Court by a circuitous route, arriving by twelve forty-five. Hope went with Dylan and Saffron to get them checked in.

"I wanted a suite," Dylan said, when he was assigned a standard double on the second floor. He glared at Hope, waiting for her to justify the mistake.

"But you asked for a double. An ordinary double or I'd have booked you a suite," she said, not sure if he was just being difficult for the sake of it.

"I'm sorry, sir, there are no suites available tonight, but there will be one available for tomorrow night, if that suits you?" the receptionist said.

"But I always have a suite," he whined, then sighed theatrically, shooting a toxic glance at Hope. "I suppose it will have to do."

"You *asked* for a double," Hope said not willing to let it go. "Why would I book you a double if you'd asked for a suite?"

"Because you're inefficient?" he offered flippantly.

Saffron looked mortified, and averted her eyes, shifting from one foot to the other. Hope recalled the feeling and empathised.

"Room 226, sir," the receptionist cut in, "and the Casement Suite for tomorrow night. May I have your credit card details, please?"

Dylan handed over his credit card then stepped away from the reception desk to let Saffron complete the check-in. Grabbing Hope by the arm he pulled her away a couple of paces and hissed, "You did that on purpose, bitch!"

"What?"

"Messed up the room booking, buggered off with my driver and left us marooned out at RTE. What else have you up your pathetic sleeve? Don't you dare try to fuck this up for me!"

Staggered by his spleen, Hope murmured, "Still just as paranoid, I see."

She felt his hand tighten around her upper arm.

"You'd better start looking for another job, lady, because I'm going to make certain you get the boot, do you hear me?"

"Oh, piss off, Dylan. Contrary to your inflated opinion of your own importance, the world doesn't revolve around you, you know. You weren't that put out. I found you in the canteen stuffing your face for feck sake." On the surface she appeared reasonably calm, but her heart was thumping and she was finding it difficult to hold on to her temper.

Aware that Saffron had turned away from the reception desk and was looking in their direction, Dylan loosened his grip, smiled at her, and to Hope said, in a reasonable tone, "Fine, tell Diana I'll talk to her later."

Hope just nodded, teeth gritted.

Then, as she turned to walk out, he called after her, "And leave the car!"

Chapter 28

Hope got a cab outside the Berkley Court and, reluctant to go back to the office until Diana had cooled down and hopefully forgotten about Dylan's tirade, headed for Amber's apartment instead. Whilst in transit, she called the florist who confirmed that the table decorations were on the way to Fitzgerald House as they spoke. Amber was in high spirits when she let Hope in. Eric was there too, so she finally got to meet him. He was older than she expected, early thirties possibly. Short for a man, around five six, and on the chunky side, with shaved head and a Celtic tattoo peeking out from the short sleeve of his T-shirt, but he had a friendly open manner and on first impressions she thought he was nice. While Amber made coffee,

Hope complimented him on his paintings.

"Thanks," he said. "I'm hoping to have an exhibition soon. I've finally got a big enough body of work together. Then maybe if all goes well, I can finally give up the day job."

"Where's the exhibition going to be held?" Hope asked, interested.

"Oh, nothing's arranged yet. It's still on the long finger, I'm afraid."

Amber returned with the coffee. "Are we all ready to go tonight?" she asked.

Hope nodded, relaxing in the knowledge that Eric's party was a *fait accompli*. "Yes. Everything's in place. I was out there this morning and the Lord Edward suite looks amazing." She took the espresso cup and saucer from Amber's hand.

"You should do it!" Amber suddenly said.

Hope stared at her. "Sorry?"

"Eric's exhibition. You should arrange it – shouldn't she, Eric?"

"Oh, right," Hope said, surprised but pleased.

"Well, that would be great, but ..." He looked a touch embarrassed. "The thing is, you're a bit out of my league. I'm afraid I just can't afford a big affair."

Amber's face fell. "Oh, sweetie? How can people recognise what a genius you are unless they see your work?"

"She's right, Eric," Hope agreed. Then, before she had time to think, added, "Anyway, it needn't cost that much. I'd be glad to do it for no fee at all."

"Oh, I couldn't expect you to do that," Eric protested.

"OK, then. How about if I do it for . . . let's say … just one canvas? A small one. The exhibition won't have to be expensive – leave it with me and let me see what I can come up with."

When Amber saw her to the door she explained, "Eric's very independent, you know. He won't take money from me."

Hope smiled. "At least it's nice to know he's not after you for your money."

"Oh, I know," Amber agreed, "but sometimes it is a bit infuriating when he won't let me help him."

"Well, maybe you can, just not with cash."

Amber's perfectly arched eyebrows crinkled. "I don't understand."

"Guerrilla PR," Hope said. "Contacts, networking. We might be able to get everything for free one way or another. Leave it with me. I'll call you in a couple of days and we can brainstorm."

"You'd do that for us?"

Hope smiled. "Oh course. You're my first private client. You had faith in me, so it's the least I can do."

"That's so nice. Thank you. Will I see you later?"

"Absolutely. I'll be out at Fitzgerald House to make sure everything's perfect."

Amber gave her a hug. "Thank you so much."

Despite the sentiments expressed to Amber, the fact

that she genuinely liked the girl and was glad to help, Hope's motives weren't entirely altruistic. She was well aware that Amber had a large network of friends, and to have her under some obligation could prove to be useful. And as for the Guerrilla PR, she'd seen Diana in action and she already had a plan in mind.

The call on Amber had temporarily put Dylan from her mind, but on the short walk back to the office she replayed the morning's events. The pettiness of him kicking up about the room, alleging that she'd made a mess of the booking. His threats to get her fired. In some respects she was surprised by how much he'd changed for the even worse. Success had certainly gone to his head and he obviously believed his own publicity, considering himself to really *be* an Important Novelist. She couldn't fault his self-belief, despite the fact that left to his own devices it was doubtful the first book would ever have been published – or even finished come to that. She felt a small knot of anger at his refusal to acknowledge her help on that score. Admittedly her motives hadn't been exactly pure, but the end result had proved to be very fortuitous for him. Obviously another case of selective amnesia, she decided. She wondered what he'd said to Saffron about her. How would he describe their relationship? Would he bother? She decided that no, he wouldn't. She was history. A nagging loose end. It was clear from his reaction that he wasn't happy to have her around though, presumably in case she made waves.

Waves?

She gave a wicked grin. How perceptive of him!

She stopped abruptly and, changing direction, headed for Elephant & Castle. The lunch-time rush was diminishing as it was coming up for two o'clock so she got a table straight away. After she had ordered a basket of chicken wings she rummaged in her bag and pulled out Diana's press release, then after a brief pause thought, feck it, and dialled Geoffrey Mandelson's number.

"Mandelson & Fenwick."

"Hello. This is …" she groped for a name then her eyes fell on the ketchup bottle, "Scarlett Heinz from Porter & French PR in Dublin. I need to speak to Laura, Dylan Jones' partner, urgently. Some of his friends over here have planned a surprise party for him to celebrate the publication of *The End of the Endgame*, you see, and they assumed that she'd be travelling with him. Sorry, who am I speaking to?"

"Tiffany Merrick. I'm Mr Mandelson's Assistant, but I'm afraid I can't hand out that information over the phone." She sounded apologetic.

"I totally understand, Tiffany," Hope gushed. "But perhaps if I gave you my number, you could contact her and get her to call me? It is rather urgent. The party's tomorrow night and Dylan's friends are really anxious that she should be there."

"I'm sure I could do that, Scarlett," Tiffany Merrick said. "I'll call her right away."

"Thank you so much," Hope said. "Dylan will be *so* surprised."

She briefly had second thoughts after she terminated the call, but the recent memory of his arrogance strengthened her resolve. Then her chicken wings arrived so, as she gnawed her way through them, she rehearsed what she would say to Laura.

Diana was out when she got back to the office. Hope was relieved, but the anxiety returned when, ten minutes later, she bustled in.

"I need you upstairs Hope – *now*," she said, without interrupting her passage through reception.

Hope shot a wary look at Sonya, who just shrugged, so Hope followed her boss, anxiously rehearsing excuses as she trotted upstairs towards Diana's office.

Diana however had other things on her mind. "Benny Harris was arrested for shoplifting yesterday."

"The poet? Good grief. What did he take?"

Diana, who was scanning her email inbox, met her eyes. "Three bottles of vodka and a case of Budweiser from Tesco."

Hope opened her mouth to express disbelief but, before she had a chance, Diana shook her head. "I know. But he claims he just forgot to go through the check-out." She paused. "Mind you, he was wasted at the time, or so his solicitor said."

"So what's the spin?" Hope asked. "Are we going to play it up or down?"

"Oh, no contest. Up," Diana said. "He has a new

collection of poetry out next month." She smiled. "*Manna from the Gods*." Sitting down behind her desk she flipped open her diary and made an entry. "I've a meeting with Hughie Montgomery in half an hour, so I'm going to give you the chance to write a press release, playing the incident up. Usual stuff, tortured creative genius. Make reference to Kavanagh, Beehan, and any other old literary soaks you can think of. Make it light-hearted, but be sure to stress how mortified and ashamed he is."

"Are you serious?" Hope said, staggered but delighted. "About me writing it, I mean?"

Diana peered at her over her half glasses. "Am I known for my sense of humour?" she asked, without the slightest trace of jest. "Don't send it out though. I want to read through it first."

Hope was still standing in front of her desk in a mild state of shock. She'd been expecting a tirade from Diana regarding the Dylan incident, but she obviously didn't think it that important and it had slipped her mind.

"Well, go on then! Don't just stand there," Diana snapped, but there was just the hint of a smile on her lips.

Hope sprang into action. "OK. Right."

As she hurried through the door, Diana shouted after her, "And I want it on my desk by the time I get back at four o'clock. I want to make the late edition of the *Evening Herald* and I'll probably have to rewrite the bloody thing."

* * *

"So remind me. Did she bin your efforts and rewrite it herself?" Reuben asked.

They were standing by the lifts in the Berkley Court close to the Casement Suite.

"Nope," Hope said, feeling strangely proud that her first press release had been sent out unedited, as written. "It was the first of many."

"So all in all it was a pretty successful weekend."

Hope nodded, wondering from which direction the sting would come. He was being way too nice. "Yes. Amber's party was a resounding success. Not a hitch," she said guardedly.

Reuben slid his back down the wall and sat on the carpet, his long legs crossed. "And what about Laura?"

"What *about* Laura?" she said, not willing to admit to anything.

The angel frowned. "Oh, please! Don't act the innocent. You know very well what I'm talking about."

As he spoke the lift doors opened and Laura walked out, a small overnight bag and a key card in her hand. Glancing first left then right, she made straight for the door of the Casement Suite and let herself in.

"That was just luck. I didn't expect –"

The sentence was cut off by a scream followed by raised voices, Laura's the loudest, a thump, a crash and another scream – then Saffron erupted from the room naked but for a cushion clutched in an effort to cover herself. In an obvious panic, after a brief hesitation, she slipped back into the room, where Laura was still hurling abuse at Dylan. She emerged a millisecond later amid a hail of clothing in all probability chucked by the incandescent Laura, who then banged the door after her. Saffron, still clutching the cushion, grabbed some of the clothes and tore off down the corridor, presumably desperate to get as far away from Laura's ire as possible.

"As I was saying," Hope continued, "I didn't expect she'd actually catch them at it. That was a bonus. I thought she'd just turn up and put a halt to Dylan's gallop."

"So why did you pinch Saffron's key card and leave it at reception in an envelope for Laura?"

"I didn't pinch it. I picked it up after she carelessly dropped it. Again, just a stroke of luck I suppose," she said unable to stop the smile.

"And you have no regrets?" Reuben asked, a touch censoriously in her opinion.

"About what? Laura wasn't exactly the innocent, Reuben. She was shagging Dylan behind *my* back, so don't expect me to feel sorry for her. And as for Saffron, well. I probably saved her a whole load of grief."

"Still," Reuben said, just as Laura stormed from the suite and made for the lift.

Hope stepped to one side to let her pass, but it was obvious that Laura couldn't see her as she punched the lift button and stood, steaming, waiting for the doors to open.

Just then Dylan hopped from the room, one leg in his jeans. "Laura, wait! This isn't what it looks like! She means nothing to me!"

Saffron, now dressed in a haphazard assortment of clothes but still clutching the cushion, unable to find the stairs, had just turned the corner on her way back to the lift. She stopped dead in her tracks when she heard that.

Hope burst out laughing.

Saffron, however, was made of sterner stuff than Hope had been at that age. Her face scarlet, she tore down the corridor and launched herself at Dylan, screaming abuse, battering him with the cushion which burst due to the force of the onslaught, covering him in feathers in an ironic reprise. When the empty cushion cover proved to be ineffective she resorted to using her clenched fists.

Laura, who had completely ignored Dylan's pathetic pleas, turned to witness the assault, and it was obvious that his stock excuse held a resonant reminder because she laughed out loud and said, "You can take him!" She laughed again as the lift doors opened. "I'll just take him to the cleaners!"

"And she did," Hope said, grinning. "The house in Wandsworth Common. Half his earnings along with the dogs, a shitload of cash and four weeks a year in the Tuscan hideaway."

Dylan, amid frantic placatory cooing to the distraught Saffron, had managed to grab hold of her wrists to avoid further injury, and coax her back into the suite.

As the door closed behind them Reuben said, "That was still a rotten thing to do."

"Oh, stop being so bloody holier than thou!" Hope scoffed. "He had it coming. Anyway, how was that worse than what he was doing? Or what Laura did to me? Or what Saffron did to Laura come to that?"

"Or what you did to Monica?" he cut in.

She conceded that point, adding, "Well, at least Saffron and I had an excuse. We were seduced by him. We believed his old guff."

Reuben glided back to his feet and pressed the lift call button. "All the same."

He was annoying her now. In all honesty she couldn't see what she had done that was so terrible. "I can't believe you're holding this incident against me. He had it coming. If I'd wanted I could have caused him far more problems by going to the papers when *Stockton Pier* was published. I had the chance to change his future if you remember and I didn't. I posted the sodding manuscript. I did him a favour. He owed me."

Reuben looked down his nose at her and gave a derisive sniff. "In all probability you only posted the manuscript so you could have the satisfaction of doing this."

"That's so unfair!"

Reuben didn't comment further which was frustrating. If her chances of leaving Crusty Heaven hadn't been dependent on the whole contrition and forgiveness thing she'd have told him to sod off. "If you're determined to be picky," she said, "you owe me one, remember? For the phantom jelly-chucker?"

The lift doors opened and Reuben stepped inside, his mouth twitching in amusement at the memory of Little Jeremy splatting the bowl of jelly and ice cream into her face. He sighed. "Oh all right then. I suppose I can scribble that one out."

Relieved, she joined him in the lift. "Good. What now?"

He pressed the ground floor button. "Diana, James, Amy?"

She hadn't seen that one coming so soon and felt a flood of relief. "Amy? I'll take Amy."

"It wasn't a list of options," he said, fixing her with a steely gaze. "I meant Diana *and* James *and* Amy."

That was a disappointment. She thought he'd just fast forwarded to Amy, but nonetheless, at least the end was in sight. At least, if she played her cards right, she knew that there was some slim chance that she could get herself out of this predicament. "OK. If you insist," she said brightly. "Bring it on."

Chapter 29

There were no repercussions after the Dylan visit. She was hoping that he had enough to worry about without attempting to chuck his weight around and get her sacked but she was still a little nervous going into work on Monday morning. She relaxed however when, after confiding in Sonya, her friend pointed out that Dylan probably hadn't even connected Laura's sudden appearance with her, and anyway, even if he had, Diana would probably have seen the funny side. Hope wasn't so sure about that, and was very relieved when her boss didn't mention the incident.

Amber contacted her later that afternoon, absolutely delighted after the success of Eric's party. They arranged to meet up at her apartment that evening to discuss the options for his exhibition. At first Amber didn't understand how it could be done for relatively nothing until Hope explained the concept of Guerrilla PR. That is to say, finding ways of getting publicity, venue etc for little or nothing. Hope, as usual, had a checklist, top of which was Amber's family, and her network of friends.

"But Eric won't take help from my family," she reminded Hope.

"No. Eric won't take *money* from your family. How about we turn it round? How about we make it so Eric's helping them?"

"I don't understand."

"OK, your mother's involved in charity work, isn't she?" Hope recalled seeing Amber's mother, Audrey, all the time in the papers, *Hello!* even, supporting one charity or another. "What's her pet project, would you say?"

Amber thought about it for a moment. "Hmmm …blind dogs. I would think."

It took a moment. "Oh, I see. *Guide* dogs." She was disappointed. "Nothing sexier than that, I suppose?"

"Such as?" Amber asked. "How do you mean 'sexier'?"

"Oh, you know. Something that catches the collective public conscience a bit more. Sick children, battered women, Romanian orphanages … something like that?"

"She was involved in this project to donate

antibiotics and cancer drugs for abandoned kids somewhere – Armenia or Kazakhstan or somewhere like that," Amber said after a further moment's thought.

"Perfect! Sick *orphaned* kids. Couldn't be better!"

Amber frowned. "But I still don't understand where this is going."

"We do a benefit," Hope said. "Eric's exhibition will be a benefit night for the Eastern European underprivileged sick kids. How sexy is that! All I need to do is find a sponsor which shouldn't be too hard if the charity endorses the event, which is where your mother comes in. One of the pharmaceutical companies maybe – the positive publicity would be well worth it for them. They might even cough up some drugs for free too." She laughed. "For the kids I mean, not the guests! Tickets at say, two hundred quid a pop. Get one of the wine wholesalers interested, maybe shell out for a few canapés and nibbles or steamed *wan ton* perhaps – that would be a bit stylish. Steamed *wan ton* or *sushi*. Invite a few celebrities, get the media interested and, *voilà*! Eric gets his exhibition, and sells some canvases as well as getting a truckload of publicity for free, and the charity gets the door proceeds. Everyone's happy."

Amber was hugely impressed. "That's brilliant! This could be Eric's big chance." And she insisted on phoning Audrey that very minute.

And that was the start of it.

Eric's exhibition/benefit was a resounding success.

All the canvases sold on the night, six of the larger ones to Sylvester Stallone who happened to be in Dublin for a film premiere, and by sheer chance attended the event as the guest of Stephen Rea who was his co-star in the movie, and was associated with the charity. Audrey and the other ladies who lunch and do charity work were deadly impressed which, in turn, led to some small (paying) gigs. The breakthrough came however the following March when Morgan Banner (heavily encouraged by Amber) contacted Hope to arrange her first corporate event. It coincided with the completion of the sale of the apartment, so she found herself with a fairly sizeable windfall. The question was, should she be sensible and cautious and put the lot down on another apartment, or take a chance and use a chunk of the money to set up her own business? One way or another she had to make a decision because the way things were going she knew she couldn't manage to organise a high-profile corporate event in her spare time. It was make-your-mind-up time.

"Go for it," was Sonya's advice.

But her father, Mister Cautious Public Servant, thought she should keep the regular job, put her cash into bricks and mortar and start a pension fund.

"Take no notice of your father," was Maisie's advice. "Far too cautious by half." Which was in itself a little worrying because she never took her mother's advice about anything.

Josh was equally encouraging, albeit over the phone

from Atlanta. He phoned her every couple of weeks, but, possibly because of the distance between them, the tenor of his calls had reverted to good-mate status which Hope found a touch disappointing and very confusing. That he was a good mate was not in dispute. In any case, she was looking forward to seeing him again the following month when his contract with CNN was up.

"I think you should go for it," he'd said. "You have a natural talent for organisation." There was a nano-pause before he added, "It's because you're so bloody bossy!"

"Cheek!" she'd replied, but she was glowing from the compliment and his faith in her.

On balance, it was Josh's confidence in her that tipped the scales and the following morning she asked to see Diana and James together.

"Look, it's not because I'm unhappy here, you've both been really great and taught me a huge amount, but, well the thing is ..." She squirmed uncomfortably.

"You're leaving," Diana finished the sentence for her. She looked at James. "I knew it! Who poached you? What did they offer?"

"Oh no. No one. It's not like that," she cut in. "If I wanted to stay in PR I wouldn't want to work anywhere else, honestly. It's just I want to go into event management. Myself. Just me. On my own. You see I've been doing some events in my spare time and I think I can make a go of it, what with the cash from the apartment."

416

"In your spare time?" Diana said, scepticism dripping from the question.

Hope nodded, averting her eyes to James. "That's right."

Diana sat down. "So when were you thinking of going?" she asked, not sounding too happy a bunny.

Hope squirmed some more. "Ah, that's the thing. You see I've been offered this big contract and I need to take my holidays today so I can concentrate on it, but I'll work out my notice after that."

"Oh, I *see*," Diana said, heavy on the irony. "Not satisfied to be working virtually part-time while you set up your little business, and no doubt at our expense, now you want us to pay you while you're doing it."

"Oh come on, Diana, that's hardly fair!" James interjected.

"Oh wake up, James! You really think she's been organising these events in her spare time? Of course she hasn't. It all makes sense now."

Hope hackles rose. "That's not fair, Diana. I've never compromised my work here for you and James. Never."

Diana glared at her. "That's a matter for debate at another time. So when are you leaving?"

"Well ...um ... like I said ... I'd like to take my holidays now so I can concentrate on Morgan Banner's event."

Diana, despite herself, looked impressed, but James's expression was hard to read.

"Morgan Banner? Good grief, you are playing with

the big boys!" Diana said. "How did you swing that in your *spare time*?"

"This is really bad timing, Hope," James started apologetically.

"I know and I'm really sorry, James, but this is my big chance. And I'll even do part-time for a while if that suits you, until I'm properly up and running, and my replacement's trained in, if that helps. I wouldn't just leave you in the lurch."

"Well, that's good of you, Hope. And we appreciate –"

"No, we do not, James," Diana cut in, her temper showing. "Well, I certainly don't appreciate her sodding off like this and," Hope was harpooned by her angry gaze again, "you *are* leaving us in the lurch, and you damn well know it."

"Look. What more can I do? I offered to do part-time. I said I'd train in my replacement. What more can I do? I want to work for myself. What's so bad about that?"

"She's right, Diana." James's tone was conciliatory. "And Hope has the ability to make a go of it, so why shouldn't she?"

"Oh shut up, James!" Diana snapped. Then to Hope, "Just sod off out of my sight!"

Hope stood her ground. "But what about my holidays?"

"Tell you what," Diana snapped. "Part-time's no good to me. Take a permanent holiday. Go now. Yes. Just go now, clear your desk and piss off right now!"

James looked startled. "Diana!"

"No, James. I don't want her ferreting through my files and pinching my contacts. Do you? And come to that, do you really think we'll get a proper day's work out of her now. No! She should go *now*. Two weeks in lieu of notice. We'll never get a decent day's work out her at this stage. Her and her *big event!*"

Hope looked at James who was thinking over Diana's proposition.

"Maybe it is for the best," he said after a couple of charged beats, which caused her some disappointment. "I'll forward on what's owed to you."

Despite knowing Diana's form, her attitude had disappointed Hope, who felt she'd worked really hard for Hackett & McAllister. James's attitude was no surprise however once Diana's stance had become clear. He was a nice man, a great PR person and hail fellow well met, but Diana was better equipped in the balls department than he was.

"What's the story?" Sonya asked when she got back to her desk. "Diana sounded really pissed off."

Hope rummaged in her bottom drawer for a carrier bag in which to put her things. "You could say that. She fired me."

Sonya was gobsmacked. "What? But you resigned."

"When she accused me of leaving them in the lurch I offered to do part-time. I offered to work my notice and train in my replacement, but she fired me. Told me to clear my desk and piss off right now."

"But that's stupid. Why?"

"She doesn't want me," mimicking Diana she continued, "ferreting through her files and stealing her best contacts."

"That's a bit strong, even for her," Sonya commented as Hope slipped the notepad containing all Diana's best contacts trawled from her files over the previous months into the carrier bag.

"I know," Hope said. "What a cheek!"

* * *

"*Thou shalt not steal?* Shalt not tell porkies?"

"Oh sod off, Reuben!" Hope snapped. "How about '*Thou shalt not cut off thy nose to spite thy face*', which is exactly what Diana did. I was upfront with them. I could have just thrown a sicky for the Morgan Banner job, but I didn't. I was up front and honest. I didn't want to let them down, and look where it got me."

Reuben gave a Gallic shrug. "I suppose you have a point."

Hope, in full indignant flow-continued, "And if you are alluding to her contacts when you accuse me of stealing, I didn't *steal* anything. I just made a list of companies and people who might be useful to me. What difference could that have possibly made to Diana?"

"None, I suppose," the angel said.

"So I think you should scribble Diana's name out

and James's come to that," she insisted. "I was definitely the wronged party there and furthermore –"

"*Furthermore?*" Reuben cut in, a lopsided grin on his gob.

She ignored him, repeating, "Furthermore, I hope '*vicious*' and '*small-minded*' have been written up in Diana's file."

"Wouldn't know about that," he said. "Haven't –"

"I know, Hope cut in wearily. "You haven't seen the file."

* * *

Since moving out of the apartment after the sale, Hope had taken a lease on a small apartment in Christchurch. Due to the miniscule size (even smaller than the Smithfield apartment), she'd had to give up on cat-swinging, but it was just as central and the rent not too exorbitant which allowed her to continue living on her own. Living solo was a state she'd become accustomed to since Luke had moved out, and she found she liked it. Liked getting home to find the apartment in the same state in which she'd left it. Vegging out on a Sunday afternoon in her PJ's if she felt so inclined without someone sighing and tramping around because they fancied going to the pub and didn't want to go by themselves. It was only ever meant to be a temporary arrangement until she made up her mind as to what she was going to do with her share of the proceeds of the sale, i.e. whether she would buy or rent. In one way the decision had been taken out of her hands when Diana gave her a hefty shove rather than letting her jump in her own good time.

"That's it," she said to Sonya over a pint on the evening she was fired. "I suppose I'm committed now. At least I had the option of a bit of creative form-filling for the Building Society when I was still working, even part-time, for Hackett & McAllister, but I'm officially unemployed now, so there's no chance of a mortgage."

"Well, really you're self-employed rather than unemployed. I thought that's what you wanted."

"I suppose," Hope conceded. "It's just when I headed out to work this morning I thought I was just handing in my notice. I thought they'd be civilised about it. I never expected her to let me go right away."

"My gran reckons things happen for a purpose," Sonya said. "Now you'll just have to make a go of things."

Now that it was a reality, now there was no going back, Hope felt a wave of mild panic. "But what if I don't? What if I make a mess of it?"

Sonya snorted. "Why would you do that for feck sake? It's not as if you haven't given it a bit of a dry run. You know you can do it. And what better start than a big corporate contract from the likes of Morgan Banner? Anyway, what's the worst that can happen?"

"I lose all the money?" Hope offered.

"Well, that too, but what I'm getting at is, succeed or

fail, unless you give it a try you'll regret it for the rest of your life."

Hope knew she was right on that score.

"And even in the event of the corporate side going belly up," Sonya continued, bringing her back down to earth with a thump, "there's always wedding planning."

"Thanks for those words of comfort," Hope muttered, anxiety returning to gnaw at her guts.

"But it won't come to that," Sonya assured her, raising her empty glass. "I think it's your round by the way."

As Hope stood at the bar waiting to be served, she realised that Sonya was absolutely right. If she didn't give this her best shot, if she didn't take the chance, she would regret it for the rest of her life.

* * *

Two weeks later Hope stood waiting near the Arrivals gate at Dublin airport, a stampede of butterflies dancing a jig in her guts. She was waiting for Josh.

In the intervening time, the panic she'd experienced after Diana and James had let her go so abruptly had subsided and she realised that, in the event, it changed very little. In fact in some ways, as Sonya had pointed out, it was all for the best as it did indeed concentrate her mind on the matter at hand, namely that she was no longer a wage slave, but a self-employed person about to embark on a new and exciting project. The cushion of cash that had so fortuitously fallen into her lap was also a comfort and she felt confident that, as James had put it, she was well capable of making a go of it. Her first expenditure was a car, a three-year-old VW Polo with low mileage. Knowing absolutely nothing about cars she had been savvy enough to get a friend of her father's, who owned a garage, to find one for her. She bought a computer, a printer, a fax, and a set of empty box files and set it all up in the tiny second bedroom and, at her father's insistence and with his assistance, contacted the Revenue Commissioners, registered for VAT, and Prior Engagements was officially in business.

Anxiously checking her watch for the umpteenth time she wondered what was keeping Josh. His flight had landed half an hour ago but there was still no sign. Then a straggle of passengers exited Customs and there he was. The butterflies started turning double somersaults. It took a moment, but she managed to catch his eye and give a shy wave. Suddenly she felt awkward, though as soon as he saw her, his face lit up, and her heart leapt. Pushing through the crowd they eventually came face to face and stood there grinning like fools.

"How's it going, McFling?"

"How's yourself, Prior?"

For a moment they just stood staring at each other, equally idiotic looks on their faces, then he grabbed her and gave her an almighty bear-hug, knocking the breath out of her and lifting her off her feet. The next thing she knew they were kissing, she hanging on to him like she never wanted to let go, he the same. Coming up for air, they were still grinning like fools.

"Better late than never," he said and they both laughed. Then as he loosened his grip and her feet touched the ground again, his face was suddenly serious.

"You are ... well, you're not involved with anyone, are you? I haven't missed my window of opportunity again?"

Hope laughed. "It would be all your own fault if you had," she mocked. "For all the encouragement you gave me since you went back!"

He gave a sheepish smile. "Sorry. I wasn't altogether sure how you felt, and I didn't want to make a prat of myself if you just wanted to be mates."

She took a small step back, and took hold of his hands. "Josh, trust me, after all this time and all the false starts, the last thing I want to be is *just mates*."

Chapter 30

After the first Morgan Banner event, Prior Engagements took off. Hope's anxiety vanished and she realised that she had done exactly the right thing. The boom was in full swing and there was plenty of corporate money flying around. After his spell writing in sound-bites for CNN, and anxious to get back into the print media, Josh took a job with the *Irish Times* and the following year they bought a house together on the North Circular Road adjacent to the Zoological Gardens. It was a big step for Hope who, from past experience, was concerned that once they moved in together the rot would set in and they'd start to take each other for granted and drift apart as had happened with Luke, or worse, all the things she loved about Josh would prove to be some kind of cunning front which would, the minute they unpacked, slip, and he would turn into Dylan. Her other concern was whether she could actually share her living space with another person again as she was so accustomed to living alone. True, she and Josh had hardly spent a night apart since he'd come home, but there was always the option. Always a bolthole to flounce out to if they had a row. The fact was, though, none of these things happened. In fact, the opposite was the case. They became even closer and she found him perfectly comfortable and lovely to live with. He didn't turn into a procrastinating slob or a paranoid, precious, control freak and she loved him to bits. Loved. Really loved.

As to space, they didn't live in each other's pocket. Apart from the time they spent together, Josh played soccer, went to matches, out with the lads and didn't sulk when she went to the gym or a movie with friends, or had to work some evenings. She did have a moment of anxiety when he started to write a book, but here he proved again that he was no Dylan Jones and just plugged away at it for a couple of hours on wet Sunday afternoons, some evenings while she watched TV or if she was out. Her mother was totally enamoured of Josh too. He charmed her without trying, and even her father took to him, their mutual lifelong affiliation to Newcastle United the icebreaker. She got to know his family too and, though she wasn't mad about his mother, for the brief spells she had to spend at his family home in Galway it wasn't difficult to keep the fair side out. The fact that Josh was no mammy's boy and had no illusions about his ma, was also a good thing in this regard.

Their house was a three-bedroomed Victorian terrace, but it had been really well refurbished and had a contemporary kitchen extension at the rear with a new bathroom overhead. It had been re-plumbed, rewired and re-plastered throughout so there was nothing to be done to it other than choosing new paint colours – which was just as well, as neither Hope nor Josh were particularly DIY inclined. Hope quickly grew to love it and her new life. As they toasted the new millennium they blessed their good luck and their lives and the fact that they had eventually managed to get together.

In the spring of 2001 as her workload escalated, Hope took on Ruby, Sonya's cousin, as her PA. They got on well. Ruby was smart and competent and soon Hope began to rely on her and managed to delegate tasks to her, which was high praise for Ruby indeed as, after being a one-man band for so long, she found delegation hard at first. Ruby however proved to be totally dependable which gave Hope more time to pitch for new business. Though she had a good name in the industry for being reliable, competitive and innovative, it was a dog-eat-dog business and she was well aware that she couldn't just sit on her laurels and wait for business to come to her. The previous three years had been a steep learning curve during which she'd sometimes had to do the wing-and-a-prayer thing by the seat of her Josephs, but she'd had no disasters. At least no *recognisable* disasters.

That autumn, persuaded that Ruby was perfectly capable of holding the fort, they took three weeks off and headed to Australia. One balmy evening, sitting together on the steps of the Sydney Opera House looking out over the harbour, Hope wondered if she could ever feel happier or more contented than she did at that moment. Then next instant she felt a stab of anxiety. The other shoe has to drop sometime, she thought. It always does. This is too perfect.

In a manner of speaking the other shoe did clatter to the floor the following August to shatter her idyll, when Josh announced that the editor had approached him concerning a vacancy for a foreign correspondent. Hope, who had just emptied a tin of red kidney beans into a pot of chilli, stopped in mid-stir. "Foreign? As in another country?"

Josh laughed. "No, Hope, Roscommon ... of course another country."

"How foreign?" she asked.

"China," he said.

Just like that. "China." As if it was just a little to the right of Roscommon.

"China? The China at the other side of the world?"

He grinned at her. "Yes. *That* China. It's a great opportunity, Hope, and you know I've always wanted to see China, the *real* China."

"But it's so far away!"

"I know." He wrapped his arms around her and kissed the top of her head. "But you'd love it, and it's only for six months."

Horrified, she pushed her hands against his chest. "Six months! I can't go away for six months, Josh! I have a business to run."

He gave a little shrug. "So come out and visit. This is the chance of a lifetime, babe. I can't turn it down."

She wanted to say "Can't or won't?" but despite feeling abandoned, she knew she couldn't stand in his way. She wanted to. But she didn't, aware that grown-up relationships involved give and take, compromise. And unlike her other relationships this was a proper grown-up relationship with compromise on both sides.

"But China!" she said wrapping her arms around his waist and leaning her head against his chest. "That's half – no three-quarters of a world away."

"Not if you go the other way round," he pointed out.

Two months later, putting on a brave face amid his oblivious and almost boyish excitement she saw him off at Dublin airport. As he disappeared with one last wave through the departure gate she reflected that this was the first time they would be apart since she had stood at Arrivals to meet him off his Atlanta flight. Returning home later after work, the house felt so empty without him she actually cried. It's only six months, she repeated. Six short months. And he'll probably be home for Christmas.

But when Josh came home for Christmas he announced tentatively that he been asked to stay on another six months.

"But that's a year!" she'd wailed. "A whole year!"

"I know, babe. Listen, why don't you clear your diary for a couple of months around Easter and come out there?"

His suggestion stunned her. "I can't clear my diary just like that. It's my busy season. If I'm out of the picture of that long I'll lose business. I haven't worked this hard for this long to chuck it all away, Josh," she'd raged. It wasn't just his offhand suggestion, it was the fact that he didn't seem in any hurry to come home that wounded her. The truth was, she missed him like mad, but he didn't appear to be missing her half as much.

"Look, just think about it," he said. "You'd love China in the springtime. Szechwan province. You've never seen landscape like it, babe. The mountains, the mist, the rivers, it's stunning. And the people. They're amazing – you wouldn't believe …."

He rattled on eulogising China but all she heard was blah, blah blah! All she heard was 'I'm in no hurry to come home. Why don't you chuck your business away and come out to me?'

Of course she didn't chuck her business away. Didn't clear her diary and go out to him. It crossed her mind, but only briefly, and as soon she considered it, it was if the fickle finger of fate decided to poke her in the eye. The economy took a downturn and the captains of industry tightened their belts a couple of notches and the corporate sector decided that frugality was the new black. Nonetheless, confident that the new penny-pinching state of affairs was only a temporary blip, Hope chased business and managed to hold it together when a number of her competitors went to the wall.

* * *

He was standing by the window of her office looking down into the narrow street, doing a rather bad hip-hop scat version of 'Can't Get You Out of My Head'. But the leather cover of her desk diary informed her that it was 2004 which was confusing.

"Why are you singing that?" she asked. "'Can't Get You Out of My Head' was 2003, if I remember correctly?" She was getting used to his obsession.

"September 2002 actually," he corrected. "Her first number one since 'Spinning Around' in July 2000. But I regard it as definitive Kylie."

"Thank you for sharing that with me," she said. "We've got to Amy, haven't we?"

"I'm thinking more Josh. You did him a great disservice, you know."

She felt a stab of pain in her heart. "I know," she said, feeling the tears well up. "If I had my time over …"

He turned his head and caught her eye. He looked sad.

"I was just afraid," she said, feeling the need to explain.

The angel's expression changed to one of pure disbelief. "Of what? You knew he loved the very bones of you."

She nodded. "I know. But I was still afraid. It was such a big step and I've known so many relationships that were nodding along nicely, thank you very much, until they got married. Then wham, inside six months they were on the rocks."

"Nodding along very nicely? I don't hear any passion in that description," Reuben commented. "You and Josh were hardly just nodding along. I mean you were always shag –"

"Just *don't* go there, OK?" she cut in swiftly. She felt colour flood her neck. The thought of Reuben standing at the foot of their bed, looking on and passing comment about their sex life to Josh's Guardian Angel like a couple of prurient old women was excruciatingly embarrassing. Do angels do that, she wondered, fervently hoping that they didn't.

"We can hardly avoid it," he said, reminding her of his mind-reading ability. "We're with you twenty-four-seven for heaven's sake. I'm just pointing out that your relationship wasn't about to flounder just because he suggested marriage, that's all. Way too passionate for that."

He had a point. Despite her fears, as soon as Josh returned from China it was as if he'd never been away.

Now she felt a huge pang of regret. She wanted to see him again. To touch his face, to kiss him, to feel his arms around her but now she never would and she hadn't even had the chance to say goodbye.

The weekend before Amy had taken the dive into the river, Josh had taken her away to Fitzgerald House. Four-poster bed. Sitting by a huge log fire after dinner drinking brandy, long walks through the gorgeous estate after lunch on the Sunday then, as they lingered enjoying the view of the lake, he'd asked her. She'd had no inkling it was coming. Marriage was the furthest thing from her mind.

Then out of the blue he'd produced a little red leather box and handed it to her. Struck dumb by the shock of it, she stared at the box in her hand for a full five seconds until he prompted, "Aren't you going to open it?"

Actually she was afraid, but had no option but to lift the hinged lid. There lying in its velvet cocoon was a stunning platinum and diamond ring. She heaved an inner sigh of relief. The ring was half an eternity ring, not an engagement ring. Five respectably sized diamonds set into the platinum band. Exquisite.

She relaxed, thrilled to bits, until he said, "I know it's not a conventional rock. And I know this might sound cheesy but I feel like I've known you for half an eternity, and I want to be with you for the whole of eternity, Hope, so I thought it was more appropriate somehow."

It took a moment for his words to register, then her smile faded. "What exactly are you saying?"

He laughed. "God! What kind of wordsmith am I? I want us to get married, bozo! Big do, the frock, the friends. I love you, Hope, and I think it's time you made an honest man of me." It must have been the look of pure fear, of shock-horror, of Bambi caught in the headlamps, and her inability to speak that prompted him to add, "Look, I know this is kind of sudden. I know how you feel on the 'if it ain't broke why fix it?' theory, and your pathological fear of the M word, but we can do this, Hope. Take some time to think it through and you'll see we *can* do this without everything falling apart."

So, strangely, and all credit to him, he didn't go into a strop when she didn't jump for joy, and for that she was grateful. She loved him, of that she had no doubt, but that was the problem. She loved him. Loved what they had and was afraid it was all going to unravel with mention of the dreaded M word. Charity and Goran had gone their separate ways after only three years together, and she'd had a string of relationships after that, none of which had lasted. And her parents – what if they turned into her parents? Maisie the nag, her father disappearing into the garage or to the golf club – anything to get away from her.

"I should have said yes, shouldn't I?" she said. "Straight away. No hesitation."

Reuben smiled kindly. "Not for me to say."

"But I should have. I love him to bits, and I know he loves me. He's the best thing that ever happened to me." She sat down behind her desk. It felt strange to be back there. Her dry cleaning was still hanging on the back of the door where Amy had left it. She was wearing the trouser suit and the Patrick Cox mules. Then it hit her. It was too late. Her plan concerning Amy was a non-runner unless she could get Reuben to rewind a few months. If she could do that she could change everything. Then she'd have the opportunity say yes. Yes! Yes! Yes!

"Sorry, Hope, he said. "Can't do it."

"Can't do what?" she asked innocently.

"Turn the clock back any further so you can change the way you treated Amy."

"But I thought that was the point?" she said, panic rising. "I thought I was supposed to right the wrongs. To acknowledge what I did wrong and where possible try and lessen the effect on others."

"Well remembered," he said sauntering over and planting his left buttock on the corner of her desk. "But I don't think that's actually what you had in mind, is it?"

She felt herself blush and averted her eyes. "I don't know what you mean," she protested. "So I was going to make Amy's life better. Isn't that the whole point?"

"It depends on your motivation," he said. "I believe you only contemplated that so you could –"

"Could get promoted to Prada Heaven," she cut in. "OK, so that was the deal. Am I right?"

Ignoring her question he finished the sentence, "So

you could change history and avoid saving Amy, and thus avoid dying."

She felt her face scarlet now. "That's so unfair!" she snapped. "True enough if I dealt with Amy differently she wouldn't have wanted to jump in the first place, but this is – this is impossible. This is Catch 22. I'm damned if I do and damned if I don't!"

He smiled at her again. It was a kind compassionate smile. Then the door opened and Amy walked in.

"Ruby said to tell you Clive might not be able to get down to the venue until three. But he said not to worry, he'll have everything finished in plenty of time."

Hope piped up brightly. "No problem! Excellent, Amy! Thanks!"

The girl looked disconcerted.

"She thinks you're being sarcastic," Reuben said.

"No, *really*, Amy, that's fine," Hope repeated, trying to infuse sincerity into her voice just as Amy noticed the BLT in the waste bin.

Horror. "You didn't like the BLT! I'm *really* sorry. Can I get you something else?"

"No. It's OK. It wasn't the sandwich, *honestly*. I love BLT's. *Adore* them, it's just that I dropped it on the floor. Yes, that's it. I dropped it on the floor so I had to dump it in the bin … I'll grab something on my way down to the venue." Even to her own ears she sounded a touch manic.

Amy gave her a weird look. "Are you sure? It's no trouble."

"I'm sure." She patted her stomach. "Anyway, I need to lose a few pounds."

"No need to overdo it," Reuben muttered.

Hope gave him a venomous glance then pushed back her chair, stood up and, in an over-jolly tone of voice said, "I suppose we'd better get down there."

"I'll call a cab."

"A cab? Oh yes – a cab. I guess the valet man picked up my car." Her face was aching from the effort of smiling like a maniac.

Amy smiled right back at her, pleased to be able to impart something positive. "Yes. He called this morning so I told him where you usually park."

"Excellent," Hope said. "Well done!"

She heard Reuben give a snort of derision as she headed out of the door, but she didn't look back.

Chapter 31

On the drive over to The Waterfront Amy sat in the far corner of the cab quietly looking out of the window. It was as if she was uncomfortable sitting in such close proximity and Hope felt bad about that. Was I really so awful to her, she wondered. Reuben's voice inside her brain replied: 'Were you ever consciously nice to her?' She had to admit to herself that actually, no, she had never made the slightest effort with Amy. But I was under a lot of stress. My business was in danger of going pear-shaped, she rationalised. I never meant to be horrid, but she did make some really silly mistakes.

'And you never made a mistake?' the voice continued, and she realised that it wasn't Reuben, but her conscience talking.

Stuff Reuben, she thought.

"Listen, Amy, your placement's coming to an end and I was thinking ..." The girl nodded, a resigned look on her face which was annoying, but Hope thrashed on. "How would you like to stay on?"

"*Stay on*?" Utter disbelief.

Hope nodded. "Yes. Ruby's very keen and I know I haven't always been the easiest boss, but that's just my way and I've been under ... well, never mind that. So what do you say?"

"You're offering me a job?"

Hope nodded, and felt a surge of relief flood through her.

"OK ... thanks."

OK? Thanks?

She hadn't expected her to burst into tears of gratitude or drop to her knees and kiss her feet, but, *OK – thanks*?

The cab drove round to the service entrance of the hotel and pulled up.

"Oh look, Gordo Whyte's here," Amy said, and she did sound more upbeat.

The Rasta banjo players were rattling through 'The Campdown Races' as Hope and Amy stepped out of the lift, then segued seamlessly into the frenzied version of 'I'm a Yankee Doodle Dandy'.

"I'm really sorry," Amy said. "I could only get three. I tried for the quartet but they only come in threes."

"That's OK, Amy. Don't worry about it," Hope said,

gritting her teeth. "Actually I meant *Benjaos*. They're a string quartet, but now I think about it, the banjos will work better because Benjaos played at the Epic Software gig and Dermot Hudson wouldn't want the same as them so really banjos are a much better idea."

She's forgotten that the Epic story had been a total fabrication for Dermot Hudson's benefit, but did realise she was babbling so she shut up.

Amy looked confused and repeated the word, "*Benjaos?*"

Walking through the next fifteen minutes, finessing Gordo Whyte, plamausing Clive about his floral artistry, talking Dermot Hudson into believing that white Rasta banjo trios were the best thing since predictive texting, felt totally surreal, then as the goody bags crossed her mind she realised that she couldn't see Amy anywhere. A stab of panic hit her in the solar plexus, and just as she was about to start running round like a headless chicken, she saw her coming out of the kitchen carrying a plate of sandwiches and a steaming cup.

"Got you some lunch," she said. "Why don't you sit down and eat and I'll go over to the office and start filling the goody bags."

Stunned, Hope complied. "Oh, OK. Thanks, Amy."

Ten minutes later, as Hope hurried over to join Amy in the office, the sandwiches having just about stuck in her gullet, her mobile rang. It was Ruby.

"Are you OK?"

"Me? Yes, why?"

"Amy phoned me and said you've been acting weird?"

"Weird?"

"She said you offered her a permanent job?"

"And that's weird because …?"

Ruby snorted at the other end of the phone. "Because you've made it pretty clear you think she's useless?"

"Well," Hope prevaricated, "maybe I've changed my mind. She is getting better. In fact she's filling goody bags as we speak. Anyway, she needs this job. She has a little girl, you know? Lily. She's a single mum. I can hardly fire her."

Ruby, obviously of the same mind as Amy, enquired, "Your cab driver didn't take you via Damascus, did he?"

Hope couldn't help but laugh. "Oh shut up! Where are you?"

"On my way over in a cab to help you fill the goody bags."

The three of them filled the goody bags together and the atmosphere was quite jolly. Ruby told her about the mega wedding booking and Hope only just stopped herself from saying, "Yes, I know, you told me," but of course she hadn't because they'd had an entirely different conversation. It got her to thinking that Ruby was right and she felt sad that she'd been so pigheaded about wedding planning. Josh had suggested it too.

They rarely talked about her business, at least not to the extent that Josh knew exactly how bad things had become. She wasn't sure why, though it occurred to her now that perhaps she was afraid he'd think less of her. She wanted him to be proud of her. How short-sighted was that? Thinking rationally now, she realised that far from thinking less of her, he'd have been totally supportive.

With the goody bags filled and one placed on every seat, Hope and Ruby surveyed the room. It looked great and as the first guests started to trickle in, the musicians launched into 'Zipppty-doo-dah'.

Suddenly Hope realised that Amy was missing again.

"Where's Amy?" she said, frantically looking around.

"I think she went outside to ring her mum to tell her the good news," Ruby said, smiling. "By the way, that was a really nice thing you did, offering her the job."

"Outside?" Hope said, a look of horror on her face.

Ruby stared at her for a beat. "Are you sure you're all right?" she said, frowning.

Hope turned on her heel and raced towards the exit, "Quick!" she shouted at Ruby. "I have a really bad feeling!"

Pushing open the service entrance she rushed outside. The wind had picked up again. She looked about wildly, hoping to catch sight of Amy, but she couldn't see her anywhere. Grabbing her mobile from her bag she punched in Amy's number with her shaking fingers. Ruby caught up with her at that point.

"What's up? What's the panic?" she said, a look of concern in her eyes, a look that said: *She's really lost it.*

Hope heard the call connect, ring, then cut abruptly to voice mail. Her heart sank. This was going exactly as it had before. But why? Why would Amy chuck herself in the river when she'd just been given a permanent job? She was in good humour. She seemed happy. It didn't make sense.

But as they rounded the corner there she was, standing on the wall looking down into the river, the wind ferociously whipping at her hair as she hugged her arms around her lean body. Then the same rogue gust of wind buffeted her, causing her to wobble and throw out her arms for balance.

"Amy! No!" Hope yelled. *"Please don't do it! Whatever's troubling you we can fix it!"* But her voice was once more lost to the elements. She ran across the grass towards the wall.

Ruby, behind her, was yelling, *"What are you doing, Amy. Don't be daft!"*

Looking wildly around to see if Reuben had put in an appearance, the elusive George, anyone at all, she saw no one.

"Amy! Get down off the wall. You'll fall in!" Ruby shouted.

Stupid thing to say in hindsight, considering that's exactly what the girl had in mind, but then maybe

Ruby's brain hadn't yet computed the visuals. Amy turned her head and, seeing Hope and Ruby coming towards her, pointed over the wall and said something they couldn't make out.

"I can't hear you, Amy!" Hope shouted. She was but ten feet away now, Ruby hot on her squelching heels, just as the same strong gust hurled Hope forward into the stonework and Amy's legs, toppling her over the wall and into the water.

Hope screamed. Ruby screamed. Where the feck was George when Amy needed him? *Crap At Being A Guardian Angel* would have to be a strong contender for his Indian name.

Hope struggled to her feet. She was soaked and muddy from the dash across the saturated grass. Shaking, hanging onto the wall, she peered into the dock, Ruby beside her.

"Where is she?" Ruby yelled. "Shit! Where the fuck is she?"

At first they couldn't see Amy, but then her head bobbed to the surface for a few seconds before disappearing under the water again.

"There. There!" Hope shouted, pointing. Then, "The life-saving thingy! Quick!"

Ruby made a dash for the ring which was hanging on a post a few yards away. Hope was careful not to go too near the wall, conscious of George. "Don't even think about it, George. I'm warning you!" she hissed, hoping he could hear her.

Amy's head bobbed to the surface again and Hope saw her gulp in a breath before a wave swamped her and she disappeared from view for a second time.

Well, at least I know she'll come up again, Hope thought.

"Where is she?" Ruby had returned with the lifebuoy.

They both peered into the murky choppy water but there was no sign of her.

"She's only been up twice," Hope said. "She has to come up again."

"That's just an old wives' tale," Ruby said. She sounded as frantic as Hope felt. "Where is she?"

"Quick! Go and get someone," Hope said. "Raise the alarm." Ruby hesitated for a second until Hope urged, "Quickly! Hurry!"

Just then Amy broke the surface again, fighting to fill her lungs. It was enough incentive for Ruby. Thrusting the lifesaver at Hope she raced back across the grass towards the hotel.

"Try and grab this, Amy!" Hope yelled as she flung the red and white ring into the river. It landed only a couple of feet away from the girl and for a split second their eyes locked, then she went under again. Just like that.

Suddenly Hope knew. Knew Reuben was right. Her fate was inescapable and she realised with an unequivocal certainty what she had to do.

Quickly peeling off her coat, jacket, pants and the

remaining Patrick Cox mule, she clambered back up on top of the wall. There was no sign of Amy coming up again. Looking left and right she shouted, "Sod off, George! I'll do it myself!" Then filling her lungs with air, launched herself off the wall.

Plunging into the freezing cold brackish water knocked the breath out of her. Kicking her legs she fought her way upwards, breaking the surface and sucking in a desperate breath. Amy was about ten feet away. She was struggling towards the lifebuoy, just as Hope remembered, then as she gathered herself together and swam towards her, Amy's head disappeared under the water again. Waiting for a couple of seconds in case it was different, in case Amy resurfaced, Hope filled her lungs again then dived under. On opening her eyes, the visibility was next to zero. She swam in the general direction of where the girl had gone down, stretching out her arms, searching the water. A strong swimmer once upon a time, Hope kicked her legs up behind her and dived down towards the bottom, recalling that Amy had sunk to the river bed. Her lungs were at bursting point. Suddenly her arm brushed against Amy's coat. Feeling her way in the muddy water she found her arm. Grabbing it, she pulled her upwards towards the surface again, praying that Amy wouldn't panic. Slim chance. The girl was drowning, totally panicked and disorientated and was instinctively fighting for her life. Hope let a little air trickle from her mouth to ease the pressure in her chest.

If I can just hang on, she thought, if I can just hang on I might make it this time. But she had forgotten about the kick, and an instant later Amy's leg lashed out in her frantic fight to reach the surface. The kick connected with Hope's stomach and it was her undoing. A cascade of air bubbles escaped from her mouth as Amy's frenzied efforts for survival knocked all the air out of her. She remembered the light-headedness from the last time. It was quite pleasant and she recalled reading somewhere that in fact drowning, once one got over the initial panic, wasn't the most unpleasant way to die.

The pretty lights danced before her eyes. The lovely warm comfortable feeling revisited. Floating. Light as a feather. Stretching out her hand, she once more gave Amy that one final push towards the surface.

Chapter 32

Beeping. *Beep, beep, beep*, like a steady heartbeat. Floating. She was afraid to open her eyes. Straining her ears she listened, and there it was. The sound of a piper and a fiddler somewhere in the distance. Her throat was very sore and her mouth dry.

Bugger it, I'm still dead, she thought, still in fecking Crusty Heaven. This is so unfair!

Then aware of someone close at hand, she cautiously opened her eyes.

Her next thought was: Shit, Mum's dead too, and I didn't even know she was sick. For there was Maisie sitting close at hand, a Walkman on her lap, the headphones on, eyes closed, gently dozing, the source of the piper and fiddle.

"She's awake!" Her father's voice. "Maisie! Charity! She's awake!"

Hope blinked. They couldn't all be dead, barring the unlikely possibility that a 747 had fallen from the sky and landed on number 56 Vavasour Gardens, Terenure.

Maisie was on her feet now, tears streaming down her cheeks, then she was replaced by a nurse who, after grabbing hold of Hope's wrist to check her pulse, smiled broadly and said, "So you decided to come back to us, eh? Good choice."

The next person she was aware of was Josh, standing at the end of the bed, four cartons of takeaway coffee in one of those egg-tray things, and if she wasn't mistaken, he was crying too.

This is a pretty sick joke, Reuben, she thought, certain that any moment they would all disappear and she'd find herself back in a yurt. And disappear they did before she had a chance to talk to them, but that was only because the doctor shooed them out until he could check her out.

"You gave us quite a scare," he said.

"A scare?" she croaked.

"You've been unconscious for three days, young lady."

She thought the 'young lady' pretty rich seeing as he didn't look old enough to have done his Leaving Cert.

"It was touch and go for a while," he added as he listened to her lungs with the aid of his stethoscope. "You might find your throat is sore. That's from the tube. We had you on a ventilator for the first twenty-four hours, so don't do too much talking for a bit."

Pushing herself up in the bed she glanced around the room. It was awash with vases of flowers and get-well-soon cards. A few candles and she could have been in a chapel of rest. Scary. But she thought she'd better check.

"I'm not dead?"

"Oh you were. Technically for about half a minute, but the paramedics brought you back. Good job they got there when they did."

"I'm not dead?" she repeated. Then a grin spreading across her face, she said it again, "I'm not dead. I'm not dead!"

She was still a touch wary though, expecting Reuben to shake her awake and tell her she was dreaming. Once the impossibly young doctor was satisfied that she was all right, that all her vital organs were functioning properly, he said he'd allow visitors again, but only one at a time and not for too long.

Some hushed voices outside, then the door opened and Josh came in. He looked tired and unshaven but very relieved. He sat on the bed and they just clung on to each other, then the tears started. Hers and his. No talk for half a minute. Just sitting motionless, holding each other.

Then he said, "I thought I'd lost you."

"Yes," she croaked, and when she realised that he didn't get it, repeated in her Marge Simpson voice, "Yes. Yes, I will marry you. I'd love to marry you. I should have said yes right away. I should have –"

But his kiss cut off the end of the sentence.

*   *   *

It took a few days before she had the full story clear in her mind. She couldn't understand how she had survived when nothing appeared to have changed, despite her efforts. As it turned out she realised that it must have been Ruby's inclusion in the equation that had swung the balance. Because she was at hand to call the emergency services, they must have got to the scene much sooner, therefore the paramedics had been able to resuscitate her. Amy's fate hadn't altered either it seemed. She was fine apart from a badly grazed shin caused by the seawall.

"But why did she try to top herself?" Hope asked Ruby when she managed to get her on her own on the afternoon of the third day.

"She didn't," Ruby explained. "She was sitting on the wall talking to her mum and just as she hung up she dropped the phone over the wall – it landed on a small ledge about three feet from the water, so she climbed up on the wall to see if it was retrievable. Apparently it was quite a new phone."

"She dropped her bloody phone? I nearly drowned because she dropped her bloody phone?"

"No. You nearly drowned because you did a very silly but heroic thing," Ruby said, and she had a point so Hope could hardly blame Amy at the end of the day.

It was only after reading an article in one of the numerous magazines that her visitors had brought in that she began to rethink matters. The article was concerning the old chestnut of near-death experience and the whole 'bright light at the end of the tunnel' phenomenon. The article explored both arguments, that is to say, those who believed that they had experienced the hereafter, and those of a scientific persuasion whose theory was that a lack of oxygen to the brain can trigger experiences similar to those caused by hallucinogens such as magic mushrooms and LSD. In a nutshell, their compelling argument was that supposed memories of the afterlife were just a trick of the oxygen-starved brain. She read the article three times, and after each reading found the premise more and more compelling. Stranger things have happened in the imagination, she decided. Look at Bobby Ewing.

On the fifth day she was allowed to go home and Josh came to collect her. "Some people will do anything for a few days in bed," he joked.

She waited at the entrance while he went to collect the car from the carpark. It was a beautiful summer day and she felt glad, really glad, to be alive. Her mind was elsewhere so she didn't notice him coming up the steps towards her, but suddenly there he was. A tall lean figure with the same long nose and shaved head, wearing hospital scrubs. Three loping paces away he caught her eye and smiled.

No, she thought, I'm imagining it. It was oxygen

starvation. It was!

But then, just as he drew level, he slowed his pace and, still in motion, whispered, "Good one, Hope. I'll tell George you were asking for him."

For an instant she was rooted to the spot, then whipped around to look for him.

But the hallway was completely empty.

Epilogue

Whoever said no publicity is bad publicity had it spot on. And the fact of Hope's newly attained hero status certainly helped revive her flagging business. She did however decide to diversify into the area of wedding planning as a hedge against any further economic downturn. But wouldn't you know it? The minute she did, the economy revived and the aged Celtic Tiger opened its eyes, stretched its rested limbs and arose rejuvenated. Sod's Law in action.

Hope and Josh got married on New Year's Day of 2005. It was an intimate affair, the reception held over a weekend in Fitzgerald House. (Hope negotiated a very special rate.) Charity, Ruby and Sonya were her bridesmaids and Charity got off with one of the groomsmen, Josh's nineteen-year-old cousin, Barry, who thought that all his Christmases had come at once. Maisie wore a rather startling magenta silk suit and matching hat trimmed with ostrich feathers. Very Mother of the Bride. She looked amazing. Tom made the wine (*Chateau Terenure*) and a good time was had by all. Especially Maisie, and Josh's mother Caroline who, after half an hour of circling each other suspiciously at the rehearsal dinner, bonded like separated twins once they got on to the subject of gardening and complaining about their respective spouses. They were really very alike. Therefore, needless to say, both Tom and Josh's dad Brian had much on common.

The bride and groom took a month's honeymoon safari in Kenya during which time Prior Engagements was left in the capable hands of Ruby and her newly promoted assistant, Amy.

Hope never actually saw Reuben again, but occasionally, particularly when a Kylie Minogue track played on the radio, she sensed his presence.

THE END

receiving the
HOLY SPIRIT
and His gifts

How to ... Study series
Series Editor:
TERRY VIRGO

receiving the HOLY SPIRIT and His gifts

TERRY VIRGO
and
PHIL ROGERS

WORD BOOKS

NELSON WORD LTD
Milton Keynes, England
WORD AUSTRALIA
Kilsyth, Victoria, Australia
WORD COMMUNICATIONS LTD
Vancouver, B.C., Canada
STRUIK CHRISTIAN BOOKS (PTY) LTD
Cape Town, South Africa
CHRISTIAN MARKETING NEW ZEALAND LTD
Havelock North, New Zealand
JENSCO LTD
Hong Kong
JOINT DISTRIBUTORS SINGAPORE –
ALBY COMMERCIAL ENTERPRISES PTE LTD
and
CAMPUS CRUSADE, ASIA LTD
SALVATION BOOK CENTRE
Malaysia

RECEIVING THE HOLY SPIRIT

© Frontier Publishing International Ltd. 1990, 1993

ISBN 0-85009-626-X (Australia 1-86258-300-5)

Unless otherwise indicated, Scripture quotations are from the New International Version (NIV), © 1973, 1978, 1984 by International Bible Society.

Created, designed and typeset by Frontier Publishing International Ltd., BN43 6RE, England. Reproduced, printed and bound in Great Britain for Nelson Word Ltd. by Cox and Wyman Ltd., Reading.

93 94 95 96 / 10 9 8 7 6 5 4 3 2 1

THANK YOU TO ...

I want to thank Phil Rogers for his hard work in the preparation of this material. He is personally responsible for the second half of the book (Chapters 8—13) and also worked hard in faithfully reproducing my own teaching material in the first half. The whole book has also been enriched by the additional work of Mary Austin and Chris Wisdom. Thanks also to John Colwell and John Hosier for their useful comments on various theological points. My thanks too to Patricia, Phil's secretary for all her practical help, and to the members of South Lee Christian Church for their support.

Terry Virgo

Also available in the *How To* series:

FOREWORD

T he *How To* series has been published with a definite purpose in view. It provides a set of workbooks suitable either for housegroups or individuals who want to study a particular Bible theme in a practical way. The goal is not simply to look up verses and fill up pages of a notebook, but to fill in gaps in our lives and so increase our fruitfulness and our knowledge of God.

Both of Peter's letters were written to 'stimulate ... wholesome thinking' (2 Peter 3:1). He required his readers to think as well as read! We hope the training manual approach of this book will have the same effect. Stop, think, apply and act are key words.

If you are using the book on your own, I suggest you work through the chapters systematically, Bible and notebook at your side and pen in hand. If you are doing it as a group activity, it is probably best to do all the initial reading and task work before the group sessions — this gives more time for discussion on key issues which may be raised.

Unless otherwise stated, all quotations from the Bible are from the New International Version.

Terry Virgo
Series Editor

CONTENTS

INTRODUCTION

The 'Charismatic Movement' has had a growing impact on the church and the world since the early 1960s. Vast numbers of Christians world-wide have come into an experience of the Holy Spirit formerly unknown to recent generations of Bible-believing churchgoers.

Early shockwaves have been largely forgotten but still many are unsure of what it means to be baptised in the Holy Spirit and how one enters into this enduement of power. Some have actually stumbled into a new dimension of the Spirit and some are not sure what has happened to them while others have even wondered if it is a true biblical experience.

'He will baptise you with the Holy Spirit,' said John the Baptist as he introduced Jesus to his hearers. Every one of the gospel accounts includes these words and Luke repeats them for good measure in the book of Acts. So there is clear ground on which we can base our faith to receive this promise of the Father.

This book in the *How to* series is an attempt to help enquirers know how to receive the Holy Spirit's fullness and an introduction to the gift of the Holy Spirit which are available to the church today.

As you work through these pages it is my prayer that you will find your questions answered and your faith quickened to seek the Lord for the promise of the Spirit. I believe that as a result your life can be transformed for the glory of God.

Terry Virgo

Chapter One

YOU SHALL RECEIVE POWER

One day, as I was strolling along Brighton seafront, I saw some people witnessing. I had just been leading the youth group Bible Study and was feeling quite pleased with my performance. There on the lower promenade were these Pentecostal, grey-haired, frail old ladies holding banners and speaking about Jesus with crackly voices. People were throwing things at them and laughing at them.

I stood there, in my dark glasses, watching what was happening. It was not a pretty sight. 'O God, why is it like this?' I thought. Then suddenly I realised that God had called young men like me to do this sort of thing, not frail elderly ladies. 'But I'd rather die than do that!' I protested.

There were two guys standing nearby. They were sneering, 'Look at those old fools, why don't they keep their religion to themselves?' The Lord prompted me, 'At least speak to them about Jesus.' But I stood there thinking, 'I can't, I just can't do it.' I went home broken.

People knew I was a church-goer, but I was frightened to acknowledge the name of Jesus. I just couldn't speak to people about Him. I felt so ashamed, and I was desperate to know how I could overcome my reluctance.

The next morning I phoned a Pentecostal friend and asked him to meet me for lunch near my work place. We often had lunch together and he would always witness to anyone who shared our table. I envied his liberty and admired his boldness. But I almost died every time he spoke about Jesus and wanted him to be quiet. When we parted, I would watch him walking down Oxford Street giving out tracts as he went.

Now I had to see him. I had to know what made him tick. So when we met for lunch I asked him, 'How can you witness so freely? What's the secret?' He replied, 'I've received the Holy Spirit.' So that was the answer to his boldness — the Holy Spirit. I had a knowledge of the Bible and could lead studies, but now I realised that I needed to be filled with the Holy Spirit as well. 'I must have what you've got,' I told him.

JUST LIKE THOSE DISCIPLES

I felt just like those disciples of Jesus. Initially they thought they were OK. James and John angled for positions at Jesus' right and left hand. Peter said he would never betray or deny Him. But they all denied Him. They all fled. They were all disillusioned and frightened. They all hid behind barred doors. The cross revealed their weakness. But Jesus did not leave them helpless. Later He appeared to them and said:

> But you will receive power when the Holy Spirit comes on you; and you will be my witnesses in Jerusalem, and in all Judea and Samaria, and to the ends of the earth (Acts 1:8).

This statement has been described as the key to the book of Acts. After the day of Pentecost, this same group of disciples were a dynamic company marching forward with the gospel, travelling all round the Mediterranean, planting powerful churches in one city after another.

What transformed a timid bunch of deserters into a courageous band? How did such fearful believers get such boldness to speak about Christ? They were filled with the Holy Spirit.

Jesus had chosen these men to be His representatives to the world. But before they could ever begin this ministry they had to have God's power. That is why Jesus said:

> stay in the city until you have been clothed with power from on high (Luke 24:49).

If we want to fulfil God's plan for our lives, we must have the same experience of the Spirit as the disciples did. God showed me my own need of His power while I was standing on the Brighton seafront. I cried out to Him not in aspiration but in desperation! He met me and filled me with His Holy Spirit.

Do you feel your lack of power? God wants to fill you with His Holy Spirit.

Go! But Wait!

After His resurrection Jesus appeared to His disciples and gave them special instructions.

> Look up the following verses to see what they were: Matthew 28:18,19; Mark 16:15; Luke 24:49; Acts 1:4.

Clearly, Jesus was keen to see His disciples spread the gospel. 'Here's the Commission,' he was saying. 'Go!' But he did not want them to begin their ministry before they had the power to accomplish it. So He exhorted them to wait in Jerusalem until they had received power from on high.

The Greek word for power is *dunamis* from which we get our words 'dynamite', 'dynamic' and 'dynamo'. The root meaning of the word is 'to be able'. Jesus promised His disciples an 'ability' or an 'enabling'. When the Holy Spirit came upon them, they would receive a dynamic ability that they hadn't had before. They would be given the power of God to enable them to do the work of God.

ANOINTED WITH THE HOLY SPIRIT AND POWER

Jesus told His disciples:

> **As the Father has sent me, I am sending you (John 20:21).**

His ministry began with baptism in water, but not only that. Even the Son of God needed power to do His Father's will.

> Read Luke 3:21–23; 4:1,2,14,18 and note the work of the Holy Spirit in Jesus' life.

Jesus did not need to repent of sin so why did He submit to John's baptism of repentance? Here are three reasons.

Jesus was anticipating the cross. By going down under the water and rising up from it He identified with the death and resurrection He was going to experience three years later (see Luke 12:50).

By being baptised along with sinners He was identifying Himself with sinful man.

He was also saying, 'I am dead to the world and to all normal human expectations.' The will of God took precedence over everything else. Jesus laid down His life to fulfil it.

When Jesus came up out of the water and was praying, the Holy Spirit descended on Him. Peter says that He was 'anointed' with the Holy Spirit and power (Acts 10:38). He was not anointed with the ceremonial anointing oil poured over the heads of priests and kings to consecrate them. He was anointed with the heavenly 'oil' of the Holy Spirit. Only then was He equipped to begin His ministry.

Jesus refused to entertain Satan's temptations. There would be no short cuts to the purpose of God. Jesus was not interested in Satan's offer of the world and immediate success. He was more concerned about fulfilling God's will for His life.

THE SON OF GOD

Even before He began His ministry Jesus was the perfect Son of God. He had been born of the Holy Spirit — conceived as the Spirit came upon Mary His mother (Matt. 1:20; Luke 1:35). But He did not begin teaching or healing until He had been anointed with power. Until that time He lived in comparative seclusion with His family, working as a carpenter and leading a godly life. But when the Holy Spirit came upon Him He suddenly broke out of anonymity and launched Himself into His heavenly Father's business.

Some have said that Jesus' miracles were evidence of His divinity, yet nowhere in the New Testament do we find Him acclaimed as God because of signs or miracles. Men in Old Testament days had worked miracles but that did not make them equal with God.

Read John 3:2 and Acts 10:38.

Of what were miracles a sign?

Read John 10:38; 14:10–11; Acts 2:22.

Who is doing the miracles through Jesus?

The Son always works in conjunction with the Father and the Spirit. They exist in eternal interdependence. At the Father's direction, the Son spoke creation into being and the Spirit immediately executed His word of command. So within the Godhead, the Father always acts through the Son, by the power of the Holy Spirit.

When He became man Jesus accepted the limitations of our humanity. He depended not on some sort of secret inner force but solely on the power of the Holy Spirit.

When Jesus became man He did not in any way lose His full divinity. He is not God because He has certain attributes or powers. He is God in His very essence. We read that Jesus 'made himself nothing' (Phil. 2:7). This literally means, 'emptied himself' and is a much debated expression. From it, we understand that He voluntarily laid aside the outward expressions of Godhood. By becoming flesh He emptied Himself of His omnipresence (being everywhere), His glory (John 17:5), His omnipotence (having all power) and His omniscience (knowing everything).

So 'being made in human likeness. And being found in appearance as a man' (Phil. 2:7–8) Jesus chose to live in obedience to His Father and in full dependence on the power of the Holy Spirit. In this way He became our pioneer, 'the firstborn among many brothers' (Rom. 8:29). He is our Saviour and our example.

What, according to 1 John 2:6, does God want us to do?

Although Jesus was fully God, He fulfilled His great ministry as a man anointed by the Holy Spirit. This is how the Father sent Him; it is also how Jesus sent His disciples.

Read John 14:12.

Who is addressed here? What is the requirement? What is the twofold result? Why?

Jesus knew that He would not always be with His disciples in bodily form. But they would not need Him if they had His power to complete His work. 'I am going away,' He said, but added that 'the Father ... will give you another Counsellor to be with you for ever — the Spirit of truth' (John 14:28,16,17). They received the Spirit at Pentecost. He gave them the power to preach and to perform signs and wonders (Acts 2:43).

Consider whether the same power is available to us today.

Chapter Two

I WILL POUR OUT MY SPIRIT

Jesus told His disciples to wait until they were clothed with power from on high. They would not have thought this a strange concept because their history was full of people who were given power from God. About half of the eighty or so references to the Spirit in the Old Testament describe this type of experience. Let's look at some of them.

CLOTHED WITH THE SPIRIT

Jesus' disciples knew about David.

Read 1 Samuel 16:13.

What happened when Samuel anointed him?

Some years earlier the Spirit had come upon King Saul and he had prophesied. It was said, 'Is Saul also among the prophets?' (1 Sam. 10:11). In those days it was evidently normal for prophets to prophesy when the Spirit came upon them. Even the godless prophet Balaam knew that he could speak only the words that the Spirit gave him.

Read Numbers 24:2–3.

What happened when the Spirit of God came upon him?

The disciples also knew about Samson. When he was a young man the Spirit of the Lord began to stir him (Judg. 13:25), and on a number of occasions gave him extraordinary physical strength.

Read Judges 14:6,19 and 15:14.

What phrase is common to these verses?

The Spirit also came upon other Judges of that period. He came upon Othniel and Jephthah, enabling them to carry out their leadership responsibilities and to defeat Israel's enemies (Judg. 3:10; 11:29).

Perhaps the most well known of the Judges was Gideon. He was a godly young man who, through fear of the Midianites, threshed wheat secretly in a winepress.

Read Judges 6:34,35.

What happened when the Spirit came upon this timid man?

Read Judges 6:14–16 and 7:15.

Did he fulfil his commission?

The New International Version says, 'The Spirit of the Lord came upon Gideon.' However, elsewhere in the Old Testament this same word is usually translated 'clothed', 'dressed' or 'wearing'. The phrase literally reads: 'the Spirit of the Lord clothed Himself with Gideon'. He put on Gideon like a suit, dressed Himself with Gideon so that He could use him to accomplish God's purposes. The Spirit came upon people in order to work through them.

There are two other places where this word is used in this same way: 1 Chronicles 12:18 and 2 Chronicles 24:20.

Look up these verses and note how the Spirit used each of the two men.

FILLED WITH THE SPIRIT

When we speak about being 'filled with the Spirit' we can slip into the unhelpful notion that God wants to pour a liquid into us. We grin and say, 'Lord, fill me with Your Spirit. I leak!' But the Holy Spirit is not a liquid, He is a person. So how can we be full of a person?

The Old Testament idea that the Spirit clothes Himself with people is a good illustration here. When I put my clothes on, they are full of me. So when the Holy Spirit comes upon me or clothes Himself with me, I am full of the Holy Spirit. When the Spirit of God wears us He can manifest Himself in us through what we say and do in response to His prompting. This is how He uses us to fulfil the purposes of God.

The Bible uses a number of different terms to describe this experience. Let's look at the way the various terms are used to describe what happened on the day of Pentecost.

Consider the different expressions used in the following verses:
e.g. Acts 1:5 — baptised with the Holy Spirit
Acts 1:8
Acts 2:4
Acts 2:17,33
Acts 2:38; 10:47
Acts 10:44; 11:15

The above terms are all speaking about the same experience of the Holy Spirit. They are therefore used interchangeably throughout this book.

Moses was evidently full of the Spirit of God — although we do not know when he had this experience. Certainly he had some exceptional encounters with God — at the burning bush and later on Mount Sinai when his face radiated God's glory. One most instructive event in his life is recorded in Numbers 11.

> Read verses 10 to 30.

> What did God do to Moses and the seventy elders? (vv.17,25) What did they do? (v.25)

Moses was extraordinarily privileged. Among the whole nation, only he knew the Spirit of God resting on him, empowering him to lead the people. When the burden became too great for him, God commissioned seventy elders to help him. But before they could share the task they had to be as spiritually equipped as Moses was. We might expect Moses to be jealous that the elders now shared his experience. When Joshua heard Eldad and Medad prophesying in the camp, he was certainly indignant about it.

> Consider Moses' response in Numbers 11:29.

Moses' desire then is shared by God now. Here in Numbers we have a most significant anticipation of the New Covenant.

FROM ONE TO ANOTHER

When Moses handed over his responsibilities to Joshua, he laid his hands on him to commission him.

> Note what happened when he did this (Deut. 34:9).

With the commission came an impartation of the Spirit that equipped him for his responsibilities. Something similar happened to David when Samuel anointed him with oil (1 Sam. 16:13) and when Elijah left Elisha to continue his ministry.

When the disciples watched Jesus go up into heaven they might well have recalled Elijah's ascension. Elisha knew that God was going to take his master away from him so he kept close to Elijah. There was something he had to have before they were parted.

What did he want? (2 Kings 2:9)

Elisha was not being greedy. He was asking for the heir's portion. He was effectively saying, 'If I am to take over the ministry that God gave you to do, then I must have the same power that you had.' He knew that it was useless to inherit the job without also inheriting the resources necessary to do it. As Elijah was taken up into heaven in the whirlwind, Elisha received his master's anointing and moved on in the power of the Spirit.

When Jesus told His disciples to wait until they had been clothed with power from on high, He was not striking an unfamiliar chord in their hearts. Their scriptures told them that many of God's servants had received the Spirit. Jesus was simply promising them that when He was taken up into heaven, they would inherit His power and be fully equipped to continue the work that He had begun.

THE ANOINTED ONE

Isaiah and other writers of the Old Testament pointed towards the coming of the Messiah or Christ (Hebrew and Greek words for Anointed One). He would be a descendant of David but would be outstandingly anointed above all others. As 'the Lord's anointed', he would receive the Spirit without measure (John 3:34).

The Christ would not only be anointed with the Spirit, He would also usher in an age of the Spirit.

Isaiah anticipated a time when the Spirit would be 'poured upon us from on high' (Isa. 32:15).

And God Himself declared:

> I will pour water on the thirsty land, and streams on the dry ground; I will pour out my Spirit on your offspring, and my blessing on your descendants (Isa. 44:3).

> I will no longer hide my face from them, for I will pour out my Spirit on the house of Israel (Ezek. 39:29).

Until now, the Old Testament experience of the Spirit was restricted to a very few choice servants of the Lord — people like Moses, Gideon, Samson, the prophets, priests and kings. They were anointed to prophesy, lead or perform some special task. God's people followed them at a distance because they were the ones with the Spirit. The experience was often only temporary. The Spirit would come upon people for a task and then leave them afterwards. Very few individuals knew anything of the abiding of the Spirit on them.

The day of Pentecost was a landmark between the old and the new. When the Spirit came, Joel's prophecy about a widespread outpouring of the Spirit was no longer a future desire, it was a present reality.

What mistakes can you find in the following?

> I will pour out my Spirit on some people. Your apostles and elders will prophesy, your housegroup leaders will dream dreams, your evangelists will see visions. Even on my servants, only women not men, I will pour out my Spirit in those days (Joel 2:28,29).

Moses and the seventy elders, and Elijah and the school of the prophets knew nothing of this widespread outpouring of the Spirit. Their experience was a shadow of something much greater — a time when God would pour out His Spirit on every one of His people and accomplish His purposes through them all.

Chapter Three

HE WILL BAPTISE YOU WITH THE HOLY SPIRIT

WHY JESUS CAME

God sent John the Baptist to prepare the way for the Anointed One. John made two statements about why Jesus came. The first is recorded only in John's Gospel. According to John the Baptist, Jesus came to:

> take away the sin of the world (John 1:29)

The second statement is found in all four of the Gospels and in Acts 1. He said that Jesus came to:

> baptise ... with the Holy Spirit and with fire (Matt. 3:11).

Most evangelical Christians tend to reverse the emphasis. They focus almost exclusively on Jesus as Saviour, not as the one who ushers in a new age — the 'ministry of the Spirit' (2 Cor. 3:8).

In view of these things, it is surprising that during His three years of ministry, Jesus said so very little about the Holy Spirit. Certainly, the Spirit is mentioned significantly in the early chapters of Matthew and Luke, but after Jesus' anointing, all we have is a comment here and there. One clue to the reason for this lies in a statement made by Jesus which is recorded in Luke 12:49,50:

> I have come to bring fire on the earth, and how
> I wish it were already kindled! But I have a
> baptism to undergo, and how distressed I am
> until it is completed!

Jesus was effectively saying, 'Yes, I have come to baptise with fire. I'm longing to pour out my Spirit. But before I can do that I must go through a baptism of my own — on the cross. I must be the sacrificial lamb of God. I must first atone for sin because only then can I baptise with the Holy Spirit.'

Redemption was only part of God's purpose for us. Paul says that:

> [God] redeemed us in order that the bless-
> ing given to Abraham might come to the
> Gentiles through Christ Jesus, so that by
> faith we might receive the promise of the
> Spirit (Gal. 3:14).

The cross was not an end in itself, but the means to a greater end. God wants to justify people, give them Christ's righteousness, fill them with His Spirit and make them a blessing to the nations.

Just as Moses saved his people from their bondage in Egypt, so Jesus delivers us from our bondage to sin. Just as Joshua brought the people into the Promised Land, so Jesus (whose name is a form of Joshua) brings us the promised Holy Spirit. Just as the Israelites were given a land flowing with milk and honey, so we can be filled with the fullness of God.

I AM GOING AWAY

The Gospels suggest that Jesus said comparatively little about the Spirit until the night before His crucifixion. Then, knowing that He would soon be taken from His disciples, He gathered them together for what we call the Upper Room discourse (John 13—17) and began to teach them about the Spirit.

Read John 14:16,17 and consider:

Who cannot receive the Spirit.

Where God wants the Spirit to be.

Read John 14:26 and 15:26.

Note what the Spirit will do.

Read John 16:7 and imagine what happens if Jesus
does not go away.

'It is for your good that I am going away,' said Jesus. Such a
statement must have stunned the disciples who had been His
constant companions for three years. They had seen the crowds
flock to hear Him and had witnessed the most amazing sights:
lepers cleansed, the sick healed and people delivered from
demons and even raised from the dead. Every question He
answered. Every need He met. Yet now He was saying, 'It is for
your good that I am going away.' Surely, it would be far better if He
stayed! But Jesus wanted to raise their faith. 'It is better for the
Holy Spirit to be with you,' He was saying. Later they realised why.

When Jesus was on earth He could only be in one place at one
time. When He was in Jerusalem He could not be in Capernaum,
and when He was in Capernaum He could not be in Bethany.

The Jews thought that by killing Jesus they would rid the world
of His influence. But then the Holy Spirit fell on His disciples and
Jesus, by His Spirit, was present with them wherever they went. So
at the same time, Peter could be in Joppa, Philip in Samaria and
Paul in Antioch and Jesus could be in all three places at once! The
same power that was with Him rested on His followers, enabling
them to teach and perform amazing miracles.

The Holy Spirit is omnipresent, which means 'all present' or
'everywhere at the same time'. This does not mean that He is thinly
spread everywhere. When Peter and John went up to the temple,

Jesus was with them — and a cripple was healed. When Philip went to Samaria Jesus went there too and many believed and were healed.

That was why Jesus said that it was better for Him to go away than to stay. The things that He had done they would do — and even greater things than these. Why? Because He was going to the Father.

> Read Acts 2:33 and consider the two things that
> happened when Jesus was exalted to the right hand
> of God.

WAIT IN JERUSALEM

The disciples' success was wrapped up in Jesus' return to the Father. It was imperative that they wait in Jerusalem until Jesus sent them the Holy Spirit.

God does not give us the Spirit so that we can enjoy a few more uptempo songs. He gives us the power that Jesus had to live as He lived, to speak as He spoke and to do what He did. He is looking for a church which will reach the nations with the gospel. When that has been accomplished, the end will come and Jesus will return in triumph for a church that has done the job He commissioned us to do.

When we understand the immensity of the task, we become acutely aware of our lack of power. We think, 'If Elisha needed power to follow the ministry of Elijah, how much more do I need Jesus' power to continue the ministry of Jesus? If I'm going to accomplish great things for Him, I must have the Spirit that He had.'

'So what am I meant to do?' we ask. 'I'm a Christian. Did I automatically receive the Spirit when I believed? Should I imitate the early disciples and wait for the power? Do I need the laying on of hands? What must I do to receive the Spirit? Where do I go from here?'

After I became aware how much I needed the power of the Spirit, I began to read book after book about the subject. But people's opinions tended to confuse me.

CONFUSING THEORIES

Depending on whom you ask, you will encounter a variety of responses to this dilemma. Let's look at four theories.

GRADUAL FILLING

Some people say, 'You automatically receive everything at conversion. You gradually become more mature as you increasingly yield yourself to the Spirit within you. So being filled with the Spirit is a process.'

HIGHER LIFE

Others suggest, 'Initially you accept Jesus as your Saviour but later you surrender yourself to Him as Lord. Then His Spirit fills you more and gives you the ability to live a higher life.' A popular illustration of this likens us to a glass that is full of 'self'. When you empty it out God can fill it with His Spirit. This full surrender and emptying of yourself is a kind of sanctification crisis. When you totally give yourself to God in this way His Spirit can fill you and you enter into the higher life.

RELEASE

Some maintain that we receive everything at conversion or at baptism or confirmation, but there comes a time when we appropriate the gift that we have already received. This is referred to as 'the release of the Spirit'. The Spirit may be locked up within us for many years, but may later be released through a crisis experience. At that time we step out in faith and exercise the gift of the Spirit within us by reaching out to the sick or speaking in tongues.

TARRYING

There are some who declare, 'The disciples had to wait in Jerusalem for the Spirit to be poured out upon them. That's what you have to do too — possibly for years — and when you speak in tongues you will know you have been baptised in the Spirit.' In the past, people would go to tarrying meetings to pray and seek God for this to happen to them. They would repent and pray and fast and try to be holy in order to make themselves fit to receive the Spirit. Some waited for years and never spoke in tongues.

Faced with such diverse theories, what are we to believe? How can we be filled with the Spirit? In our next chapter we shall see what happened to the earliest Christians.

Chapter Four

THE SPIRIT IN ACTS

God wants us to build His church on the pattern of the one in the New Testament. Much modern church life is unrecognisable when compared with the early church because of so-called 'historical development' — which is actually historical deviation.

The New Testament tells us what to believe and shows us how to behave in the church. It tells us how we should function and what we should experience. Some say that we cannot establish doctrine from narrative passages in the Bible, arguing that we must focus on the solid teaching in the epistles and on Jesus' words in the gospels. But this belief undermines the truth of 2 Timothy 3:16 which declares that:

> All Scripture is God-breathed and is useful for teaching, rebuking, correcting and training in righteousness.

God did not have the inspired book of Acts preserved purely for the sake of historical interest. If the Old Testament narratives were written to instruct us (1 Cor. 10:11), surely the New Testament account of our church origins is of equal or even greater value. We ignore to our cost the ministry of our predecessors, the ones who paved the way and show us how to walk in the purposes of God.

The book of Acts is of vital importance to today's church and we would benefit from reading it again and again. It inspires and motivates us with a realistic picture of our calling and destiny. In it we discover how the early Christians first received the Spirit and how their experience provides a pattern for us today.

ACTS 2

Since this outstanding passage is so familiar, we will not spend a great deal of time on it.

> Read through the chapter now to familiarise yourself
> with its contents.

Acts 2 documents the first outpouring of the Spirit. About a hundred and twenty people were gathered in one place when they were suddenly clothed with power from on high. The Spirit fell upon them and they all began to worship God and speak with tongues. Following this experience, they became a dynamic, forceful company who turned the world upside down.

ACTS 8

The second account of the outpouring of the Spirit occurs in Samaria.

> Read Acts 8:12–17 and consider:
>
> What Philip was preaching.
>
> Whether people actually became Christians.
>
> Why Peter and John were sent to them.
>
> Why this was necessary.
>
> What they did and what the result was.

There is no mention here that the new converts spoke in tongues or prophesied. But Simon the Sorcerer saw something happen to them that so impressed him, that he offered the apostles money saying, 'Give me also this ability so that everyone on whom I lay my hands may receive the Holy Spirit' (v.19). There must have been some sort of manifestation to impress him so much.

Acts 9

In this chapter we read of the apostle Paul's conversion. He was on the Road to Damascus when the Lord came to him in a blinding light. Three days later, Ananias visited him.

> Read verse 17.
>
> What were the first two words that Ananias said to Paul (Saul)? What does this say about Paul's spiritual state? Why did Ananias visit Paul?

Who was Ananias? Was he some great apostle like Peter? No. He was just an ordinary believer who obeyed Jesus. We have never heard of him before and we never hear of him again. But he was chosen to minister to the man who would one day become the most significant of all the apostles.

The next outpouring of the Holy Spirit took place in the house of a man called Cornelius. Peter would never have set foot in this Gentile home unless God had told him to do so. God overcame Peter's scruples by giving him a vision of unclean food — unclean to the Jewish mind that is — and commanding him to eat. While he was pondering this vision, God told him that He had sent three men to see him. Peter welcomed them and the next day went with them to Cornelius' home. When he arrived he spoke to the assembled company about Jesus. But while he was in full flow, something extraordinary and unexpected happened. The Holy Spirit fell on them.

> Why were the circumcised (Jewish) believers so astonished? (Acts 10:45) How did they know what had happened? (v.46) On what basis did Peter order them to be baptised? (v.47)

Here we see a different sequence of events. Peter was preaching the gospel message to the heathen. While he was doing this, faith was rising in their hearts and they were agreeing that Jesus was the Christ. Then the Spirit fell on them. There was no delay, no three day gap, no tarrying! They were born again and filled with the Holy Spirit all in a moment. Peter did not even get the chance to finish speaking, let alone lay hands on them! Yet the same supernatural things were happening now as they had in the upper room on the day of Pentecost.

When Peter returned to Jerusalem, he faced criticism from the Jewish believers who wanted to know why he was associating with the Gentiles. Peter effectively said, 'But I never touched them! I never laid a hand on them! While I was speaking, the Holy Spirit fell on them just as He had fallen on us. It was the Lord, not me! If you have questions, you had better take them up at a higher level!'

I believe that this is the reason why the account of Cornelius' conversion is so different from the others. God had to prove to the Jewish believers that He wanted to include the Gentiles in His purposes. So He had to break in sovereignly and unexpectedly in order to change their thinking.

In John 3:8 the Spirit is likened to wind.

Where does this wind blow? What do you hear?
What can't you tell?

Cornelius' experience warns us not to be too dogmatic about the way the Spirit moves. The Spirit is likened to wind, fire and water — all unpredictable elements. So when we are developing a doctrine of the Holy Spirit and His ways, we can really only say, 'It's usually like this.' As soon as we try to define Him too much, He will do something unexpected.

Not only must we avoid being too dogmatic about the Spirit, we must also beware of the opposite extreme and fall into a sort of mysticism which says, 'Who can know anything about the Spirit? We'll just have to see what happens.' The Bible gives us objective truth about the Spirit and how He operates. It describes His activities and gives us a basis for expectation. But we must leave room for Him to break in sovereignly on us — as He did in the life of Cornelius.

ACTS 19

The final account of the outpouring of the Spirit is found in Acts 19 (although we have not looked at Acts 4 where the Spirit filled again those who had earlier received Him at Pentecost).

Arriving at Ephesus, Paul found a group of disciples and began talking to them.

> Read Acts 19:1–7.
>
> Paul must have sensed that there was something lacking in these men which is why he quizzed them.
>
> What question did he ask them? (v.2) What was their reply? (v.2) What was Paul's next question? (v.3)

If these men had received Christian baptism they would have heard about the Holy Spirit. It was all part of the same package — as Peter had outlined on the day of Pentecost:

> Repent, and be baptised, every one of you, in the name of Jesus Christ for the forgiveness of your sins. And you will receive the gift of the Holy Spirit (Acts 2:38).
>
> John's baptism was a baptism of repentance. He told the people to believe in the one coming after him ... in Jesus (Acts 19:4).

People from all over Palestine went out to hear John the Baptist. These men in Ephesus had evidently heard his message, either directly from the prophet himself or from someone like Apollos (see Acts 18:24,25). They would have known about the Coming One who would take away sins and baptise in the Spirit — because that was John's message. Apollos taught accurately about Jesus, though he knew only the baptism of John. Priscilla and Aquila had to take him aside and explain the way of God more adequately (Acts 18:26).

Paul also had to explain the way of God to these men too. When he told them about Jesus they readily believed in Him and were baptised into His name (v.5). Whatever has been deficient in their previous experience was now made up. But notice that Paul did not leave it there.

What did he do next? What happened?

There was a gap between conversion and the outpouring of the Spirit at Pentecost, in Samaria and in the experience of Paul. Here these men were converted and filled with the Spirit on the same day, although their experience differed from that of Cornelius. In whatever way God chose to work, there are three distinct elements present: hearing the gospel, believing the Lord Jesus and receiving the Holy Spirit.

Paul underlined this progression in his letter to the Ephesians (which would have included this original group of a dozen men). He wrote:

> In Him, you also, after listening to the message of truth, the gospel of your salvation — having also believed, you were sealed in Him with the Holy Spirit of promise (Eph. 1:13 NASB).

First they had heard the message of truth, the good news of their salvation, secondly they had believed and then they had been sealed with the promised Holy Spirit. The process is this:

Hearing — believing — receiving the Spirit.

As we have seen, these elements may all happen together or there may be minutes, hours or days between them. The question is, have you experienced them all? Let me repeat Paul's question of Acts 19:2.

Did you receive the Holy Spirit when you believed?

Chapter Five

RECEIVING THE SPIRIT

So how do you receive the Spirit? We have looked briefly at the theories, but how do they square with the experiences that people had in the book of Acts? Let's see.

GRADUAL FILLING

Do we automatically receive everything at conversion? Certainly, Cornelius' story indicates that an individual can be saved and filled with the Spirit at the same time. But for Paul and those in Samaria and Ephesus, the case was very different. They heard the Gospel and believed it, but they received the Spirit later through the laying on of hands. Clearly the teaching that we automatically receive the Spirit at conversion is not borne out by these examples in the book of Acts.

Coupled with this notion that we receive everything at conversion is the idea that being filled with the Spirit is something that happens gradually. If you ask someone who holds this view, 'Have you been filled with the Spirit?' he will usually reply, 'As I walk with God and grow in grace I'm steadily being more and more filled with the Spirit.' This may sound spiritual but it is not biblical.

When Paul asked the Ephesian disciples if they had received the Spirit, they didn't say. 'We're steadily moving into the fullness.' They were quite clear that they had not had this experience. But if Paul had asked the same question after he had laid his hands on them, they would have responded with a very definite, 'Yes!'

In the New Testament, the people were not vaguely aware of the Spirit. Either they had received Him or they had not. When the Spirit came upon them they knew all about it and so did everyone else present. Simon the Sorcerer saw something happen and wanted to buy the ability to give the Spirit. Certainly we need to grow in grace, but this has nothing to do with receiving the Holy Spirit.

HIGHER LIFE

Is there a later step of sanctification? Do we receive Jesus as our Saviour at conversion and then, as we grow in our understanding of God and our weakness, bow the knee and accept Him as Lord? Is the filling of the Spirit linked with a new kind of surrender?

Certainly, Christians do give themselves to God more fully; they deal with their sin; they know a greater reality of God and may even have an experience of being filled with the Spirit. But the idea that there is a 'higher life' is neither taught nor demonstrated in the entire New Testament. Nowhere do we find the apostles saying, 'It's great that you've made Jesus your Saviour and have been baptised. Later, as you grow in your faith, you will need to make Jesus your Lord, then you will receive the fullness of the Spirit.'

What do we confess at conversion? (Rom. 10:9)

If you cannot confess this, then it could be questioned whether you are a Christian at all.

Peter and Paul did not tell new converts, 'Now, you must wait until you have a more mature grasp of your salvation before you ask for the Spirit.' Not a bit of it! Immediately the new believers were baptised, the apostles laid hands on them and expected them to receive the Spirit — which they did.

Some people have protested, 'Isn't this rather dangerous? Shouldn't we hesitate to furnish young Christians with such power and gifts? That's rather like giving a loaded gun to a small child. The wisest course of action must be to wait until people are more mature and can handle such things.'

Paul did not seem to think like that. The church at Corinth was in a mess, but Paul said:

> I always thank God for you … For in him you
> have been enriched in every way — in all your
> speaking and in all your knowledge … There-
> fore you do not lack any spiritual gift (1 Cor.
> 1:4–7).

Paul's way of handling their immaturity was not to say, 'Wait until you're more experienced and can cope with these spiritual things.' On the contrary, he effectively told them, 'Here's the dynamite. This is how you use it properly. Get on with it and God will sanctify you as you go.'

God wants us to be zealous about maturity, but He does not want us to think that by trying to be holy we can somehow earn His power and a gift or two. This is not a biblical idea. God loves to lavish His gifts upon all Christians — the young, the middle-aged, the old and even the irresponsible! Indeed, we are currently seeing all sorts of amazing signs and wonders in very young churches — particularly in the so-called 'Third World'.

RELEASE

Do we receive the gift of the Spirit at our 'Christian initiation' (conversion, baptism or confirmation) and then seek to 'release' the Spirit from within us? According to the New Testament — No!

When Peter and John went to Samaria they did not tell the newly baptised believers, 'You've been baptised, so you've got the Spirit, now just release Him. Speak out in tongues.' We know that the new converts were believers but we also know that 'The Holy Spirit had not yet come upon any of them' (Acts 8:16). Only when Peter and John laid hands on them did they receive the Spirit.

Consider the following false statement:

When Paul placed his hands on them, the Holy Spirit welled up from within them, and they spoke in tongues and prophesied.

You will find the correct version in Acts 19:6.

Do you get the point?

TARRYING

Must we wait for the Spirit? When I was first seeking the Spirit some friends told me that I should 'tarry' until something happened. I met people who had been 'tarrying' for ages. One of them had been waiting ten years but had received nothing.

Those of us who have recently been involved in the charismatic movement may find these things hard to believe. But a few years ago, tarrying meetings were important among Pentecostals if you earnestly wanted to receive the Spirit. The people who attended them kept pleading with God to fill them. They were saying to themselves, 'When I speak in tongues I'll believe I've got it, but until I speak in tongues, I won't believe.' Although they did not realise it, they were actually putting the cart before the horse. They were looking for a sign before they believed, when God wanted them to believe because He had promised.

Why did they teach the need to tarry? Because Jesus told the disciples to stay ('tarry' AV) in the city until they had been clothed with power from on high (Luke 24:49). At Pentecost we see the result of this waiting.

> All of them were filled with the Holy Spirit and began to speak in other tongues as the Spirit enabled them (Acts 2:4).

The filling of the Spirit was evidenced in the gift of tongues. After the day of Pentecost, no one was ever again told to wait. When Ananias was sent to Paul he did not say, 'Now Paul, you're going to be an apostle. Since all the other apostles had to wait for the Spirit, you'd better find a nice quiet upper room somewhere and do the same. The power will come eventually.' No! He went up to Paul, laid his hands on him and the Spirit immediately came upon him. Similarly, after Paul had baptised the men in Ephesus, he laid his hands on them and they were instantly filled with the Holy Spirit.

So why did Jesus tell the disciples to wait for the Spirit? The Bible teaches us that they were not waiting until they were ready, they were waiting until Jesus was ready.

The outpouring of the Spirit was dependent not upon the performance of the disciples but on the position of their Saviour. Until Jesus had been exalted to the right hand of God, He could not pour out the Spirit. That is why they had to wait.

> Read Acts 2:38,39 and identify the four groups of people who may receive the promise of the Holy Spirit.
>
> Are you included?

Having established that the outpouring of the Holy Spirit flows from the ascended and glorified Christ, let's see how we can receive the gift for ourselves.

IF ANYONE IS THIRSTY

The Feast of Tabernacles lasted a whole week. Every day, water from the Pool of Siloam was ceremonially poured out in the centre of Jerusalem to symbolise God's provision. The last day of the feast was the greatest day — the choicest time for Jesus to stand and declare Himself to be the source of living water and the one who would pour out the Holy Spirit. Jesus said:

> If anyone is thirsty, let him come to me and drink. Whoever believes in me, as the Scripture has said, streams of living water will flow from within him (John 7:37–39).

If you had been there at the feast, you might have gone up to Jesus and said, 'Yes, Lord. I'm thirsty for your Spirit. I want Him to flow through me. Please give Him to me.' Had you done that, you would have been disappointed. He would have responded, 'I'm sorry. I can't give you the Spirit now.'

Hearing this you might have protested, 'Why not now? Didn't you promise ..? Am I disqualified for some reason? Why can't I receive the Spirit now?' In reply, He would have said, 'It's nothing to do with you. I'd love to give you the Spirit now but I can't. You must wait.'

According to John 7:39 why couldn't Jesus have given you the Spirit?

On the high day of another feast, the Feast of Pentecost, Jesus poured out the Holy Spirit upon His church. Did He delay because they needed time to prepare themselves to receive the Spirit? No. They had to wait until Jesus was ready. Only when He was exalted in heaven could He fulfil His promise and give the Spirit to His church.

Let faith rise in your heart. The Spirit is given because Jesus has been glorified. No one need ever wait for the outpouring of the Spirit again.

JESUS IS WORTHY

When we start seeking the outpouring of the Spirit, the devil will do all he can to discourage us. He does not want to see Christians full of the Holy Spirit and will try to make us look in at ourselves and despair at what we see. 'It's OK for others,' we conclude. 'I'm just not good enough.'

The devil is quick to agree. 'I saw what you did the other day,' he says. 'Call yourself a Christian? You're not worthy to receive the Spirit.' We then embark on a strict self-preparation programme which includes things like Bible study, prayer, fasting, confession, self-surrender and general waiting for it to happen.

I do not want to discourage anyone from praying or fasting or hungering after God. But the believers in the New Testament were never told, 'You must make yourself worthy to receive the Spirit.' What we are is not the issue. Our focus must be on the one who is worthy. Jesus is the Lamb of God who has taken away our sin. He is now glorified and has received from the Father the promised Holy Spirit. He wants us all to be filled with the Spirit and is ready to give the gift to anyone who wants it.

LIVING PROOF THAT JESUS IS ALIVE

Jesus told His disciples:

> you will receive power when the Holy Spirit
> comes on you; and you will be my witnesses
> (Acts 1:8).

This does not mean that when we are baptised in the Spirit we will suddenly become fantastic orators! The Scripture speaks of our being witnesses, not doing witnessing. If you are a witness, you have see something, you can testify to what you know and give evidence that it is true.

Every Spirit-filled person is proof that Jesus is not a corpse rotting in a tomb in the Middle East. Dead men cannot give the Holy Spirit. Only someone who has ascended to the right hand of the Majesty on high can do that. So when we are full of the Holy Spirit we automatically become witnesses to Jesus' resurrection and ascension. We are living proof to the world that Jesus is alive. Peter said:

> he has ... poured out what you now see and
> hear (Acts 2:33).

The evidence of Jesus' resurrection was right before their eyes.

THE SPIRIT IS ACCESSIBLE

Jesus once said, 'If anyone is thirsty, let him come to me and drink.' But He did not mean, 'Come now.' He meant, 'Not yet. Not until I'm glorified.' Since Jesus has been glorified the 'not yet' clause no longer applies. There is a waterfall of God's grace and power available for us right now.

I remember speaking to a couple about this many years ago. I was taking them through various passages of Scripture and we were about three quarters of the way through the evening. I was about to bring it all to a conclusion when the husband asked his wife to make some coffee. She went out into the kitchen, but before she had finished making it she ran back in declaring, 'It's wonderful! It's wonderful!'

We asked her what had happened and she replied, 'The Holy Spirit has come upon me.' I hadn't even finished my explanation! I hadn't laid hands on her. But she had understood and believed and reached out to Jesus. You can receive the Spirit before you finish reading these words. The Spirit is available — to you.

IF ANYONE IS THIRSTY

Are you thirsty? I hope so. You probably would not be reading this book if you were not thirsty for God. Jesus did not say, 'If anyone is holy' or 'If anyone is special' or 'If anyone is a super-saint'. He was looking for thirsty people.

God made me thirsty by showing me the desperate need in the world and my inability to communicate Jesus with those who did not know Him. After that painful experience on Brighton seafront I became extremely thirsty. Have you become thirsty?

LET HIM COME TO ME

The weekend after my lunch appointment with my Pentecostal friend, I joined him at his church and sat in a circle with others who were seeking the baptism of the Spirit. A man was laying hands on each person and praying for the power of God to come on them. Seeing the joy on their faces, I thought, 'This looks good. This is why I came. I'm going to receive the Spirit through this man.'

Then he laid hands on me, prayed and went on to the next one. Everyone around me was worshipping and encouraging me to do the same. But I was thinking, 'Hey, wait a minute! What's all this? Come back! Nothing has happened.' People around me were saying, 'Praise the Lord.' But I was thinking, 'Why praise the Lord? Nothing has happened! Then they exhorted me, 'Say "Hallelujah!"' By this time I was thinking, 'This is desperate! I've come all this way to meet with God These people are trying to get me excited and I'm dead on the inside.'

Why was this happening to me? Perhaps because at that moment my faith focused on a man when I should have been going to Jesus. The man had no power of his own. He could not fill me with the Spirit. Only Jesus could do that. By all means ask someone for the laying on of hands for the Spirit but remember to look beyond the servant to the Master. You must make sure you come to Him.

AND DRINK

Jesus did not say 'and beg'. He did not tell us to prostrate ourselves before Him and plead, 'Oh God! Oh Jesus! Please give me your Holy Spirit. Please do it for me. Oh Lord! Please! Please!' He said, 'Come to me and drink.' 'Take it,' He is saying. 'Just come and receive.'

God is a loving Father who wants to give us His Spirit (Luke 11:11–13). He wants us to ask with the expectation of receiving. We do not have to plead and beg, neither do we sit back passively and just wait. We drink.

Suppose it is a hot sunny day. My young children are playing in the garden when they hear an ice cream van playing its tune in the neighbourhood. They race in and say, 'Dad, can we have an ice cream?' Knowing what a meany I am, they are probably thinking as they ask me, 'Not a chance!' And of course I say, 'Not on your life!'

Suppose the following day is equally hot. I am looking out of the window at the kids as they play in the sweltering heat and I am thinking, 'Poor things, They'd love something nice and cool.' So I go in the car, drive to the shops, buy some ice cream and drive home again. Then I open the back door and call out, 'Hey! Come and get your ice cream!' Before I know it. my youngsters are all round me asking for their refreshments. I went to a great deal of trouble to make them available, and my children come to me with confidence that I will give them an ice cream because it was my idea, not theirs.

The baptism of the Spirit is not our idea, but God's. Jesus went to an enormous amount of trouble to make it available to you. He removed your sin and ascended into heaven where He received the promised Holy Spirit from His Father. Now He says to you, 'Are you thirsty? Come to me and drink.'

God knows your heart. He understands your doubts. You question: 'Does God really want to give this to me?' And He replies:

Ask and it will be given to you (Luke 11:9).

He also understands your fears — You wonder: 'What will happen to me if I yield to this? Will I fall on the floor? Will I shake about uncontrollably?' and you conclude: 'I'm not sure if I really want the Hoooly Ghooost!' But God reminds you that He is more loving and faithful to you than your earthly father. He will not give you something that is dangerous or spooky — any more than a good father would.

Read Luke 11:12,13.

Consider the way that a good father responds to his children when they ask him for things.

If you ask your heavenly Father for the Holy Spirit, what will He give you?

Are you thirsty?

Jesus offers you a drink.

Take it.

Chapter Seven

THE STEP OF FAITH

J esus calls thirsty people to come to Him and drink. Then He goes on to say, 'Whoever believes in me ...' Clearly, the exercise of faith is vitally important when we come to receive the Holy Spirit.

Answer the question posed in Galatians 3:5.

The New American Standard version translates the last few words of this verse: 'by hearing with faith'. There is a faith element to receiving the Spirit, so we have to shake off passivity.

When they were praying for me to receive the Spirit and were exhorting me to praise the Lord, I was desperate for something to happen to me. The trouble was that I was passive. 'I'm not going to make up some silly language,' I told myself. Then they took me back to the promises in God's Word and showed me how faithful He is to give to all who ask. As I listened I began to believe God for His Spirit. 'Surely ...' I thought, '... the Lord has brought me this far. I can't believe that He wants me to go home empty.' So instead of sitting there passively waiting for something to happen, I reached out to the Lord and began to drink and to believe.

Faith without action is dead (James 2:17). It is not real faith at all. Many miracles in the Bible happened when people actively responded to the Word.

If we had been standing with the Israelites on the edge of the River Jordan we might have been tempted to fast and pray all night for God to part the waters.

Read Joshua 3:8–16 and consider:

What God told the priests to do.

What He promised would happen.

Whether the priests heard with faith.

Whether God fulfilled His promise.

When Jesus told the ten lepers to 'Go, show yourselves to the priests' (Luke 17:14), they probably looked at their hands and feet and said, 'What's the point of doing that? Nothing's happened!'

When were they cleansed?

'Stretch out your hand,' said Jesus to a man whose hand was withered (Matt. 12:13). I can imagine the poor man saying to himself, 'That's my problem, I can't stretch it out.' But what did he do? He did what he knew he could not do. He heard Jesus, reached out in faith and found that he could do what he could not!

Jesus said to a paralytic, 'Get up, take your mat and go home' (Mark 2:11). He said to a man born blind, 'Go... wash in the Pool of Siloam' (John 9:7). They heard Him and said to themselves, 'Jesus says I can do it and I believe Him!' They heard with faith. Jesus wants you to hear with faith as you come to Him for the outpouring of the Holy Spirit.

Jesus' promise of the Spirit was based on what the Scripture had said. God had declared that He would pour out the Spirit on all flesh. He is the source of living water. Jeremiah took up this theme, but what he said to the people was not encouraging:

> Be appalled at this, O heavens, and shudder with great horror... My people have committed two sins.

Read Jeremiah 2:12,13.

What were those sins?

Sadly, some Christians are doing the same thing today. They are neglecting the power of the Spirit and trying to serve God out of their own resources. They are so busy striving to please God by works of evangelical law that they fail to realise that what they are digging does not hold water. They have forsaken the spring of living water. They are devoid of the power of God.

Many of them have never received the Spirit's power simply because they have never been told about it. Like the twelve men at Ephesus they have not heard that the Holy Spirit is available. They have been led to believe that they must automatically have received the fullness of the Spirit at conversion. Assuming that their experience is normal, they restrict all supernatural activities to the Bible.

If preachers do not preach about the availability of the Spirit's power, Christians will not hear it. If they do not hear it, they cannot believe and receive it. On the other hand, when Christians are taught these truths from the Scriptures and hear with faith, they will receive the Holy Spirit.

A young married couple were in leadership in a church where the teaching emphasis was: 'You received everything at conversion'. The use of tongues was forbidden and no other viewpoint tolerated. Then they attended a conference where a large number of the delegates were Spirit-filled. They enjoyed the lively worship but could not enter into it themselves. When they began asking questions about receiving the Spirit, we lent them a manuscript of this book which, at that time, was incomplete. As they saw what the Bible said about the outpouring of the Holy Spirit, they began to reach out. What happened? They were gloriously filled — just as the Scripture says.

STREAMS OF LIVING WATER

As my friends prayed with me, I began to believe and to thank God for the gift of His Spirit. Then they said to me, 'Now just speak in tongues.' 'Oh no!' I thought. 'If I try and do that I shall say "blublublublublub", then dry up and feel a right idiot.' At first I was not prepared to step out in faith and risk the embarrassment if nothing happened. But then, as faith started to rise, I broke the sound barrier and spoke in tongues.

Remember, God doesn't speak in tongues, you do! Initially, I did not realise this. I sat there waiting for God in some mystic way to speak through me. But I had to take the first step. I had to operate my diaphragm and vocal chords. I had to speak — with the Spirit's enabling.

The Old Testament tells us the story of a woman who had run out of oil. Elisha told her:

> Go round and ask all your neighbours for empty jars. Don't ask for just a few. Then go inside and shut the door behind you and your sons. Pour oil into all the jars, and as each is filled, put it to one side (2 Kings 4:3,4).

This woman could have thought, 'That's daft. If I tip this little drop from this jar into that one, I'll just have a little drop in there instead.' It could be argued that the miracle did not happen when she started to pour, it happened when she continued pouring and the oil kept flowing and multiplying. How similar to speaking in tongues!

As I prayed on in tongues I began to have serious doubts about what I was doing and a spiritual battle started to rage inside. 'You're just making this all up, Terry,' the devil argued. 'There's nothing supernatural about this. It's just a lot of rubbish.' I wanted God — not something unreal. But as I listened to myself making these funny noises, I was frightened of fooling myself that I had something genuine when it was not. So I stopped speaking. My friends had to encourage me to recognise the enemy and to overcome my doubts, fears and unbelief.

The devil does not want Christians to be filled with the power of the Holy Spirit. It is therefore not surprising that he stirs up so much controversy about the subject, and tries to discourage any who reach out in faith. Tongues does sound weird, but so too do many of the world's languages. Sometimes when I'm abroad I hear the most strange sounds from people's mouths! I ponder, 'Is that a language?!' They answer my question by communicating with one another in it! So when you speak in tongues, don't try to analyse your vocabulary and recognise the enemy's temptation to doubt. I had a battle but I got through it — and so can you.

> Submit yourselves, then, to God. Resist the devil, and he will flee from you (James 4:7).

Phil Rogers' battle over tongues was similar to mine. He wanted to be filled with the Spirit on God's terms, not his, and decided that if tongues was part of the deal, then he would have to have that as well.

As they prayed for him to be baptised in the Spirit, someone told him that the Lord was saying, 'Open your mouth and I will fill it.' They continued to encourage him to step out in faith and speak in tongues. But he just stood there with his mouth open, waiting for something to happen and thinking, 'Perhaps my tongue will start thrashing about inside my mouth of its own accord.' Then some wise person said, 'In Acts 2 we read that they began to speak in other tongues as the Spirit enabled them. Once you start speaking, the Holy Spirit will give you the words and the flow will come.'

He began thinking of the disciples in the boat on the sea. He imagined Peter looking at the raging water and then at Jesus standing there inviting him to 'Come'. The only way he would know if the waves would hold him up was to get out of the boat and try walking on them. Phil stood there for what seemed like an eternity of self consciousness, then he started to speak out odd words like those around him. The initial trickle became a great surge and he suddenly found himself caught up in a great flow of tongues.

TONGUES FOR ALL

Simon the Sorcerer was evidently impressed by something when he saw the Samaritan believers receive the Spirit (Acts 8:18). Clearly there is some outward manifestation when people are filled with the Spirit. Speaking in tongues seems to be the most common occurrence, although prophecy is sometimes mentioned (Acts 19:6).

Some people question, 'Does everyone speak in tongues?'

Read Acts 2:4; 10:44–46; 19:6,7; 1 Corinthians 14:23.

Note the frequency of the word 'all' in respect of speaking in tongues.

Certainly, not everyone is required to speak in tongues in a public context, but God wants us all to use tongues in a private capacity.

Maybe you have already been baptised in the Holy Spirit but have never spoken in tongues.

The devil 'comes to steal and kill and destroy'; Jesus wants to give us 'life ... to the full' (John 10:10). These two individuals are opposed to one another. Jesus wants only what is good for you and freely offers you the gift of tongues. Ask Him for it. Step out in faith. Speak out and you will discover that the Holy Spirit will give you the enabling.

When I finally left all my doubts and fears behind me and poured out my praise in tongues, I felt a surge of power go right through my body. For the first time in my Christian life I experienced the intimacy of the cry, 'Abba Father'. Suddenly I knew that He was right there with me and I loved Him in a way that I had never loved Him before.

Gone was my old reluctance to speak about Jesus to others. Now I wanted to tell them about Him. And I wanted to explore the other spiritual gifts available to the believer too. I had been brought into an exciting supernatural dimension and was hungry for more. The baptism of the Spirit was not so much a goal as a gateway of discovery which would lead on to many more good things ahead.

Peter said that the promise of the Spirit is for all whom the Lord our God will call (Acts 2:39). If you know that you are a believer, you have a promise to claim. Jesus wants to fill you with the Holy Spirit. If you are thirsty, hear His invitation to you, 'Come to me and drink.' Come with expectation. Ask Him for the Spirit. Receive the Spirit. Take a step of faith and speak out. Streams of living water will flow from within you.

Having received the Holy Spirit, you may have the opportunity to counsel others to receive. If so, see further notes in the Appendix.

Chapter Eight

SPEAKING IN TONGUES

My early opinion of the gift of tongues is reflected in the prayer I prayed when I was a nineteen-year-old student. 'Oh Lord, please fill me with Your Spirit, but skip the tongues!' At the time, I was kneeling in my study-bedroom in a hall of residence in Bristol. I had become a Christian at the age of fourteen. Now I was at university and was eager to serve God in my new situation.

Some Christians invited me to a half night of prayer which I attended with a great sense of anticipation. I had been to many prayer meetings but this was different. Never had I experienced such a sense of God's presence in a meeting before. It was the leader who particularly provoked me. He had not been a Christian very long and belonged to a denomination that I did not view very charitably. But when he prayed, he spoke to God with such intimacy and reality that stirred up great yearnings within me. I found myself longing to know God as he did.

I got to know him and discovered his secret. He had been baptised with the Holy Spirit and spoke in tongues. I had already heard about the baptism of the Holy Spirit and had read a number of books about it. Indeed, my pastor back home in London had quietly admitted to praying in tongues in private. So I accepted that the experience was biblical and that it was for today's pastors. But when I began to encounter people of my own age who were involved in these things, I started feeling terribly thirsty.

Certainly, I was privileged to have been brought up in a Christian family. But in spite of that, and in spite of all the sound teaching and enthusiastic activity, I knew that I lacked something.

My God lived in unapproachable transcendent glory! I longed to be close to Him, to have His Spirit inside me. But I dared not reach out because I was hung up on speaking in tongues.

This gift offended me. I could not see the point of speaking words that I could not understand. And I was frightened that the Spirit would, like some alien brain invader, take me over and control my life.

I was not the first or the last person to have such anxieties. Maybe you share them today. Let's look more closely at the gift and see what the word of God says about it.

NEW LANGUAGES

'These signs will accompany those who believe...,' said Jesus to His disciples. 'They will speak in new tongues.' Tongues, healing, miraculous protection and the authority to drive out demons were seen as evidences that God's power was with His people (Mark 16:17,18). Even after the apostles had died, these signs continued for many years. Then they became less common and finally, for 1600 years, all but disappeared.

We are living at an exciting time, a time of church restoration. God is moving among His people and we are again seeing manifestations of His power both in our own nation and throughout the world. One of these manifestations is 'new tongues'. An increasing number of Christians are beginning to speak in languages that are totally new and unfamiliar — to them.

TONGUES AT PENTECOST

On the day of Pentecost, the believers who were assembled in the upper room spoke in 'other tongues' (Acts 2:4). The crowds who gathered to listen heard their own native languages being spoken by working class Galileans!

What was their reaction? (Acts 2:12,13)

In the other accounts of the outpouring of the Holy Spirit, tongues was not generally understood by the bystanders. On those occasions there was not the international context that we see on the day of Pentecost when the languages were recognised by the hearers.

What were the disciples declaring?

Clearly, the disciples were not preaching to the crowd. As they were speaking in their unlearned languages, the bystanders found themselves eavesdropping on Psalm-like declarations.

TONGUES IN CORINTH

Read 1 Corinthians 14:2–5 and consider the following:

When people speak in tongues, to whom are they speaking? What sorts of things are they saying? How do they do this? How does speaking in tongues benefit them? What did Paul think about Christians speaking in tongues?

Paul wrote this section of his letter because he wanted to correct the Corinthians' misuse of tongues. Today we do not suffer the misuse of tongues so much as the disuse of tongues! So we must keep in mind the context of his comments. We misinterpret Paul if we think that he is either undervaluing tongues or dismissing the practice.

According to Paul, how important is speaking in tongues? (1 Cor. 14:18)

When Paul refers to his speaking in the 'tongues of angels' (1 Cor. 13:1), he is probably speaking rhetorically. In other words, he is saying, 'If I speak in tongues — whatever language it might be (even if it were the very language of angels) — but do not have love, then all I am is a resounding gong or a clanging cymbal.' Even angelic languages without love are futile.

PRAYING WITH MY SPIRIT

Paul says:

> if I pray in a tongue, my spirit prays, but my mind is unfruitful (1 Cor. 14:14).

When we speak in tongues, our prayer bypasses conscious thought and comes directly from our human spirit. At first, this can seem really strange because we discover that we can pray in tongues while our minds are preoccupied with numerous other things. In the context of a meeting it is possible to pray in tongues and think about the Sunday lunch, plan what to do in the afternoon and arrange the schedule for the week. When we pray in tongues we clearly need to discipline our thoughts and focus on the Lord.

One young man who had received the Spirit and spoken in tongues was terrified that his experience had been of the devil. He found that by leaving it empty the devil was stirring up all sorts of filth. Then, I told him how to focus his mind on Jesus and prayed for him. At the meeting later that day he was worshipping the Lord in tongues with a huge grin on his face.

Read 1 Corinthians 14:15.

What was Paul's practice?

God wants to hear us glorify Him in our own language and in His. In our regular devotional times we can switch naturally from one to the other whenever we pray or praise the Lord. In our own language we pray rationally about things we know and understand. In tongues we pray about things that are given to us by God and answered by Him.

LORD, HELP US TO PRAY

It may sound peculiar to pray prayers and get answers to prayers when we have no idea of their content. Paul gives us some insight into this.

> Read Romans 8:26–27.

> In what way does Paul say that we are weak? How does the Spirit help us in our weakness?

The Spirit is always willing to pray — even when the flesh is weak. When Paul says that 'He intercedes for us' he means that the Spirit prays not for us but through us. When we pray in tongues or groan in prayer we are interceding according to the will of God. We may not understand what we are saying but we can be sure that our prayers are accomplishing God's purposes.

Tongues is a great help when we do not know what or how to pray. When we begin interceding in tongues, we may find that we are very moved. The Spirit may give us strong feelings: groanings, pleadings, anger, burdens, aggression ... On occasions we may even weep. After a time of such dynamic praying, there may be a sense of breakthrough and release — a conviction that we have been heard and that God is going to act.

GIVING PRAISE AND THANKS

Luke tells us that at Pentecost the disciples were praising God in tongues (Acts 2:11). Paul talks about our praising God and giving thanks with our spirits (1 Cor. 14:16). Although no one except the Lord understands what we are saying, we could easily be giving thanks when we pray in tongues (v.17).

There are times when we simply run out of words which are adequate to express praise to the Lord. Tongues goes beyond our mental limitations and offers Him an expression of sublime praise from our spirits. From time to time we will have feelings of great glory, exhilaration, wonder, awe, reverence, love and adoration. Our worship may be accompanied by tears of joy.

My initial fear of being taken over and of not being in control has proved groundless. I think it arose from the reference to tongues as 'ecstatic utterances' or 'languages of ecstasy'.

What does Paul say in 1 Corinthians 14:32?

This means that when we speak in tongues or prophesy, we are always in control of our actions and emotions. We can stop whenever we wish and we can choose to respond emotionally or not. Much of the time we pray in tongues without any feelings at all — as we do in our own language. In fact most of the time praying and praising in tongues is a very normal, down to earth sort of practice.

People who cry out or behave in an abnormal way cannot blame the Holy Spirit. They choose to react like that and are responsible for their conduct. The Spirit does not give us weird and mystical 'ecstatic experiences'. But He does live in us and intercede for us according to God's will. If we pause to think about it, that is quite an amazing idea for us to grasp.

SPEAKING IN TONGUES TODAY

Before the twentieth century, the experience of speaking in tongues had become generally regarded by Christians as peculiar to the New Testament era and of no relevance for us today. Then, in December 1900, a group of students at Bethel Bible College in Topeka, Kansas, were set the task of searching the Scriptures to see what they taught about the Baptism in the Holy Spirit. When the founder of the college, a Methodist evangelist called Charles Parham, returned from a three day preaching trip, he found the students very excited with their discoveries.

That evening they met together to pray that they would be baptised in the Spirit and speak in tongues — just like the disciples on the day of Pentecost. One of the students pointed out that in the New Testament the Spirit had often been received through the laying on of hands and suggested that they try this. At first Parham refused, but after praying a little longer, he decided to take God at His Word and step out in faith. He asked Agnes to sit in the centre of the room. As he laid his hands on her head 'a glory fell upon her, a halo seemed to surround her head and face' and she began to speak in tongues. Parham and many of his students were similarly filled with the Spirit.

In the face of much hostility, this New Testament teaching was passed on. Today, millions of Christians throughout the world have believed and experienced the baptism of the Spirit and can speak in tongues. They will never regret the day when they reached out in faith and received the promise from God.

Chapter Nine

ABOUT SPIRITUAL GIFTS

In recent years Christians who have been baptised with the Holy Spirit have generally been known as Charismatics. The term comes from the Greek word *charismata*. *Charis* means 'grace', so *charismata* are 'grace things' or 'free gifts' — gifts that the Lord delights to give us even though we do not deserve them. Paul uses the word in Romans 12 and in 1 Corinthians 12 — the two main New Testament passages about spiritual gifts.

> **There are different kinds of gifts (1 Cor. 12:4).**

> **We have different gifts, according to the grace given us (Rom. 12:6).**

Charismatic Christians have discovered that the gifts of the Spirit were not intended just for New Testament times, but for today as well.

The word, 'charismata' is not used for Spiritual gifts alone, it also refers to salvation itself — the greatest free gift of all (see Rom. 6:23).

Read 2 Timothy 1:6,7.

What sort of spirit (Spirit) did Timothy receive?

Since the 'gift of God' was received through the laying on of hands, it could refer to the Holy Spirit Himself. Certainly He is a wonderful free gift of God's grace that we do not deserve nor could ever earn. Alternatively it may refer to the special gifting that Timothy received when he was appointed as Paul's companion (see 1 Tim. 4:14). Either way, when we receive the gift of the Spirit, we also receive the gifts that the Spirit brings with Him.

Read 1 Peter 4:10.

How should we use 'whatever gift we have received'?

Note the two types of gift that Peter mentions.

We shall call these gifts of revelation and gifts of power — for in order to speak words from God, we need the Spirit's revelation, and in order to serve the needs of others we need the Spirit's power. We will be looking at each of these in the next two chapters. But before we do that, we will examine Paul's teaching about spiritual gifts in Romans 12.

Read verses 3–8.

What do we not all have? What do we all have? On what basis are they given? How are we to use them?

Paul wrote similar things to the Corinthians about our being part of Christ's body.

Read Romans 12:12–21.

ONE BODY OF MANY DIFFERENT PARTS

We are all individual parts of the body of Christ, the church, and every member has a different role to play. God gives us all the appropriate gifts and abilities that we need and fits each one of us into our own particular place with our own special function. I love the way Paul describes this in Ephesians 2:10 and in the second half of Philippians 3:12:

> For we are God's workmanship, created in Christ Jesus to do good works, which God prepared in advance for us to do.

> I press on to take hold of that for which Christ Jesus took hold of me.

God wants us to do the works that He has prepared for us in eternity. When we do what God has given us to do, we act with faith. But when we try to do things for which we are not gifted, we cannot do them in faith because God has not given us the grace we need to accomplish them. Then we find ourselves striving in the flesh and failing to achieve the purposes of God.

> Consider the seven gifts that Paul mentions in Romans 12:6–8.

This is just a small sample of the many ways in which we can serve the Lord and each other as members of the body of Christ. Some of these gifts may not seem particularly spiritual. The first certainly needs some special inspiration of the Spirit. But the fifth seems to be more dependant on financial circumstances, the fourth, on personality and the third and sixth on developed abilities.

Don't be too spiritual about these things. People often get confused and uptight about identifying their spiritual gifts and the role that God has for them in the Body. God has created us as we are and wants us to be ourselves. Our natural abilities, our gifts and our achievements are just as much God-given as things like speaking in tongues. God calls us to be what He created us to be and to do what we can do best. One of my favourite texts is Ecclesiastes 9:10.

Consider the first part of this verse.

Life is too short to mess around wasting time. If something needs doing and you think you can do it, don't worry whether it is your gifting or not — just get on with it. If you are not meant to be involved in this particular thing, you will not be very successful at it. But that does not matter. Next time you can let someone else have a go.

All too often we talk about our giftings as strengths and our lack of them as weaknesses. This is unhelpful. By attaching emotional terms particularly to our so-called failures — we only make ourselves feel inadequate and defensive. So get stuck in and do whatever comes to hand. By trial and error you will soon discover what you can and cannot do in faith.

MANIFESTATIONS OR ENDOWMENTS

The classic passage on spiritual gifts is, of course, 1 Corinthians 12.

Read verses 1 to 11.

In verse 1 Paul introduces us to the subject of 'spiritual gifts'. He does not use 'charismata' but a different word that can be literally translated 'spirituals'. 'Spirituals' are things that have to do with the Spirit — what He does and the way He operates.

Paul did not want the Corinthians to be ignorant about the ways in which the Holy Spirit works in the church. He therefore described how the Spirit gives us various gifts (v.4) and different ways of serving (v.5) and how He works in such diverse ways (v.6). Then in verse 7 Paul made a statement which is essential to our proper understanding of these things.

Now to each one the manifestation of the Spirit
is given for the common good.

Paul listed nine ways in which the Holy Spirit manifests
Himself. These manifestations are usually referred to as the gifts
of the Spirit. The list is representative, not exclusive, since such
things as visions and dreams, mentioned in Acts 2:17, are not
included here even though they are clearly the same type of
phenomenon.

To be completely accurate we should call these things manifestations of the Spirit, because they are not strictly gifts. If someone
gives me a gift for my birthday it is mine. I own it and keep it with
my other possessions. It is at my disposal to use whenever and
wherever I choose. But we cannot treat the Spirit's manifestations
like this.

What exactly is a manifestation? It is a means by which the
Holy Spirit manifests or reveals Himself. It is something that
makes evident His presence and power. In many church services
nothing extraordinary happens because nobody expects the Holy
Spirit to manifest Himself in a powerful way. The congregation
assume that He is among them simply because He is omnipresent.
But they do not worry much about it. They just plod on as usual.

This sort of service is totally alien to the New Testament. When
the early Christians met together they had a personal awareness
that the Spirit was with them and saw clear evidence of His work
among them. They would never have imagined it possible to meet
without there being any sense of the Spirit's presence or any
manifestations of His power! If this had happened, they would
have been on their faces seeking the Lord, searching their hearts,
repenting of sin and crying out for the Spirit to move afresh among
them.

How tragic it is to see many of our present day churches meeting
week after week oblivious of these things! Some are even hostile
to the very idea that the Spirit should manifest Himself in their
services.

RECEIVING MANIFESTATIONS

In 1 Corinthians 12 there are three principles which form the basis upon which the Holy Spirit manifests Himself in the church.

SOVEREIGNTY OF THE SPIRIT

Read 1 Corinthians 2:10,11.

What does the Holy Spirit do and know?

Since the Spirit is in touch with God and with the church, He can, at His own discretion, give manifestations according to the need of the moment. So what happens when the church meets together?

The Holy Spirit reveals His presence and power among us by distributing to individuals the various manifestations mentioned in the 1 Corinthians 14 list. He makes a sovereign choice to give a prophecy to this person and a vision to that one, a gift of healing to another and word of knowledge to a fourth. We cannot work to order because we do not possess these things as gifts. The Spirit controls their use and He decides who has them and when.

BENEFIT OF THE BODY

The Spirit does not give someone a manifestation for His own benefit, but for the common good (1 Cor. 12:7).

Read 1 Corinthians 14:12 and consider the gifts in which we should try to excel.

These believers were keen to see the Holy Spirit working in the church and Paul encouraged them to pursue the 'gifts' that edify (1 Cor. 14:4,5,17) and strengthen (1 Cor. 14:3,26) others.

God wants you to be motivated not by personal ambition but by a desire to see the church built up. Is that your aim? Then be available to the Spirit and move out in faith when He prompts you.

EAGER DESIRE

What, according to 1 Corinthians 12:31 and 14:1a, should we eagerly desire?

The manifestations of the Spirit will not be given to the satisfied, the indifferent and the unbelieving. They will come to those who covet and value them, to those who long to see the church strengthened, the purposes of God fulfilled and the name of Jesus glorified.

> Read Matthew 7:11 and James 4:2,3.

> To whom does God give good gifts? Why don't we receive good gifts from God?

If you put aside your own desires and seek the blessing of the church as a whole, then God will be happy to manifest Himself through you. So if you have received the baptism of the Spirit, don't sit back as if you have arrived. You have not. Be diligent. Seek God earnestly. Ask Him to give you His 'gifts'. Put yourself at His disposal. Be eagerly available at any time — especially when you join others to worship.

THE MANIFESTATIONS OF THE SPIRIT

Here is a list of the various manifestations of the Spirit that we find mentioned in the New Testament. It has been taken largely from 1 Corinthians 12:8–10.

Word of wisdom
Word of knowledge
Faith
Visions
Dreams
Working miracles
Healing

Discerning of spirits
Interpretation of tongues
Interpretation of dreams and visions
Prophecy
Tongues
Deliverance

Some of these involve a revelation from the Spirit that is then spoken out, while others involve a supernatural empowering.

Have a look at the list and consider those you think could be called 'gifts of revelation'. We shall be describing them in the next chapter.

Chapter Ten

GIFTS OF REVELATION

PROPHECY

This is the most frequently mentioned of the spiritual gifts. Much could be written about it, but here we will limit ourselves to such manifestations of prophecy that any member of the body may receive and which we are all encouraged to eagerly desire. Paul wrote about prophecy in 1 Corinthians 14:1–5 and 26–33.

> Read these passages through again and notice particularly what is said about prophecy.

When someone prophesies, he is essentially acting as a divine spokesman. He is speaking words that are not his own but which are given to him by the Lord. For this reason, we must not treat prophesying casually. On the other hand, we must not be so afraid of misinterpreting the Lord that we avoid it altogether.

> Read 1 Corinthians 13:9 and note what we must remember about prophecy.

No prophecy will ever be 100 per cent from the Lord. It will always be limited by our sensitivity to Him, our ability to express ourselves, our theological views and our preconceived ideas. So when we prophesy, we will be genuinely speaking from God, but will be bringing in a lot of ourselves too.

According to 1 Thessalonians 5:20, what must we not do with prophecy? According to 1 Corinthians 14:29, what must we do with it?

God does not want us to think, 'Oh, that's just Fred!', neither does He want us to assume that every word is Spirit-inspired. In spite of our limitations, God does speak His word through those of us who are eager to be used in this way.

Read 1 Corinthians 14:1,39.

With reference to prophecy, what does Paul want us to do?

EAGERLY DESIRE IT

Ask God for a prophecy. It may help to ask someone to pray for you to prophesy. I received my first prophecy when I was sitting in a small group. Someone laid hands on me and prayed for the Lord to speak through me. For a few moments I had no thoughts at all but then a simple phrase came clearly into my mind.

SPEAK OUT IN FAITH

I took a step of faith and began to speak out the phrase that had come to mind. As I spoke, more words came and then they flowed and flowed — just like the first time I spoke in tongues. I was amazed as I listened to myself because my words were so relevant to my situation at the time. My first prophecy was a word of encouragement just for me.

SPEAK NORMALLY

It is not more spiritual to speak in old fashioned English or to punctuate your prophecy with liberal doses of 'thus says the Lord'. Don't do strange things — huff and puff or shake your head. Don't speak in an odd way and get louder as you continue. These things do not enhance your message so speak naturally.

BE SENSITIVE

Sometimes we may get physical sensations like a thumping heartbeat, butterflies in the stomach, sweaty hands or trembling in our arms and legs. This could be the Spirit prompting us to speak out in faith, or just plain nerves. As we become more sensitive to the Spirit, these feelings often decrease and may even disappear altogether.

We need to work out whether the prophecy is intended for others or is a personal word to us. We must also consider whether the content is appropriate at that particular time. The fact that we receive it now does not mean we have to say it now. We may have to hold the prophecy and let it settle in our hearts until a more suitable moment arrives.

DON'T ABUSE IT

In 1 Corinthians 14:3 Paul specifies three purposes of prophecy. What are they?

Prophecy is not for rebuking the church, nor is it for off-loading our frustrations or current gripes. If we prophesy without love, we are nothing (1 Cor. 13:2). We must be prepared to have our contribution weighed (1 Cor. 14:29) and be willing to receive correction as is necessary.

VISIONS

Compare Acts 2:17,18 with Numbers 12:6. With what are visions and dreams associated?

God wants to give His people visions and dreams. A vision is most commonly a picture in the imagination, a fleeting image given by the Spirit. This may on occasions be a vivid picture which we 'see' in full technicolour. People have had visions when their eyes have been open too. They have seen angels, evil spirits and invisible words written on foreheads.

When we receive a vision we can usually understand and explain its meaning, but sometimes we may be completely stumped. Then we must allow someone else to make sense of it for us. This manifestation of the Spirit is very similar to tongues and interpretation.

Read Daniel 5:5, 26–28.

DREAMS

The Bible makes no great distinction between dreams and visions.

According to Job 33:15, what is a dream?

The main difference between a vision and a dream is that you are awake when you have a vision but asleep when you have a dream. When Jacob set out for Egypt he had a vision, not a dream — because, he was awake when God spoke to him (Gen. 46:2). We are unlikely to have dreams during meetings because we do not sleep at those times!

Visions tend to edify others while dreams tend to edify you. Dreams may even be life-changing.

What did Joseph do in response to a dream? (Matt. 1:24)

Early in our marriage my wife was troubled with a fear that I might die. One night she had an incredible dream in which she saw the Lord on His throne and Jesus' second coming. It was so vivid that it not only delivered her from her fears but gave her a whole new perspective on eternity as well.

Other examples of dreams in the Bible can be found in Genesis 20:3–7, 1 Kings 3:5–15, Daniel 2, and Matthew 2:19–20.

Dreams, like visions, may need interpretation. Clearly we must be careful not to become preoccupied with the meaning of dreams — as men in the past have done. And we must not be sucked into the modern psychological interpretation of dreams either. The Bible distinguishes between ordinary dreams and specific messages from God.

> According to Ecclesiastes 5:3, when do dreams come?

We must beware of looking for hidden meanings in every dream that we remember. If it comes from God, we will be aware that it has been given to us and understand its purpose.

WORDS OF KNOWLEDGE

Sometimes the Holy Spirit gives us information that we did not know and, humanly speaking, could never have known. It is a very useful tool in counselling. The Spirit impresses thoughts on the counsellor's mind and enables him to get to the root of a person's problems and bring resolution to them. The knowledge usually comes through words, but it may also come in pictorial or other forms.

While counselling a young woman with chronic asthma I saw a fleeting image of a white statue of an angel in the middle of a lot of nettles. As I described this to her she suddenly burst into tears. The Lord had given me a glimpse of her mother's grave. This exposed the root of her problems and enabled us to minister healing to her.

Words of knowledge may also be given in public meetings. The Spirit reveals information or brings images to mind. He may even give us a physical sensation, such as a feeling of sudden pain in a certain part of our body, indicating that someone present has a complaint in that region. The Lord may even show us the person in the congregation to whom such a word of knowledge applies. Naturally, before we speak out, we do need to check that the pain is not ours!

Sometimes we may receive a word that would expose or embarrass someone. Then we must be extremely sensitive and caring. When sharing such things publicly it would be better not to demand an immediate response but to invite whoever it might be to see you privately after the meeting.

Jesus used a word of knowledge when He spoke to the woman of Samaria.

> What two things did He tell her? (John 4:18) What did she tell the Samaritans? (v.29)

Such revelations tell us that God knows about our situation and that He wants to encourage, help, release or heal us. When such a word is shared publicly and when someone responds, the faith of the whole company is stirred.

WORDS OF WISDOM

Closely related to a word of knowledge is 'a word of wisdom'. This is not the wisdom that we acquire through experience, but a revelation of the Spirit who tells us what to do or say in a specific, often difficult, situation. This manifestation is often needed in leaders' decision-making meetings, in confrontation situations or in counselling.

Jesus used the word of wisdom when the Pharisees tried to trap Him.

> Read Matthew 22:17–22.
>
> What were Jesus' words of wisdom? How did the Pharisees react?
>
> Read Luke 12:12.
>
> When will we need wisdom from the Spirit? Other possible examples can be found in Acts 6:1–7; 15:28–29 and 27:10,31.

INTERPRETATION OF TONGUES

Some people who work as interpreters are fluent in several languages. Their skills are in great demand. The manifestation of interpretation of tongues is quite different from a learned ability to interpret. When someone speaks aloud in tongues, the Spirit will inspire someone else (and sometimes the original speaker) to translate, interpret or explain it to the people in the meeting.

When God wants you to interpret tongues, you will not understand what the speaker is saying but words will start coming into your mind and you will have the distinct impression that the Spirit is revealing their meaning to you. Since the language will be foreign to everyone, no one will ever be completely sure that your interpretation is accurate. You must take a step of faith, speak out and let others weigh your words.

Someone who speaks in tongues speaks not to men but to God. He utters mysteries with his spirit which no one can understand (1 Cor. 14:2).

What response is desirable from the listener? (v. 16)

An utterance in tongues will generally be a prayer or an exclamation of praise addressed to God rather than a message from God to us. We would therefore expect an interpretation of tongues to reflect this Godward movement. Sometimes, however, we hear interpretations given like prophecies (e.g. 'My people, I alone am to be your heart's desire. Let your soul long after me as a deer pants after the water brooks').

If the original tongue was spoken to God then the interpreter has turned round his interpretation. Let us turn it back again: 'O Lord, You alone are my heart's desire. My soul longs after You as a deer pants after the water brooks.' See how this lifts the spirit. Instead of feeling that God is demanding something of us, we find ourselves identifying with the one speaking in tongues, caught up with his praise and able to say 'Amen!'

Some interpretations are turned round like this because of

preconceived notions that a 'message in tongues' requires an interpretation that sounds like a prophecy. But the phrase 'message in tongues' is not biblical since Paul plainly says that when we speak in tongues we speak not to men but to God (1 Cor. 14: 2). When we interpret, we must address our thoughts to the Lord. Then we will more faithfully reflect the content of the original prayer. This is what makes tongues and interpretation distinct from prophecy.

When we are waiting for an interpretation of tongues, the silence can make us all rather tense. Paul encourages us not to be passive at this point.

> anyone who speaks in a tongue should pray that he may interpret what he says (1 Cor. 14:13).

God wants us to overcome our uncertainties and fears and reach out in faith. As we begin to interpret, we will have the joy of lifting the spirits of those around us and of encouraging them in their own prayer and praise.

DISCERNING OF SPIRITS

This gift of revelation enables us to evaluate, identify or distinguish between spirits and is particularly necessary when dealing with powers of darkness. It exposes the demonic so that we can effectively deal with it and bring deliverance to the victim. The Holy Spirit may impress on us the identity of a demon, or give us a visual image, such as a large dark object on a person's shoulders. He enables us to recognise when a demon is speaking through a demonised person and when that person is speaking himself.

Jesus helped the demonised, so too did Paul. We will doubtless be very eager for this manifestation when we encounter the demonised too. (See Matt. 9:32; 17:18, Mark 1:25; 5:8, Acts 16:18.)

In other situations, the Spirit may also give this ability to show us the spiritual source of a person's words, motives or deeds. In meetings He may identify contributions or events that are demonically inspired (e.g. false prophecy), or ones that are purely fleshly and not from the Holy Spirit.

Read I John 4:1 and note:

What John encourages us not to believe.

What he encourages us to do.

Why?

Chapter Eleven

GIFTS OF POWER

SPEAKING IN TONGUES

It is impossible to speak in a foreign language which we have never learnt. So when we pray in tongues, we are using a gift of power. If the Spirit can work this miracle in us again and again, then He can certainly give us other manifestations. Speaking in tongues quickens our faith for other works of the Spirit and is often the first step to receiving prophecy, and other gifts of revelation.

When we have received the gift of tongues we can use it privately whenever we wish. We do not need any special prompting from the Spirit nor do we need any interpretation. But when the Spirit provokes someone to speak out loud in tongues during a meeting, then we naturally need an interpretation so that everyone can understand.

In 1 Corinthians 14 Paul discusses tongues in quite some detail.

For whom are tongues a sign? (v.22)

Since the uncontrolled use of speaking in tongues might make such people think we are mad, Paul puts certain restrictions on the use of tongues when the whole church comes together.

Read 1 Corinthians 14:26–28.

How many people should speak in tongues? How should they speak? Who must also be present?

Paul does not discourage speaking in tongues when we come together. In fact, he expects there to be such manifestations. If we handle the gift wisely and follow his practical guidelines, unbelievers among us will understand what we are saying and be amazed. Then, when prophecies come that lay bare the secrets of their hearts, they will acknowledge that God is among us.

GIFTS OF HEALING

Paul did not say that God gives us a gift of healing. He used two plural words, 'gifts of healing' (1 Cor. 12:9). Some commentators have suggested that every individual healing is a special gift of the Spirit, and that we are totally dependent upon Him on every occasion. The Spirit delights to give gifts of grace to those who are sick. To the lame He gives the gift of being able to walk, to the one with cataracts, the gift of clear sight, to the asthma sufferer, the gift of being able to breathe freely. These are His healing gifts to those who are sick.

The Spirit is the Healer. We are like His postmen. Now and again He gives us a healing gift for someone and we simply deliver it. Since a postman is neither the sender or the owner of his letters and parcels, so no person is the healer or can be said to possess the gift of healing. We are always totally dependant on the Lord — as Jesus was. Luke writes:

> the power of the Lord was present for him to heal the sick (Luke 5:17).

Healing comes in God's time. Peter and John would often have seen the crippled beggar who sat at the temple gate. But one day, when he asked them for money, the Spirit of God gave them a gift of healing for him instead. They acted upon the prompting of the moment and the man was instantly healed.

Consider what the following statement should say and check your answer in Acts 3:16.

It is our gift and the faith that comes through us that has given this complete healing to him.

DO ALL HAVE GIFTS OF HEALINGS?

No, we do not. God clearly calls some people to specialise in gifts of healing. A number will have some success, while others will seem not to be particularly gifted in this area. The Christians who do not see much result from their praying for the sick must not, however, assume that the Spirit will use only those who frequently see the sick healed. The Spirit will often use someone who is keen, available and willing to step out in faith.

> Read Matthew 10:1.
>
> To whom was Jesus speaking? What authority did they have?
>
> Read Luke 10:1,9.
>
> To whom was Jesus speaking? What did He command them to do?
>
> Read Mark 16:17,18.
>
> To whom is Jesus speaking? With reference to healing, what are they encouraged to do?

HOW TO BE INVOLVED IN HEALING

Someone has calculated that about one fifth of all the verses in the four Gospels relate to healing, deliverance or raising the dead. The phrase, 'gifts of healings' implies that there are many different kinds of healing. Jesus did not come to save us from spiritual disability alone. He wanted to see us physically and mentally whole, to give us life to the full. But how do we do His works?

In the Gospels we find Jesus using many different methods to heal. Sometimes He touched or laid hands on the sick. Sometimes

He spoke to the sickness. Sometimes He took someone by the hand and raised him up. Sometimes He told people to go and show themselves to the priest. Sometimes He did some very odd things like making a mud pack for a blind man's eyes and sticking His fingers in the ears of a deaf man. We have to conclude that there is no hard and fast, 'You do it this way' rule. We are utterly dependent on the Holy Spirit.

When the Spirit gives us a gift of healing for someone we must try to discern how He wants us to pray. Should we lay hands on the sufferer? Should we pray in tongues? Should we address God or rebuke the sickness? Does the Spirit want us to anoint with oil? Clearly, we must be alert to the Spirit's prompting and then take a step of faith. If we are unwilling to reach out, we are not likely to see anyone healed.

One night my wife had a severe stomach ache and could not get to sleep. While she was crying out with the pain I was wondering what on earth I could do. Then, suddenly I began to feel very angry. I rebuked the pain and prayed over her strongly in tongues. She was instantly quiet and soon fell asleep in my arms.

God wants us to reach out to people who are suffering. We do not possess the power to heal them, but He does. All He needs is our availability and willingness to be used. The simplest question, 'May I pray for you?' is often all we need to ask. Even unbelievers respond positively to it. They need to see that we, like Jesus, are not concerned simply for their salvation but for their wholeness. God will act — but we must step out in faith and trust Him.

Read Hebrews 11:6.

What is it impossible to do?

WORKING MIRACLES

Miracles and healings are very closely allied. In the Gospels the supernatural actions of Jesus, including all kinds of healings, are called miracles (see Mark 6:5). Jesus' miracles also included turning water into wine, calming a storm, walking on water and multiplying food to feed the crowds. Some miracles, like the amazing catch of fish and the finding of a coin in a fish's mouth, are like divinely-managed coincidences. Sometimes a miracle will defy natural laws. At other times God's involvement will be clear from what happens in a particular situation.

Paul is probably referring to these types of activities (excluding healing) when he speaks of 'miraculous powers' (literally, 'workings of powers') in 1 Corinthians 12:10. We also read of miracles in Romans 15:19, Galatians 3:5 and in Hebrews 2:4. We read that:

> God has appointed ... workers of miracles (1 Cor. 12:28).

Read Hebrews 2:3,4 and note the purpose of signs, wonders and miracles.

When we were first married, Sandy and I were given an old twin tub washing machine. One day while Sandy was using the spin dryer it began to make a strange noise and emit acrid smoke. We unplugged it but it was no use my trying to mend it because I am not mechanically minded. Then Sandy suggested that I prayed for it. I walked out of the room struggling with the absurd idea — which was more a challenge from the Lord than a request from my wife. I sheepishly returned, laid my hands on the poor old machine and prayed for it. Then I took a step of faith, plugged it in and switched it on. It worked perfectly — no smoke, no smell, no funny noise. We never had any trouble with it again, and it was still working well when we eventually bought a new automatic machine.

FAITH

Hearing with faith — that is the crucial factor in receiving salvation, the Spirit and His gifts (Gal. 3:2,5. Rom. 10:14,17).

Consider the definition of faith in Hebrews 11:1.

We read that God gives 'to another faith by the same Spirit' (1 Cor. 12:9). All faith comes by the Spirit, but here Paul is referring to a special manifestation of faith which is given for a specific occasion. It is a sudden surge of confidence and certainty and often comes in some crisis situation. We suddenly know that what we do not see will come to pass.

What does this faith do? (Matt. 17:20)

Consider three biblical examples of faith (e.g. Elijah calling down fire from heaven).

DELIVERANCE

One in four of all the people that Jesus healed was afflicted by evil spirits.

When He sent His disciples out what did He give them? (Luke 9:1) Why were they so excited when they returned? (Luke 10:17) What is the first sign that will accompany those who believe? (Mark 16:17)

Sometimes a demon may suddenly manifest itself. This happened when Jesus was in the synagogue (Mark 1:23–25). Sometimes the Holy Spirit will enable us to discern the spirits and we will then know that we have the authority to tell them to go.

Read Acts 16:18.

What did Paul say to release the slave girl from the spirit of divination?

By faith, we must do the same. The demons must submit to Jesus. Like Paul, we have the authority and power of the Spirit to speak firmly to them and command them to go.

Read Luke 11:24-26.

How can a person who has been delivered and saved guard against further intrusion from Satan?

When we deal with this subject we must avoid extremes, Some err because they see demons under every chair. They try to cast out spirits when the real problem is to do with the flesh. On the other hand, some categorically declare that Christians cannot possibly be troubled by demons. They leave believers struggling with demonic problems that could have been dealt with by a word of authority.

GIFTS OF POWER IN THE TWENTIETH CENTURY

In today's rational and scientific climate, modern man cannot entertain the idea that demons actually exist, let alone that they affect others, Society suggests that someone is not demonised, he is simply mentally ill or suffering from a perplexing affliction like epilepsy.

The Bible gives another option. It clearly presents to us the realities of a positive and a negative spirit realm. We see the Father, Son, Holy Spirit and angels, But we also see Satan, demons, principalities and powers of darkness. The Christian knows that these spiritual beings are real and that they interact with people on earth,

People in the New Testament expected to see the miraculous, We often encounter it in the so-called Third World. Healings, deliverance and miracles seem to be taking place with great frequency and there are even reports that people are being raised from the dead. Sadly, we in the West seem largely sceptical of these things and our expectation level is low.

> Why couldn't Jesus do many miracles in His home town? (Matt. 13:58)

The problem for the believer tends not to centre round a sense of personal weakness: 'I find it so hard to believe. I just don't seem to be able to find the faith.' It is actually more to do with a positive refusal to accept the truth: 'Miracles died out with the apostles. I can't believe that they happen today. I don't believe you and I'm not going to change my mind.'

Jesus was grieved at the hardness of men's hearts and could do no mighty miracles when He was in the company of people who had no faith in Him. He must react the same way today. Even those of us who believe that the Spirit still gives supernatural manifestations are often infected with disbelief and cynicism.

> According to Mark 16:14, how did Jesus handle the stubborn unbelief of His disciples when they refused to believe those who had seen Him after He had risen from the dead?

Clearly, Jesus wanted the disciples to repent of their unbelief. He longs to see us repent of our unbelief too. Don't allow our worldly wise, scientific society to dictate to you what you must believe. You serve a God for whom nothing is impossible. Rise up from unbelief and into faith. Be available. Be willing. Move forward.

Chapter Twelve

GIFTS TO THE CHURCH

God gives some giftings on a more permanent basis. We have already looked at the list of gifts in Romans 12. There is another list in 1 Corinthians 12.

Read verses 27–31 and consider the nine giftings mentioned there.

What important statement does he make about you? (v.27)

Read Ephesians 4:7–13.

In recent years the Holy Spirit has drawn a great deal of attention to this key passage and its relevance for the restoration of the church.

After Jesus had ascended, He sat down at His Father's right hand, poured out His Spirit and gave gifts to men.

Note the gifts that are listed here.

As people have been baptised in the Holy Spirit and have been gifted in various ways, some have discovered that they have been given a specific role in the church.

FIRST APOSTLES, SECOND PROPHETS

Traditionally it has been taught that apostles and prophets existed only in New Testament days. The Bible does not accommodate such a belief. If we say that we need pastors, evangelists and teachers, for what reason do we omit apostles and prophets? The Corinthian and Ephesian passages tell us that apostles and prophets are vitally important for the church in every age.

The comment, 'First of all apostles' does not refer to time. It does not mean 'in the days of the early church but not later on'. Rather, it indicates the priority or importance of these particular ministries. If they were so important to the New Testament church, we dare not try to operate without them today.

> Read Ephesians 2:20 and note what the church is built on.

Some commentators say that this refers to the founding of the early church and conclude that after the original apostles died, their ministry became obsolete. These commentators also seek to back up their argument from Revelation 21:14.

> What is written on the twelve foundations of the wall of the city of God?

The church was initially founded and governed by the twelve apostles, including Matthias who replaced Judas (Acts 1:26, 2:14, 6:2). But very soon other apostles were raised up.

> Note those mentioned in the following verses: Acts 14:14; Rom. 16:7; Gal. 1:19.

Also included among the apostles, although not mentioned as such, were probably Mark, Timothy and Titus. Evidently there were not just twelve apostles but many more. By the grace of God, they established churches in town after town throughout the Roman Empire and beyond.

What applies to the worldwide church also applies to the local church. In Ephesians 2:20–22, Paul is saying that the apostles lay the foundations on which the whole (global) church is being built. Then he turns his attention to the Ephesian church and includes them in God's plan. During the three years that he had spent with them he had laid the foundation of the local church in Ephesus.

Earlier, he had done exactly the same thing in Corinth.

> How did he lay a foundation as an expert builder? (1 Cor. 3:10)

Paul knew that he had been gifted by God as an apostle. He had the expertise to lay proper doctrinal and structural foundations and had authority to appoint elders. Wherever he went he established churches — with the help of gifted companions like Silas, the prophet, and Timothy (Acts 15:32; 18:5).

So in Bible days, each living church was individually built on an apostolic and prophetic foundation. Indeed, a living church cannot be properly established without it. Today it is just as essential for each local church to be built on the foundation of apostles and prophets. That is why the ascended Christ is restoring the baptism and gifts of the Spirit and the gifts of apostles and prophets to His Church.

Apostles and prophets have not been entirely absent in previous generations. Men such as John Wesley and Charles Haddon Spurgeon were undoubtedly gifted apostles even if, in their day, they were not acknowledged as such. Jesus wants to restore all the New Testament giftings, that through them He might build His church in this generation according to His Father's specifications. The goal of these Ephesians 4 ministries is this:

> to prepare God's people for works of service, so that the body of Christ may be built up until we all reach unity in the faith ... and become mature, attaining to the whole measure of the fulness of Christ (Eph. 4:12,13).

The fragmented church will become the radiant bride of Christ (Eph. 5:27) only as we recognise the ministries of apostles and prophets and allow them to function in the way that God originally intended.

EQUIPPING THE SAINTS

In the Authorised Version Ephesians 4:12 reads, 'for the perfecting of the saints, for the work of the ministry, for the edifying of the body of Christ'. This gives the impression that all the work falls on the shoulders of the full-time minister. He has to perfect his flock, do all the work of ministry and edify the body of Christ as well! But this is not at all what Paul meant. The task of leaders is not to put on services for the saints (believers), but rather to equip the saints for service. As the Christians then give themselves to the work of serving the body, so the whole body is strengthened and built up.

If the church is to be fully equipped we must have not only pastors, teachers and evangelists, but apostles and prophets as well. All these ministries also need each other because they work as a team, each complementing and harmonising with the others. While apostles and prophets may head the team in their gifting, the others must be brought in if we are to see the local church grow in unity and maturity.

> Note who went to, Samaria (Acts 8:14), Antioch (Acts 11:25,26), Phrygia and Galatia (Acts 16:6).

> Who were the leaders in the church in Antioch? (Acts 13:1)

In the early church there was always a plurality of elders (see Acts 14:23; 20:17; 1 Tim. 5:17, Titus 1:5, James 5:14 and 1 Pet. 5:1). Today we have drifted away from the biblical norm and instead load one man with the responsibility of leading the church. While the elders share their giftings, the full-time leader struggles alone with limited abilities and is expected to do everything.

If a full-time minister is an evangelist, he will equip his people for outreach. They may see many new converts but will not know how to encourage them and build them up. The pastor is not gifted in this area. But if a church is led by an apostle, a prophet, an evangelist and various pastors and teachers, then they will interact together and the whole church will be edified.

A small local church will not have all these ministries. But it would benefit greatly from at least two full-time leaders, along with regular input from those who have the gifts that it lacks. As the saints are equipped and give themselves to the work of ministry, so the church will grow. God will then raise up more apostles and prophets, evangelists, pastors and teachers until the whole church reaches unity in the faith and attains the whole measure of the fullness of Christ.

LAYING A FOUNDATION

Read Romans 15:20.

Why did Paul only want to preach the gospel where Christ was not already known?

In those days Paul never needed to re-lay the foundation of a local church. But today God, the architect, is inspecting the church's foundations and He wants them re-established according to His original plan. If our church is not built on apostolic and prophetic foundations, it must be built on something else. What? What does God see as He inspects the foundations? He sees churches that are built on:

INSTITUTIONALISM

In this country we have an institutional state church. If one of its ministers wants to bring in biblical practices and make changes, he has to make a formal application to do so. He may say 'The Bible says ..., so I'd like to ...' but he will probably be told, 'That's not the point. You can't do that. We don't allow it in this institution.' Although great progress has been made by some local state churches, they have always to battle with problems related to institutional factors.

TRADITION

Take another church where the pastor also wants to make certain changes in order to be more biblical. 'It's in the Bible,' he says. 'So what?' comes the reply. 'We've never done it that way before.' 'But,' he protests, 'the Bible is our final authority in all matters of doctrine and practice.' 'Yes,' they say, 'But we don't do it that way here. We never have done it like that and we don't mean to change. We like things the way they are.' Tradition prevails.

SENTIMENT

Another church has for years had a certain organisation which is now ailing and is no longer relevant today. But the leaders cannot bring themselves to close it down. 'Old Sid's been doing that for thirty-five years. He'll be ever so upset if we stop it. And his wife plays the piano. We don't want to distress her or we'll have to find another pianist.'

DEMOCRACY

In another church the leaders want to give opportunity for personal ministry at the end of each service. But first the idea has to go before the church for a vote. Some of the members who oppose the present day move of the Spirit, stand against the motion. Then some of the more unspiritual people begin abusing the leadership and stirring up those who feel threatened and apprehensive. The proposal fails to get the necessary majority and thus the church becomes more deeply divided than it has ever been before.

> Read Luke 11:47–49 and note what happens to prophets and apostles.

Read Jeremiah 1:10 and note why prophets are so unpopular.

When many Christians attend conferences they say, 'This is superb teaching. It's such an exciting vision. But we can't do it in our church.' Often they cannot do it because their church is built on a wrong foundation. Such churches today are in urgent need of a prophet to reveal what is not of God. When he comes, the people can choose to stone him or hear what he is saying and respond.

BUILDING ON THE FOUNDATION

Churches which have a prophetic vision welcome the prophet and are ready to listen, repent and make necessary changes — just as God's people did in Haggai's day (Hag. v.1). The prophet keeps the church sharp and on its toes. The evangelist helps it to take the gospel into the locality. The pastor maintains a caring community and the teacher stimulates a healthy appetite for the truth of God's Word.

We do not all respond to these ministries equally. Some will be keen to follow the evangelist and will be involved in all sorts of evangelistic activities. Some will prefer to care for those who have difficulties. Some will love teaching new converts or bringing prophecies in different situations. Our interest in these things does not make us evangelists, pastors, teachers or prophets, but it does show us where our measure of gifting is likely to be.

We still have not looked at all God's gifts to His church. In Romans 12:7–8 and 1 Corinthians 12:28, Paul mentions others whom God has given special gifts to serve the church. They are:

ADMINISTRATION AND LEADERSHIP

These two terms are quite similar. The first of them is derived from sailing ships. A steersman, captain, or pilot has the ability to give direction, to take charge, to set course and to take the lead. The second literally means 'standing in front' and means giving direction, leading, managing, caring for and helping.

How should leaders govern? (Rom. 12:8)

Since elders have oversight of the church, they will obviously require this gift. But others will need it too — when they take charge of meetings, lead worship, direct a group of people or supervise an activity. These leadership, management and administrative skills are vital for a church to run smoothly. The gift involves the ability to organise and motivate people lovingly.

Read John 13:12–17, 1 Timothy 4:12 and 1 Peter 5:3 and note how this leadership gift should be exercised.

ENCOURAGEMENT

Encouragement involves coming alongside others to help and fortify them.

Read Acts 9:27, 11:22–25 and 15:35.

How did Barnabas encourage others?

GIVING

Some are given special faith and grace to contribute to the needs of others. The capacity to give financial and material help may come because God gives success in business or a skill in making money. Or it may happen as a result of God's promise to bless those who give so that they can give more (Luke 6:38).

How should givers give? (Rom. 12:8)

HELPING AND SERVING

Helping is a term used to describe what happens when an

individual sees someone struggling with something, goes over and 'takes hold of the other end'. Helpers share burdens and are always there to give their support when you need them.

Servants, similarly, are always there when a job needs doing. The servant or steward of a household originally saw to all the practical affairs of running the home. While we must all have a servant heart, some are particularly gifted in serving and getting things done.

According to some commentators, the distinction between these two gifts is that the ministry of helpers is more people oriented while that of servants is more task oriented.

SHOWING MERCY

Paul wrote that the person showing mercy, kindness or compassion should do it with cheerfulness (a Greek word from which we get 'hilarity'). People who often give themselves to caring for the sick, the troubled, the bereaved, the weak and the needy can find their spirits becoming affected by the sadness of others and the enormity of the needs. This will make them ineffective. Along with their practical support, they need to bring a cheery disposition that will bring a ray of light, comfort and hope to the suffering.

OTHER GIFTS

Sometimes it is difficult to determine whether we are exercising a general responsibility or a specific gifting. It probably depends on the extent to which we are involved. Sometimes such things as hospitality and intercession are described as gifts.

> Read Romans 12:13 and 1 Peter 4:9 and note what we are all exhorted to do.

Paul said that we should also:

> pray in the Spirit on all occasions with all kinds of prayers and requests. With this in mind, be

alert and always keep on praying for all the saints (Eph. 6:18).

According to 1 Timothy 2:1, what should be made for everyone?

Clearly, we must not excuse ourselves from these things by saying, 'They're not my gift.' We are all meant to be involved in them. Undoubtedly, some in the church will be noted for their hospitality and others for their prayer life. While these are not specified as gifts in the New Testament, some people do seem able to exercise them with a degree of faith that surpasses most of us. So maybe we can consider them as gifts.

Creative abilities such as music, drama, dance, graphic arts needlework, painting and writing, are often considered to be spiritual gifts. Craftsmanship and musical skills are mentioned in the Old Testament (see Exod. 35:30–35 and 1 Chron. 15:16–22). Dorcas used her needlework ability to help the poor (Acts 9:36,39). Let us devote to God whatever skills or gifts we have received from Him. Let us be grateful for them, pray for His help as we use them, and serve one another with faith and by the power of the Spirit.

Chapter Thirteen

GO ON BEING FILLED

T hey're drunk!' That is what some of the people in the crowd said when they heard the disciples praising God in tongues on the day of Pentecost. The disciples evidently displayed a happiness and lack of inhibition that suggested that they were intoxicated. Had they been drinking wine — that makes life merry and gladdens the heart of man (Eccl. 10:19, Ps. 104:15)? Was it oil that made their faces shine like that? No, it was the new wine of the Spirit, the fresh anointing oil running down from the Head upon the body of Christ.

The effects of alcohol soon wear off, often leaving a heavy feeling that makes people want more to drink. Excess leads to drunkenness, confusion and loss of control.

> What does Paul say that drunkenness leads to? (Eph. 5:18) What does this word mean? (You may need to look it up.)

The newness of life that we have in Christ is too precious to waste on happiness that will not last. God wants us to be filled with the Spirit.

In Ephesians 5:18 Paul uses a continuous tense that could be translated 'be being filled' or 'go on being filled' with the Spirit.

When we receive the baptism of the Spirit we do not sit back and think that we have arrived, that we are now living in all the fullness of God. We need to have fresh fillings of the life, love, power and joy of the Spirit.

A few weeks after the disciples' experience at Pentecost, Peter and John were brought before the Sanhedrin and told not to speak in the name of Jesus. When they were released, they joined the other believers for a prayer meeting (Acts 4:23–31).

> What did they ask God to give them? How did they want Jesus to demonstrate His power?

The disciples were faced with new challenges and needed a fresh empowering from the Spirit. They did not pray that God would baptise them with His Spirit. He had already done that. They needed boldness, but they received it by being filled with the Spirit.

Like the disciples, we too face new challenges and need God's power to cope with them. Since boldness, faith, love, joy and peace have their source in the Spirit, it is not surprising that God's answer to our cry, 'Please give me more courage ...' may come in the form of a fresh filling with His Spirit.

A FRESH ANOINTING?

The experience of Pentecost was not repeated in Acts 4:31. Many of the disciples present at this later prayer meeting had received the Spirit on the day of Pentecost. Others had doubtless already received the Spirit before this later event. There is only one baptism in the Spirit. The apostle John wrote:

> the anointing you received from him remains in you (1 John 2:27).

The baptism of the Spirit is a once for all experience that can never be repeated. John the Baptist's testimony about Jesus was this:

> The man on whom you see the Spirit come down and remain is he who will baptise with the Holy Spirit (John 1:33).

Read 1 Corinthians 6:19.

What is your body? Where is the Holy Spirit? From whom did you receive Him?

It has become popular to pray for 'a fresh anointing' but from the examples above we see that the anointing never left Jesus and never leaves us. We so often want to feel that He is there rather than believe by faith that He is committed never to abandon us.

So when Satan whispers in your ear, 'You need a fresh anointing before you can do that,' don't listen to him. Remind yourself that you already have the anointing and pray for the help you need to do the task that God has set before you. He may choose to give you a fresh filling of the Holy Spirit, as He did with Peter and the other apostles.

DON'T GRIEVE HIM

The Spirit is a person, so He can be grieved (Eph. 4:30). He is also Holy. Unbelievers belong to the evil one and display his unholiness by the way they live. Believers belong to God and must display the Spirit's holiness by they way they live. When we behave in a manner which is inconsistent with our new nature, Satan rejoices but the Spirit is grieved. If we are living in harmony with the Spirit, the slightest sin we commit will rob us of our joy and we will feel the Spirit's sadness.

Jesus came to baptise us with the Spirit and with fire. The Spirit is jealous over us. He blazes against anything that hinders His work in our lives. When we sin through unbelief, disobedience, hardness of heart and the like, we grieve Him and quench His fire within us. He remains, but we can lose His dynamic energy.

Read 1 Thessalonians 5:19 and note what we are exhorted not to do.

Read 1 Corinthians 6:20 and note what we are exhorted to do.

God wants us to keep short accounts, to confess our sins and repent of them.

Read Psalm 32:3,4 and note how a guilty person feels.

Read Psalm 32:1,2 note how a forgiven person feels.

Are you quenching the Spirit in any area of your life? Take this opportunity to question the Spirit about this. Don't harden your heart against Him. Respond to His voice. Know the joy of full restoration with the Lord.

STIR UP THE GIFT

'Fan into flame the gift of God, which is in you,' said Paul to Timothy (2 Tim. 1:6). How do we do this? By faith. We confess the truth, pray, speak in tongues, worship and reach out believing that God will use us to bless others.

PRAYER

When we get alone with God we take a step of faith. The Bible tells us that we cannot pray as we ought to, but that the Spirit within will help us. As we pray in the Spirit, both in tongues and in our own language, the fire within us is fanned into flame. The more we pray, the hotter it becomes. On sleepy mornings, it is good to remember that Jesus told His weary disciples that the Spirit is always willing to pray, even when the flesh is weak!

WORSHIP

One of my favourite verses is Philippians 3:3. In it Paul describes some of the characteristics of an authentic Christian.

What is the first of these?

He is referring to worship in its broadest sense. Since the Spirit brings joy, peace, thanksgiving and praise, we will stir up the Spirit within us when we take a step of faith and engage in these things. So much the better if we 'live joyful' too. The Spirit loves to see not just two hour praise times, but lives which are characterised by enthusiasm and joy.

Read Ephesians 5:20.

How often we should give thanks to God? For what we should thank Him?

SERVICE

It is said that the devil finds work for idle hands to do. God wants us to occupy ourselves with His work.

Read Romans 12:11,

What must we never lack or keep or do?

Other translations speak of our being 'fervent in spirit' (NASB) and 'aglow with the Spirit' (RSV). Paul uses the image of water bubbling over a fire. The same phrase is used of Apollos who 'spoke with great fervour' or, as the margin says, 'with fervour in the Spirit' (Acts 18:25).

By faith, let us give ourselves to love and good deeds. Let us care for one another, testify about Jesus, speak His word and use the gifts He has given us. By doing these things, we will continue to keep the Spirit's fire burning and our lives bubbling with zeal for the establishment of Kingdom values on earth.

THE WORK OF THE SPIRIT

The greatest work of the Spirit lies not in the giving of gifts but in the transforming of lives that are having increasing revelation of Jesus, bringing individuals from spiritual darkness into Christ's marvellous light.

There is another very specific work of the Spirit that we need to consider briefly.

> Read Romans 15:16; 2 Thessalonians 2:13 and 1 Peter 1:2.
>
> In one word, what is this work?

The Spirit is Holy and part of His divine brief is to make us holy too (1 Thess. 4:3).

> According to Romans 8:29, what does God want us to be?

This process continues throughout our earthly lives. As we go through life and experience various trials, faith-testing situations and challenges, the Spirit puts His finger on certain specific areas of ungodly and unrighteous behaviour. Then He brings us to repentance, cleansing and change. It is vitally important for us to understand the sanctifying work of the Spirit. He is not out to get us. He is trying to make us like Jesus. It is in our best interests to yield to Him and change accordingly.

NO CONDEMNATION

The Bible says that there is

> **no condemnation for those who are in Christ Jesus (Rom. 8:1).**

The devil condemns, the Spirit convicts. The condemnation of the devil goes on day and night. It tends to be vague and makes you feel miserable and hopeless. By sharp contrast, the conviction of the Spirit is always clear and specific. It hurts but makes you feel hopeful. We must learn to reject the one but recognise and respond to the other.

FORGIVE US OUR TRESPASSES

In the Lord's Prayer this plea for forgiveness does not come near the beginning of the prayer, but at the end. This is because it concerns not justification (getting right with God — becoming a Christian) but sanctification (allowing the Spirit to deal with sins in our lives). When we become Christians we are justified by faith in Christ. He makes us 100 per cent righteous for ever and gives us unrestricted access to the Father

YOU FACE TRIALS

James warns us that we will experience trials. These are sometimes so severe that we may be tempted to think that God has deserted or is punishing us. Job was never given an answer to his suffering and the subject is often shrouded in mystery.

Read Hebrews 12:1–13.

What are the two things that we must not do?

Whom does the Lord discipline and punish?

115

Why does God discipline?

How does the discipline feel?

What does it produce?

Consider the way you react to trials.

A MAN REAPS WHAT HE SOWS

Church history is littered with people who have been mightily used by God while they have been living in immorality and avarice. We would expect God to withdraw His blessing from these individuals. But He is merciful. He does not use us because we are worthy. He works by grace and will continue to use us even when we sin.

We might be tempted to think that if God is going to use us whether we sin or not, it is almost worth carrying on in sin! We deceive ourselves if we think this. Paul makes it quite plain that whatever we sow we will reap (Gal. 6:7). We may be able to carry on an effective and powerful ministry, but if we are sinning behind the scenes, we will one day reap the consequences.

There's a difference between gifting and holiness. On the one hand, some people do not step out in faith and use their gifts because they think, 'I'm not holy enough.' On the other hand, some minister powerfully to others while thinking, 'It doesn't matter that my life isn't right. God is blessing me anyway.' The Lord may not withdraw His power but He will call them to account.

While power operates quite apart from holiness, holiness produces character and a godliness that affects the way in which we minister and use our gifts. We can use God's gifts with the wrong motivation: a desire for recognition or praise, a need for identity or purpose, self-importance, self-promotion, pride or the need to dominate or control others. If our motivation is selfish, our service will have a 'clanging cymbal' feel about it. The Corinthians had the gifts, but they needed the love to go with them. So do we.

THE SPIRIT AND THE FLESH

The major area in which we need the constant sanctifying work of the Spirit is in overcoming the flesh.

Paul rebukes the Galatians, 'Are you so foolish? Having begun by the Spirit, are you now being perfected by the flesh?' (Gal. 3:3 NASB). Some versions of the Bible unhelpfully translate 'by the flesh' as 'by human effort' or 'by the sinful nature'. In Romans Paul makes it plain that when we believe in Christ our old sinful nature dies and we are given a new nature, a new heart that loves righteousness. Our struggle against sin is nothing to do with our trying to overcome our sinful nature — which died (Rom. 6:6–7). The battle involves resisting temptation in an earnest desire to live out the righteousness that Jesus has already given to us.

(For a more detailed study of this subject see Terry Virgo's book *Enjoying God's Grace* which is in this series.)

We live in a sinful worldly environment which tempts us to give in to fleshly desires. The Spirit helps us to overcome these temptations.

> According to Galatians 5:16, what will we not do if we live by the Spirit?
>
> NB If you are answering from the New International Version, please substitute the word 'flesh' where you see the words 'sinful nature'.
>
> According to Romans 8:13, what does God want us to do by the Spirit?

Be encouraged! The Spirit will give you the power you need to overcome all temptation.

All over the world Christians are acknowledging their spiritual poverty and are reaching out to Jesus for His power — the baptism of the Holy Spirit. They are receiving His gifts and using them, and

God is honouring their faith. The Spirit is equipping them to face difficulties and temptations, working on their lives to conform them to the image of Jesus, building them into a company of men and women who have the power of God and who can wield it against the forces of darkness.

Don't be left out. Don't be an observer when God is blessing and using others so powerfully. God wants you to be involved. 'The promise of the Spirit is for you,' He says. 'And the time to receive is now.'

APPENDIX

HELPING OTHERS TO RECEIVE BAPTISM IN THE SPIRIT

Let us suppose that someone comes to you saying. 'I want to receive the baptism in the Holy Spirit.' Can you lead them into the experience?

Here are a few guidelines:

Acts 2:38,39 is a key passage. The Holy Spirit is the promise of the Father to everyone who is called. Are they called? Then the promise is for them. Do they understand this? Answer questions. Don't pray if there is unbelief.

Allow them to talk and ask questions until they are clear on the subject and say that they confidently expect to receive because of the clear teaching of Scripture and the clear promises of God to them.

Do not focus too much on tongues. You are not encouraging them to do strange things with their voice, or seek odd feelings. You should be exhorting them to reach out in faith to God.

Pray and encourage them to pray out loud. Listen to their prayer. Are they asking for the Spirit now? Make sure that they are and they are not simply praying around the subject.

There is sometimes a pause at this point. Ask more questions. What is happening? Be cautious — don't give tongues too much or too little importance. Differentiate between the baptism in the Holy Spirit and speaking in tongues. If they believe they have received then don't allow them to get uptight about speaking in tongues. They may receive this gift later.

However, people who speak in tongues tend to have a greater sense of assurance. Don't tell them that they have received the Spirit, ask them. We cannot impose faith on them. They must be able to reply with faith even if they have not spoken in tongues.

If they begin to speak in tongues, encourage them not to be satisfied with a quiet mumble. Encourage them to open up their heart to God, to speak out, sing or even shout. They will then have much more opportunity to be aware of having received this dynamic experience.

The reason for this is that we are not advocating a nice little prayer language, but looking for a praise which bursts out. Some people are satisfied with too little. They are not receiving a thing but God Himself. So encourage them to open up, reach out for more from God and give themselves to God in a new way. Don't let them be too easily content. Encourage them to believe for spiritual gifts.

If they seem to be having difficulty, don't pressurise them. If there is time, go over any points of which they seem unsure. It is best to make sure that they have understood the truth and that their faith is rising. If you sense that they have not actually come to a place of confident expectation, you may have to postpone praying with them.

When they have been baptised in the Holy Spirit, follow through. Encourage them by reminding them of what has happened. Help them to be more involved and more expressive in worship — to pray and sing in tongues. Remember that this is all new to them and they need to gain in confidence.

Look for the development of spiritual gifts and be encouraging. Correct them if necessary. Look for changes in their life and relationship with God. Receiving the baptism in the Holy Spirit should have a powerful and lasting effect.

Acts 1.15   120
Acts 2.41   3000 in a day
Acts 3.37   365 at least (1/day)
Acts 4.4   5000 men
                      women
                      children

Acts 21.20   250,000.

PRAYING THE LORD'S PRAYER

Praying the Lord's Prayer, also by Terry Virgo, is a practical
workbook for maintaining a consistent and effective prayer
life. It can be used by individuals or groups. Taking Jesus'
prayer structure as a model, it develops the themes of the
fatherhood and names of God, the nature of God's will, reign
and Kingdom and His gifts and forgiveness in our lives.

Catalogue Number YB9627   £2.50

ENJOYING GOD'S GRACE

Enjoying God's Grace is a workbook which will help us to understand what God has done for us and to rediscover excitement in our walk with God. If we were honest, some of us might admit, 'I'm bored with my Christian life,' while others might confess, 'I feel constantly condemned.' This book examines the Scriptures and shows us how we can be set free to begin and maintain a brand new relationship with God.

Terry Virgo has written several books, including *Restoration in the Church* and, in the Oasis Bible study series, *God's Amazing Grace*.

Catalogue Number YB9183   £1.95